JULIA VANISHES

THE WITCH'S CHILD, BOOK 1

VANISHES

CATHERINE EGAN

ALFRED A. KNOPF

NEW YORK

THIS IS A BORZOI BOOK PUBLISHED BY ALFRED A. KNOPF

Visit us on the Web! randomhouseteens.com

Educators and librarians, for a variety of teaching tools, visit us at RHTeachersLibrarians.com

Library of Congress Cataloging-in-Publication Data is available upon request.
ISBN 978-0-553-52484-0 (trade) — ISBN 978-0-553-52485-7 (lib. bdg.) —
ISBN 978-0-553-52486-4 (ebook) — ISBN 978-1-524-70084-3 (intl. tr. pbk.)

The text of this book is set in 13-point Adobe Jenson.

Printed in the United States of America
June 2016
10 9 8 7 6 5 4 3 2 1

First Edition

For Mick,
who keeps this ship afloat
while I am conjuring sea monsters

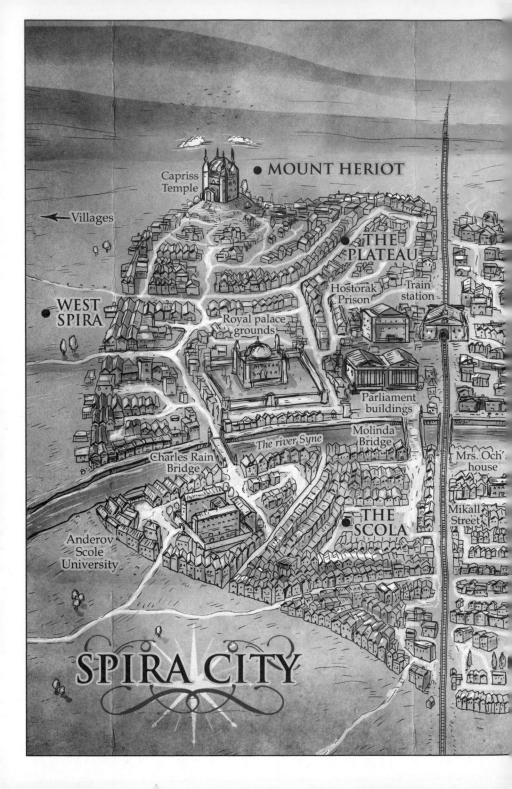

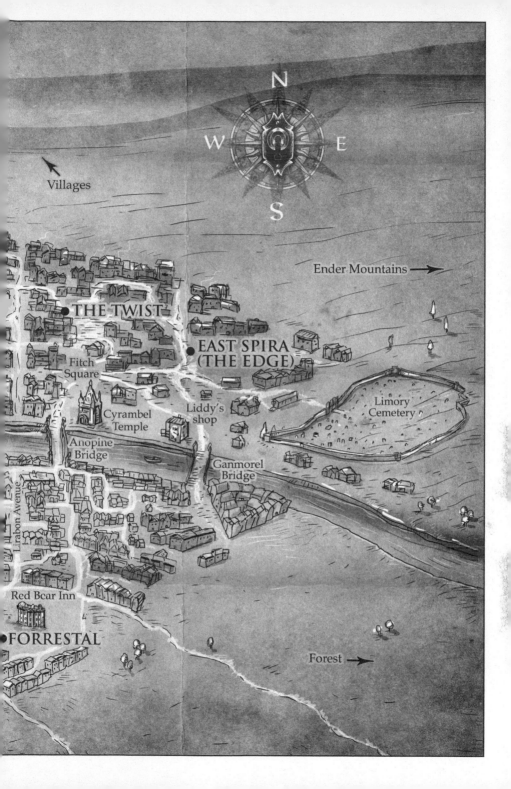

The cab crosses the bridge by Cyrambel Temple, and Jani hears herself say, "I'll get out here."

"Here?" asks her companion, still bouncing the sleepy baby in her lap. "Surely not. I don't know Lord Snow, but I can tell you he doesn't live here. Nobody lives here."

"It isn't far," says Jani, laughing, though she cannot remember at the moment where Lord Snow and his family reside. She has the address in her purse; she just needs to get out, gather her thoughts. She doesn't know and will not have time to wonder what compels her. She is sorry to leave her companion and the beautiful child. They have traveled by train all the way from the south together, agreed to share the cab because they were going to the same part of the city.

"You sure?" asks the cabbie, also skeptical. There is nothing here but the temple, the river, the empty bridge.

"I fancy a bit of a walk," she says.

"'Tisn't safe, miss," says the cabbie.

"I'll be fine." She turns to her companion. "Thank you for keeping me company. Please give me your address. We're both new to the city—we could get to know it together."

"Of course." Her companion takes a pen and a bit of notepaper from her own purse, writes swiftly, folds the paper, and presses it into Jani's hand. The smell of rotten flowers wafts through the cab. "Take care," she says.

"You also," says Jani. Impulsively, she leans over and kisses the woman on her cheek. She kisses the baby too.

"Say bye-bye, Theo," says her companion, and little Theo waves a fat hand. "Bah-bah."

The cabriolet pulls away into the night, and Jani is alone in the shadow of the temple. Someone is waiting for her. She knows that much. She is afraid too, and yet here she is. She unfolds the paper her companion gave her. She can only just make out the words in the dark:

Forget me

She looks after the cab, puzzled, trying to remember who gave her the paper. Lord Snow's house in Forrestal is a long way off, and the night is cold.

"What am I doing?" she says aloud.

The soft hand on her throat comes like an answer to her question, choking off her scream. In one swift motion the blade cuts her loose of the dark night and all that was to come.

ONE

The floor is cold under my bare feet. Florence and Chloe are breathing deeply, not stirring. I would guess it to be an hour or more after midnight. The rusted springs of my cot shriek when I rise, but the two sleeping figures are undisturbed. They are used to the sound, no doubt, as the beds scream like murder victims whenever we roll over. I step past their beds lightly, let my hand slide around the doorknob. The door doesn't squeak—just last week I oiled the hinges and took apart, cleaned, and reassembled the knob. There was nothing to be done about the bedsprings. Moonlight slips between the curtains, giving some light to the little attic room where we housemaids sleep, but the staircase is dark. In one hand I have a candle, unlit in its iron holder. With the other hand I shut the door behind me.

The main bedrooms are on the third floor, along with the bathroom. The clock on the landing tells me it is nearing two in the morning, but I can still see a light under Frederick's door. That doesn't worry me. Most likely he fell asleep over a book. The stairs leading to the second floor are wider. I skip down them quickly, a hand to the wall to guide me in the dark. I know every floorboard that creaks, and my descent is soundless. Here is the library, the music room, Mrs. Och's reading room, and my destination tonight: Professor Baranyi's study. We do not clean this room, so I have never been inside. It is locked at night.

Not that a lock is any great impediment.

There is no light coming from under the door, but I press my ear to it and listen just in case. With my free hand, I slip a pin from my hair and flatten it out. I'm not a practiced lockpick, but I have the basic skills and get it open in under a minute.

I've stitched a match into the hem of my nightdress. Shutting the door behind me, I feel my way to the hearth and strike the match against the stone. Once the candle is lit, the room leaps into view around me, bookcases looming, the furniture sending monstrous, grasping shadows my way. I've never been one to quake at shadows: I make my way straight for Professor Baranyi's desk.

The professor is not a tidy man, to put it mildly. Precariously stacked books and papers cover every inch of space. Three ashtrays overflow with cigarette butts, there are two half-full glasses perched dangerously atop a pile of large leather-bound folders, and his inkpot lies open, pen leaking onto the blotter.

It would help if I knew what I was looking for.

A soft sound behind me—my imagination turns it into a handkerchief being pulled out of a pocket—and I freeze.

"*Hooo,*" comes a fluting little voice. I nearly laugh aloud with relief. On a perch in the corner is a small brown owl, blinking at me.

"Sorry," I whisper. "Go back to sleep."

"*Hooo,*" murmurs the owl, shrugging its wings and resettling itself.

I turn back to Professor Baranyi's desk, lift my candle, and scan the books and papers around the blotter, whatever he was looking at before he retired to bed. Esme taught me to read, and I can read quickly and well, even the most ungainly, misspelled scrawl. I shuffle through his papers: an old clipping from a journal about a lake somewhere that has mysteriously dried up, lists of names with some of them crossed out, figures without context, lists of cities and countries. A circle around one name in a long list: *Jahara Sandor—Hostorak 15c.* That brings me up short. Hostorak is the impenetrable prison where witches and folklore practitioners and other abusers of magic await execution. It is a great gray monolith behind the parliament, the ugliest building in all of Spira City, and the most terrifying. I commit the name, Jahara Sandor, and 15c to memory, without knowing what they might mean.

At the back of the study, there is a long workbench with scientific instruments, but I don't know how they work. I turn to the bookshelves instead, which line the entire room. At the bottom of one shelf, I find a locked glass cabinet full of books. There. Anything with a lock on it is bound to be interesting. I wiggle the hairpin until the lock gives and slide the case open. I can see why these books are locked up, with titles like *A Scientific Analysis of Elemental Forces at Work* and *Legends of the Xianren I* through *Legends of the Xianren VII*. I've heard of the Xianren—mythical, winged wizards in the old days who could supposedly speak their magic. Folklorish stuff. I shouldn't be surprised—Professor Baranyi spent a number of years in prison for heretical writings, and you can go to prison just for owning books like these. So you see, I'm not snooping through the private rooms of honest, upstanding citizens of Frayne. Criminals every way I turn.

My hand is on *Legends of the Xianren I*, pulling it off the shelf, when I hear a creak on the stairs. I push the book back and slide the glass door shut, blowing out the candle. I work the cabinet lock shut again, but there is no time to get to the door. I hear a key in the lock as I tread softly through the dark. I bump against a sedan chair piled with books and freeze, afraid of knocking something over. There is some fumbling with the door, as I left it unlocked, and whoever is at the door has mistakenly locked it again. But he tries the key again, and opens the door.

I draw in a slow breath and release it. The door opens and light pours into the room. It is Professor Baranyi with a lantern. He is wearing a thick robe and house slippers. By day he is an affable, genial-looking man, but the light from the lantern makes his swarthy, bearded face look sinister. He drops the key into his robe pocket, glances around the room, and then goes to the owl on its perch and scratches it under its beak. The owl nibbles at his fingers and bobs its head in my direction. Treacherous little thing. But Professor Baranyi does not look my way, going instead to his desk. He places the lantern atop a pile of books on the floor that reaches to the height of the desk, and fumbles in the drawer for a cigarette.

I bite back my curses. He's going to be a while.

$\sim$

In my sixteen years, I've seen as much as, or more than, someone five times my age, and I've acquired a number of unusual skills. Some of those skills required endless practice, while others came to me more naturally. One particular skill has always been mine. I don't know what to call it, except to say that I have the ability to be unseen. It's not invisibility or anything so absolute—this I learned from hard experience when I was a child. But there is a space I can step into, a space between being myself in the world and I know not what, where people's eyes simply pass over me, as if I were a piece of furniture so ordinary they barely take it in. Since I got the hang of doing it on purpose, only one person has been able to see me when I did not intend her to.

I watch the professor as if through a fogged window now, everything slightly blurred. He reaches for one of the leather folders, moving the glasses of who knows what. I clench my jaw to keep my teeth from chattering. The house is frigid at night, and I hope he will think to light the fire.

He licks his finger and turns a page. I try to warm myself

by thinking about Wyn. Wyn feeding pigeons on the roof. Wyn pulling off his boots and tossing them aside. Wyn by firelight, reaching for me. Wyn's mouth. I feel something run through me whenever he flashes his wild smile or throws his head back to laugh so you can see his back teeth and the brown stretch of his throat. That laugh! How it shreds me, every single time. I think of Wyn's fingers brushing up and down my arms, his hand moving around to the small of my back, his breath like wine and smoke and something else, something sweet. Now I'm warming up, and the minutes fly by for a time.

But even thoughts of Wyn, with his clever fingers and his sweet lips, can only get me through so much of the night in phantom form. Shivering violently, toes curled against the icy floor, fingers aching from gripping the candlestick, I run through every curse I know in my head. Professor Baranyi is deep in his leather-bound volume and shows no sign of returning to bed. Soon Florence and Chloe will be rising to begin the day's work. I imagine them waking up, finding me gone from my bed and nowhere in the house. What will they say to Mrs. Och? How will I explain my absence? I can't leave the room without being caught, and I can't *not* leave the room without creating a whole new set of difficulties for myself.

I am weighing the possible disastrous outcomes of this night when a great crash comes from below us, followed by a long, low howl. The professor's head shoots up. Another crash, like steel on stone, and a roar to wake the dead. It's not the first time I've heard such sounds from the cellar, but never quite so terrible as this. The professor leaps from his seat and goes straight for the locked cabinet of books. My heart gives a jump as he fumbles it open. Footsteps on the stairs above, and a moment later Frederick bursts into the room, gangly and half-awake.

"Is it a reaction?" he asks.

The professor is pulling all the books out of the cabinet. He reaches behind them and appears to slide open a panel. I can hardly contain my delight—this night will not be a waste after all. He emerges with a black case. The sound of wood splintering makes us all start. The professor curses. He takes something out of the case and hands it to Frederick, but they have their backs to me, and I can't see what it is. I am distracted, anyway, by the sound of something on the lower stairs, and then a snarl in the hall, chillingly close.

Frederick and the professor run together to the door just as a large, dark shadow flashes past. Frederick aims some kind of triangular instrument about a hand's width in size. There is a hissing sound, a strangled cry, then a thud as something hits the ground, hard. The two men seem to exhale as one, Frederick leaning against the doorjamb, Professor Baranyi taking a handkerchief out of his robe pocket and mopping his brow.

"So much for the soothing properties of amethyst, eh?" says the professor, and Frederick gives a short laugh. I think he is trembling, but it is hard to be sure from my blurred vantage point.

"We need a new door," he says. "Steel."

"Yes. We'll see to it in the morning."

"And then what? Surely we've tried everything."

"Not everything," says the professor. "But close."

They are silent for a moment, staring into the hall at whatever it is. Then Frederick hands the professor the peculiar instrument—like a miniature crossbow, I see now—and says, "I'll take care of this."

The professor nods, and Frederick closes the door behind him, blast him. Professor Baranyi seems quite steady now, muttering to himself as he returns the black case to its hidden compartment, arranging his set of forbidden books in front of it. Back at his desk, he stares harder at the volume before him. I don't know how to make sense of what I've just witnessed, but my heart is thundering, and I can't stand still any longer. I begin to make my way across the room.

When I am in a crowd, the movement of others seems to open pockets of space that I can vanish into and move within. Moving through a still room while keeping myself behind that membrane of the visible is much more difficult—sort of like trying to write different things with each hand. But the professor doesn't look up as I head for the door. I wait until he seems entirely lost in his book. Then, too fast, I reach for the knob and open the door, losing my equilibrium. Everything comes sharply into focus.

He starts and stares, and I am caught.

"Sir!" I cry, pivoting on my heel as if I were coming in rather than going out. "I heard terrible sounds coming from downstairs, sir!"

Professor Baranyi pushes his spectacles up his nose to look at me in the dying lanternlight. "Miss . . . ?" he says, not remembering my name.

"Ella," I say. "I was going to the privy, sir—sorry, sir—and I heard the most awful bashing and hollering. I'm sorry, sir; I was afraid, and I saw your light."

"*Hoo-hoooo*," says the little brown owl, shifting from one foot to the other, delighted by all the excitement.

"I don't hear anything," says the professor, rising. I can see his confusion at finding me in his room fading already as he accepts the more reasonable explanation: that I was coming in, not going out.

"It's stopped," I say. "Is it something got into the cellar, do you think? Is Mr. Darius all right down there?"

Mr. Darius is the ailing, aristocratic houseguest who has a room in the cellar and, as far as I can tell, keeps a very unhappy nocturnal pet. I only hope he is not the cause of the suffering down there. Wondering about it gives me chills every time I have to pour his coffee.

"There's no need to worry, Edna," says Professor Baranyi soothingly.

"Ella," I correct him, then bite my tongue, wishing I hadn't.

"Quite—pardon me. There is a door down there that needs fixing, you see. The wind catches it sometimes and makes some awful echoing sounds in the passageway. We must see to it, but please don't be frightened."

He's not a bad liar, if not near as good as I am.

I look down at my bare feet. "I shouldn't have barged in on

you. I was ever so frightened. But I ought not to have bothered you. I'm so embarrassed, sir."

"Nobody need hear about it," he comforts me, and I hope he means it. Mrs. Och would be less inclined to credulous sympathy, I somehow think. "Now, perhaps you had better get back to bed."

"Yes, sir. Sorry, sir." I duck out the door.

The relief of moving again is tremendous. I nearly fly up the stairs, slipping back into the housemaids' room as quietly as I can. I ease myself onto the cold sheets. The bed screams its usual protest, and Florence's eyes fly open.

"Where were you?" she says, in a cold and alarmingly awake little voice.

"Privy," I grunt back, pulling the blankets over me. After a minute I give a snore, but I can feel her beady little eyes still watching me.

TWO

The following day is Temple Day, and we housemaids are given the day off. Besides Florence and Chloe, Frederick is the only member of the household to attend temple with any regularity. I am supposedly going to my hometown of Jepta, a nondescript village about an hour north of Spira City. Gregor even took me out there once in case I encountered anyone who knew the place, made me walk around memorizing alleyways and chatting with grocers and cobblers so that I would know their names. Esme, for her part, concocted an impressively dull family for me; I have endless dull details about them and their dullness to share should anybody be interested, but nobody is. After all, I'm just the new housemaid.

Except, of course, that I'm not.

Mrs. Och generously gives me the fare to Jepta, so I buy myself a hot breakfast on Lirabon Avenue, sitting shoulder to shoulder at the bar with the students and artists and poor aristocrats who live in the area. Mrs. Och's house is on Mikall Street, in a well-to-do neighborhood near the bustling center of the Scola, the university quarter, which hugs the southern bank of the river Syne. The Twist is just across the river from here, an easy walk, but a gray sleet is falling, and I am bristling with impatience, so I flag down a motor cabriolet. It is still early, and the streets are relatively quiet. There are a few miserable-looking horses pulling old-fashioned carriages over the cobblestones, and I see one silent electric hackney slipping by us down a side street, its occupants dressed all in white. As we near Cyrambel Temple, hulking darkly between the Scola and the Twist on the very edge of the river Syne, the street becomes impassable. Carriages and cabriolets are stopped, pedestrians in their temple-best clothes are milling about and talking to strangers in an avid way that can only mean one thing: a death.

"I'll get out here," I tell the cabbie, and pay him with Mrs. Och's coins. I figure I'll be faster on foot.

I fight my way through the crowds to Anopine Bridge, where I see the blue coats and feathered hats of the soldiers, the police officers drab and glum in comparison. At the center of the fray is a blanket laid over what I assume is a body. The pavement all around it is dark with blood.

"Back off, girl," a soldier snarls, aiming a shove my way, but I dodge his arm neatly and wink. His mouth twitches and he turns his broad back on me.

"What happened?" I ask a gossipy-looking old hen in an apron.

"Girl from Nim!" She rounds on me, delighted to have

somebody new to tell the story to. "They've just identificated her! She was to be governess to Lord Snow's little ones!"

That's a shock. You don't often find wellborn girls dead on bridges. The old hen sticks her face right in mine, and I can smell her breakfast of salty broth and weak tea. "You hear about the banker in Nim they found just yesterday? The cabaret dancer the day before that?"

I shake my head. I've not left Mrs. Och's house in a week and don't pay much attention anyway to news from far-off places. Nim is a port city in the south of Frayne. My mother was born in a village not far from there. I've never seen the sea, myself.

"Tops of their heads sliced off," she carries on gleefully. "And their *brains*'d been messed with! This one is just the same, and this girl, she *came from Nim on the train yesterday*. They found her ticket in her purse!"

"You reckon it's a copycat, or the killer came with her?" someone asks. A small crowd is forming around us now to hear the story told again.

"Oh, the killer's here in Spira City now, no doubt about that," declares the hen authoritatively. "I saw her body meself before they covered her up. Shan't recover from that sight, I tell you!" She affects a tragic mask, though as far as I can tell this is the most exciting thing that's ever happened to her.

"Move along, all of you!" shouts one of the soldiers, but the mass of bodies keeps pressing in, gaping and gossiping, wanting a glimpse of the body. Soon the soldiers will start threatening violence, and then the crowd will disperse.

I make my way across the bridge and into my old familiar

territory. Narrow streets wind their way between the cramped apartments, groceries, and tobacconists. Stray cats seek shelter from the sleet; glowering faces peer out of fogged windows. Despite the weather, the market stalls are already set up in Fitch Square and are spilling out into the surrounding alleyways. The broken statue of some kind of sea beast burbles a bit of water into the fountain at the center of the square. Esme owns several rooms on the east side of the square, including mine and Dek's. We get room and board, and sometimes a little extra, depending on the job.

Esme was born the day of old King Zey's coronation, the illegitimate daughter of a courtesan. Her mother died in childbirth, and Esme grew up in the brothel, raised by seventeen whores, if you can imagine that. Now she's got a finger in every unlawful pie but that one, having no taste for the selling of bodies, and presides over her own little empire in the Twist. Crime doesn't pay what it used to, with the Crown building more prisons north of the city and hanging folks left and right, but it still pays better than honest work. Since the big men who used to run the Twist are mostly dead or in jail, half the crooks around here work for Esme, who keeps a low profile and doesn't take risks.

I head straight up to the main parlor, technically part of Esme's apartment, but it is always open to us. Benedek, my brother, is tinkering with a flat metallic object, but he raises a distracted hand in greeting. A lock mechanism is in pieces on the table in front of him. For the past few weeks, he has been working on a magnetic lockpick that he claims will open anything. Esme is kneeling by the fire, blowing on it vigorously.

She rises, clapping the ashes from her hands, and gives me a warm smile. I am of an average height, but Esme dwarfs me. She wears men's trousers because she's impossible to fit for dresses and can't be bothered to go to the expense of having them made specially. Her short hair is nearly white, but her face is only subtly lined.

"I'll get you some coffee, love," she says, and hands me a towel to dry my hair with. "Good to see you."

"You too," I say, toweling off and then throwing the towel at Dek to make him look up. He catches it and laughs at me. I peel my wet coat off and throw myself down in a chair. The fire is blazing nicely now, and I shift a little so my feet are closer to it. It's such a blessed relief not to have to scrub a floor, carry water or coal up the stairs, polish a grate or another blasted candlestick. To be *home*.

"Saw a dead girl over by Cyrambel," I tell them, and repeat what the gossipy old hen told me.

"Poor thing," says Esme, handing me a mug of steaming coffee. "This city is a dangerous place for a girl on her own. You be sensible, my Julia. I don't want to hear about you on a bridge one day."

"Wouldn't happen to me," I say, slapping my boot where I keep my knife tucked away.

"It won't happen to you because you'll be smart and not go wandering about on your own at night," says Dek, giving me a hard look. "Not because you've got a six-inch knife so snug in your boot lining it would take you five minutes to get it out."

"Nine inches," I say, grinning at him. "And look."

I whip the knife out at the same moment that he lunges for me, twisting my wrist back so the knife falls to the ground with a clatter and I spill my coffee.

"Flaming Kahge, Dek, relax!" I shout.

He is breathing hard, his bad leg twisted beneath him. Esme chuckles, sips her coffee.

"My point," he says slowly, "is you be smart, Julia. You be careful."

"I'm careful," I say, shoving him away from me. I'm only a little bit angry, though. He worries about me, I know, and the truth is, it makes me feel safe to have him worry. Like his love can keep me safe. You'd think I'd know better; love doesn't keep anyone safe. But he's my older brother, and worrying about me is what he does.

∾

Dek and I were born in the Twist. I was seven and he was ten when our mother was killed and our father disappeared. Dek begged, I stole, according to the fortunes the Nameless One had bestowed upon us. That was the summer after the Scourge swept across Frayne, decimating the population. It was the worst Scourge in living memory—corpses were rotting in ditches and people barely went out. In our house, it touched only Benedek. I was sent to stay with an aunt in the countryside who beat me, and I cried every day, not because of the beatings but because Dek was going to die.

Only he didn't. A child surviving the Scourge was unheard of. Dek not only survived; he survived with his *self* intact, unlike the trembling, ravaged, half-witted survivors you some-times see begging along the river. A decade later, he wears his curling black hair long to cover the scars and the unmistak-able dark blots of the Scourge that deform the right side of his face, the empty eye socket now sewn shut. His right side is blighted, the arm and leg withered and nearly useless. It is as if the Scourge raged through him but stopped halfway and turned back again. From the left, he is quite handsome, with a strong jaw and a straight nose. He gets around well enough with a crutch. Most days he counts himself lucky to be alive, but I know there are dark days too, when it doesn't feel so much like luck.

People are terrified of Scourge survivors, as if the contagion might still be present in them, but Esme never flinched at the sight of him. She'd lost her own son to the Scourge, and her husband to a failed revolution, and I don't think anything frightens Esme anymore. She took us both in, taught us how to read and a great many other things besides. They became our new family: Esme, her colleagues Gregor and Csilla, and beautiful Wyn, her adopted son, a lanky ten-year-old then. I fell in love with him on first sight, when I was barely eight years old. He winked at me, and I was lost.

∾

Gregor and Csilla arrive midday, after temple, as I am writ-ing up my report. They come sweeping in and have a way of making the comfortable parlor seem suddenly dingy and small. They are recently back from working a long con in

Ingle—one of their classics. Csilla plays the damsel in distress, a Fraynish lady trapped in Ingle with her abusive husband, lacking funds to escape him and flee to her powerful family. Each time, several rich, besotted gallants come eagerly to her rescue and provide her full fare home, that she might be free of her monstrous husband. I'm sure Gregor has had a wonderful time playing the ogre. Needless to say, they've both been having a better time than I have.

"Hallo, everyone!" says Csilla, pulling off her white gloves. "Gracious, Julia, I've got to give you something for those circles under your eyes. Don't housemaids sleep?"

"Not this one," I grumble, stretching my legs out self-consciously.

"Poor thing," says Csilla, settling into a chair and taking out a silver cigarette case. "We'll take you to the cabaret when the job is done; won't that be fun? You can borrow one of my dresses."

I laugh. I'd never fit into her clothes, which require all bust and no waist.

"Everything went smoothly, I take it?" says Esme. "No angry Inglese aristocrats chasing you across the channel?"

"See for yourself how smoothly it went," says Gregor, tossing her a thick packet of Inglese bills. "Csilla charmed them senseless, of course, and I was a drunker lout than you've ever seen."

"Really?" I ask, raising an eyebrow. "Hard to imagine."

Dek shoots me a warning look.

Gregor was, once upon a time, the wayward son of an aristocrat executed for treason. Following his expulsion from high society way back in his unimaginable youth, he became a revolutionary, and when that didn't work out, a thief, a con, and a hopeless drunk. He still has those upper-crust manners, though, that way of walking into a room like the whole bleeding place belongs to him, and when he flashes a smile at you, there's a glimmer of his former charm, buried under years of booze and despair. Esme's husband was his best friend, and she's kept him on in spite of everything. Csilla, for her part, was a well-known actress before she married Gregor and gave up the stage for good. What Csilla sees in Gregor is one of life's great mysteries. She is ten years younger than him at least, and a true northern beauty, all porcelain and gold except for her eyes, which are dark and deep enough to drown in. She has no family that I know of.

"We'll take our cut to the track tomorrow," says Gregor, ignoring my dig. "Belle Sofe is a sure thing, make us a fortune!" He winks at Csilla, and she smiles back moonily. The two of them are fanatics for horse racing, in spite of the fact that they never win anything. "Now, what have you got for me, Julia, my dear? I've an appointment with the client this afternoon."

While Esme rules the criminal underworld, Gregor is our point of contact with Spira City's elite. They don't invite him to their parties, but they all know who he is, and a well-paid case of blackmail or spying often comes our way through him.

"I could come with you," I suggest. "I've got the whole day off."

Gregor shakes his head. "When the client wants to see you, I'll let you know."

"Fine. Makes no difference to me," I say, but I can't deny I'm disappointed. I am dying to find out more about this mysterious client.

I have been sent to Mrs. Och's house with a rather vague set of questions: Who is in the house? What are they doing? What do they talk about? What are they reading? Where do they go? Every week I give Gregor a report and he takes it to my employer. It's a far cry from the usual sort of thing— digging up material for blackmail, following misbehaving spouses, locating hidden safes—but my mysterious employer gave us six silver freyns at the start of the job, and offers *twenty* upon completion, whatever completion might mean in this case.

The six silver freyns are spent already. A thief who worked for Esme was arrested just last week, and half the money went to bribing officials so that he'll do prison time instead of being hung. The other half went to his family. Esme might be rich if she didn't take such good care of her people and their families. Then again, if crooks weren't so loyal to her, she might be in prison herself. I negotiated hard with Esme and will get a quarter of the final payment for myself. More than enough for a few fashionable gowns and weeks of dining out at fine restaurants with Wyn. Perhaps we'll go mingle with the lords and ladies at the opera.

I hand Gregor the report I've just written out on Esme's good paper. I don't dare keep pen and paper at Mrs. Och's house; a housemaid with a pen might well be taken for a witch, and though I could prove my innocence quickly enough, there's no need to arouse suspicion.

"I got into the professor's study last night," I tell him. "I found a name written down that could be important. Jahara Sandor at Hostorak Prison. Fifteen-c might be a cell number."

"Hostorak!" exclaims Dek. "These aren't just some rich nambies, then, are they?"

Gregor skates his eyes across my awkward handwriting and takes a swig from his hip flask.

"Then there's the houseguest in the cellar," I continue. "I have this horrible feeling he's doing experiments on animals. They shot something in the hall the other night, maybe with sleeping serum, but I didn't see what."

"Yes, I mentioned the houseguest to the client last week. Mr. Darius, isn't it? You're to find out who he is and exactly what he's doing there."

"Hold up, Gregor. I thought she was just snooping on a rich old lady, but this sounds like something else," says Dek. "How dangerous is this job?"

"Julia won't get caught," says Gregor unhelpfully.

"Of course I won't," I say, not admitting how close I had come. "So when am I done? If I find out what Mr. Darius is doing in the cellar? Or what interest they have in a prisoner at Hostorak?"

Gregor shrugs.

"Look at these blisters!" I show him my hands. "I've been

scrubbing a blasted privy! Peeled so many vegetables I never want to look at a carrot again! Have you ever scaled a fish? Your hands stink for days afterward!"

"At least now you know you're luckier than half the girls in Spira City," says Csilla, pointing her unlit cigarette at me. I slump back in my chair.

The talk drifts to gossip about Marianne Deneuve, an actress Csilla used to know, now wanted as a witch.

"She's disappeared without a trace!" says Gregor while Csilla shakes her head and says, "I can't believe it; I just *can't* believe it."

"You never had a hint of it, then?" asks Esme.

"Not at all!" says Csilla. "She was kind to me back then, when I was the new face. She taught me a thing or two."

I am barely paying attention. It's almost noon, and I can't wait any longer. I slip out, skip up the stairs to the room at the very top, and bang on the door. When there's no answer, I shove my bent hairpin into the lock and wrestle with it clumsily, noisily, until it gives.

It's a sad little room, not unlike the attic room I'm staying in at Mrs. Och's, but this one I love. The tiny window looks out over the square and the spiky rooftops of the Twist, but the curtains are shut now. A few embers still glow in the grate, so it must have been a late night. There is a pistol on the table, next to a half-finished charcoal sketch of Fitch Square. He's captured the broken fountain, the mad pigeon lady with birds all over her. Wyn has a way of drawing ugly things and making them seem beautiful.

He is sprawled across the bed, half-covered by his blanket. His long brown back is exposed, and one leg with black hair on it too. His face is turned away from me. The sight of his back and leg undoes me, my joints suddenly loose and weak. I cross the room, heart leaping against my rib cage, blood singing and rushing.

"Wyn," I whisper, and he stirs. I run my hand down his spine, and he rolls over slowly. Dark hair on his chest, long thick lashes, stormy green eyes, and, oh, those lips, parting in a sleepy smile.

"Hullo, Brown Eyes," he says. "How did you get in here?"

I hold up the hairpin.

"Nowhere is safe from Spira City's fearsome thieves," he intones.

"Lock up your handsome young men!" I mimic, sitting down on the edge of his bed and bending to kiss him.

"I thought we just established that locks are useless against these fearsome thieves," he says, and kisses me back, but lightly.

"You call that a kiss?" I protest. "I've been slaving day and night for a week now—I think I deserve better than that!"

He laughs, starting to get up. "Hounds, Brown Eyes, I haven't even eaten breakfast yet."

I push him back down and say, with mock severity, "Breakfast can wait."

*W*ithout knowing why, the cabbie leaves the still-busy nighttime streets of the Scola and crosses Ganmorel Bridge, heading into the Edge, where Spira City's destitute and desperate make their way. He passes the cheap brothels and opium dens, and the cab climbs the hill toward Limory Cemetery.

Something follows on swift, dark legs, unknown to him but pushing him on.

He parks the motor cab and gets out, pulling his coat around him, confused. Winter is in the air already, and the street is deserted. He walks uncertainly through the cemetery gates, then stops, turns, and looks around.

"Hullo?" he says. His breath puffs out in a great white plume.

He hears something move in the shadow of his motor cab, or sees it perhaps, but then there is nothing, silence.

"Flaming Kahge," he mutters. He reaches into his pocket for a pipe and then changes his mind. Turns to head deeper into the cemetery, then stops again. His mind is a fog. Why has he come here?

The air gets colder, and now he hears, clear as anything, something breathing nearby.

"Who's there?" he calls. Fear surges in and clears his mind. Get out of here. Dangerous. He heads back toward his motor cab at a trot, but there is something at the gate, barring his way.

The moon is behind the clouds, and he doesn't see the thing clearly. It stands upright, but the face is not a human face, the body too tall and lithe to be a human body. He lets out a strangled yell, turns, and runs.

There is a sound like a growl, and he finds himself facedown in the gravel. He thinks of his wife, at home waiting for him, their child about to be born any day now, his fear dissolving into another horror, for how will they survive without him? A hand jerks his head up by the hair. A wetness at his forehead, a spreading blackness. He thinks of struggle, but fleetingly, as if from a great distance—already this sudden, brutal ending has become part of somebody else's story.

THREE

My stomach growls, but I ignore it, as it's only ten o'clock in the morning. I grit my teeth and beat the great parlor rugs so the dust flies. It is a crisp, fine day, likely the last fine weather before winter comes to claim the city. From the terrace, I can see Florence and Chloe hanging laundry to dry down by the pond, where turtles have crept out to sun themselves. Soon the scullery will have to do on laundry days, but today it is pleasant out, the sky a piercing, cloudless blue, blackbirds shrieking in the trees, which shed their bright, dying leaves all over the lawn.

Mrs. Och's large, walled back garden would be very picturesque if not for the great mound of earth marring the lawn between the terrace and the pond. Mal, the groundsman, told me that until a few months ago a towering old cherry tree stood there. Had to be hundreds of years old, he said, and then one summer day it was gone, leaving behind the ruptured lawn, as if someone had come along and simply plucked a forty-foot tree out of the ground and walked off with it. He shook his head a great deal and scratched his ear as he told me this, and I agreed with him that it was quite the strangest thing I'd ever heard of. Sometimes Mrs. Och goes out with a blanket wrapped around her shoulders like a shawl, kneels next to the spot, and sifts the earth through her hands. That made it into my first report but elicited no hint of interest from the client, whoever he is.

Though it's only midmorning, we have served all the household members their breakfast and coffee; lit the fires and taken water up to the bath for Mrs. Och (the only one who uses the giant tub, as far as I can tell—I'm dying to try it myself); scrubbed down the scullery; prepared the makings of lunch for Mrs. Freeley, the cook; emptied Mrs. Och's bathwater (which I have noticed is always remarkably clean and smells like apple blossoms after she bathes); polished the silver; brushed the curtains; and soaked, washed, rinsed, blued, and wrung out the laundry. My arms are stiff and sore, and I am desperate for a cup of coffee and a cream pastry.

"Fine day," says a voice behind me, and all the hairs on the back of my neck stand up. I turn and give a little curtsy, pausing from my attack on the parlor rugs.

"Yes, sir," I say.

"Sorry to interrupt. Will you light this for me?" Mr. Darius gestures with his pipe. "I've injured my arm."

Indeed, the hand not holding the pipe is thoroughly bandaged and he is holding his arm gingerly, as if it hurts him.

"Of course, sir," I say. "Let me have a match."

He gives me a matchbox and bends at the waist with the pipe in his mouth so I can reach to light it. As I do, I glance up into his face. He is looking right at me with those slate-gray eyes of his. I hastily drop my gaze, focusing on the pipe.

"There you are, sir," I say.

"Thank you." He straightens up and puffs on the pipe. He is a handsome man, between forty and fifty years old, well built and well bred. The sort of man whose pockets I might pick if I passed him on the street. I've no idea what his relationship to Mrs. Och is or why he is staying in her cellar. For a moment I think he's going to stay to talk with me, but then he makes to leave and so I venture to ask, "What happened to your arm, sir?"

His face registers immediate disapproval. I should not have asked a personal question. I smile, all innocence, but he doesn't soften.

"An accident," he says gruffly.

"Is it very painful?" I ask. "Can I get you anything?"

He shakes his head and walks away from me. I watch him stride across the lawn, blowing smoke all over the clean laundry. Florence and Chloe bob awkwardly as he passes them. I wonder if they have heard the noises from the cellar. It was bad again last night, but neither of them has mentioned it.

I give the rugs a couple more bangs, then haul them off the terrace railing and drag them back into the parlor in a great hurry. Mrs. Och will be in her reading room now or lying down, Professor Baranyi and Frederick at work as usual.

Mrs. Freeley is in the kitchen. I fetch a mop and a pail of water from the scullery and head for the cellar stairs.

I don't know how long Mr. Darius will walk in the garden, but this is a rare chance and I dare not waste it.

The hall at the bottom of the cellar stairs is unlit, but that doesn't deter me. I hurry on, sloshing water from my bucket, and find myself in a cavernous wine cellar. I touch one of the bottles and my finger comes away thick with dust. I turn back and take the corridor to the right.

I'm just wondering if I should have brought my knife when I am dazzled by light as someone comes around the corner and runs right into me. I yell, fumbling with the bucket, and the lower half of my dress gets soaked with soapy water.

"Hounds!" comes a curse. I recognize the voice before the lantern swings out of the way, and I can see Frederick standing there, his feet wet and the shattered pieces of a wooden chair under his arm. Immediately my fear leaves me. Frederick is only a few years older than I am and he is, I think, a kind person, unlikely to tell Mrs. Och that I have been where I should not be. Chloe tells me that he was a very promising student at the university but left to work for the professor. His parents were devastated, she said. He has fair hair and skin, a rather untended beard, and he always looks vaguely surprised—perhaps an effect of his round spectacles. Of course, at the moment, he is genuinely surprised.

"Sorry, sir!" I say.

"Haven't they told you that you don't need to clean down here?" he asks.

"They did, sir," I say. "But I saw Mr. Darius was outside and thought it would be nice to surprise him with a clean room for once. It must get filthy. There are so many rooms here we hardly tend to."

Frederick laughs uncomfortably. "Best not to surprise anybody, Miss . . . it's Ella, isn't it?"

Three weeks I've been here, and nobody remembers my bleeding name. Fake name, but still.

"Yes, sir," I say.

"Well, in all seriousness, nobody in this house is keen on surprises," he tells me. "Even if that surprise is an unexpected mopped floor."

"I see, sir," I say.

His eyes crinkle a bit at the edges.

"You don't need to call me sir," he says. "I'm just an employee here too."

That's nonsense, of course. He eats with Mrs. Och and the others, and we serve him his breakfast and his coffee every morning. He is not on the level of a housemaid, but I say, "All right," because I get sick of the yes-sir-no-sir business anyway. I smile at him, to soften it.

"What happened to the chair?" I ask him.

"Broken," he says.

"I can see *that*," I say, and he laughs.

"It was no good anymore," he says. "We'll use it for firewood. Come on, shall we go up?"

I have no choice but to go up the stairs ahead of him.

Florence is at the top, her nostrils flaring wildly. Her hair has come loose a bit from under her cap, and her hands are on her hips. Florence is all sharp angles and edges, her eyes a bit too wide, her mouth a bit too small. She and Chloe are cousins and look very alike, except Chloe's features are more proportional and so she is quite pretty, whereas Florence always looks a bit crazed.

She bobs her head at Frederick, who says, "Hello, Florence," and gives me an apologetic look over his shoulder as he heads past us. He knows I'm in for it.

"You aren't supposed to go down there," she says.

"I thought I could clean Mr. Darius's room while he was outside," I say. "Doesn't it get filthy?"

"I wouldn't know," she says. "I don't go where I'm told not to."

"I thought— Well, it was my mistake," I say humbly. This doesn't mollify her much. I think Florence has an ear for insincerity. She gives me a sour look and says, "Go be scullery maid, then. Mrs. Freeley needs one of us."

Florence is only a couple of years older than I am, but since my predecessor left, she is now the senior housemaid and takes her role very seriously. Reluctantly, wearily, having seen nothing of the cellar except that it is unlit and needs dusting, I go to the scullery, followed by Florence's suspicious gaze. Mrs. Freeley is waiting there, a hulking ham of a woman, all red meat with watery little eyes and some gray hair on top.

"Oh, you," she says with a sigh. She is the only one to have really noted my inexperience; I know nothing about kitchen work. "We're making custard pie. Does that frighten you, girl?"

"'Tis the custard pie that ought to be afraid, ma'am," I reply. "Pie mamas tell their little pie babies tales of Terrible Ella to scare 'em into behaving, you know."

Making Mrs. Freeley laugh is something I take seriously, as I think it is the only reason she tolerates me at all. Her hammy body shakes as she laughs; then she points to the counter and says cheerfully, "Roll the dough, my girl, and no more of your lip."

❧

At lunch, one housemaid stands at attention in the high-ceilinged dining room while Mrs. Och, Professor Baranyi, Mr. Darius, and Frederick eat. I am always struck by how this particular aspect of servitude mirrors my own gift. You are there, but you are invisible, at least until somebody needs a cup filled or a plate cleared away.

Mrs. Och comes in on Professor Baranyi's arm, the two of them deep in conversation. Due to his time in prison and his reputation as a heretic, the professor is the subject of awed disapproval and gossip among the housemaids. However, his association with Mrs. Och lends him a sheen of respectability, for Mrs. Och is rich enough to be respectable no matter how eccentric she might be or whom she might choose to associate with. Chloe tells me that the professor works for Mrs. Och and has lived in her house for more than a decade now, but nobody seems to know exactly what the nature of his work is. "Something to do with translation," Florence said vaguely. "Restoring old books," said Mal, the groundskeeper. "None of your beeswax, little miss," said Mrs. Freeley. The professor is wielding a newspaper emphatically as they talk.

"It is disturbing, to be sure, but I do not think it has anything to do with *me*," Mrs. Och is saying.

"But why else should he be *here*, in Spira City?" protests the professor, waving the newspaper.

"First Nim," says Mrs. Och in a low voice. "He is looking for someone."

"No, it cannot be a coincidence, first the tree and now this—" But she shushes him, angling her head at Mr. Darius, and he helps her into her chair.

I eye the newspaper as the professor sits down. It is folded over and I cannot see the front page, so I step forward and say, "Shall I take this away for you, sir?"

Florence would be horrified, and Mrs. Och looks rather surprised as I lay my hands on the paper.

"You can leave it there," says Professor Baranyi, unbothered.

But I've flattened the page out enough to see the headline: *Cabdriver Murdered in Limory Cemetery*. Farther down the page I see, in smaller print, mention of Marianne Deneuve, Csilla's old friend from the theater. I've no time to read more, but if a dead cabbie is bigger news than a glamorous actress revealed as a witch, I reckon his killer is the same one who left the governess without the top of her head on the bridge. The one who traveled from Nim. I shudder a little inwardly.

Why should Professor Baranyi think it might have anything to do with Mrs. Och?

She is watching me closely. I step back, murmuring an apology.

"Can you read, Ella?" she asks, addressing me directly. Frederick and Mr. Darius had been chatting idly about something else, but they stop and look up at me also, surprised.

"No, ma'am," I say.

She stares at me a moment longer. Mrs. Och is, I suppose, a fairly ordinary-looking woman. She is of an average height and build, wears her white hair tied back demurely, and dresses in an elegant but not showy style. I cannot guess her age. My impression is that she is frail and unwell, for she spends a good deal of the day lying in bed. Frederick and the professor always seem terribly concerned about her health. Today, though, there is a vigor and clarity about her that is almost unsettling.

"The way your eyes moved as you looked at the paper," she says, "it looked as if you were reading. It's quite all right, you know. Reading is nothing to be ashamed of!"

Of course not. But it would be highly unusual in a housemaid, and I do not wish to appear in any way unusual.

"I wish I could, ma'am," I say softly. "I just like the way the words look."

She smiles a chilly little smile and begins to eat, which signals the others to begin also. Frederick is giving me a rather pitying look, I think. I step back against the wall. I don't need to disappear for them to forget all about me.

In the afternoon Florence is to assist Mrs. Freeley at the market, leaving Chloe and me alone together. Florence is terribly anxious, as if Chloe and I can't manage to clean up the scullery, fill the lamps, and ready the hearths on our own, but she is also proud to be doing something so important as watching Mrs. Freeley select fish and fowl and fruit from the market. Perhaps she will be allowed to carry the basket, lucky girl. In any case, I am glad to have some time with Chloe. She lost her entire family to Scourge and was taken in by Florence's family, so although they are cousins, they have grown up more like sisters. She and Florence came to work here together two years ago. In general, she does, and no doubt thinks, whatever Florence tells her to. Unlike Florence, though, she is pliable, and not averse to gossip.

"How long has Mr. Darius been staying here?" I ask her once we're upstairs, filling the lamps in the bedrooms.

"Oh, weeks," says Chloe, eyes widening. Which is not terribly specific, but then weeks are not months, nor days, and the timing of it strikes me.

"He came not long before the last maid left, then?" I say. "What was her name? Clarisa?"

"Yes, Clarisa Fenn. She'd worked here for ages. She was ever so nice." Then she looks uncertain, as if maybe Clarisa was not nice after all or, I suspect, not approved of by Florence.

"Wasn't it quite sudden, her leaving?" I say.

Chloe nods, eyes wide and shining. She wants to tell me, I can see. I just need to push her a little more.

"It wasn't because of those . . . *sounds* in the cellar, was it?" I ask, with a perhaps too theatrical shudder.

Chloe looks as if she might topple over from excitement. "She was scared," she whispers.

I lower my voice, widen my eyes: "You've heard it too?"

She nods wildly. "Clarisa thought . . . well, she thought it was a demon!" She looks sheepish at this.

"What do you mean?" I say.

"Demons aren't real," she says hastily, as if I'm going to report her for having folklorish beliefs. "Clarisa is Lorian, though."

I'm right, then, that Florence likely disapproved of her. Lorians are the oldest sect that worship the Nameless One and still have the most folklorish elements in their religious practice. They used to portray the Nameless One as a white stag, until the Crown declared it blasphemy, twenty odd years ago. The year before I was born, angry Lorians joined forces with folklore practitioners and element worshippers and all those that opposed the Crown for other reasons. The goal was to oust the childless King Zey in favor of his half brother, a Lorian by marriage, but it was a short-lived revolution. The king's brother was hung, along with his wife and children, and the revolutionary forces were slaughtered. It gets called the Lorian Uprising, but the Crown claimed the whole thing was orchestrated by a power-hungry coven of witches. The Spira City of my childhood was still reeling from the aftermath, and there is plenty of ill feeling left, to say the least. The first thing Florence asked me when I was hired on was "What religion are you?"

"Rainist," I answered promptly.

I'm not, but the king is Rainist, and it is the only unassailable answer. When I declared myself so, Florence gave a stern little nod of approval and Chloe looked relieved. Most people in the Twist go to the big Baltist temple, where there is lots of music and dancing and round honey cakes after service. I'd never go to a Rainist temple, where they all wear white and kneel, praying in silence for hours, and seem to be constantly fasting. In any case, Lorians must tread carefully these days. The white stag has disappeared from their temples, and talk of demons is imprudent at best.

"Do you know why she thought such a thing?" I ask.

"She saw something," says Chloe. "We all heard a noise on the landing one night. A sort of . . . grunting noise. Clarisa got up to see, and then she was screaming and screaming and everybody was up, and Mrs. Och told us to go back to bed, and that everything was fine. But Clarisa left the next day. She was a wreck, and all she said was, *I saw it.*"

This is maddening. "But what did she see?" I press her.

"I don't know!" says Chloe, delighted with our conversation. I swallow my sigh of frustration and file away the name Clarisa Fenn. It shouldn't be difficult to find her.

"Mrs. Och is very kind," I say, changing tack as Chloe piles wood in Frederick's fireplace.

"Oh yes," she says.

I'm not sure how to follow this in a way that will get Chloe to open up about Mrs. Och but am interrupted, anyway, by Frederick coming in.

"Excuse us," I say. "We're nearly done here."

"Not at all," he says, with that startled look he always seems to have, as if you've just walked in on him in the privy. "I was looking for you, in fact. Would you mind helping me for a moment in the library?"

"Both of us?" I ask, because he's just looking at me.

"No, just you, Ella," he says, and I get a little chill. Have I left some evidence of snooping? I follow him down the stairs to the library, a large book-lined room with comfortable chairs and a fireplace full of barely glowing embers.

He seems oddly nervous. I look up at him expectantly.

"At lunch . . . you said you wished you could read."

"Yes," I say.

"I could teach you, if you like," he blurts. "It seems a shame not to . . . well, I can't imagine not being able to read."

He looks abashed then, like he might have offended me, but I understand the sentiment and am rather touched by it. My mind moves quickly. I don't need to add pretended illiteracy during reading lessons to my lengthy list of tasks here.

"I've not much time," I say.

"I'll tell Florence I need your help sorting the books," he says. "Just a short time each day would be enough to get a start."

That settles it. If it will give me a break from housework, I'm delighted. And who knows where a greater intimacy with

Frederick might lead? He is the professor's assistant, and it could be very useful indeed to be friends with him.

"Thank you," I say, breaking out my best smile for him. "I can't begin to . . . It's very generous of you, sir. I've always longed to be able to read."

He flushes, and smiles back.

"Do call me Frederick," he says.

FOUR

Here is what I have learned over the past couple of days: First, inside the black case Professor Baranyi keeps hidden in the secret compartment behind his forbidden books are two vials of liquid, one amber, one clear, and five darts with hollow centers, along with the ingenious little handheld crossbow. Second, Mr. Darius's room in the cellar is bolted *from the outside*. In other words, he is not keeping people out; somebody else is locking him in. The wooden door has been replaced by a steel one, and there is also a very sturdy key lock. A pick might do for it in the hands of an expert, but I am no expert and have not managed to open the door in spite of two attempts. Third, Frederick is an appallingly bad teacher. It is a very good thing I already know how to read or I would be making no progress at all, and while I consider myself a reasonably good actress, pretending to fumble through the alphabet is a trying sort of performance. Frederick, however, is delighted with my progress and declares we will be reading the classics in no time. Florence is highly suspicious of my new task "sorting books" for Frederick but dares not challenge him. She probably thinks we're having an affair.

Midweek, we are all abruptly given the afternoon off.

"I have a visitor," Mrs. Och tells us. "We will require privacy."

This is extremely interesting, and I have no intention of leaving the house, except that Florence is dogging me everywhere in a disturbingly friendly way, right into my coat and boots.

"There's to be a Cleansing at the river, in front of the parliament buildings," she tells me in a whisper at the doorway, as if I didn't know.

Chloe is bundled up next to her, eyes wide and frightened.

"Come with us," says Florence.

She needs to work on her invitation style. I'm tempted to reply tartly that she can't give me orders if we have the afternoon off and I have other plans. But the two of them look so pale and eager that it's almost pathetic, and the truth is, I never miss a Cleansing. The prospect of missing this one had me feeling an uncomfortable kind of irritation that I can't explain and don't care to think on too deeply.

"Have you ever been to a Cleansing?" I ask.

Chloe shakes her head vigorously. Florence hesitates, not wanting to admit to any gap in her experience. Then she says, "My duties keep me far too busy to attend such events."

"It's not much to see," I tell them. "A few ragged witches get tossed in the river. Sometimes, if you're lucky, there's a bit of a scuffle. But it always ends up the same. Witches in the river."

Florence nods solemnly and then says, "Mrs. Och gave me some money to buy us hot buns."

She's resorting to bribery. They both seem to desperately want me along. I decide I'll go for a bit, then lose them and come back on my own.

"All right," I say, and I can see how relieved they both are. I feel something like relief myself—some loosening inside. "But honestly, I think you'll be disappointed."

∽

There is already a crowd along the river when we arrive, crossing Molinda Bridge to the Plateau, where the parliament buildings squat, stubbornly practical, next to the palace grounds. The palace itself is hidden behind thick walls, but from Mount Heriot you can see the tips of its elegant spires.

The sky is clear, but the wind has winter in its fingers. I notice that Chloe's and Florence's boots are nearly worn through, and their coats have seen many winters. While my clothes are nothing to brag about, at least my coat was new a little more than a year ago, purchased off a job at a wealthy collector's home, and I get boots whenever I need them. The lesson for housemaids of Spira City being: Crime pays. Florence buys three hot buns for us at a stall on the bridge and then I lead them to the narrow steps that take us down from the road to the low path hugging the river.

"Won't we have a better view above?" asks Florence, following me and nibbling at her bun. I want to tell her to eat it while it's hot. Really, I want to snatch it out of her pale little hands and eat it myself. I've already finished mine.

"It gets too crowded up there," I say. "Have you any money left?"

She is startlingly passive now that we're off her turf. The bustle of the city is my domain, and although she has no reason to know this, it's as if she senses it, and suddenly I am the one in charge. She holds out a few pennies, almost apologetically.

I take them and wave down a man smoking in a little rowboat.

"Three pennies?" he says with a raised eyebrow.

"And the charming company of three girls," I say with a wink.

He laughs a bit sadly at that but lets us on.

"Is this safe?" asks Chloe.

"Of course it is," snaps Florence, white-faced.

Before long, the low path and the road above are packed with bodies and the river is full of little boats like ours, anyone with a vessel making what pennies he can by giving spectators a better view. I flirt halfheartedly with our man so he doesn't decide to throw us off for someone offering more, but he is uninterested, tossing his cigarette into the water and withdrawing into himself.

"I'd like to see that Marianne Deneuve drowned!" Florence pipes up. "The vile beast!"

"Those poor children," agrees Chloe.

"What children?" I ask.

It seems that the story going around is that Marianne Deneuve cursed her lover *and* his wife and children with long monkey tails before fleeing Spira City. I give a snort, and Florence looks appalled.

"It's not funny in the least!" she cries. "Their lives are completely *ruined.*"

They go back and forth about how awful it is and what a fool he was and what a monster she is, and I do my best not to pitch myself into the water out of sheer boredom with their conversation. At last the long government barge pulls into view and everybody begins to shout and throw things into the river. I wish I'd remembered to bring an umbrella to shield us from the rotting fruit and debris raining down.

"What are they doing?" screams Chloe, panicked. Florence is gripping her hands together in her lap, her nostrils working, as if *she* were about to be tossed into the river.

"They're just excited," I say. "Trust me, we're safer out here."

It's true, sometimes the crowd goes a bit wild, and people have been killed in the crush and stampede. Our man rows us lazily around so that we can see the witches standing in a row on the deck of the barge. They have silver chains around their ankles, wrists, and necks, supposedly to impede their magic. A witch cannot cast a spell unless she writes it down, but witches are nevertheless preternaturally strong, and a superstitious fear of them makes their captors bind them in silver. There are eight of them today, and no children, thank the Nameless. Only one of them looks a proper witch—an old crone with a wicked face and bony hands like claws that grip the silver binding her. There is a giantess too, fair-haired and hideous, towering over the guards. A plump, dark witch sobs and sinks to her knees again and again, but the guards behind her keep forcing her back up. The rest of them mostly look like the kind of women you'd find selling silks or bangles at markets in the Twist. I find it interesting how convicted witches seem to come mostly from the lower classes, though now and again a rich girl just learning to write reveals her power and gets turned in by her parents or her governess. One year, the wife of a wealthy banker was drowned as a witch, and the excitement of it rippled through the city for days, but that sort of thing is rare.

"More guards than usual," I say, frowning, for they line the entire deck, dressed in their royal white and blue, rifles at the ready.

A moment later a slender man in a fur-collared black coat steps out of the cabin and climbs up onto the platform at the stern of the boat. The crowd roars—an ambiguous response, it seems to me. I've never seen him in person before, but I recognize him from likenesses in the newspaper: This is Agoston Horthy, the prime minister, and arguably the most powerful man in Frayne, for old King Zey reportedly spends his days in prayer and fasting and has little to do with affairs of state anymore. No wonder there are so many guards.

When King Zey came to the throne, nearly half a century ago, he outlawed element worship, potion making, palmistry, wish writing, elemental charms, tattooing and any other form of writing on the skin, even the old songs and stories—but still those practices flourished in secret for a time. Then Agoston Horthy came to power. For twenty years now he has been the king's bloodhound, a young man from a landowning family, handpicked by the aging king himself, nosing out all hidden corners where the old ways still hung on. Soldiers have destroyed the last of the shrines to the elements, and there aren't many folklore practitioners left, even in the Twist. Those who love him claim that he used to work the fields side by side with the farmers on his land and that he holds the common people close to his heart. Others remember only his ruthlessness in crushing the Lorian Uprising and the stern line he has hewed to since then. In my lifetime, the king has been a vague, holy figure, growing older and vaguer and, by all accounts, holier, behind the palace walls, while Agoston Horthy has emerged as the terrible, unswerving captain of the ship of state.

In person, he does not look nearly as formidable as his likenesses would have him. He is thin and small, with a lined, doggish face, pouches under his eyes, and gray in his hair. His coat is worn at the shoulders, and the fur collar is rather shabby. In fact, he looks like a weary grocer, but that impression is erased as soon as he speaks.

"Like you, I am here to bear witness," he says in a thunderous baritone. The crowd falls silent. "For the glory of the Nameless One and the safety of Frayne, we do not tolerate unnatural magics within our borders. Helmed by our great king Zey, Frayne is a holy nation, a nation that thrives on the hard work and honest faith of its people, a nation that rejects false worship and evil magics. We have led the way, and the rest of the New Porian kingdoms have followed. It is our duty to show the world what a holy nation looks like, but more than that, it is our duty to keep our children safe, to protect one another and be true to one another and to the Nameless One. I am here to witness the blessed waters of the river Syne wash away the poison that threatens us all, that threatens our children: this dark magic, the terrible power of the witch." He pauses and then leans forward and says: "I derive no pleasure from death, from killing. But what would you do, you mothers and fathers, to protect your dear children? Would you not do whatever was required? Would you not murder those that threaten them, and think it just? *You,* the honest Fraynish people, are my only children, and without qualm I shall put to death all those that wish you harm."

Wild applause follows. I'm worried Florence is going to fall overboard, she's clapping so hard. It is a masterful bit of oration, delivered with every appearance of absolute sincerity. Whatever resentment common people may feel about his stamping out the old folklorish ways, the prime minister's implacable pursuit of witches has earned him widespread admiration, and it is said that no country in the world is less disrupted by magic than Frayne.

Agoston Horthy bows his head, clasps his hands before his chin, closes his eyes. I think there are tears on his cheeks, but it is difficult to tell from here. A Rainist holy, all in white, speaks a blessing, while his devoted lights the torch to prove that these are witches. There is one witch with brown hair, a bit younger than the rest, keeping very still, although she is next to the witch who keeps sobbing and collapsing. I watch her as the Rainist holy gives the order and his devoted lays the flaming torch on the bare arm of each witch, one at a time.

A couple of them scream and pretend to burn, and the crowd laughs. The devoted holds the torch to them for longer to show the crowd that they do not burn. The crowd shouts and stamps. I think I hear an odd sound from Chloe, or maybe from Florence, but I am too busy watching the young brown-haired witch. She doesn't move when the torch touches her. She shuts her eyes.

Somebody shouts, "Catch it, Agnes!" and a small thin object goes sailing through the air. Whoever threw it is trying to escape through the crowd, but they have him already; they are beating him without knowing yet what he has done.

The giantess and another witch, one of them presumably Agnes but perhaps not, lunge for the object. There is a shot and the giantess staggers, a red stain bursting across the front of the man's shirt she wears. She falls against the rail of the barge. We have drifted so close that we are looking right up into her face, twisted with rage.

"Pen," she says hoarsely, as if she is asking us for one.

I suppose that's what was thrown. But neither witch got it. The giantess is hauled back into line, bleeding heavily as our man rows us a little farther out. She is unsteady on her feet, but it takes more than a gunshot to kill a witch. Drowning is the surest way, for no witch can swim, or even float. Water is their great enemy; fire their friend.

It is a small bit of drama to liven up the Cleansing. A year or so back, a witch actually managed to snap a guard's neck before being shot three times and hurled overboard. I still remember the look on her face as she twisted his head, the horrible sound it made. Agoston Horthy watches expressionlessly, one hand on his gun, and the holy rambles a bit about the Nameless One showing us grace for doing His bidding while the man who threw the pen is beaten to an immobile, bleeding heap on the low path. I fix my gaze on the young witch again, her eyes and mouth squeezed shut, her fists clenched. Something is building in my chest, some terrible pressure.

The witches struggle, some of them, but there on the ledge with a row of soldiers behind them, there is nowhere to flee to. They are hurled untidily into the water, clothes flapping, screaming or silent. The young witch just holds herself tight and falls. Like all of them, she sinks like a stone. The crowd roars, a deafening sound.

Nine years ago, I watched my mother die like this. I cheer myself hoarse.

∽

This is what I remember: My parents were in love, and they were unhappy. My mother was a washerwoman who did a bit of palm reading too—a dangerous side job, in Agoston

Horthy's Frayne. She wouldn't read my palm, though. "It's mostly bunk," she said lightly. "The lines on your hand might tell your path, but you can surely wander off it." The brick courtyard behind our flat was always hung with other people's laundry, and when we were very small, Dek and I used to play hide-and-seek among the great white sheets and fading underthings of Spira City's residents. My father was a famous jockey before I was born, but I knew him only as an opium addict.

My mother was pretty, with olive skin and thick hair, but I find it harder and harder to recall her face exactly, its proportions and expressions. I remember better her hands, both the feel of them and the look of them: small, brown, callused hands, deft and clever, *moving* hands. I remember her hands folding paper scraps into little animal shapes to delight us, working a hairbrush through my tangles, cutting bread, pouring milk, reaching to wipe a smudge from my face. I can see vividly, still, her fingers striking a match or pinning laundry to the line. The way she gestured when she and my father were arguing, her hands like twin knives slicing the air asunder. Afterward, the air was in shreds, but nothing had changed.

If anyone asked, we said proudly, "Our mama is Ammi, the washerwoman." We called her that—everyone called her that—but we all knew she was more than that. Sometimes she'd be gone for days, and when she came back her hands moved even faster than usual, her worried fingers never still. Cloaked figures turned up in the middle of the night to whisper and pass messages that she burned in the stove. By day, the denizens of the Twist tipped their hats to her, gave her a good price at the market, called out "Good day, Ammi!" from across the street. The big men of the neighborhood nodded to her when they saw her pass. The old crones who had seen everything and knew everyone had things to whisper in her ear. She was at the heart of it all, connected deeply to the very pulse of the Twist, the secret and the not so secret, but more than that, people respected her and they *liked* her. They gave my father more chances than he ever deserved, for her.

My father's name was Jerel. I remember him giggling in a corner of the room at nothing, and sleeping in the stairs, and promising my mother, promising us, promising the landlord, promising the cabbies in the street, that he was going to quit and get a decent job.

"Don't believe him," Dek told me, so I didn't.

My mother believed him, though, for years. Or maybe she didn't, maybe she was just pretending to believe him, but she stuck by him, anyway. I think he was a handsome man once, but there wasn't much left of that by the end.

Dek took care of me most of the time, though he was only three years older. We ran wild with the other children, little bands of troublemakers in the Twist, always getting dragged home by the ear or whipped by whoever we were irritating that day. I learned early on that there was a secret space I could retreat to, sort of out the back of me, a shadowy place like a pocket in the world I could pull myself into, and nobody would see me. When I told Dek what I could do, he told me not to let on. So I was careful, and guarded my special skill. My secret. I liked having a secret, and somehow it made sense that it was dangerous. Maybe it's because my mother was a witch that I can do it, but I am no witch myself. I burn very well and am a fine swimmer. A pen in my hand is just a pen; it wields no magic.

I was still very young when I understood about my mother. I knew what witches were, of course: wicked things wielding their pens to disrupt the natural order, masquerading as human, always plotting to rule over the rest of us, worshippers of the Dark Ones who live under the earth in Kahge. They'd give you boils and eat your guts for supper without the slightest pang of remorse. Fire in their veins, pitiless, soulless.

We were outside throwing stones at rats, of which there were a great many that summer, when somebody hollered out a window, "Raid! Soldiers! Raid!"

We all scattered, making for home. Dek and I ran up the stairs to the little flat our parents kept above the laundry. There was a smell of burnt cardamom. Our mother was sitting at the table scribbling something awkwardly on a piece of paper. I don't know where she learned to read or write, and she didn't do it well, but well enough, as it turned out. Her face was flushed and slightly damp.

"There's a raid," said Dek, almost angrily.

"Hush," she said, rising. She fed the paper she'd been writing on into a little fire in the gas stove and turned to me with a pen and inkpot. "Go and hide these out of the building," she said. "Hurry. Don't be seen."

I look back on that sometimes and think: She knew. *Don't be seen.* That's why she gave the things to me and not to Dek, who was older.

Proud as anything, I ran out of the building and into the street. Soldiers were coming around the corner, row after row of them, dazzling in their white and blue. They wore long shining boots, swords at their hips, and rifles on their backs. I huddled against the wall, withdrawing into my secret space, so they would not see me. They were breaking off into smaller groups at each building, barging into shops and apartments. Two of them went stomping up the stairs to our flat in those magnificent boots, hat feathers waving. I shoved the pen and ink into a gutter pipe, deep as they would go, and ran up the stairs after them.

The smell of burnt cardamom was now covered by my mother's perfume, which she had sprayed around the room. Our flat looked so small and dreary with the soldiers in it, the white feathers in their hats brushing the ceiling. One of them was short and fat, with a double chin and kind eyes. The other had a mouth like a trap, and he was going through our few belongings.

Dek looked scared and uncertain next to our mother, but she was smiling up at the soldiers and touching a hand self-consciously to her hair.

"Your papers, ma'am," said the fat soldier.

"Of course."

Our mother crossed to the other side of the room, where she pulled a brick out of the wall. Behind it was a little tin box, which she took out and opened, handing over her papers.

"My husband's too," she said. "He's at work now."

"What does he do?" asked the soldier, looking at the papers.

"Carpenter," she lied blandly.

"This your son?" he asked, gesturing at Dek. I had disappeared myself near the door.

"No," she said. "This is Benedek, just an errand boy. I believe he lives the next street over. Who are your parents again, dear?"

Dek gave her an openmouthed stare. She waved a hand dismissively.

"Rosalie Tish," she said. "I remember now. Two streets over." She added in a loud whisper, "No father."

But the soldiers weren't interested.

"Nothing," said Trap Mouth, having rooted through everything we had.

"Well," said the fat soldier uncomfortably. "I suppose we could just carry on."

"We've got to check, though," said the other, taking out a box of matches.

"I suppose so. Apologies, ma'am. Orders, you understand. Would you give me your hand, please?"

"My hand?" She looked alarmed, withdrawing slightly. "What's going on?"

"I'm sorry, ma'am," said the fat one, and Trap Mouth went over and grabbed her by the arm. She gasped but did not resist as the fat one took the matches and lit one.

"Oh, please don't," she whimpered. Trap Mouth gave her a hard yank by the arm, then staggered as Dek went catapulting into him. I ran at him too, wanting to tear his eyes out, but he hurled Dek straight into me, and we both went tumbling across the floor.

"Little beasts!" said Trap Mouth as my mother gave a shriek.

"She burns," said the fat one, blowing out the match. A red welt was rising on the back of my mother's hand.

"Barbaric!" she cried, clutching her burnt hand to her chest.

"Sorry, ma'am," said the fat one.

"Where did this one come from?" Trap Mouth pointed at me with his foot.

"No idea," said my mother angrily. "Scat, both of you!" This at Dek and me. We ran down to the street, me shaking with sobs. The soldiers followed us out, but ignored us, instead joining their company and disappearing around a corner. No witches were taken from our street, though we heard later that four were arrested from the Twist, including Ma Rosen, who sold cinnamon buns in Fitch Square. They were drowned a few days later.

When Dek and I returned to the flat later on, our mother looked even more exhausted than usual.

"What did they want?" I cried, although Dek had already explained it to me.

"Just soldiers up to mischief," she said.

"I hate them!" I said. She smiled wryly at me and said, "So do I."

"Why did you say we weren't yours?" Dek wanted to know, still hurt.

Our mother reached out and drew us both close to her in a hug.

"Because," she said, "when you have an enemy, you must never let them know what matters to you the most. Or who."

I nestled against her, breathing in the soapy smell of her— soap with a hint of burnt cardamom and perfume. My heart was racing, but I did not say to Dek what he also must have noticed: The blister on her hand was gone, the skin as smooth as if it had never been touched by fire.

∾

The next time I smelled that same smell was when Dek had the Scourge. I remember her bent over his bed, her child- ish scrawl on the sheets of paper scattered across the floor, the inkpot nearly empty. She was whispering something over and over again while she wrote, and the smell of burnt car- damom was so heavy in the air I could hardly breathe. She sent me for more ink. I had no money, and she told me to steal some, so I did. Then she sent me away, to the aunt in the country.

When I came back, Dek was half-blind and crippled, but he was still Dek, and still alive. My mother too was changed. Whatever she'd done to save his life, it had taken something from her, and she did not recover. She was thin and faded and quiet, a shadow of her former self. I suppose I knew the truth by then, but I didn't allow it to the front of my thoughts. Witches were evil, and my mother was not evil.

But my mother *was* a witch. A few months later, Agoston Horthy offered a reward of ten silver freyns to anyone turning over a witch. This was an outlandish sum for most in our neighborhood, and there were Cleansings every week for a time. I don't know who turned her in. The soldiers came in the night, filling our flat, hauling her out of bed. One of them knocked out my tooth when I tried to stop them. I lay in Dek's arms, swallowing mouthfuls of my own blood, and watched them hold the flame to her arm. She stood motionless, casting only one unreadable look at us when they dragged her away down the stairs.

Our father sobbed, and did nothing, and disappeared from our lives the next day. We never saw him again. I suppose he only hung around for her and not for us, which ought not to have come as a surprise, but you never really expect a parent to abandon you, no matter how useless a parent he might be.

The next time I saw her was on a barge like the one today, still in her nightgown, before a shouting, hateful crowd. She didn't tremble or fight. She searched the crowd, maybe for Dek and me, but did not see us. They threw her overboard and the river closed over her and my screams were lost in the rising chorus of cheers.

Chloe throws up on the low path as soon as we get off the little boat. Afterward, she stays crouched there, weeping.

"You ought not to be upset," Florence tells her harshly. "The will of the Nameless One was done! They were evil things, and we've rid the earth of them! It's no good pitying them."

"I don't," sobs Chloe. "I don't!"

Florence herself is white as a sheet, not quite as hard as she'd like to think herself.

"It shakes you up, the first time," I say.

Florence looks rather relieved at this.

"Do you hear that?" she says to Chloe. "It's quite normal to be upset. Do pull yourself together."

"Perhaps we ought to get some more hot buns," I say wistfully, but none of us has any money and I can hardly pick a pocket right in front of them.

"Have you seen many Cleansings?" asks Florence.

"I go to all of them," I answer without thinking.

She looks impressed and asks me something, but I don't hear her. I feel as if somebody has run me straight through the heart with a bayonet. For there on the street above, I've just seen Wyn. Just for a moment, a flash—laughing Wyn with a bottle of something in his hand and a black-haired girl on his arm. I recognize her too: Arly Winters, the herbalist's lazy daughter. She is supposed to be learning that profession, but instead she poses for art classes with no clothes on. She has dimples and an enviable figure.

"Come on," I say, pulling Chloe up by the arm. I hurry

up the stairs, and the two of them follow, calling after me to wait. Out in the street, I can't see him. I push through the crowd, looking about wildly, heart thumping, but it's no good. I tell myself I imagined it. I've lost Chloe and Florence, so I steal another bun. Still, I can't slow the painful *thump thump thump*ing in my chest. Wyn and Arly? No. No. *Thump. Thump.*

I should get back to the house and see who Mrs. Och has visiting, why she wanted us out of the way. As the crowd thins, I hear a policeman saying to a gentleman in a dark suit, ". . . should have been nine of them."

"You can't mean one of them escaped from Hostorak?" says the man. I slow my step, edging closer.

"Not from Hostorak. On the way to the river! They switched her off somehow. Some ordinary girl all in chains, declaring her innocence. One guard realized he didn't recognize her, held a match to her and burn she did. They're still holding her, trying to figure out what happened. But they're one witch down for now."

"Unbelievable!" says the man in the suit.

"It was something unnatural, all right," says the cop. "No way it could have happened, else. They're under guard from the prison to the boat, watched every second."

"Speaks to the importance of drowning every last forsaken one of them, doesn't it?" says the man. "They get organized again and there's no telling what they'll do! We'd all end up their slaves, by the holies!"

"Terrifying things, aren't they," mutters the cop.

I walk the rest of the way back to Mikall Street. The streets are quiet now, most people still milling about by the river. From the front, Mrs. Och's house looks rather forbidding, gray stone and a black iron gate, windows like cold, reflecting eyes, door shut to me. I slip through the gate and over to the side door, next to the outdoor privy, letting myself into the scullery. The house is still and silent, the scullery cold. I expect to find visitors in the parlor, but it's empty. Climbing the stairs, I hear voices coming from Mrs. Och's reading room.

The door is closed. I go and put my eye to the keyhole, but I can't see much besides Professor Baranyi's trousered legs.

". . . a letter for my friend in Tulles," Mrs. Och is saying. "From there, she can make arrangements to get you across the border."

A muffled voice protesting.

"They do speak Fraynish in Sinter," says Professor Baranyi, his voice clearest, as he is closest to the door. "It's colder than Frayne, but the capital, Zurt, is a lovely city, and you will be safer there—that is the most important thing."

Again the muffled voice, upset. Mrs. Och replies this time, but I only catch snatches. Something about contacts, and help. Then somebody inside is coming to the door. I spring back against the wall, vanishing myself as quickly as I can. Frederick comes out, a middle-aged woman in a gray shawl on his arm, her eyes red-rimmed.

"It will be all right, Mrs. Sandor," he tells her quietly as they pass me. "They seem strange and brusque, I know, but they have done this before, and they are good people. You'll be taken care of."

Professor Baranyi follows, closing the door behind him. Mrs. Och remains in her reading room, and so I go downstairs and make myself something to eat in the scullery. Frederick goes out and returns some time later in an electric hackney. The woman, dressed quite finely now and holding a ruffled carrying case like a wealthy lady off on holiday, is bundled into the hackney, and it glides quickly and soundlessly away.

Mrs. Sandor. *Jahara* Sandor—Hostorak 15c.

If Mrs. Och is smuggling witches out of the country, I'll need some proof of it beyond what I've just overheard. I remember the lists of names and places in Professor Baranyi's study. I will have something impressive to put down in my next report, but the thought gives me no pleasure. I beg off my evening duties, claiming a headache, and go to bed early, but I can't sleep. I lie on my cot and stare at the peeling paint on the ceiling, imagining my mother whisked away to safety in Zurt. We might have joined her there. I push the thought away and instead wonder, why Zurt? Are the laws different in Sinter? I'd thought witchcraft to be punishable by death across the whole of New Poria, an alliance of nations formed after the Magic Wars. I will have to ask Esme about it.

I am still awake when Florence and Chloe come to bed, Florence muttering about how some people like to take it easy. I lie awake half the night, thinking of the witches who drowned today and Jahara Sandor's setting off in the hackney, saved from that fate, it would seem, by Mrs. Och. Over and over, I think of the way Frederick held Mrs. Sandor's arm in the hallway, the kindness in his voice when he spoke to her—like she was just a woman, and not loathsome, not evil, not at all to be feared.

T*he innkeeper looks over the account book, reading the same page twice without taking it in, before he sighs and closes it. He is thinking about the woman who left today with her baby. He'd fetched Jensen, his regular driver, to take her, though she would not say where she was going. He would ask Jensen later. "I need someone I can trust," she'd said. Now the sun has gone down, but he is still thinking of her with an odd sadness he can't place. Perhaps he'd gone a bit sweet on her. She was very pretty. No ring on her finger, despite her having the little boy.*

The front door blows open with a bang, and the wind comes howling in, sending his papers flying. He gathers the pages and finds among them a folded piece of notepaper. It has her scent on it. For a moment he dares hope it might be a message to him, something saying where to find her. He unfolds it, his heart beating a little faster. Another great gust of wind comes, and he hurries to the door to shut it. But in the doorway, he stops. The street is quiet, the moon rising above the rooftops, almost full. It is a clear night, bearing winter's chill. He is cold in his shirt, and yet something compels him to step out into the quiet street. His inn is brightly lit and inviting, with its great fire blazing in the hearth, he notes with satisfaction from outdoors. Almost empty now, though. Not many travelers this time of year.

He walks to the end of the street, shivering, and turns the corner. Not so far to walk to the river, see if there's any ice yet. He should fetch his coat. He should go indoors and finish the accounting. He walks down the street, whistling a little, then stops.

There is someone under the streetlamp. Something.

"What the . . ."

A blade in a black-furred hand. Soft black feet, like great cat paws, walking toward him. But walking upright, like a man.

"Nameless One, protect me," he whispers, unable to move, even as the thing draws close, towering over him, even as it grasps the back of his neck and raises the blade to his forehead. The piece of notepaper flutters from his hand to the ground:

Forget me

FIVE

When I get to the library with coffee for Frederick, wondering if it is more painful to sit there and pretend to read poorly or to clean the inside of the grandfather clock on the landing, he is wearing his coat and putting a piece of paper into the pocket.

"Oh," I say, feigning disappointment. "Are we not reading today?"

He looks up as if I've startled him, but he always looks that way.

"I'm so sorry, Ella—I've got to run an errand for the professor," he says. The way he says it, a little grudgingly, I smell an opportunity.

"Let me do it," I say. "Heaven knows you have more than enough to do as it is."

He grins. "That's kind, Ella. But really, I must go. It's a ways from here."

"All the more reason you ought to let *me* go," I press. "I

thought you were trying to finish that history of Old Poria this week?"

I know all of Frederick's private pet projects now. He is passionate about history and language study and longs for more time to read. If he could give up sleeping and eating, he would.

He hesitates, and I push on.

"I'm feeling so cooped up today, you'd be doing me a favor! I'll run the errand for you, and you just hole up in your room and get some work of your own done. You deserve the break, Frederick; you're much too busy."

He shakes his head. "Really, you can't, Ella. It's . . . I've got to go to East Spira. It's not a nice area."

"I know the Edge," I say boldly. "My family is in Jepta now, but we lived in Spira City for years before moving out there."

"Did you?" he looks astounded. "I took you for a country girl."

Well, the more fool you, then.

"I suppose I am, at heart," I say, laughing. "But I know Spira well enough, and I know my way around the Edge. Nobody will bother me. I'll be in and out as quick as you please. You're the one who'd look out of place there."

"You hardly fit in there either!" he protested. "A pretty, fresh-faced girl like you!"

And then he blushes. I hold my hand out for the paper. "Go on, we'll be doing each other a favor. Tell me what the errand is."

He relents. Poor Frederick, such an easy target, always.

"There's a parcel for the professor at an alchemist's shop," he says. "This is the address—can you read it?"

I frown at the paper. "I know the number," I say. "What's this? Fi-ling-ton . . ."

"Fillington Street, the Adder's Switch," he rushes in, like he always does. "Just tell them you're there for the professor and they'll give it to you. Oh heavens, I'm not sure— Is it safe for a girl?"

"It's broad daylight!" I laugh at him. "You don't think there are girls in the Edge?"

After a bit more of my teasing and persuading, he gives me the scrap of paper and money for a hackney. I tell Florence I'm running an errand for Frederick and her eyes nearly drop out of her head, but what can she say? On Lirabon Avenue I flag down a hackney pulled by a miserable-looking gray horse. Freed from the day's drudgery, neither pretending to read poorly nor cleaning a clock, I hum all the way out to the Edge.

∾

The Edge squats in a little dip between sprawling Limory Cemetery and the Twist. Most of the streets are so narrow that a hackney can't even fit down them. Unlike the Twist, with its hustle and bustle and smells, the Edge always feels deserted. You see faces at windows sometimes, but they disappear fast when you look at them. People in the streets keep their heads down. Nobody smiles or stops to chat. Nobody shouts rude comments from windows. It is quiet, and damp, and full of rats.

At the alchemist's shop, a pale young man with black hair and blisters around his nostrils opens the door and stares at me.

"I'm here for Professor Baranyi," I say. When he just keeps looking at me blankly, I add, "I'm supposed to pick something up for him."

"Hold on," he says, and slams the door on me.

I stand shivering, holding my coat around me. A light snow begins to fall, the first snow of the winter. I look up into it as the sparse white flakes quickly become a flurry. Some movement to my left startles me, and I flatten against the wall, ready to disappear.

It is a boy, no more than nine or ten. His coat is poorly patched and his boots have holes in them. He has a scruff of gingery uncombed hair and freckles across his nose. He's been in a fight recently, earning him a cut lip and a black eye.

"You work for that lady in the Scola?" he asks.

"Who's asking?"

"I got a message for her. I tried to go to the house yesterday, but the police told me to get back across the river."

"I'm not surprised," I say, looking him over. "You've got the Edge written all over you. Was it a cop gave you that busted lip?"

He shrugs.

"Who is the message from?"

He frowns suddenly, as if confused. "I dunno, someone at the inn—I don't remember, but it was for the lady in the Scola. I heard she sends her people out here for things."

Are the professor's orders a subject of gossip in the Edge? Perhaps the alchemist's boy has a big mouth, and I wonder if I should tell Frederick this. But then, who am I trying to protect them from? It's rather a silly idea, if you think about it, since I'm as likely to be their undoing as anyone.

"Well, give me the message," I say. "I'll take it to my mistress."

The boy hands me a sealed envelope and waits for a tip. I give him a penny and ask him, "Who do you work for?"

"I run messages for Morris at the Red Bear in Forrestal, him and his customers," he says, and then scampers off when I give him another penny.

I tuck the letter into my coat and bang on the door again. It swings open right away and the boy with the blistered nostrils peers out, giving me a baleful look.

"Well?" I say.

He hands me a brown parcel and slams the door again. Just the sort of exuberant fellow you so often encounter out here.

The snow is coming down hard now, but I've got another stop to make.

&

On the slope between the Edge and the Twist, there is a shoe shop. A picture of a boot hangs outside it, and inside, you can be fitted for a pair of custom-made shoes or boots at a very reasonable price. The workshop is clean and smells of leather. Repairs can be done on the spot. In a small room at the back of the shop, a kettle is always hot on the stove. Fresh coffee is either ready to be drunk or in the process of being made. Warm, soft rolls come out of the little oven.

The shop is quiet, but I can smell the coffee and the bread. I make for the door at the back and tap lightly with my knuckles.

"Come in."

It is an extraordinary voice, neither male nor female but somewhere in between, and it is attached to an extraordinary person. I first heard that voice some months after my mother was drowned. I was stealing apples in the market when it rumbled behind me: "You have an interesting talent, my girl." I spun around and looked up into a face that had almost folded right in on itself, a swarthy mass of wrinkles and creases, fringed by a mane of wild silver hair. Nobody should have been able to *see* me. But Liddy could.

"I've been talking to people," she'd gone on. (I have been given to understand that Liddy is a woman, though I might not have guessed it myself.) "I've some employment in mind for you and your brother."

She had seemed to know all about us. I got used to that, eventually—how Liddy seemed to know everything and everyone. My curiosity about her has become almost a game between us, but she never really tells me anything, and I do not know why *she* can see me when I vanish, while others can't. I have asked her, of course, but she only says that perhaps she is better at looking than most people.

She came to Spira City, so she says, the year after the Lorian Uprising, though she does not say where she came

74

from. The very day she spied me thieving in the market, she brought us to Esme, and Esme opened her home to us, maybe just because Liddy said it was a good idea. Later, Esme told me, "I've known Liddy as long as you've been alive, and if she says a thing is so, it's likely to be so." If she is the subject of gossip hereabouts, it is gossip without malice, for she has done many a good turn for those down on their luck.

"I thought I might see you today," says Liddy when I come in, brushing snow off my sleeves. She is resting in her rocking chair, still wearing her leather apron and smelling of shoe polish. "Isn't that odd? Sometimes I feel as if we are acting in cycles, or patterns. We think we are free to choose whatever course we wish, but a certain pattern holds us, keeps us to our set course, and we do not vary it. It brings us around to the same places, again and again, to the same feelings, over and over. Here you are, and I, expecting you for some reason I do not know. Could be a coincidence. I don't want to give up on the idea of free will—what would I make of my life, if I didn't believe in my own choices?"

It's hard to know what Liddy is talking about sometimes.

"Hello," I say.

Liddy chuckles, a deep growl of a sound.

"You are hungry, I expect. Help yourself."

I devour a couple of the fresh rolls and pour myself a cup of coffee. Liddy has the best coffee in Spira City, though she is secretive about her source.

"Do you mind if I use your kettle?" I ask. "I need to open a letter."

"Ah," says Liddy. "Your new job."

"Yes. Have you heard of Mrs. Och, in the Scola?"

"Philanthropic, eccentric," says Liddy vaguely. "Old."

I steam the envelope open and take out the letter.

"Have you pen and paper? I should copy this down."

Liddy fetches me an old-fashioned quill pen, a pot of ink, paper, and a blotter. I sit myself at the table and set about diligently copying down the letter the messenger boy gave me.

Dear Mrs. Och,

You do not know me, but I know of you from your brother Gennady. I am mother to his son, and he once told me that if ever I needed help, I could ask you for assistance. He said you would not judge me and I hope that he is right. My son and I are in terrible danger. I have arrived in Spira City but I dare not stay in one place for long. Today I go to Madam Loretta's in East Spira. You may send me a reply there. When I move on, I will be sure to return for any messages. Pray you, help me.

Bianka Betine

So Mrs. Och has a brother: Gennady. I wonder about this Bianka, staying at a brothel in the Edge with a child. Madam Loretta is known for taking in women in trouble, women afraid of husbands or fathers or employers. Her whores have a well-fed look about them, unlike so many of the starved waifs selling their bodies in this part of the city, and I have heard she never shuts her door on a woman in distress. A softy, in other words, though her brothel has stood for a good many years, so she must be a decent businesswoman too. I reseal the letter, fold up my copy, and tuck it away in a pocket. Then I turn to the brown parcel, plucking the knots in the twine apart and unwrapping it. Inside I find a book in Inglese, a vial of powder, and a small leather pouch.

"I thought I might need your help," I say to Liddy, who has been sitting in silence all this time, lost in her own thoughts, I suppose. "What have I got here?"

Liddy takes the stopper from the vial and sniffs the powder. My bet is that she was some kind of lady alchemist in another life, wherever she lived before she came here, though when I suggested this to Esme she just snorted.

"Rifolta," she says. "Poison."

Inside the pouch is something that looks like a piece of bark or a dried mushroom. It is brown and withered and gives off a pungent, moldy smell.

"Oxley root," says Liddy, examining it. "Good for snake-bite, among other things, and might go a ways toward neu-tralizing the effects of the rifolta too. It was used long ago for combating sickness caused by magic."

"What's the book?" I ask. I recognize Inglese, but I can't read it.

Liddy glances at the title, then opens the book and flips through it.

"About the absorption of poisons."

I wonder if any of this will be significant to the as-yet-unknown client I am writing my reports for.

"So the person who wants all this . . . is he planning to poison somebody? Or cure somebody who's been poisoned?"

"My best guess, dear, is that he wants to poison somebody *and* cure them, at the same time."

"What in blazing Kahge is the point of that?" I ask.

"He wants to use a poison but mitigate the effects in some way," says Liddy. "Fascinating. I can't imagine why."

I ponder this a bit, and not knowing what to make of it, I let my mind wander. It wanders where it always wanders, straight into Wyn's arms, and I think again of what I saw, or thought I saw, at the Cleansing. Liddy watches me, black eyes just visible in the folds of her remarkable face.

"Are you well, Julia?"

"Yes, fine," I answer distractedly.

"And Benedek?"

"We're both fine," I say.

Liddy looks up at the ceiling. So do I. There are patches of mold on it.

"I wonder sometimes about the pattern that holds you. The places you return to."

Heaven help us. "You mean like here?"

"No." Liddy smiles—a fearsome expression, on her face. "I mean like the river Syne whenever there is a Cleansing."

My heart skips a beat. "How did you know I was there?"

"Because you are always there," says Liddy. "You are caught in something that takes you back. But I think it does you no good, Julia."

I shrug. "I almost *didn't* go yesterday. I got talked into it. Does it matter?"

"That depends," says Liddy. "Maybe nothing matters. But here we are. What can we do?"

I don't know what Liddy's getting at. Well, besides maybe not approving of my going to Cleansings.

"I don't think about it much," I say. "Life is short."

I think of Wyn again. If I go to the river Syne to stare at Death, I go to his bed to drink my fill of Life. I want love and good food and adventure. I want my days to hold the possibility of surprise and joy. I want to see the sea someday. I don't care about the patterns Liddy is talking about, as long as I don't have to break my back working for pennies, as long as my life gives me room to breathe, something to laugh about, a lovely boy to keep me warm when winter sets in.

"Sometimes life is short," says Liddy. "Sometimes life is very long. It's always all we have. Do you want to spend yours at the bottom of the river?"

A shudder runs through me, and I leap to my feet.

"It's cold, Liddy. Should I light the stove?"

"No," says Liddy.

"I'd better go," I say.

Liddy nods and parcels up the book, the root, the vial, tying the twine around the parcel just as it was. Liddy never asks questions about that sort of thing.

"Be careful, Julia," she says.

"I always am," I call back over my shoulder. I'm already halfway out the door.

∽

I should go straight back to the house. They will be wondering where I am if I don't, and Frederick will surely be worried now, having sent me to the Edge. I hope his gallantry doesn't provoke him to go looking for me. But I can't help myself. I'll think of some excuse for why I got held up. I have to see Wyn.

Esme is alone in the parlor, seated on the floor in a bizarrely contorted position, eyes closed serenely. She is burning scented herb sticks on the table and the room is a dizzying mix of jasmine and foxruth. Suddenly she raises her arms up over her head, palms together. I jump, and her eyes open.

"Julia," she breathes.

Esme is a great believer in some very strange exercises practiced in the far eastern isles of Honbo.

"Hullo," I say, looking around hopefully for something to eat but finding nothing. Three emerald necklaces are laid out on the table on handkerchiefs. Stealing jewels is easy, Esme always says, but fencing them is getting harder all the time. I doubt whoever brought her these got what he'd hoped for them.

"Esme, what happens to witches in Sinter?" I ask. "Aren't they drowned, like here?"

"Witches are drowned across New Poria and beyond," she says, rising to her feet. She moves with surprising grace for someone so tall and powerfully built. "But I don't believe the queen of Sinter is quite as invested in rooting them out as is our esteemed prime minister."

"So Sinter would be safer for a witch than Frayne," I say.

"Anywhere in the world is safer for a witch than Frayne. But a witch would have to go a long way—Yongguo, perhaps—to wield her pen freely."

Yongguo is the terrible empire in the Far East, half the world away. It is a lawless, barbaric place, where the emperor is rumored to keep witches at court.

"Why do you ask?" She fixes me with her clear gaze.

"There was a Cleansing yesterday," I tell her. "Agoston Horthy was there and made a pretty speech."

"He has a gift for speeches," says Esme, her lips tightening at his name.

Like any sane person, Esme gave up on the revolution after the Lorian Uprising. I asked her about it once, and she told me tersely that there were not enough courageous oppositionists left alive to effect a revolution anymore. We used to play revolutionaries and soldiers when we were little kids, but now that I am older, I don't waste much thought on it. Let the powerful run around having their wars and chasing their witches if they want to. It's no business of mine. Not anymore. They've taken everything they can from me already.

"Well, and I heard a cop telling someone that one of the witches had got away. I wondered where a witch might run to."

"And you thought Sinter?"

I shrug. Even those that supported the uprising and who long for the old ways are uneasy about witches. Esme knows what my mother was, of course, and she has never been twitchy about my own abilities, but I am not sure what she would say if I were to tell her that I suspect Mrs. Och of helping witches.

"I imagine it is rather like Frayne used to be before King

Zey's rule," she says. "If a witch kept her head down and didn't do anything nasty or show-offy, she'd likely be left alone. There were even some who'd seek out a rumored witch to buy a spell in those days, if they were desperate enough."

"Weren't people frightened of witches back then?" I ask.

"Oh, I reckon they were frightened," she says, and I think of how, after my mother was drowned, the same people who used to greet her in the street spat on me, and those that had loved her best avoided my eyes and said nothing, did nothing for us.

Esme takes my chin between her thumb and forefinger, looking right into my eyes. "You look tired, my girl. How is it, at that house?"

"I'll have the job wrapped up soon," I answer lightly.

"Good." She lets go of my chin. "I'll be glad to have you home."

"And I'll be glad to be home," I say.

I am always taken aback by these odd moments of tenderness from her. She was a hard schoolmistress, and she is an uncompromising employer. I have watched her coldly break a man's kneecap for cheating her and then head straight out to take a warm supper to a sick employee. For all the kindness she has shown me, I wouldn't want to cross her.

"Is Wyn here?" I ask.

Her eyes cloud slightly. I do not think she likes it much, this thing between Wyn and me, but she has said nothing of it to either of us.

"Upstairs," she tells me.

I leave her to her exercises and climb the stairs, heart in my throat. I knock on the door, too loudly. Wyn opens it, shirt open to the waist, eyes bloodshot.

"Julia Brown Eyes," he says with a warm smile, and swings the door wide, stepping aside for me. "You're not scrubbing floors and spying today?"

"I'm working," I say. "I had an errand to run, but I need some lunch. Join me?"

"Just had breakfast," he says, gesturing at a greasy plate on the floor.

"Oh well," I say. "Look, I need you to do me a favor. Can you track down a girl named Clarisa Fenn? She used to work for Mrs. Och just a few weeks back. She's Lorian, so I'm guessing she lives in Mount Heriot. Eighteen, I think."

"I'll ask around," says Wyn.

"Good. That's all I wanted to ask you." I find myself backing out the door, suddenly wishing I wasn't wearing this horrid maid's uniform with its ugly buttons. I need Csilla's advice if I'm going to buy a gown with my earnings, I think wildly. I know nothing about fashion. I forgot to brush my hair.

"Hang on, stay a minute," he cries, grabbing me by the wrist and pulling me to him. "I haven't seen you in days! You're going to run off without even giving me a kiss?"

"If you insist," I say. I try to sound lighthearted, but my heart is weighing me down so I can hardly move. He bends toward me, and I blurt out: "I was at the Cleansing. I saw you with Arly Winters."

"Why didn't you say hello?" he asks in surprise, straightening up.

"I was with the other housemaids," I say. And you were with Arly.

"You could have passed me off as a relative," he says. "Shock seeing Agoston Horthy there, wasn't it?"

"Quite a speech," I say, my mouth dry.

"I heard one of those witches tried to kill him, and that's why he was there. To watch her drown."

"Charming."

"I wish you'd joined us. I went to a pub with Ren and Arly afterward, and if I'd had a belt on me I might have hung myself from boredom. The pair of them! Ren spent the whole time trying to talk me into a game of King's Heir with some scoundrels from the Edge who would have cheated him blind, and Arly's still convinced some rich man is going to marry her for her dimples and take her away from all this. Their mother is too soft on them."

"Well, the housemaids aren't exactly thrilling company either," I say, beginning to relax. Maybe I didn't see what I thought I saw; maybe it didn't mean what I thought it meant. It's not as if I saw them kissing. We've known Arly since we were kids; why shouldn't he have his arm around her?

He fingers the buttons on my dress, thoughtful for a moment, then says, "Arly said she might be able to talk to the teacher of the class she's sitting for, get me a spot."

"Wyn! Could she really?" At once, I forget my jealousy and fear. Of course he wasn't with Arly, not like that. They were with Ren as well, and a spot in an art class could change everything for him.

"I don't know. You know how she talks. But I'm wondering if I'd want to do it, anyway."

"Well, why wouldn't you? Wouldn't it be an amazing opportunity?"

"I'm not sure," he says. "That's the thing. Real artists get apprenticeships at studios or find a mentor, right? These sorts of classes are really just a way for less successful artists to make some money. Rich boys who can draw a bit paying for some technical training that won't really get them anywhere, you know?"

"It might be a place to start, though," I suggest.

"Lorka did it all on his own," he says, not looking at me. He goes and sits down on the edge of the bed. I follow and sit next to him.

There are a few things Wyn only talks about in the dark, when we can't see each other's faces. One of them is the seven years he spent in an orphanage just outside the city. The other is his dream of being an artist—a real artist, like his hero, Emil Lorka. This is the first time he has spoken of it to me by daylight.

"That's true," I say carefully. "But there might be a hundred other Lorkas that nobody has ever heard of because they thought they were too good for art classes."

He laughs, and I'm relieved. "Well, I didn't tell her no, but it got me thinking. I've been trying for over a year to get an apprenticeship at Lorka's studio, but when I tried to buy a spot after that last museum job, his assistant told me out-right that they weren't taking a known thief. He's probably never even mentioned me to Lorka. I thought if I just went to his studio and showed him some of my drawings . . . well, it might not do any good, but if he liked them, maybe . . . who knows. . . ." He trails off, not daring to say out loud his dear-est hope, and my heart gives a painful squeeze of sympathy.

Lorka is one of the only famous artists in Frayne to have risen to prominence without sponsorship from the Crown. He paints the city as it is, not as the well-to-do see it: the wid-ows, orphans, and Scourge survivors, the derelict buildings, the painted whores and opium addicts, the starving dogs, along with ruthless, excruciating self-portraits slashed upon the canvas like an assault of paint. He built his own studio in the Scola a few years back and takes on one or two students a year. Wyn sees his own world in Lorka's work, and a good deal of himself in Lorka, no doubt. I know he hopes that Lorka might see some of his youthful self in Wyn, a boy with no connections and a gift for capturing real life. But where Lorka's work is all pain, mauled out with heavy paint and blazing color, Wyn's light charcoal sketches are alive with joy and a wicked humor that no amount of hardship has been able to drive out of him. I may not know a thing about art, but I'd take Wyn's drawings of barefoot kids playing jacks over Lorka's miserable, hunched widows any day. That said, a mentorship with Lorka would mean a real career as an art-ist, and as far as I'm concerned, it's far preferable to a class that involves drawing pictures of naked Arly Winters. I don't think Lorka does nudes.

"Can you do that?" I ask. "Just . . . go to his studio?"

"Well, I'd have to hang around and wait for him to come in or out," he says. "Is that a terrible idea? I know it's bad form to accost an artist in the street, but if anyone can understand how hard it is to get a break without money or connections, it'll be Lorka."

"It's worth a try," I say. "What's the worst that can happen?"

He forces a laugh. "I suppose my dignity isn't worth much."

"Bah, who needs dignity," I say, kissing him playfully.

He kisses me back, and there is nothing playful about his kiss.

"I have to go," I whisper, but his arms wrap around me and everything else falls away from me fast. When Wyn draws the Twist, he makes all the ugliness, filth, and poverty beautiful somehow—this is his gift, his magic: to transform with love. And he works this magic on me as well, so that when he touches me, my horrible dress and uncombed hair are nothing, nothing at all to the beauty he draws forth. I am not the same Julia—motherless, broke, badly dressed, a crook. In his arms, for a short while at least, I am perfect.

In a windowless room far from anywhere, a man lies dreaming. A yellow serum works through his veins. The room is lit with amber lights. His only companion is a squat, hunchbacked woman with sad eyes and fair hair fading to gray. She watches him, a syringe in her hand.

Some hours later, the woman steps out onto a balcony. Below, ridged gray waves come rolling in from the horizon. The sky is stormy. A man watches the sea, his back to her. He is wearing a silk robe that catches the wind, and his feet are bare. His hands are clasped behind his back, fingers rich with rings.

She clears her throat, but he does not turn around. You would have to know her well to read correctly the tightness around her mouth or the single furrow in her brow. Perhaps nobody knows her that well.

"My lord."

"You haven't found it," he says. "What use are you to me, Shey, if you cannot find what I seek?"

"It is not there to be found," she says. "He has no shadow."

"That is impossible," he says.

"What he has done with it and how, I cannot yet tell," she says. "Even in his dreams, his secrets are hiding. But I can find them out."

"His shadow," says the man, his voice rising.

"He has no shadow," the hunchback he called Shey repeats levelly. "Forget his shadow. It has become something else."

"How? What?"

"I don't know. But I think I know who has it."

He turns to face her.

"A woman," she says. "A beautiful woman from Nim. The mother of his son."

"Gennady has a son?"

She raises an eyebrow. "I imagine he has many. But he is hiding this woman deep inside him. She is his secret."

"Then get me her name."

"Yes, my lord."

SIX

I lie in the dark and listen to the awful shrieking of Florence's cot as she tosses and turns, until I can't bear it any longer.

"Would you lie still?" I say crossly.

"Sorry," she mutters, and there is a minute of blessed silence.

Today we had to beat out all the bedding, and I am beyond exhausted. I think I may strangle Florence if she makes another peep.

But peep she does.

"Why have you been to so many Cleansings?" she asks me.

"I don't know," I say. "I'm trying to sleep."

"But I mean, being from Jepta. Did you come into the city specially? Wasn't that very costly?"

Ah. She has me there. I'd forgotten my cover that afternoon, a stupid mistake.

"I came in to sell my mother's wares," I say. "Jepta wool

is well known in Spira City, and she makes beautiful dyed shawls and other garments. We'd always come to the city if there was a festival, or something like a Cleansing that would draw a great crowd."

Florence seems satisfied enough by that, but thinking so quickly of an explanation has pulled me further from the sleep I'm longing for, which is annoying.

"I wonder how long it takes to drown," she says thoughtfully.

"A minute or so at most, I expect," I say. I don't like to say how often I've wondered this myself. Liddy told me it doesn't take long, and that those who have almost drowned describe a moment of peace when they ceased to struggle, unconsciousness coming painlessly. I think Liddy would not lie, but perhaps it is different for witches. Perhaps it takes longer; perhaps they suffer more.

"They didn't look the way I expected," Florence adds.

"Who, the witches?" I ask.

"Yes."

"Witches look like everybody else," I say, thinking that sometimes she seems much younger than eighteen, much younger than me. "That's why it's hard to find them."

"That seems wrong," says Florence. "They *aren't* like everybody else. They have evil magic in them. They shouldn't look like ordinary people."

I want to say snidely that I'll pass that suggestion along to the Nameless One, but it would be blasphemous and I don't know how she'd take it.

"Do you think they know that they're witches when they're born?" asks Chloe. Her voice is rough, as if she'd been asleep. We probably woke her, though I'm amazed she was able to fall asleep in the first place with Florence rolling around on the screaming cot.

"I don't imagine so," I say.

"So how do they find out?" asks Chloe.

"They must know they are evil as soon as they can know anything," says Florence with conviction. "They worship the Dark Ones, by all the holies!"

"But witch babies don't worship the Dark Ones, not when they're newborn," says Chloe logically. "Does anyone who decides to worship the Dark Ones *become* a witch? Or do witches naturally decide to worship the Dark Ones and that's when they find out they're witches? Scripture says that we are all born pure."

"That's *people*, not witches," scoffs Florence, and I think of the young girls I've seen, terrified and screaming on the barge, *I didn't mean it; I didn't mean to*, before being tossed into the river. "A witch is born a witch, you ninny. They have no souls!"

"They looked like people," says Chloe softly.

"But they were witches," says Florence.

I roll over onto my side, the bed howling beneath me, trying to shut them out. I think about Wyn, his eyes up close, his lashes nearly touching mine when he says *Look at me— look at me*.

"What if they don't want to be witches?"

This from Chloe, followed by an angry snort from Florence. I pull the covers over my ears.

∾

My reading lessons with Frederick have built a certain flexibility into the day. There is now a set time when I am accounted for and Florence does not expect me. It is not long, half an hour at most, but that is long enough.

"I can't do it today," I tell him. "There's far too much to do."

He looks crestfallen.

"Tomorrow, I promise," I tell him.

"Well, never mind," he says. "If you're busy."

"Yes. Well, it will give you time for your own work too," I say.

"Yes," he says sadly. Funny how he looks forward to our lessons. I think it would be impossibly dull trying to teach some poor illiterate to read. Then again, I am an astonishingly quick student. Frederick has declared me extremely intelligent, and said it was proof that class has nothing to do with intelligence. Or beauty, he added, and then blushed. It's very convenient, his coming to fancy me. It's not terribly surprising, though, given that he's twenty-one and the only females he ever sees are Mrs. Och, Florence, Chloe, and me.

I leave him in the library and wait in the hall, vanished, until he leaves with the books he'd readied for our session. Then I dart to the third-floor landing just to make sure I can still hear the sloshing and humming of Mrs. Och taking her bath, which she always does after breakfast. I scrubbed it out yesterday, climbing right inside to do so, and wondered what it would be like to sit in warm water up to your neck. She should be another quarter of an hour, I am guessing. The grandfather clock ticks at me scoldingly, but I stick my tongue out at it and hurry back down to the second floor.

The door to Mrs. Och's reading room is unlocked. I slip in and close it behind me. It is an ordinary sort of room, and quite bare compared to the professor's study, with a writing desk by the window, a comfortable chair to sit in, and a number of books on the shelves, no more than that. I search her desk first. It is locked, but the lock is a weak one and I get it open quickly. Her account book reveals little upon first glance, besides the fact that she is very rich, which I knew already. She has her own shorthand or code, and I cannot make out the purchases, only the amounts. Looking more closely at the dates, however, I can see that she spends large quantities in bursts, including cabling money abroad. This week she put out a princely sum and cabled money to Zurt. Lucky Jahara Sandor, I assume. Besides the account book, she has a notebook full of addresses all over New Poria and beyond, some attractive stationery still tied in a ribbon, and a bundle of maps. The map of Frayne is marked up with lines and circles and stars, none of which mean anything to me, and there are other maps too, of unfamiliar cities and countries. If all this is related to the smuggling of witches, then she runs quite the operation.

Tucked into the account book are some folded newspaper clippings. I flatten them out on the desk and look at them.

They are murder reports. The governess on the bridge by Cyrambel, the cabriolet driver in Limory Cemetery, and a new one, dated yesterday: KILLER STRIKES AGAIN! RED BEAR INNKEEPER FOUND DEAD IN FORRESTAL. The messenger boy who gave me the letter from Bianka said he worked for Morris at the Red Bear in Forrestal. I tuck the clippings back into the account book, feeling slightly sick, remembering how the professor had seemed to think the murderer had something to do with Mrs. Och. *He is looking for someone,* she'd said. And here is Bianka Betine, newly arrived in Spira City, just like the killer. Perhaps it is a coincidence, but I think not.

At the back of the account book, there is a loose sheaf of paper—an unfinished letter, it appears. I draw it out and scan it quickly.

> *Casimir,*
>
> *What have you done? What can you be thinking? I do not wish to believe it of you, but I can think of no other explanation for the Gethin. You do not answer my letters anymore; the green lake has dried up; my tree is gone. If you are behind this, I fear you have gone mad, or worse.*

I hear someone at the door and startle; I hadn't heard footsteps in the hall. Panicked, I put everything back in the drawer and pull back quickly—much too quickly, overshooting that familiar pocket of invisible space. The room fades. Where am I; where am I? For one terrible, dizzying moment, I can see the room from every direction as Mrs. Och comes through the door. Then I find myself again, my own two feet, but I am standing over by the window now. I am trembling violently—I have a feeling, now, about the awful nothingness that lies behind me when I vanish.

Mrs. Och looks right at me, and my blood freezes.

"What are you doing here, Ella?"

For once, I am completely at a loss for words. I stare at her. She should *not* be able to see me. She raises an eyebrow.

Pull yourself together, Julia, I tell myself harshly.

"Florence said you wanted to see me," I blurt, easing myself back into the visible room, so she comes clearer. It's a bad lie, a very bad lie. Too easy to disprove.

"Did she?" says Mrs. Och, frowning and raising a hand to her temple, as if she has a headache.

I nod miserably. I don't like getting caught. I also can't understand *how* I got caught, let alone how I ended up crossing the room without actually, well, *crossing the room.*

"I gave her no such instruction," she says, reaching for the bell at the door that she uses to call the housemaids.

"Don't do that, ma'am," I say hurriedly. "I think I've been a fool. I think she was playing a joke on me."

"Odd sort of joke," says Mrs. Och. I cannot read her voice or face at all. It makes me nervous.

"She said I should go wait for you and shut the door," I say. "She's trying to get me in trouble, I suppose. She won't admit to it, ma'am; I know she won't. She doesn't like me. I do my best here, but she doesn't like me."

"And why is that?" asks Mrs. Och, looking suddenly very

old and tired. She makes her way to her desk. I am gambling wildly that she has enough on her mind, what with smuggling witches and whatever else she's up to, and won't want to bother with a dispute between housemaids.

"I don't know, ma'am," I say, adopting an irritating sort of drone just shy of a whine. "I'm not quite fitting in, I reckon. I know some of these city girls look down on those of us from the villages. But it doesn't matter; I'm sure it was just a little joke. I'd rather pretend it never happened. If that's all right with you, ma'am."

She waves a hand dismissively, and I am out of the room like a shot, heart pounding. *What just happened?* I run down the stairs and nearly trip right over Mr. Darius's writhing form on the ground.

"Sir!" I shout.

He rolls onto his back. His face is a terrifying white-gray, exactly like a marble statue that has been exposed to a good deal of weather. There is a grayish foam coating his lips. He bares his teeth at me.

"They are killing me," he hisses.

My mind darts immediately to the rifolta I fetched for Professor Baranyi from the alchemist's shop in the Edge.

"What? Who?" I fall on my knees next to him, feel his forehead. He is cold, very cold.

"Pretenders and murderers!" he raves. "We can help you, they say; we can make it right. Then they feed me poison and what do they care? I can't go on this way!"

"I'll get help," I say, starting to rise, but he grabs my wrist, pulls me close to him, so I can smell his acrid breath. His eyes are wild, rolling, and the grip on my wrist is shockingly strong for a man who cannot stand up.

"Help me," he whispers. "I have to get home. My *daughter*. This place is unnatural."

"You are very cold, sir," I say, frightened now. "Come into the scullery, by the stove. I'll warm you up."

I manage to help him to his feet, and he leans heavily on me, lurching on trembling limbs. I sit him down in the scullery and stoke the oven with coal so it blazes hotter.

"I hear them in the night; I hear everything in the night," he mutters. "It is not natural. Misery. They deal in misery, girl. You should flee. Where is your father?"

"My father?" I look at him, startled, and he falls right off the chair. His teeth are chattering like mad.

"Sir, I am going to get help for you!" I cry, and run from the room while he protests loudly.

He's right to be afraid, no doubt, but I am as confident as I can be that Frederick would never do anybody harm, and so I go to him. He is in the library, deep in one of his histories.

"Frederick, it's Mr. Darius!" I cry. "He's very ill!"

Frederick leaps to his feet, dropping his pen and splashing ink all over the page he was writing on. He follows me down to the scullery and we find that Mr. Darius has dragged himself halfway out the side door into the snow.

"No—no more of your witchery!" he screams at Frederick. "You are killing me!"

"We need to get you into bed," says Frederick gently. He turns to me. "Can you help me, Ella?"

"Of course," I say.

"Take his legs," says Frederick, hauling Mr. Darius up and grasping under his arms. I grab Mr. Darius's weakly thrashing legs. For a moment, I think I'm going to get to see his mysterious room in the cellar, but Frederick takes us upstairs, to his own room. There he has me light the fire while he arranges Mr. Darius in bed and gives him a bit of brandy. Mr. Darius twists under the heavy covers, muttering: "All liars . . . infection . . . this cannot be . . . witchery . . . it's a dream. . . . I'll see you all hanged yet," and so on.

"Thank you, Ella," says Frederick, guiding me to the door. "As you can see, Mr. Darius has a very serious condition, but we are taking care of him."

"He said the professor is trying to poison him," I tell Frederick, to gauge his reaction.

"The professor means to help him," he says firmly. The way he says it, I believe him, but still the rifolta niggles at me, and so does Mrs. Och's connection to the murders in the city, whatever that connection may be.

"Whatever is the matter with him?" I ask.

"Oh, it's complicated . . . some tropical illness." He fumbles a bit. "The professor is out at the moment. Can you fetch Mrs. Och for me?"

I am not keen to go back to her reading room, but I don't have much choice. I knock dutifully on the door. When she opens it, she looks faded, washed out. She stares at me like she doesn't even remember who I am.

"Frederick is asking for you," I say, bobbing a curtsy. "He's in his room. Mr. Darius is unwell."

"Thank you," she says. She shuts and locks her door before sweeping past me. I wait a minute and then follow.

I can hear them arguing before I even reach the door to Frederick's room.

"He is running out of time," Frederick is saying. "We have done nothing to help him, and the things we are trying are more and more dangerous."

"More dangerous than what awaits him?" demands Mrs. Och.

"We are adding to his suffering, nothing more, and perhaps endangering everyone in this house."

"The professor tells me you have an unusual mind," says Mrs. Och. "Think of something unusual. We need him."

"Mrs. Och, I entreat you to consider other options."

"There are no other options."

"And if we fail?"

She answers that by opening the door abruptly, and I leap back.

"Is he all right?" I ask meekly, pretending concern.

"Come with me, Ella," she says. I follow her back to her reading room again. She sits down at her desk and begins to write.

"Ma'am?" I ask tentatively after a moment, but she shushes me.

When she is done writing, she slips the notepaper into an envelope and writes upon the envelope. Then she hands it to me. It is addressed simply: *Miss Bianka Betine, Madam Loretta's, East Spira.*

"I need this delivered," she says. "Find a hackney to take you. It's not a safe area. You may ask Mrs. Freeley for money for the driver."

"Yes, ma'am," I say.

"And, Ella," she calls after me as I back out the door, "tell the girls to set up the back parlor as a guest room."

"Yes, ma'am," I say again. And then, because I cannot help myself: "For whom?"

"A woman and a child," she replies.

SEVEN

Dek and Gregor are the only ones in the parlor when I arrive. I used the hackney money to pay a messenger boy to take the letter to Bianka Betine, freeing myself to take care of a few other things in the meantime, before anyone expects me back. Wyn is out but has left me a message: *Clarisa Fenn at Ry Royal Pub Mt. Heriot*, and beneath, a quick sketch of a pointy-faced barmaid offering me a drink. I smile and put it in my pocket.

Dek and Gregor are sitting with a large bottle of cheap whiskey between them, lists and charts spread all across the table.

"I was hoping you'd turn up soon," says Gregor. "The client is waiting for a report, my girl."

I give him the copy of Bianka's letter, along with a hastily scrawled note about the things I fetched from the Edge for the professor and about Mr. Darius's sudden illness. I've left out the witch-smuggling business and the rest of what I saw in Mrs. Och's study. I don't know enough yet. I don't know anything yet. Or that is what I tell myself. I can't stop thinking about that witch they sent off to Sinter. Perhaps she has children, and they didn't have to watch her drown.

"It's not even noon," I say, nodding at the whiskey.

"All the more day to get through," says Dek, giving the bottle an affectionate pat. I don't like to see him drinking with Gregor but I can't very well tell him not to. He's a grown man. I know he keeps his mouth shut when he doesn't approve of things I do. Wyn, for example. The two of them got on very well until I took up with Wyn. Wyn still makes a brave attempt at camaraderie, but Dek has turned chilly toward him. We've never spoken of it.

"How is that magnetic opens-everything lockpick coming along?" I ask. "Am I going to get a crack at it? I've got a room I can't get into."

"The mysterious Mr. Darius," says Gregor, and takes a long drink straight from the bottle. "Taking your time with that, aren't you?"

"Because I can't get into his room," I reply coldly.

"Oh, that?" says Dek, brightening. "I got sidetracked, but I'll finish it if you need it."

"What's all this, then?" I ask, picking up a sketch of what looks like a cannon.

Dek snatches the paper from my hand and says, "You wouldn't believe what a couple of Lorian thugs have offered to pay for this. If I can make it and it works, that is."

"I am advising your brother that if he's going to design

weapons, he needs to be careful who he sells them to," says Gregor, slurring a bit. He's drunker than I realized.

"But ten silver coins!" cries Dek. "Only Julia is likely to bring in anything like as much right now."

"Twice that," I say quickly.

"Well." Dek gives me a look.

"I didn't like the look of those fellows," Gregor says. "If we were selling to some nice, wholesome revolutionaries, that'd be one thing, but there was the stink of the opium trade about them."

"Ten silver coins," repeats Dek sadly.

"Revolutionaries, or those that are left of them, don't have any money," I point out.

Gregor gives me a hard, sober look suddenly and says, "You'd be surprised, my girl."

"Would I?" I know Gregor's revolutionary days are long behind him, but I've never heard him speak of them, and I find myself suddenly curious. Gregor, Esme, and her husband all dreamed of a different Frayne when they were young. They dreamed hard enough to risk their lives for it. But things are different now. Nobody dreams of anything much in Frayne anymore.

For a moment, it looks as if Gregor might say more, but then his face changes, to careless and jovial again. He pushes the bottle of whiskey toward me. "Go on, Julia, sit down and have a drink with us," he says. "We hardly see you anymore!"

"I'm not drinking that swill," I say. "If you're going to drink in the middle of the day, you could at least get something decent."

"Good liquor is a waste," says Dek. "After the first couple of drinks, you can't tell the difference anyway." He doesn't slur or loll about when he's drunk. It's hard to tell how much he's had. The real change is that he seems, sadly, more himself. When he isn't drinking, there is too often a hardness about him, like he is clamped shut so tight around his own private pain you can't gain access at all. But then, he is not that way every day.

"Come on, what's the beef, my girl?" says Gregor. "It can't be the poor quality of booze that offends you. Tell me why you don't approve of me today."

"You're drunk," I say. "As usual."

"Not so very," he slurs at me. I think he's exaggerating now, just to annoy me.

"Stop it, Julia," says Dek wearily, gathering up his papers. "A fellow can drink whiskey if he wants to."

"I'm not telling him what to do," I argue, hurt to find Dek taking Gregor's side just because he's sharing his cheap liquor.

"It's because of your da, isn't it?" says Gregor. "But I'm not like him, you know."

The anger comes so fast, it leaves me breathless. I want to hit him. For a moment, I think I might actually do it, but then I get a handle on myself. Dek has gone rigid.

"It has nothing to do with my father," I say.

"He chose the drug over you and your ma," Gregor carries on.

"Shut up, Gregor," warns Dek.

"I'd never do that. I would never choose the drink over Csilla or any friend. Never."

"You choose the drink over Csilla every blasted day," I say.

He gives me a lopsided, uncomprehending stare, and I leave quickly, banging the door behind me. He'd better drop that line of thought or Dek will be the one to hit him.

I take a motor cab to Mount Heriot, a hill topped by Capriss Temple, the great white Lorian temple that overlooks the whole of Spira City. It's the most beautiful part of the city, the tree-lined avenues and steep stone staircases winding up the hill toward Capriss Temple's shining dome. From here, I can see the river Syne cutting the city in two, the Scola and Forrestal in the south, the Twist and the Edge to the East, and at the very center of the city, great Hostorak lurking behind the parliament. The wooded grounds of the royal palace lie in West Spira, where the most elegant shops and houses and hotels are.

There is a dearth of men of a certain age here—Gregor's age, my father's age—for so many of them were killed in the uprising. I can't believe Gregor is right that any remnant of that old guard still exists, in Mount Heriot or anywhere. To be sure, in certain bars you'll find miserable old dissenters muttering the same far-fetched rumors about the king's brother's newborn baby smuggled out of the country to return one day and claim the throne. But most people in Mount Heriot aren't holding their breath for a Lorian prince to come marching back to Frayne and take revenge. They are just getting by, like the rest of us. More than hoping for things to get better, they are praying things don't get worse.

It is easy enough to find the Ry Royal Pub. There is a large poster of the now infamous Marianne Deneuve on the wall outside, offering a substantial reward for her capture. I stop and look at her for a moment—this imperious, fair-haired beauty. I wonder if it's true about the monkey tails, and what kind of creature would think up such a thing. Then I shrug it off and go inside. There is a thin girl with straw-colored hair and a sharp chin behind the counter. I recognize her from Wyn's sketch, so I go and order a coffee and pastry and wait for things to die down a bit. It's mostly young men on their lunch break at this hour, and I am drawing a lot of stares but I ignore them, and nobody bothers me, which says something about Lorian manners.

"Busy day?" I ask the girl when things are quieter and she is wiping down the counter.

"Much as usual," she says. She is a raggedy-looking thing, with sunken cheeks and the glassy-eyed expression people get when they are bored too often. The kind of girl who reminds me why I do what I do for a living and why I'll never take an honest job.

"How long have you worked here?"

"About a month."

"You're Clarisa, aren't you?" I say. "You used to work for Mrs. Och in the Scola?"

She looks merely surprised when I say her name, but when I mention Mrs. Och, she becomes more guarded.

"Yes," she says.

"I'm Ella," I say. "I'm working there now."

"Ah." She keeps wiping the same spot on the counter methodically. "Going well?"

"I suppose, well enough," I say. "I came to talk to you. Perhaps you can guess what it's about."

She gives me a blank stare. This is a bit risky, but I don't think she has any contact left with anyone in the house, and I doubt there's a great sense of loyalty there—at least I hope not. So I say, "This is a secret, but my brother's a policeman. He got me the job there. He said I just had to work there a few months, have a look at the place. Something's up, he says, with the houseguest."

Clarisa blanches. She stares down at the counter, wipe, wipe, wipe.

"Mr. Darius," I press. "There's something horribly wrong with him. And I heard that you know something about it."

"So why don't the police come talk to me about it?" she says.

Fair point.

"I haven't mentioned you to them," I say. "No need to get you involved; I just want to know if my hunch about him is right. Can't you tell me what you saw, the night before you left?"

She frowns hard at the counter, her knuckles white around the rag.

"Something horrible," she says. "I don't like to think about it. I still have bad dreams."

"You poor thing," I say. Nameless One, give me patience. "If you can tell me, it would help so much, and then we'll be done with it."

"I heard a sound," she whispers, leaning over the counter toward me, though the pub is nearly empty now, and there is nobody close enough to overhear. "Florence and Chloe were frightened. I thought it sounded like an animal or some such thing, and I am good with animals, so I told them I would go to see. I thought perhaps a fox had got into the house. I don't know why I thought that. It didn't sound like a fox. It didn't sound like anything I'd ever heard before, but somehow I decided it must be a fox."

"Had you not heard any odd sounds at night before?" I ask.

"Mr. Darius hadn't been there long," she says. "Barely a week. I'd heard some strange sounds and told Mrs. Och. She said it was a broken door in the cellar and the wind. But I know she was not telling me the truth."

So they had been using that broken door story for a while now. Bit feeble.

"So you went down the stairs, expecting to see a fox," I pressed her.

"Yes. Only I saw a man, or so I thought. I had my candle with me, and I saw a tall man with dark hair sort of curled up on the stairs, making this strange groaning sound. I had met Mr. Darius a few times and thought it must be him. I thought him drunk, or ill. I went closer and said, 'Mr. Darius, are you all right?' Then he looked up at me."

She begins to cry. I pat her hand ineffectually.

"It's all right, Clarisa. Tell me what you saw."

Good girl, she keeps talking in spite of the sobs and sniffles.

"That face . . . it was not Mr. Darius, though it was wearing his pajamas. It had hair everywhere, on its face, even on its hands and feet. Its eyes were like the eyes of a beast, huge yellow things, and teeth . . . it was not a human face. It was not human."

"What sort of teeth?" I say.

"Like an animal," she cries, unhelpfully. "Terrible! An animal's mouth!"

"What did it do?"

"It looked at me, and it *snarled*. It wasn't like a dog snarling. It was something else. I didn't just hear it; I *felt* it in the very pit of my being! I screamed. I couldn't stop screaming. Then . . . I don't remember, I think I fainted, but Frederick and the professor were there, and the beast was gone. The professor told me I'd had a nightmare, but it was no dream. It was no dream."

"Can you tell me more about what the thing looked like? Was it shaped like a man? Only the face was monstrous?"

"It was curled up on the stairs, so it's difficult to say," she says vaguely. "The face is what I remember. That terrible face, all hairy and yellow-eyed, with those big teeth."

"The nose? A regular human nose?"

"No," she says. "I don't remember. Its face was an animal's face. A monster's face."

Her descriptive powers leave much to be desired, but I am getting the idea. Either there is some beast in Mr. Darius's room, something he brought with him (that wears his pajamas, if Clarisa can be trusted on that point) or, as seems more likely given what I have seen, Mr. Darius himself undergoes some nightly transformation and becomes a kind of beast. I have heard of such things in old, forbidden stories—stories of the kind of terrible creatures that used to walk the earth long ago. Can such things really be, in modern-day Frayne? In Mrs. Och's genteel house? Why not, in a house where giant trees go missing and witches are whisked to safety from the waiting river Syne?

I ought to be afraid. Surely a natural reaction would be to tell Gregor and Esme that the house is too dangerous, that there is more to it than we had imagined, and then never set foot there again, in spite of the promised silver. But, in fact, I feel strangely exhilarated. How it all ties together I do not know, but uncovering the secrets of Mrs. Och's strange household is far more interesting than turning up illicit love letters or nicking someone's jewels. I thank Clarisa and wish her well, then head down the hill toward the river. The whole way back, I am thinking of Mr. Darius on the floor, his foam-coated lips, and Mrs. Och's voice, like ice, saying to Frederick, *We need him.*

∾

When I get back, the household is in a flurry of activity, preparing for our guests. Mrs. Freeley is terribly upset about having to accommodate an additional member for supper.

"What do they think I am? I've got four pork chops! How can I make five suppers out of four pork chops?" she complains.

A fair question, but I assure her I have no doubt she is up to it.

Florence slips in a snide comment about how long I was about my errand, but she is too excited to expend much energy on being cross with me, and I play the deferential underling when she snaps orders, to cheer her up. We sweep and dust the back parlor and make up a comfortable bed with a little nest of pillows and blankets for the child next to it, and then set about tidying the front parlor, though really we are just waiting for the hackney. When it pulls up outside the front gate, Chloe gives a squeak of excitement, and all three of us stop pretending to clean and run to the window. It is frosted over, and so I pull it open. A toothy, long-jawed driver helps his passenger out: a dark-skinned woman in a fur coat, holding a baby. I judge her to be not much over twenty. The child is wrapped in a colorful blanket, large eyes peering about him. I can hear her clear, pleasant voice from the gate, saying, "Thank you, Jensen," to the driver.

"Isn't the baby sweet!" cries Chloe.

"Shh," says Florence.

I am not on duty in the dining room and do not see our guests again for the rest of the day, though I hear the woman's voice from the parlor, and the child's high-pitched babble. Chloe and I are still cleaning up the supper dishes when Florence comes in.

"They went to bed early," she says smugly. "Must have been exhausted."

"What are they like?" Chloe presses her, so I don't have to.

"She's a southerner, perhaps with Eshriki blood too," says Florence. "Brown as a nut, and too pretty for her own good, I reckon."

"What do you mean?" asks Chloe.

"I mean that she doesn't have a ring on her finger," says Florence pointedly. Chloe gasps, shocked.

"Not wellborn either, for all that she's well dressed," Florence continues. "She was trying to chat with me. She's not used to servants."

I wonder if Bianka Betine will find Mrs. Och's house the safe refuge she'd hoped for. In the back parlor, she's sure to hear the nighttime howls from the cellar.

∿

I am fetching water from the outdoor pump next to the scullery the following morning, shivering, the snow almost knee-deep, when I hear a sharp whistle from the gate. I look up and see a boy gesturing at me from the street. I know him—everyone calls him Boxy, and he delivers messages for Gregor. I leave the great copper tub in the snow and struggle over to him.

"They can see you from the windows, fool," I scold him.

He gives me an impudent little smirk and hands a folded paper through the gate. "You caught me by surprise; I've nothing for you," I say, snatching the paper.

114

"He paid me already," says Boxy, trudging off, sadly under-dressed for the snow but seeming not to mind.

I unfold the paper then and there, not very prudent, given I might be seen and am not supposed to know how to read, but I am too impatient to wait even a moment.

The client wants to meet you next Temple Day, it says.

EIGHT

Coming back inside with the copper tub full of water and snow, I find Bianka Betine in the scullery, wearing an expensive-looking white nightgown with a heavy robe of blue silk hanging open over it. She has beautiful fur slippers on her feet, and her hair springs and tumbles in tight, dark curls.

She is indeed very pretty, as Florence said, with a rather impish face and a good figure. She is not doll pretty like Csilla or nude-illustration pretty like Arly Winters, however. It's just as easy to imagine her decked out like a queen as it is to picture her barefoot in a village with her hair in a kerchief. There is something sly and clever about her face too, like she is guarding a private joke that may be at your expense. I put the copper tub on the stove, grunting with the effort, and drop her a curtsy.

"Hullo," she says. She has a very direct gaze. It feels like staring, but perhaps that's because she's from the south. Her accent is soft and pleasant to the ear, her speech slower than that of Spira City. Like she has all the time in the world. "I've lost the baby."

"What?" I say stupidly.

"Baaaa!"

I nearly jump out of my skin. A curly-headed moppet pops out from the laundry basket, shedding towels and underthings. I am not particularly fond of small children, but even I can see he is a beautiful child. He is lighter than she is—golden-cheeked, with a hint of red in his dark hair. He has two top teeth, four bottom teeth, and a winning smile.

"How did you get in there?" Bianka drawls at him, as if it's entirely normal to let one's children go crawling into laundry baskets in strange houses.

"It's not clean," I say.

"It won't kill him," she says as he tips out onto the floor and then begins to wail. She pulls a delicate brown foot out of her slipper and wiggles the toes at him, which distracts him from his tumble. He reaches for her foot, and she puts it back in the slipper.

"Hide-and-seek is his favorite game," she says. "I find it a rather tiresome game, myself. Do you work here too?"

"Yes, ma'am," I say.

She looks me over curiously. "This house has so many servants."

I have no idea what to say to this. Three housemaids, a cook, and a groundsman do not amount to a great many servants for a rich lady in a fine house.

"Theo and I have been exploring and got lost," she continues. "My name is Bianka. That little rat is Theo."

"Pleased to meet you, ma'am," I say, bobbing another stupid curtsy. She raises an eyebrow in faint surprise. "My name is Ella," I add.

"Well, pleased to meet you too, Ella."

The little boy pulls himself to standing holding on to the edge of the laundry basket and totters over to his mother, with his arms out for balance. He walks like a tiny drunkard. He collapses against her leg, delighted with himself.

"So this is where you do the cleaning up and so on," she carries on conversationally, looking around the scullery.

"It's the scullery, ma'am," I say awkwardly. Has she never been inside a fine house like this one? "You're not from Spira City, are you?" I go on. "Your accent is different."

"From Nim," she says absently, as if she's suddenly lost interest in me. She shakes the baby off her leg and wanders out. He goes wobbling after her, clinging to the edge of her robe and saying "ma, ba, ma, ba, ma, ba," with great concentration.

∼

The rest of the day is busy, and I cannot seem to get out from under Florence's watchful eye. Mr. Darius stops me as we are clearing supper and draws me aside. His hand is heavy on my arm, and my heart speeds up a little, even though I am sure I am safe here in the dining room, in plain view.

"I want to thank you for helping me yesterday," he says. "You were very kind."

"Of course, sir," I say. He is still holding my arm. I look pointedly at his hand, large and bristled with black hairs, and he lets go.

"Frederick tells me I was raving utter nonsense," he continues with a forced laugh. I wonder if he remembers what he said to me. "I hope I did not alarm you."

"No, sir," I say. "I am only glad to see you recovered. You're quite well now, sir?"

"Quite well," he says, though he doesn't look it, gaunt and wild-eyed as he is. "Thank you."

"Not at all, sir." He doesn't seem about to leave me, so I curtsy again, slide past him, and duck into the scullery. After supper has been cleared away and everyone has retired to the front parlor, I find Chloe watching the baby in the music room. He is gnawing on the piano leg, and there are papers all over the floor.

"He just chews on everything," says Chloe despairingly. "I don't know how to make him stop!"

"You're bigger than him," I point out. "Besides, shouldn't he be in bed?"

"I tried. I rocked him and sang to him. He bit my nose, Ella!"

There are indeed two red indentations on either side of her nose. The baby grabs hold of a piece of paper in his fat fist—it is sheet music, though I've no idea where it came from—and tears it cleanly.

"Stop it, baby!" cries Chloe, near tears.

"Don't be pathetic," I tell her. "He just needs a smack."

I snatch the paper from him and make to slap him across the face. I wasn't going to hit him hard, but if I've learned anything from the harried mothers and grandmothers in the Twist, it's that babies are too stupid to learn anything without a good smack now and then. Before I can slap him, my wrist is caught in an iron grip and twisted back, and a tug sends me staggering right across the room into the bookcase. I gasp with shock and pain, sliding to the floor.

"There will be no smacking of Theo by *you*," says Bianka acidly. She had crept up so silently, I had no idea she was there. Chloe looks petrified.

"I wasn't going to hurt him," I say, still stunned. She is no taller or bigger than me. But she is *strong*. Too strong.

She scoops up the baby and swishes out before I even have time to get angry at the way she just chucked me across the room. I get to my feet and look at Chloe, whose mouth is still hanging open.

"You'll catch a fly if you don't shut your trap," I say nastily, and limp out of the room, cradling my throbbing wrist.

༄

"Is Miss Betine all right?" I ask Frederick at our next reading session. "She wasn't at breakfast this morning."

"I believe she slept late," says Frederick.

"She is very beautiful," I say. "And the baby! Such a little poppet!"

"Yes, indeed." He gives me the sort of tender smile that

people give to young women when they talk about babies, and it is a tribute to my acting skills that I do not laugh in his face.

"What is her relationship to Mrs. Och?" I ask. "She said something about her brother."

Frederick looks startled at this and begins to stammer. "Oh—oh . . . yes, I believe . . . a distant cousin." He is a terrible liar. When he has to tell a lie, he sweats and fidgets and can hardly get a sentence out. It must be an awful handicap. I suppose it would keep one honest, for whatever that's worth.

"Will her husband be joining her?" I ask, all innocence.

"Ah! No . . . no, I believe not."

"It seems very sudden, her visit," I say. "Had Mrs. Och no warning of it beforehand?"

"I think . . . not," says Frederick.

"And Mr. Darius? I was glad to see him at dinner last night—he is better, I take it?"

"Much," says Frederick, beginning to sound exasperated with me. "Aren't you interested in reading today?"

I give up. "Of course I am. I only wondered about our guest. She is rather mysterious, appearing out of nowhere all of a sudden!"

"I suppose she is," says Frederick.

I pick up one of the books in his pile and immediately sit up straighter. On the cover, a white stag stares at me from a copse of silvery trees. I open the book and gather it is a collection of Lorian nature poetry.

"What's this?" I ask, scanning a few pages quickly.

"Mrs. Och recommended that one for you," he says.

That gives me another start. "Mrs. Och? Does she know about . . . this?" I almost say "about *us*," but I wouldn't want to give Frederick the wrong idea.

"Yes, yes, I told her," he enthuses, glad to be off the topic of Bianka, I expect. "She was all for it. She greatly approves of the education of the lower classes. It's one of her causes, you might say. She suggested poetry, said the rhythm would help with learning, and I expect she's right. This kind of poetry doesn't get read much anymore. I suppose some people think it has folklorish elements."

"Well, that's illegal," I say.

"It's illegal to worship the gods of the elements," he says plainly. "It's not illegal to write poetry about nature, and indeed it is a sad state of affairs when simple appreciation of beauty becomes conflated with archaic beliefs. Besides . . . well, as a scientist, of course, I am in favor of dispelling ignorance, and there is no doubt that the old folklorish beliefs were often very ignorant, but I do not see the purpose in banning harmless practices outright. I think education is a better way to reach the people. Then, understanding more of the world, they would abandon their foolish old practices on their own."

I am shocked that he would so openly criticize the Crown, but intrigued too. Frederick has never struck me as much of a rebel, but then again, he left a promising career to come and work in isolation for a man whose career is utterly dead.

There is some kind of wrong-headed principled stand in there somewhere.

"How would educating people change anything?" I say.

"It was Girando's telescope that struck the first blow against the old beliefs, three hundred years ago," says Frederick, smiling at me. "Before that, even educated people believed that all the power in the world was *of* the world. Earth, fire, air, water—the spirits or gods called *Arde, Feo, Brise,* and *Shui.*"

It gives me an odd little thrill to hear him say this in such an ordinary way, as if we were talking about the weather. You can go to prison for invoking those deities.

"But when scientists such as Girando were able to see the heavens, they recognized how small we are, merely a part of something far greater, something we cannot see or comprehend or name. Worshipping the elements of the world was revealed to be terribly naïve."

I shake my head, not understanding him but not knowing what question to ask to make it clear.

"Look, I'll show you." He leaps up and pulls a few large books off the library shelves. When he opens them, I see pictures of variously sized spheres around one giant sphere with flared edges. Lines curve out and away from the smaller spheres, encircling the larger one.

"What is it?" I ask.

"That is the sun," he says, pointing at the large flare-edged sphere in the center of the picture. He points at one of the smallish spheres. "That is our planet, Earth. Do you see? We are not even the largest of the planets circling the sun. Here is the moon, circling us. This nearest planet to us is Merus, the Red Soldier. And here is Valia, the Silver Princess, Earth's twin."

Of course I know that the earth circles the sun, along with a number of other planets. Though I have not been formally educated, Esme has made sure we are not ignorant. But I have never seen it laid out in this way.

"Where is Spira City?" I ask, peering at the small ball that is meant to be our entire world.

"You would need a larger map," says Frederick. "Spira City, on this scale, is so small as to barely exist. Look at this."

He takes down another book and opens it before me. I don't understand the illustrations I am looking at. Great spirals of . . . what? Something that looks like a giant eye, with dust swirling out around it. Tendrils of light.

"The heavens," he says in a hushed voice. "We cannot even find our own sun in this vastness."

I point at the thing that looks like an eye. "What is it?"

"Millions of stars," he says. "Planets too, probably. All impossibly far from here. It is unimaginable, Ella, unfathomable. The great mystery of it. The enormity of it. Once you have seen it, the very idea that the water here, or the air here, might have any significance whatsoever in that great realm is simply absurd. It is awe-inspiring. It feels like looking into the face of the Nameless One."

Frederick is full of surprises today.

"What religion are you?" I ask.

He smiles easily. "I am Rainist, like you," he says. "I can appreciate, on an artistic level, the calligraphy of the Simathists, the music of the Baltists, the poetry of the Lorians. But on a spiritual level, only the Rainists understand that all the decoration and fuss is mere distraction from contemplating the vast mystery of the Nameless One. Only through deep, undistracted meditation can we hope to reach Him. I consider my studies a form of worship also, in the sciences, in any case. In seeking to know the universe, I seek to know its maker and be closer to Him."

"So you agree with the king," I say slowly. "But you think he shouldn't have banned folklorish religions?"

"I have never met the king," says Frederick. "Not every Rainist is Rainist for the same reason. But there is a great deal of beauty in the folklorish ways that is lost to us if we stamp them out. It is *ignorance* we should be doing away with. Not beauty."

I consider this.

"Mrs. Och must think so too, if she has this book," I say, pointing at the white stag on the cover.

"Yes," says Frederick. "I believe she does. Mrs. Och is very open-minded. Perhaps she would let me take you to the university to look through the telescope there. I'm sure we could get in some clear night—I still have a few friends there, even if they don't approve of my decision to leave."

"Why *did* you leave?" I ask boldly. "It's the best university in Frayne, isn't it?"

He nods slowly. "People come from all over New Poria to study there," he says.

"So?" I press him. "You didn't like it?"

"I began to see that if I continued on that path, my studies could only follow a very narrow, prescribed course. Many of my questions were ... unwelcome, to say the least. History is being rewritten, Ella, and it is crucial that some of us preserve the truth."

"What truth?" I push. "How is history being rewritten?"

He hesitates, and I think, he doesn't know if he can trust me.

"My primary area of study is the Old Porian kingdoms, before the Magic Wars and the Purges and the New Porian alliances. The facts as they are taught to children in school ... the key players and so on ... there are a great many inaccuracies. The truth isn't necessarily ... convenient. I see my role as preserving the history that everyone used to know and which hardly anybody knows anymore."

I almost want to laugh and ask him if it is possible to be any more vague, please. But then, the truth is that if Frederick's secrets might put him in danger, he is quite right not to trust me with them.

"I see," I say.

"With Professor Baranyi, I can think and work freely, and I believe very much in the work he is doing," continues Frederick, relieved. "That is more important than a fine career and everybody tipping their hat to you in the streets."

"Then you made the right decision," I say, rather impressed

in spite of myself. "How did the professor come to work for Mrs. Och, anyway?"

"I'm sure you have noticed she is unwell. He helps her with her, ah, philanthropic projects, and she funds his work in exchange. She is a generous patron, and she admires his work very much. Professor Baranyi is responsible for the preservation and translation of a great many rare, important texts that would be lost to us by now if not for him. He is still well respected abroad. He has given lectures in Yongguo, you know."

I had no idea the professor had traveled so far.

"Didn't he spend some time in prison?" I ask. I think I am pushing it too far now, but Frederick answers as if it were quite natural for me to be asking him such things.

"That was a grave injustice. He published an article . . . perhaps it was unwise, but this was before the Lorian Uprising. He was trying to educate the Fraynish intellectual class about Yongguo policy. . . . In any case, his findings were not welcome and the punishment unduly harsh." He peers at me anxiously over his spectacles. "Have I shocked you with all this, Ella?"

I smile up at him. "No, not at all. It is very interesting."

"I'm very glad to hear it." He smiles back warmly. "You have a keen intelligence. That is clear from how quickly you learn. But more important, your mind is *open* and curious. There is no need to let your position here interfere with educating and elevating yourself. I wish to help you. We all do."

I am so startled by this, I don't know what to say. Frederick has got a rather soft, silly look on his face. He is so overwrought with sympathetic feelings for me that I think if I were to cry now he would be all but a slave to me.

I have ways to bring on tears when I need to. Half-reluctantly, I push myself to the dark place. I imagine the drop toward the cold water as the crowd roars; I imagine that struggle at the bottom of the Syne, before she cannot hold out any longer, before the black river fills her lungs. I am again the girl on the low path, half-crushed in the cheering crowd—understanding fully for the first time that the world is my enemy, not my friend, that nothing is safe, that nobody can protect me. I bring it all back, merely another tool for opening doors, now.

"Oh, don't cry!" Frederick protests. "Why are you crying?"

"You're all so kind," I sob. "To help a poor girl like me!"

He looks dazzled and unhappy and pleased all at once. Cautiously, he puts his hand on mine. He has very clean fingernails.

They *are* kind, it's true. But I am not kind. I'll find their secrets, turn them over, and be gone. How they will all hate me then. For a moment, I am terribly sorry for what I'm doing here. They are nothing but good to me, and whatever else they are doing, they are *helping* people too, people like my mother, long after the rest of Frayne has given up on opposing the brutal laws of the land. And here I am, a spy in their house, working for some mysterious enemy who may mean them great harm.

I banish the thought. I think, instead, of silver, cakes, and coffee, a pair of fur-lined gloves, sitting in a fine café overlooking the parliament gardens with Wyn, until I am myself again. The six silver freyns we got up front are spent already. It's no use going soft now. I close the book on Heaven.

NINE

I've missed you. I say it in my head, propped up on my elbows in the bed, watching him sleep. The dark curve of his brows, that beautiful mouth, his cheeks rough and unshaven.

It is Temple Day, the day I am finally to meet the mysterious client. I left Mrs. Och's before daybreak and let myself into Wyn's room to surprise him. His breath smelled like stale wine, but I didn't care. He's gone back to sleep now, and I am hungry, so I creep out and go down to the room I share with Dek to cook some eggs on the griddle. Dek is awake or perhaps never went to sleep. He is poring over some designs spread out across his desk, and looks up in some surprise when I come in.

"Didn't realize it was morning," he mutters, then crumples up one of the papers in his fist and tosses it into the corner of the room with a great many others.

"What are you working on?" I ask.

"Something for you, actually," he says, with a hint of a smile.

"My lockpick?" I ask.

"No, I'll have that for you tomorrow. It just needs assembling. I'm going to the Edge this afternoon—I've had to change the size, and need some new metal."

"Well, what's this, then?" I peer at his papers, but he turns them over and gives me a wicked grin.

"Patience, dear sister. You'll like it, don't worry. Listen, was it still dark when you left?"

"Darkish," I reply, knowing already what he is going to say. "Cusp of dawn."

He gives me a long, hard look.

"I know," I say. "I'm *careful*, Dek."

"*Three* murders, Julia. What are you thinking, going out alone in the dark with a madman on the loose?"

"There's no shortage of madmen in Spira City," I argue. "This may be a particularly gruesome sort of killing, but you end up just as dead even if you're killed by a more run-of-the-mill murderer. I don't see the need for extra caution."

"How about *any* caution? You think you're untouchable because you have a knife in your boot?"

"No," I say. "I think I'm untouchable because I can be invisible."

He sighs and shakes his head at me.

"Well, not invisible, but as good as," I say.

"It scares me that you aren't scared," he says.

I change the subject abruptly. "Dek, what if I told you that Mrs. Och helps witches? Gets them out of the country?"

His one eye bores into me. "*Does* she?"

I nod.

"Is that what the client wants to know about?" he asks.

"I don't know. I'll find out today, I suppose. Gregor's taking me to meet him, soon as he and Csilla get back from temple. It might be to do with the houseguest, or something else. There are plenty of strange things going on in that house. But it got me thinking."

"Ah."

"I mean, I was thinking about Ma."

His gaze shrinks, his lips thin, his whole body seems to tighten and withdraw, but his voice is mild when he says, "Thinking what?"

"That she was . . . nice. I mean, she was nice to us, wasn't she? And people liked her. She was good to our dad, for all that he didn't deserve it. She never harmed anybody, not that I know of. Even when I knew what she was, I never believed she was evil. Did you?"

He shakes his head, once. "No. She wasn't evil."

"Well, suppose none of them are? Suppose it's all bunk about witches worshipping the Dark Ones, witches out to rule the world?"

"Who knows?" he says. "There are plenty of witches who've done harm, though, this Marianne Deneuve being the latest—"

"If it's even true, the story about her," I break in.

"Well, and we've read about the Eshriki Empire, the Parnese Empire. Those were witch empires, and regular folk didn't fare well at all. Or the Magic Wars, all those covens competing for control of Old Poria. There were plenty of witches then that thought they ought to rule over the rest of us."

"So the Purges were all right, then? Tossing witches into the sea by the hundreds?"

"That's not what I'm saying. I mean that a witch who wants to do harm is a very dangerous creature indeed. They are capable of so *much* harm, and how are we to know their hearts? I'm not saying I like to see them drowned. I'm saying I understand why they are feared. If you knew that a neighbor of ours could just write something down and make things happen, unnatural things—wouldn't you be scared?"

"It would depend on the neighbor," I say. "If witches can do such terrible things, couldn't they also do wonderful things, if they were kind? Cure illness and such? Ma saved you. She saved you with witchcraft."

We've never said these things out loud, and the air in the room feels strange and alive.

"She did," he says slowly. "And maybe there are others who are good, as she was. But what do you do about the likes of Sybil the Bloody, who murdered her enemies with her pen? Just sat quietly at home, writing down who should choke, whose hearts would stop, and so on? Hundreds dead, and it was years before they could pin it on her."

The case of Sybil the Bloody, ten years back, was a particularly horrific one, and public support for Agoston Horthy's witch-hunting campaign rose quickly after that.

"I don't deny there are some evil witches," I say. "But d'you remember old Ma Rosen? She couldn't even read or write!

Some said she'd no idea she *was* a witch, that she was as surprised as any at the raid when she didn't burn."

"Not sure I believe that," says Dek. "Even if she couldn't write, wouldn't she have noticed sometime in her life that she couldn't *burn?*"

"Well, I don't know, I just mean that if she couldn't write, she couldn't do any harm anyway." We are silent for a minute, and then I say, "I've been to every Cleansing since she died."

"I know," says Dek.

That shocks me. "You do? I've never told you."

"I know when there's to be a Cleansing," he says. "You go off, and when you come back, you're odd and jumpy for days. It was obvious. I can't fathom wanting to see it myself, but I thought it best to let you be."

I ponder this. I hadn't thought myself so transparent.

"Well, I go to see the witches," I say. "And they seem ordinary, most of them. Just ordinary and scared."

"I can't tell you the answer, Julia," says Dek. "For all that I loved our ma, still I fear witches. I fear what they can do, but I don't know what ought to be done about them."

"I'd like to know what Mrs. Och thinks, if she's helping them," I say. "They're an odd bunch in that house. They think differently than most."

The truth is, in spite of being the daughter of one, I know no more than what everybody else knows about witches: that somehow they have the power to bend the world to the will of their pen, and that history is full of murderous, power-hungry witches trying to overthrow honest kings and queens.

But then, Frederick said history was full of untruths. Again and again my mind throws up the image of him in the hall with Jahara Sandor on his arm, knowing what she was and still bent on helping her. Somehow the sight of it changed everything, thrust all my secret questions and doubts into the light, and I've no desire to push them aside anymore, as has been my habit. If there is any place where I might learn the truth about witches, about what my mother was, surely it is in Mrs. Och's house.

"What if the client asks you about it, this business with witches?"

"I don't know."

"You don't know who this Mrs. Och is helping, or why," he points out. "Could be she wants to help witches like Ma, who never did anything to deserve drowning. But she could have other reasons for helping witches too."

"I guess I'll have to find out," I say, and he sighs.

"I'm not sure I like this job of yours."

"It isn't boring." I grin at him. "Gregor'll be back soon. Make me breakfast?"

He pulls himself up, hefting his crutch under his arm, and sets about lighting the stove. Soon our room smells of frying eggs and sausages. I curl up in his ragged chair and watch him, feeling I might burst with love. He used to make me breakfast when we were small. I always woke early, and hungry, and he'd fry some bread in butter if we had it or boil me an egg while our mother slept and our father was who knows where. He hums while he gets the food ready, and I doze right off in his chair, into a sudden, dreamless sleep, waking only when he sets my plate in my lap.

∾

Gregor finds a motor cab to take us out to West Spira. I knew the client must be rich, so I shouldn't be surprised. It's intimidating, though, chug-chugging down the broad avenue with all the quiet electric hackneys, not a horse-drawn in sight. Gregor seems unusually jittery. We stop in front of a great white monolith of a hotel.

Gregor is wearing his temple-best suit, and he looks all right here, if a little shabby. But I look plainly ridiculous in my leather boots and heavy gabardine coat that barely reaches my knees, my hair tucked untidily into a wool hat. Gregor hands the doorman a slip of paper. A porter comes and takes us straight into the hotel lobby. It is gigantic. I try not to gape around me like a village girl. The ceiling is as high as that of a temple or opera house. Great crystal chandeliers hang from it, and the carpet is so thick I long to kick off my boots and dig my bare toes into it. The porter hustles us along to the elevator, pulling the gate closed after us. I wish Dek could be here. He is obsessed with elevators but has never ridden one. It jerks and clanks and then moves up. And up. And up. I cannot believe how high the building is, and that we are moving through its belly in this way. I want to ask Gregor if elevators ever fall, but the porter is right there and I don't want him to know I've never been in one. Though I don't know why I care what the blasted porter thinks.

At last we jerk to a halt and he pulls the gate open. We step out, facing a large white door with a gold embossed number 10 on it. Gregor tips the porter and then murmurs to me, "Listen, the client's . . . a bit odd-looking, all right? Just keep your game face on, my girl. Ready?"

He knocks on the door. I tilt my head back, trying to look confident and not cowed by my surroundings.

The door swings open almost immediately. I drop my attempt at composure entirely and stare. There before us stands the strangest-looking woman I have ever laid eyes on. She is clad in dark trousers and boots, like a man (though certainly not like the men in West Spira), and she wears a fitted, brown leather jacket with matching fingerless gloves. Her black hair is so sleek it looks like a helmet, framing her paper-white face and ending in a sharp line at her chin. Most bizarre of all, a pair of metal goggles with protruding lenses that adjust and readjust all by themselves are fixed over her eyes, seeming to emerge from the flesh of her face. In plain view, at her hip, she carries a long, cruel-looking knife.

She looks at me with those alarming goggles. The lenses swivel and focus.

"This is Julia?" she says. Her voice is high, clear, and sharp as breaking glass.

"This is she," says Gregor with a little flourish.

"Come in," she says to me, swinging the door wide open. To Gregor: "Wait outside."

He opens his mouth as if to protest, then closes it again and puts his hands in his pockets. I want to protest too; I do not want to be alone with this woman or whatever she is, but I am whisked inside, and the door shuts on Gregor.

The room is like a miniature version of the lobby, with a high ceiling and a chandelier. White curtains are pulled back to reveal two glass doors leading out onto a balcony. The woman taps her long fingernails against her knife, looking at me. I think about the murders, the newspaper clippings in Mrs. Och's desk, and for a moment I am certain that I am standing before a mad killer. I feel a scream rising up in my throat.

"Don't be frightened," she says in that voice like falling icicles. "My name is Pia. Sit."

She gestures with one gloved hand at a sofa. Heart hammering, I sink into the cushions.

"Would you like a drink?" she asks me.

"Coffee," I say.

She rings a bell near the door. It is connected to a little wire going into the wall.

"I thought it time we met face to face," she says. "It's very interesting, this skill of yours. Have you always been able to do it?"

"Yes," I say. "It doesn't work on everybody, though. It didn't work on Mrs. Och."

"I suppose that is not terribly surprising."

I want to ask why not, since I myself was terribly surprised, to put it mildly, but there is a knock at the door. Pia swings it open. The uniformed man there looks petrified.

"Coffee," says Pia. "And mango, uncut."

She closes the door again. I do not know what mango is

but presume it to be some kind of foreign drink. The way she speaks, I do not think she is from Frayne, though her Fraynish is flawless.

"Can you do anything else?" she asks.

I'm not sure how to answer this. "I'm a decent lockpick," I say. "I can read and write well. I can scale a wall, carve out a window; I know some good knots if it comes to tying someone up, and how to use a knife and fire a pistol."

Pia waves a hand dismissively. "Anything unusual," she says. "Like being unseen."

"Oh," I say. Half-swallowed by the plush cushions, looking up at her, I feel about five years old. "No. Just that."

Her goggles swivel out with a whir, and then back in.

"Tell me about the woman who arrived from Nim recently," she says.

I describe Bianka as best I can, and she taps her fingernails against the knife as I do so, which is most disconcerting. When I tell her about Bianka practically hurling me across the room with one arm and no apparent effort, she smiles thinly.

Another knock at the door. She opens it, and the terrified man in uniform wheels in a silver cart with a pot of coffee, a cup and saucer, and a large piece of red-orange fruit.

"Take away the tray," says Pia imperiously, removing the items to a lacquered side table. The poor man slips out again. Pia pours my coffee and hands it to me. I wonder if Gregor is still in the hall and if she decided to scalp me and I screamed, would he come and save me?

Pia unsheathes her curved knife, nearly giving me a heart

attack, and begins peeling the fruit, letting the peelings drop to the lush carpet. She slices off a piece of orange fruit and takes it straight from the knife between her small white teeth. I watch, enthralled, while she eats the entire piece of fruit this way.

When she is finished, she tosses aside the pit and says to me, "You are to find out everything you can about this Bianka Betine. My employer believes she may be of particular importance."

"Your employer?" I say faintly. "I thought *you* were the client."

"No," she says, and grins. "I am a slave like you."

"I'm not a slave," I say.

"We're all slaves," she says. And since she is holding a long and very sharp knife, I don't argue with her any further.

"What does ... your employer want to know about Bianka?"

"She may have something that belongs to him," she says. "Go through her things. See what you can find."

"What am I looking for?"

"A shadow." Pia gives me another horrible grin, and her goggles whir in and out. "That's what it used to be. It could look like anything now. Bring me a list of everything she has."

These people. They are just terrible when it comes to specifics.

"What about Mr. Darius?" I ask.

She waves a hand dismissively. "I've read your reports. He is obviously a wolf man and they are trying to cure him. Trying and failing, it would seem."

I nearly fall off the sofa at this. "He's obviously a *what?*"

Pia answers as nonchalantly as if she were talking about the weather: "Savage wolves, terribly strong, with human intelligence. During the period of transformation, in the first months following a bite, the man becomes a wolf only by night, but once the transformation is complete, he will be trapped by his wolfish form and appetites forever. Unlucky fellow. Or perhaps lucky, depending on your opinion of being human."

"What is he doing at Mrs. Och's house?" I ask.

"The desperate often find their way to Mrs. Och," says Pia.

"But she said to Frederick . . . I heard her say that they *needed* him."

"Ah." Pia takes this in. "That is interesting. Yes, that is very interesting." Her voice turns sharp. "You should be telling *me* what he is doing at Mrs. Och's house. Find out."

"He couldn't be . . . I mean, he's locked in his room at night, so he couldn't be behind the murders in the city," I falter.

"No. That is something else."

She knows. My blood chills, but I force myself to ask: "What kind of something else?"

"The kind that will not rest until he finds his prey or is killed himself," she replies.

At least she says *he* and not *I.*

"Who is his prey?" I ask. "He seems to have a lot of prey."

She looks at me for a long time and then says, "I want a list of all Miss Betine's possessions, and I want to know about the wolf man. If Miss Betine leaves the house, follow her. She is your priority. We will speak again soon."

I flee the room. Gregor is pacing the hall outside. He grins with relief when he sees me and claps me on the shoulder so I stagger a bit.

"All right, then?" he asks, and I glare at him. I'll give it to him later for not properly warning me about her, but right now I just want to get out of here. I am relieved that she didn't ask me about the witch smuggling, and that I didn't get my head sliced off. Still, I don't have a good feeling about whoever employs such a woman, and I suspect things won't end well for Bianka Betine.

*T*he boy stares up into the snow. It's late; he shouldn't be out, but nobody at home will notice or care. It's just that it isn't safe. Especially not now. He knows that. But the silent, snowy rooftops beckoned, and he couldn't resist. No one is out but him, and so he is king of the sleeping Edge up here. The sky is black and starless, and the snow comes down heavily, soft on his upturned face. He whispers the forbidden word, the one his mother made him promise never to say, when she took him to the tiny shrine in the woods beyond the cemetery: "Arde." More daring now, loud and clear: "Blessed be Arde." He giggles and then jerks to the right, seeing movement.

Something is crossing the rooftop, coming toward him through the snow. A shadow bearing a weapon. It comes close, eyes glinting in the dark. Terror roots him to the spot, and the hand at the back of his neck is very soft. When he sees the blade, he can only think this is his punishment.

"I'll forsake . . . ," he whispers, but does not finish.

TEN

"I'm looking for Torne," I say, all too aware of the eyes on me.

"Are you, now?"

Raucous laughter comes from the dark corners of the room. The woman at the bar leans across, her tremendous wrinkled bosom nearly spilling out of her dress. She has only a few teeth in her stinking cavern of a mouth, one of them bright gold, and a purple scar running from temple to chin, right down her face, shutting one eye. She is not, I mean to say, a beauty, and she is the only other woman here. A beefy fellow has moved to block the stairs I came down—the only way back out to the street, as far as I can tell. His bare, tattooed arms are folded over his massive chest. One tattoo on his bicep is a triangle with a line through the tip of it—the symbol of the air spirit, Brise. They are element worshippers, then. An old man at the bar has a ferret draped over his shoulder. He strokes it methodically, grinning at me with blackened teeth.

"I've come on behalf of Professor Baranyi," I say, hoping his name will carry some weight here. Frederick was unhappy about my going to the Edge again, but I convinced him I knew the address, that it was just a bar with a harmless reputation. He didn't know any better, of course. I am beginning to regret my powers of persuasion. "He told me Torne would have something for him."

"Torne might have something for him," says the woman, and one of her breasts finally does fall right out of her dress and onto the bar. She shoves it back into her dress as if it were nothing. "But that'd be between him and Torne."

One of the shadows from the corner emerges into the dim light of the bar. It is a man in a stained shirt, reeking of gin, scraps of food dangling from his long gray beard.

"Why didn't your professor come hisself?" he demands. "Why'd he send his mule girl instead? Are you a peace offering, then?"

A peace offering? I have no idea what he's talking about, and I don't like the way he is looking at me. I have five silver coins from the professor but don't like to say so when I've seen no sign of Torne yet. Whatever I am getting for the professor today, it is not cheap.

"I'm just here to collect," I say evenly.

"Here to collect, says she!" he cries. "Not here to give?"

His arm slides around my waist. I step away quickly and find myself in the grip of the tattooed fellow who had blocked the door.

"Easy there," he growls at me.

"This professor of yours," says Graybeard. "He works for the lady in the Scola, that right?"

I nod, truly frightened now.

"See, I'm thinking they sent you 'cause they feel bad not backing Torne when he asked 'em to. Sometimes you think you're all on the same side and then turns out your friends ain't there for you at all. I'm thinking they sent you along to cheer us up."

"G'wan," says the man with the ferret, with a glimmer of what I hope is sympathy in his eyes. "They got him out of prison, didn't they?"

"He was asking more'n that, and deserved it," spits Graybeard. "What are they doing, hanging about in the Scola, living like rich farts, eating ham and drinking fine brandy? I hear things about that lady. Why doesn't she help us?"

The man with the ferret shrugs. "It's all just stories, about her," he says. "Still seems to me they've done us no harm."

"No harm at all!" says Graybeard. "And now they've sent us this lovely piece of arse."

He yanks my coat open.

"I have money!" I cry.

"She has money!" crows the woman at the bar.

Brise Tattoo reaches into my pockets.

"Not there," I say miserably, sliding a hand inside my coat to the hidden pocket I sewed there last winter. I don't know if the professor will believe the silver was taken from me or if they'll all assume I stole it myself. The silver may yet be the least of my worries. I pull out the purse and toss it a few feet away, hoping Graybeard will scurry after it. But nobody touches it. Graybeard tears my coat at the shoulder seam getting it off me while I struggle uselessly in the iron grip of Brise Tattoo.

"It's known I'm here! If something happens to me, you'll be punished. You'll all pay!"

"Yes, your dreaded professor," mocks Brise Tattoo.

I wrench away from him, enough to kick out at Graybeard, who grunts angrily, and I pull the knife out of my boot. Brise Tattoo twists my wrist sharply and has the knife before I can even think how best to use it. Graybeard hits me across the face. I hear myself scream. Brise Tattoo clamps a hand over my mouth. I bite him hard and he cries out, an ugly, rage-filled sound. He shoves me into the wall and for the second time in a week I am on the floor, reeling with pain. But I still have my stockings on and my wits about me. Even before I've properly got my balance, I make a mad scramble for the stairs and the door. Somebody else is there now, a ghoul, his face a blob of melted scar tissue, lashless eyes peering out from his shiny burnt skin. His fingers are webbed. He shoves me up against the wall, pulls at the front of my dress. I kick him hard in the groin and then Graybeard has me again. The woman at the bar is clapping and cheering now, and the raucous laughter from the corners is a chorus, more men pouring out of the shadows to join in the sport until I am surrounded, a dozen hands pulling at my dress, ripping the front right open, buttons popping, scattering.

"You'll be punished!" I'm screaming as I fight. "My mother is a witch! She'll curse you all to Kahge! I work for Pia! Heard of Pia? She'll cut you to ribbons!"

"Hold up."

The voice is not loud, but immediately all the hands drop away. I fall against the wall with a long, shuddering sob.

"What is this, then?"

A blond man in pajamas is standing over me. He has a horsey face, long teeth, drooping gray eyes. One ear is missing, a whorl of scar tissue in its place.

"Sorry to wake you, sir," says the woman at the bar. "This little thing come looking for you, and the boys was having some fun of it."

"Looking for me?" he says to me. "You?"

"You're Torne?" I can hardly get control of my voice. I hear more laughter. If I ever have a chance, I vow to myself, I'll come back here and burn this place to the ground with every single one of these bastards inside it. I button up the front of my dress as best I can, though most of the buttons are broken and I can't find them in the dark. Lucky for heavy winter petticoats and stockings is all I can say.

"Yes," says Torne. "Who are you?"

"I'm here for Professor Baranyi," I say. "I had money, but they took it."

The purse is not on the floor anymore. Torne looks around and somebody comes forward and hands him the purse. He empties the silver coins into his palm and looks at them carefully.

"I don't know where my coat is," I say. "These men are animals."

"Men are animals," he says. "Women too."

That's so helpful and illuminating—thank you, good sir. I think I'll leave him in the place too when I torch it.

"I need my coat," I say.

"She's a spitfire, sir," says Graybeard. "She works for that bitch in the Scola, the one who didn't want to fund your arsenal. Go on, shall we have some sport with her?"

Arsenal? Perhaps Gregor is right that there are still a few revolutionaries left in Spira City. I can hardly blame Mrs. Och for thinking it unwise to arm this rabble.

"Hush," says Torne, and looks at me again. "Who did you say you work for?"

"Professor Baranyi," I say.

"No, when I came in. You were a bit overwrought, perhaps. You said you worked for . . . Pia?"

Does he know her? I wonder whether to deny it or not, whether it might get back to the professor. I am guessing the professor is not on chatting terms with this man, whoever he is, and I am curious to know his connection to Pia. "Yes," I say at last.

"You don't mean . . . ? No, of course you don't. Do you?"

"Do I what?"

"You work for Professor Baranyi," he says.

He is so uneasy that now I'm really intrigued. "I'm a freelancer," I say. "I also work for Pia. With the mechanical goggles."

He goes very still at that. "Casimir's Pia," he says.

150

I nod slowly, remembering the letter in Mrs. Och's desk. *Casimir, what have you done? . . . the green lake has dried up; my tree is gone. . . . I fear you have gone mad, or worse.*

"Do you know her?" I ask.

"Do *you?*" he returns, studying me.

I fold my arms over my chest and stare him down.

"What do you do for Casimir?" he asks me.

"That's not your concern," I reply, sensing my advantage. He's shaken. "I'll just say Pia knows I'm here. She always knows where I am. Because she needs me, and she needs me in one piece, so I'll thank your nasty friends here to keep their stinking hands to themselves. I'm here for the professor now, and if you breathe a word of this to him, you'll have to answer to Pia. Do you have something for him or not?"

Torne nods his head, still staring at me.

"Nobody touch her or talk to her," he says, and disappears through a door behind the bar.

Now everybody is very subdued.

"My coat and knife, please," I say imperiously. The burnt man brings them to me. I tuck the knife back in my boot and wrap my coat tight around me. The men all slink back to the shadowy corners, and the woman behind the bar busies herself wiping glasses with a filthy rag. My heart is still thundering in my chest, but I feel almost triumphant at having so powerful a name to throw out and terrify them with.

Torne comes back with a small steel box. "Be careful with this," he says. "They aren't easy to come by anymore, with all the nests being destroyed."

"It's going straight to the professor," I say, staring at the box.

There is a raised star on top of it—the symbol of witchcraft, or magic, the signs of the four elements combined. Air, or the spirit *Brise*, represented by the triangle with the line through the top; Earth, the spirit *Arde*, an upside-down triangle with a similar line through it; Water, *Shui*, an upside-down triangle; and Fire, *Feo*, a plain triangle; all brought together to make a star. Whatever he's up to, the professor has moved well past roots and poison. I put the box in my coat pocket.

"You're very young," says Torne. His voice is almost kind. "Too young for this."

Whatever that means.

"Tell Pia that Torne sends his regards," he says, touching one hand to the place where his missing ear had once been. I don't bother to answer. Once I've got a clear line to the stairs, I point a finger around at the men who attacked me, skulking in the shadows now.

"You lot, I wouldn't shut my eyes at night, if I were you. I won't forget this."

Satisfied by the fear I see on their faces, I bolt up the stairs to the street and run for the Twist. Once I'm at a safe distance, I take out the little box Torne gave me and open it carefully. Inside, there are six silver bullets and, next to those, a glass vial holding two spiders, each the size of my thumbnail, with great long legs. The spiders are a bright, poisonous green, with a single gold line down their backs. They crawl around the inside of the vial, looking for a way out. I snap the lid back on with a shudder and shove the box deep into my pocket.

I need to stop at home to change and clean up, or Frederick will have a fit. I let myself into our flat, which is cold and dark, and nearly have a heart attack when I see the figure slumped in Dek's chair.

Wyn looks up when he hears me gasp.

"Hounds, Wyn, you scared me half to death!" I shout. "What are you doing in here?"

Then I see the look on his face. There is a bottle of cheap wine on the floor next to him, sitting on top of a scrap of paper.

"What's the matter?" I go to him, dropping to my knees and taking his hands in mine. His face is shut tight like a steel trap, the smell of booze a thick haze all around him. I've seen Wyn drunk and jolly, but I've never seen him like this, and it frightens me. "Talk to me, Wyn."

"Hullo, Brown Eyes," he says, his voice blurry. "Sorry to scare you. I'm all right, just wanted some quiet."

I notice the pile of drawings in his lap. I pick them up and look through them. Some of these I've seen before, but a number I haven't. His sketch of Fitch Square is finished. Then there's old Ma Fartham at her market stall with a far-away look in her eyes; a small girl playing with a dog; bare-foot boys fishing in the river; a woman with a baby strapped to her chest, carrying a basket of fruit; two old men playing King's Heir in the street. Here is life in the Twist, captured with light lines, with wit, and with love.

"Wyn, these are wonderful," I say.

"My best ones," he says expressionlessly.

I stand up and put them on Dek's worktable. "I'm going to make you some coffee," I say. "And then you tell me what this is all about."

He grabs my wrist and pulls me into his lap, wraps his arms around me, buries his face in my chest. I put my hands in his hair and kiss the top of his head.

"Wyn," I whisper. "My darling boy. What is it?"

His voice is muffled against the torn front of my dress.

"I went to Lorka's studio," he says. My heart sinks. I can guess the rest of the story before he pours it out in a rush. "I've been hanging around there every day this week. Finally got him alone. I can't even remember what I said to him. Something stupid, probably, but he looked at the drawings. I mean, just quickly, you know. Sort of flipped through the bunch of them. Then he says to me, 'So you can draw. Lots of kids can draw. Learn a trade.'"

Wyn makes a funny choking sound that might be a laugh. I'm so angry, I can hardly speak for a minute, but I master it. "Well, he's wrong about you. Lorka isn't the final authority on talent, with his nasty, smeary paintings."

He just hangs on to me, breathing slowly. I stroke his hair, and in some strange way I feel closer to him now than ever before. I've been so many things to him—a little sister and a friend and a lover and a colleague—but I don't know that I've ever been a comfort before.

"He's a bleeding genius, Julia," he says at last, and makes

another odd chuckling sound. "Poor man, he was coming from the market, arms full of winter squash. He must be crazy about squash. Look, I drew this when I got back."

He looks around on the floor and finds the picture under the wine bottle. It is a sketch of a startled-looking Lorka, his face all severe lines and annoyance, clutching a great bundle of vegetables. The picture is rather crumpled, with a circular wine stain on it.

"What a pity it's spoiled," I say. "It's a good likeness. Clever."

"Sorry to be such a child about it," he says, releasing his grip on my waist a bit. "I'd hoped . . . well, I hoped too much, is all. I'll keep drawing, of course. I like it, even if I'm not any good at it."

"Wyn, you *are* good at it. Maybe Lorka was in a bad mood, maybe he paid too much for his squash, or maybe his tastes are just very specific. You . . . you don't draw like he does, but it's special, what you do. It's real without being miserable. It's *life*, it's *our* life, and our world. You can't give up on yourself just because Lorka is an old crank. What about the class Arly Winters said she could get you a spot in?"

"Oh, that." He shrugs. "The teacher said no. I suppose Arly thought she had him wrapped around her finger, but it turns out that's not the case."

"Well, soon enough we'll have plenty of silver and you can pay for a class if you want," I say.

He manages a small grin. There's my fellow—never one to wallow. "I wouldn't waste your money that way, Brown Eyes. No, I'll draw my pictures like I've always done, and we'll have a good time, live like lords and ladies for a while." He kisses me, hand straying to the front of my dress, and then draws back. "What happened to your dress?"

I jump up off his lap. "Got it caught on something," I say. "I just came back to change it quickly."

I don't want to get into what happened to me in the Edge. Wyn might get reckless, in the state he's in. I shrug off my coat and snatch my other dress off its hook on the wall, irritated that I'll be up late mending by candlelight.

"I'm sorry I startled you," he says. "I wanted to see you but couldn't, so I just . . . came down here. I couldn't bear all the noise upstairs. Solly's there, getting drunk with Gregor and regaling them all with ridiculous tales of the latest murder."

"What murder?"

Solly is a cop, but he's an old friend of Esme's husband and keeps her abreast of police business, including any interest they might have in *her* business.

"This serial killer who's going around slicing heads," says Wyn. "Solly's of the mind it's something unnatural."

A ripple of alarm crawls up my spine.

"He's still up there?"

"I reckon so. Haven't heard anyone leave."

I button up the fresh dress quickly and grab my coat.

"Listen, Wyn, I'll be right back, all right? I just need to find out what he's heard."

"You won't be long, will you?" he says, looking maudlin again.

"Just a few minutes," I promise. I take his face in my hands and kiss him gently on the mouth. "You're brilliant. Lorka's a fool."

"What would I do without you, Julia?" he sighs.

"I don't care to find out," I say. "You don't want to come up with me?"

"I'll wait here," he says, holding up the nearly empty bottle.

I kiss him again and dash up the stairs.

∾

The whole crew is there in the parlor, seated around the crackling fireplace, and Esme's broken out the good brandy. They are talking about Marianne Deneuve now. Apparently she's been caught near the border between Frayne and Prasha.

"Offer enough silver, and yer own brother'll turn you in," opines Solly. "But thank the holies, eh? She was a nasty piece of work."

"She was my friend," says Csilla, teary. "I still can't believe it of her."

"She weren't what you thought, my dear," says Solly. "She weren't what you thought."

"Hullo, Julia!" calls Dek, waving me over to the fire.

Csilla leaps up and embraces me. "We never see you anymore. How is the house of monsters and secrets?"

Esme shoots her a look. Solly may be a friend, but he doesn't need to know the details of my job.

"Monstrously secretive," I say, and nod toward Solly. "Hullo, Solly."

"My goodness, you've grown up, haven't you!" he says.

Solly says that every time he sees me. I think the truth is that he doesn't remember any of the times he's seen me in recent years, and so I remain imprinted on his memory at around age twelve.

"I hear there's been another murder," I say.

"That's our Julia. A taste for the gruesome," says Gregor. He holds the bottle of brandy out to me and I glare at him.

"Now that he's sobering up, perhaps Solly will admit to embroidering the truth a bit," teases Dek. "According to him, there are great big paw prints in the snow where this last murder happened, and the blade being used is sharper than any man-made blade on this earth. You stand by that, Solly?"

"It's true," says Solly, goaded. "I heard them talking about the cuts. No ordinary knife or sword could do it just like that, so thin and fine, so delicate. And I heard about the prints from an officer who was there the next day. He's not the type to make stuff up. He was good and scared."

"Who was it this time?" I ask, running through the list of victims in my head. A dancing girl and a banker in Nim. A governess arriving from Nim. A cabriolet driver. The innkeeper at the Red Bear, where Bianka stayed.

"Just a kid in the Edge," says Solly. "Sad. Little boy on a rooftop. Kids found 'im. Holes in his boots, poor tyke."

"Gingery hair?" I ask, feeling sick. "Freckles?"

He gives me a sharp look, shaking off the drink. "What do you know?"

That's as good as a yes. "I don't know anything. I heard a rumor."

He relaxes slightly. "Poor little kid."

The boy who delivered Bianka's letter to me—the one who ran messages for the murdered innkeeper. *He is looking for someone*, Mrs. Och had said of the killer. Bianka knows it too—she said in her letter to Mrs. Och that somebody was after her. And if I'm right, it's not only this killer hunting her but our client too. *A shadow*, said Pia, *but it could look like anything now*. Oh, Bianka—what have you got?

Esme takes me by the arm and I jump. "I need to talk to you," she says, drawing me aside, over to the door. Gregor and Solly are noisily arguing over the reliability of Solly's fellow police officers now.

"What is it?" I ask distractedly, but when I meet her eyes, I get a start. The look on her face is pure murder.

"Somebody hit you," she says, very quiet.

I touch a hand to my cheek. I don't bruise easily, but trust Esme to notice, no matter how bad the light.

"Who was it?"

It is tempting to tell her—very tempting to imagine what she might do, how she'd make those bastards pay, every one of them. But I don't know enough about Torne and his fellows, and Esme doesn't need more trouble.

"I don't know them," I say. "It was just a scuffle. I was fetching something for the professor in the Edge. I'm not really hurt."

She gives me a long look, and I can't hold her gaze.

"Somebody *hit* you," she says again. "I want a name."

"I told you, I don't know," I say impatiently, and then Dek appears to save me, swinging over with his crutch and saying, "Here, before you run off—I've finished your lockpick!"

That perks me up. I turn away from Esme and say, "Let's see it!"

Esme folds her arms across her chest, watching us. Dek passes me a smooth metal disk. It fits neatly into the palm of my hand.

"Want to show me how to use it?" I ask.

"What, now?"

"Tomorrow," I say, handing the disk back to him. "At the house. I thought you could take me hostage. What do you think?"

Dek grins. "What time?"

"Come round the side, the scullery door, around half past four. Everyone should be busy then. And bring a pistol just in case."

"Why does he need a pistol?" asks Esme.

"He wouldn't be very convincing as a hostage taker otherwise, would he?" I say. "Look, I've got to get back."

"Julia," says Esme, her voice deadly calm.

"I'll tell you all about it later!" I say desperately, opening the door.

"All about what?" asks Dek, puzzled.

"Stay and have a drink!" Csilla calls over, wiping her eyes with a handkerchief, but I wave goodbye and run down the stairs.

I am halfway to Mrs. Och's before I remember I've left Wyn waiting in my flat, but it's too late to turn back.

ELEVEN

Between my job as a housemaid and my job as a spy, I am finding no time to do any snooping of my own. I know I will have to get back into Mrs. Och's reading room at some point if I want to find out more about witches, but I have been putting it off because, frankly, I'm frightened. The fact that Mrs. Och can see me even when I vanish has left me uneasy, but more than that, I'm afraid of what happened the last time I vanished. The way I was *nowhere* for a moment and then found myself on the other side of the room. In any case, right now I have other things to take care of.

It's easy enough to persuade Chloe to leave Baby Theo in my care while she and Florence set the fires and fill the lamps in preparation for evening. He is an inconvenient alibi, given what I need to do now, but watching Theo is the only thing I can come up with to get me out of my regular duties. Now they are carrying firewood up the stairs and Mrs. Freeley is lying down in her little room just off the kitchen, so I hoist him onto my hip and hurry to the scullery to open the side door.

"Good afternoon, miss," says Dek, leaning on his crutch and tipping his snowy cap at me.

"Hush," I say. "There's a lantern over the woodpile—grab it for me."

"You look good with a baby on your arm," he teases me, swinging into the scullery and taking the lantern off its hook on the wall. "And that outfit! I've never seen you in a cap and apron."

"Don't even start," I say, glowering at him and touching a hand self-consciously to my frilled white work cap. He follows me to the cellar stairs. Stairs are a chore for him, but he manages well enough with a shoulder to the wall for balance as he descends. Bianka is in the library, tinkling away on the piano. Mrs. Och is in her reading room. Mr. Darius, Frederick, and Professor Baranyi are in the professor's study, where they have recently been meeting for the hour before supper. If we are caught, Dek is a burglar and has taken me hostage. He'll get out of here with a pistol to my temple.

"So tell me what we're looking for," he says once we're in the dark of the cellar.

"Whatever we can dig up on him," I say. "Listen, Dek. . . ." I haven't told anyone the extent of the strangeness in the house. I don't know where to start. "Mr. Darius is . . . well, the client says that he's a wolf man."

"A *what?*"

"That's what I said."

"Clearly we're related. Both geniuses. Did you get an answer when you said it?"

"It's a man who turns into a monster at night," I say. "Eventually he turns into a wolf all the time. And I've heard him roaring away down here. There's no doubt he's . . . *something*."

"Stars, Julia! No wonder the client offered so much silver. This all sounds like something out of a folktale."

"I know."

Even folktales are illegal in modern Frayne, but growing up in the Twist, we heard them anyway—grandmothers whispering about lights in the woods, spirits that would borrow your body for a night of revelry, fiends that would crawl out of their graves to drink human blood before dawn. I used to have nightmares, and Dek would beg Ma to tell us the stories weren't true, but she would only say, "Such stories are half truth, half lies—that's what makes them stories." Now I think there was a little more truth to them than even she let on.

Dek still sounds skeptical. "So you're thinking about what Solly said, paw prints and the like, and wondering if you've got the killer here in the cellar?"

"No," I say. "I don't think so. He's locked in at night, and Pia told me it wasn't him, not that I trust her, really. I *am* sure the killer is connected to Bianka and Mrs. Och somehow, though."

"If your Mr. Darius has paws, there could be something or someone else with paws," says Dek.

I wonder if *Pia* might have paws under those boots of hers.

"Mama," says Baby Theo in a small voice.

"Hush, your mama is upstairs," I say. "Here's the door. Shall I light the lantern?"

"Not yet," says Dek. He lays his crutch to one side and the lantern with it, kneeling in front of the door on his good knee, folding the other leg awkwardly under him. He feels the lock, feels the door, and says, "My, they don't want *this* door opened, do they?"

He takes the little metal disk, his magnetic pick, from his pocket and puts it over the lock. He shifts it about a bit, listening intently. Theo is sliding down my hip, so I jostle him back up. "Mama," he complains, wriggling in my arms, trying to get down, but I hold on tight and pin him to me. Then there is a click and the lock gives way.

"Not bad," I say, impressed. This lock has bent all my picks easily.

Theo yanks my cap off my head so that my hair tumbles loose, and the door swings wide. I try to get my cap back but Theo screams in protest.

"Have it, then, but be quiet," I hiss at him.

Between Dek and me, we get the candle lit and shut the door of the lantern, creating a warm, flickering light that makes Theo go, "Aaaaaah."

And here is Mr. Darius's room at last. It has a high ceiling, with thick rugs on the floor and tapestries on the walls to keep out the chill from the stone. His bed is large and unmade. Next to the door there are heavy silver chains attached to the wall, with thick arm and ankle cuffs.

"Charming," I say.

"Who does he chain up down here?" asks Dek, interested.

"Himself, I think." I put the squirming Baby Theo down and tell him, "Don't get up to any mischief."

Silly. Like telling a dog in a very friendly voice not to wag its tail. Theo makes for the big trunk by the bed.

"Just what I was thinking," I say. "Wonder if that'll be locked too."

The trunk isn't locked. It's filled mostly with clothes and a few dull-looking books: a tepid-sounding novel about war in Ishti, a history of Fraynish kings and queens, and a book of theological philosophy called *What We Are*, so famous as to be banal. You see it on any moderately educated person's bookshelf. Mr. Darius is not a particularly adventurous reader. There are also pouches of tobacco and packets of shoe polish and hair grease packed away in there.

"Enjoy yourself," I tell Baby Theo, who proceeds to take everything out of the trunk and pile it on the floor. That should keep him occupied at least.

"Not a very glamorous existence, living in a rich old lady's cellar," says Dek, looking over the mostly empty shelves and a broad side table with a few dirty cups on it.

We search the room, checking the mattress, pulling back the edges of the rug, looking under the bed, and feeling all along the walls. I lift the tapestry at the head of the bed, and there it is: a little cupboard in the stone wall.

"Found it!" I cry.

"Found what?" asks Dek.

"Something secret," I say, trying the cupboard. It's locked. "Let me try that pick."

"You can have it," he says, tossing it to me. "I'll make another."

I pass it over the lock a couple of times, feeling the answering tug. Then something shifts and there is a sharp click as the lock opens.

"It's bleeding genius, Dek," I say admiringly. "You could make a killing selling these."

"Maybe," he says.

"What, maybe?"

He starts talking about patents and how you can live forever on a single invention if you handle it right, and how we could be leading a very different kind of life, the two of us, but I'm only half listening now, taking a thick envelope from the cupboard and sitting down on the bed with it.

"You know—we could get a flat in the Plateau, or even the Scola, if the price was right."

"I like the Twist," I say, pulling a sheaf of documents out of the envelope. "His papers!" I say triumphantly, waving them at Dek.

"I mean that things could be different for us, Julia. We could even leave Spira City, start over somewhere. You could be anyone, somewhere else. You're educated, or as good as, anyway. You could marry a wellborn fellow if you wanted, have a brat or two."

I look up at him in amazement. "Bleeding Kahge, Dek! Why in the name of all that's holy would I do that?"

"I don't know," he says, looking suddenly terribly unhappy.

"Maybe it's a fantasy. Who'd give *me* a patent? It's just ... I get sick of the whole thing."

"What whole thing?"

"Stealing."

I'm speechless for a moment. I knew that Dek was often dissatisfied, but I'd assumed it was with the limitations of his own body, not with our work. I can imagine no other life for myself and am unsettled that he has clearly spent a good deal of time and energy imagining it.

"I *like* my job," I say at last. "This is the *life*, Dek! Loads of excitement, free to do as we please."

But he is shaking his head. "Esme did us a good turn when we were kids. I'm grateful to her, but I'm a man now, and you're practically grown up too. I want more for us."

"You make it sound like we have a wealth of options," I say, more bitterly than I intend to. "Can we have this conversation another time? When I'm *not* in the middle of working?"

He gives me a ridiculous bow, and I turn to Mr. Darius's papers, my exuberance rather dampened.

Mr. Darius is not Mr. Darius, of course. According to his travel documents, his name is Sir Victor Penn Ostoway III. He is forty-six years of age and was born in Spira City to Sir Neer Liam Ostoway and Lady Emma Voltaire. I'd assumed him to be a man of business, but it seems that he is a diplomat of some kind, having risen rapidly through the officer ranks in the military. Near the top of the stack of papers is a letter dated two months ago. When I see the signature at the bottom, my heart gives a jolt.

"Listen to this!" I say eagerly, and read it aloud to Dek.

Dear Sir,

You are hereby granted the ten weeks you requested for research and the assembly of a new team. The king joins me in sending his condolences for the men you lost. They died bravely in the service of their king and the Nameless One.

I am distressed to find the Parnese wolves giving you such difficulty. They are wily and resilient, as you say, but nevertheless I assumed you were the man for this job. I hope I am right. In the meantime, Elisha seems content at court and, as always, we will keep her close to us while you are gone.

Best regards,
Agoston Horthy

"Agoston Horthy!" cries Dek. "Holy Nameless, your wolf man has friends in high places! Remember our assassination plan?"

I can't help but laugh, though it isn't very funny, really. As kids, Dek and I held the witch-hunting prime minister responsible for our mother's death. Not long after moving in with Esme, we started hatching a plot to assassinate him with poison darts. The hours we spent! In the end, the chemist we tried to buy poison from told Esme about it, and that was the end of that. It seems childish now, but in a way I miss how I felt while we were working on our ridiculous plot. Like there was something we could do about the rotten way of things. Like vengeance against all the injustice of the world was somehow possible.

I leaf through the other papers. Letters bearing Agoston Horthy's signature date back for years, referencing locations all over the world. I wonder how much Mrs. Och knows about this connection, or if she knows about it at all. The letters are concerned with the assemblage of teams, numbers of men, and sinister-sounding assignments well beyond the borders of Frayne: *You will need skilled trackers. . . . You must enlist some of the T'shuka tribesmen to lead you to the nest. . . . I cannot provide the firepower you ask for. . . . The coven is rumored to be hidden in the Tikali Mountains. . . . If what you describe is true, we have no choice but to flood the entire valley.* At least half the letters make some reference to Elisha and her activities at court. At the back, a letter seven years old bears no signature but is in the same hand, neat and cramped. It says only: *Did you think you could hide her from me? I have a proposal for you. Come to my office an hour after midnight.* There are a great many more papers, but we have been here too long as it is and I daren't stay longer. I take a sampling of the letters from Agoston Horthy out, fold them up, and tuck them into my stocking.

"Where's the baby gotten to?" I ask, looking for Theo. When I find him under the table I can't help but laugh. He has worked open a jar of shoe polish and smeared it all over his face and hair and clothes.

"Daaaaaabudabudabu!" he says triumphantly, holding up his tarry hands.

"How am I going to clean him up?" I say, my amusement quickly giving way to alarm.

"I saw a basin of water on the stove when I came in," says Dek. "Shoe polish won't be any great trick."

I try to pack everything away again the way it was. Once the room is in reasonable shape, we snuff out the lantern and make our way back to the scullery in the dark. I check ahead of Dek that nobody is there. Then I strip Baby Theo as fast as I can. I can still hear the piano tinkling upstairs. I don't have time to heat up the basin of water, and Theo screams blue murder the second I put him into it, clawing and wriggling to get out again, and who can blame him? I grab a dish brush and make a desperate go at the shoe polish matted into his hair.

"You're going to take his skin off with that thing," says Dek, reaching for a thick bar of soap above the dish rack. Somehow, between the two of us, we hold Theo in the water and I lather my hands and, thank all the holies, the shoe polish comes away easily. Dek sings a folk tune our mother used to sing us, a morbid tune about a father and son visiting a grave together, though the song doesn't say whose grave. It's a pretty song, but I wish he wouldn't sing it.

"There!" I say, pulling the wet, howling baby out of the water and bundling him into a dish towel. He quiets immediately, shivering against me, still shaking with breathy sobs.

"You've a real way with children," says Dek.

"You're the one picturing me married off on a farm or something," I snarl at him.

He laughs, and I'm glad. "Never mind it, if you're happy," he says.

"As a clam," I say, drying Theo's wet curls with one end of the towel. "You'd best get going. Listen, if you see Wyn, will you tell him something came up yesterday but I'll be over to see him as soon as I can?"

"I found him passed out in our room last night, waiting for you," says Dek dryly.

"I know. Sorry." I feel a pinch of guilt.

"Well, I'll tell him, if you want." He pauses. "This thing between you two. It's been going on a long time now."

"If you're worried about me being no good with babies, we're careful, all right?"

"It's not that," he says. "I want you to be careful in other ways too. I know you care for him, and I've no doubt he cares for you too, but you can't trust him, Julia."

My anger flares, then fizzles fast. Dek isn't one to make accusations lightly.

"What are you telling me?"

"I don't know anything to tell," he says. "Not for sure. But he's out a lot."

"You don't know him," I say, feeling sick. "You don't know him at all."

"I know him well enough, though I'll grant you know him better," says Dek. "I'd like to be wrong about him."

I hug Baby Theo to me and manage to say, "Fine, noted."

"I'm sorry, Julia. Here, I'll make it up to you—I've brought you a present."

He reaches into his coat and pulls out what looks like an odd, twisty bracelet. He fastens it on me while I bounce Baby Theo with one arm and his breathing goes back to normal, the cold bath all but forgotten already. The bracelet winds around my wrist, along my palm, and around my little finger. There is a sliding mechanism on my palm and two tiny nozzles, on the wrist and at the finger.

"You see here, on the palm?" he says. "If you can make a fist, you can push it or pull it. Pull it, and capsicum gas will come out here, at the wrist. Push it, and it'll come out here, at your finger. If you can direct it at someone's face, it'll burn their eyes and throat like you wouldn't believe. They won't be able to see at all for at least a few minutes, and it'll hurt much longer than that."

"It's brilliant, Dek!" I say, amazed.

"If you can't get your knife, if someone's got you pinned, you should still be able to use this. You just make sure the wrist or finger nozzle is pointing at their face, and be careful not to spray yourself."

"You made it just for me?" I say. I wish I'd had something like this yesterday, when Torne's men had a hold of me.

"I might make one for myself too—I'm at a disadvantage in a fight, after all—but yes, I made it for you. There are a good six shots in there, and then I'll need to refill it. Anyone that tries to mess with you will get what's coming to him."

I put Theo down, and he wobbles away naked.

"Thanks," I say, and I give Dek a hug to show him I forgive him for what he said—or almost said—about Wyn. "Now please go."

He gives me a rough kiss on the top of my head. Baby Theo comes wobbling back and flings his arms around my leg.

"Lala," he says, beaming up at me with his silly six-toothed grin.

"Clever fellow, he knows your name," says Dek.

"That's not my name."

"Don't you go by Ella?" asks Dek.

"Oh." I look down at Baby Theo in some surprise. He clings to my leg, cackling like a tiny, naked lunatic, and I'm struck by how beautiful he is, how new-looking, with his shining eyes and soft skin. I almost understand the way people get about babies, cooing over them like fools. He's so himself, and such a pretty thing, and he doesn't know yet what a nasty world he lives in. He still thinks it's a good place, that we are all good people.

"Say, what happened to your fetching cap?" asks Dek.

I touch a hand to my hair, which is still loose. "Holy Nameless," I whisper. "I've left it in his bleeding room."

∼

I send Dek on his way; I can't risk having him around any longer, and I reckon I can work his magnetic pick as well as he can. I plop Theo in the basket of clean laundry, toss a sheet over him, saying, "Hide-and-seek!" and then dash back down to the cellar. I get to the door and strike a match against the wall. Thank the Nameless, the cap is right there; Theo dropped it before we went into the room. I snatch it up, blow out the match, turn around, and run back down the hall—smack into a body coming the other way. The pick drops out of my hand with a clink as I fall backward onto the floor.

"What's this?"

It is Mr. Darius's voice. Or, Sir Victor Penn Ostoway's, rather. He bends down toward me and grabs my face in his big hand, squeezing my cheeks. I grope behind me in the dark for the pick. My fingers find it and close on it as he pulls me to my feet.

"Ow!" I squeak, and get the pick into my apron pocket.

"What are you doing prowling about here?"

"I'm looking for the wine cellar!" I cry. "I didn't think it would be so dark. Mrs. Freeley wants a white for the soup."

"The wine cellar is at the bottom of the stairs. You must have been there before." His voice is terrible, nothing like his usual voice. A sort of feral growl.

"Why would I have been there before?" I protest. "I never come down here. Please, sir, you're hurting me."

"What are you up to, girl?" He squeezes harder. Fear is pouring through my veins now, burning in my throat, and I am horribly conscious of the bundle of letters in my stocking. I think of the weapon Dek gave me, of using his real name, but both options would mean the end of my cover as Ella.

It is not easy to speak with his hand on my face, half covering my mouth, but I cry out, "Mrs. Freeley is waiting on the wine, sir! Please let me go, sir, if you are a gentleman!"

He releases me suddenly, as if he hadn't realized he had my face in a viselike grip. I can't see his face well in the dark, but some of the menace in his voice is gone and I can feel his uncertainty.

"I am that," he says.

"I'm sorry, sir," I say, allowing a half-real sob. "I wasn't trying to go to your room—they told me not to—I just want to find a white for Mrs. Freeley. Please don't be angry with me."

"Get your white, then, go on," he says roughly, stepping aside. "Do not let me find you here again."

I push past him and run down the hallway, pausing only to grab the first bottle of white that I find in the wine cellar, and then dash back up the stairs. Theo is still contentedly hiding in the laundry basket. "Lala!" he crows when I pull him out, and I am laughing with relief until I find he's pissed all over the clean bedsheets.

"Oh, you monster!" I moan. "I'm going to have to do it over. Bleeding Kahge. Well, let's get you into a fresh diaper and some clothes and have a look at your mama's things while we're at it. I've got a list to make."

He throws his arms around my neck happily, and I surprise us both by planting a kiss on his cheek.

*S*he slides the needle into the vein.

He tries to speak. His eyes are held open with clamps, and he is strapped to the bed with strong leather bands. He cannot turn his head or his eyelids will be ripped off. So he stares at the lamp swinging in slow circles from the ceiling and at the ghostly dancing girls around it whom he cannot blink away, kicking their stockinged legs in unison.

The serum gathers in his chest like a fist, or so it seems to him. A poison seeking out his secrets. He forces his tongue and mouth to make the sound he wants them to:

"Shey," he says.

Shey steps back against the wall, her eyes hooded. They have been here for hours today, and she is tired, but she does not flag. She waits.

"Please—" But it's no good. If he were free to speak to her, free of poisons and bindings and sleep and the dreams she forces out of him. If he had time, if he could take a breath, clear his head for just a moment, he could speak to her, and perhaps she would listen. For months, her subtle potions, her dazzling lights and sharp needles, have become the whole of his life. Parts of him cut out, cut away.

Bound in ways he hadn't known were possible. He clings to the only thing he needs to remember: not to tell them ... not to tell them ... what? And who is it he mustn't tell?

"It hurts," he says.

"What hurts?" asks Shey. "Her name?" Softer: "Does my name hurt?"

She steps forward, her black hair tumbling, eyes dancing, her shoulders bare, soft and brown. She is smiling, and it is dark outside the dance hall, the streets of Nim quiet under the sharp glittering stars. They can smell the sea from here.

"Yes." Her name, burning in the place he has locked it away.

"Then we must get it out, and the pain will stop," says Shey from a great distance. "Then you can rest. Then you can close your eyes."

Sympathy brims in the dark eyes and he reaches for her, but no, he cannot, his arms are bound. There is something important, something he should do or should not do, but he cannot remember. Best to stay silent, do nothing.

"I'm afraid," he tells her.

She laughs, and he feels something like peace. She always gave him that.

"Nothing to fear," she says. "I'm fine. Aren't I always fine? Can you really imagine me any other way?"

"That's why," he says. "That's why I chose you. Forgive me."

"There's nothing to forgive." She leans in close, and tears fill his eyes, but he cannot blink them away. The clamps.

"We'll take those off," she promises. "You need to rest. It's all right. It's over. Who am I?"

The name slips out of him like a sigh upon waking: "Bianka."

"Yes. That's right." She strokes his cheek. "They have you, my love. They have you. There is only me now, protecting your shadow. You must tell me where it is, so I can keep it safe."

Dancing girls spin in the sky; stars catch at his skin; yellow smoke fills his blood. She takes the clamps from his eyelids so gently, and his tears fall, washing everything away.

"Tell me, love," she whispers. And he tells her.

TWELVE

After lunch I overhear Bianka and Professor Baranyi agreeing that she will come to his study as soon as she has washed up. I intend to make it there first, but Sir Victor Wolf Man stops me on the stairs.

"Ella," he says gruffly.

"Yes, sir." I avoid his eyes, bob a curtsy.

"I want to apologize to you," he says. "I behaved very badly when we met in the cellar. I was surprised, and rather out of sorts."

"Of course, sir, I completely understand," I say.

"You're a good girl," he says. "I wish I could explain it, truly. I am not myself these days."

An understatement if ever there was one.

"I am sorry to hear it, sir."

I want to get up the stairs, get to the professor's study before he does, but Sir Victor seems to want a heart-to-heart all of a sudden.

"I was not planning such a long visit here. I have a daughter, you know."

"She must miss you very much, sir," I say.

"Yes, yes, I expect she does. Her mother died when she was a baby, and we have had only each other. She is your age now, and a very fine violinist. She studies with Bartole."

Oh, by all the holies, is he really going to start telling me about his daughter's musical talent? I wonder if this is Elisha from Agoston Horthy's letters. I hear Professor Baranyi giving Mrs. Freeley some instruction in the kitchen, which means he is on his way.

"Sir, I must hurry, I've got to fetch something for Mrs. Och. I am so sorry!" I cry.

"Of course, of course, I do not mean to hold you up," he says, flustered. "I only wanted to . . . to apologize to you. And here, here you go." He thrusts a coin at me, and I take it. A copper. He's no cheapskate when apologizing, anyway. "You are a fine girl, a good girl. I hope I did not frighten you."

Only half to death, monster.

"Only a little, and I quite understand," I say in a rush. "Thank you, sir; you are very generous, sir."

He gives me such a lost, unhappy look then, half reaching for me from a few steps below, as if he's going to take my hand. "I am not who I mean to be, Ella."

"I suppose none of us are," I say. "We must pray to the Nameless One to make us better. Thank you, sir."

"Of course, yes." He steps back, away from me, his face falling into shadow. "Go on, then. Good girl."

"Thank you!" I say, tearing up the stairs and dashing into

the professor's study. I make myself comfortable on the divan at the back of the room, carefully vanishing mere moments before the professor and Bianka come in together. It is the first time I have vanished since getting caught in Mrs. Och's reading room, and I do it with some trepidation, but it is just as it has always been, an easy step back, a slight blurring of the world. Bianka has Theo with her. He waves at me, delighted. Blasted hounds of Kahge, the little rotter can see me! I am tiring fast of the occupants of this house. I give him a stern look, and he laughs.

"That's right, an owl," says Bianka. At least she doesn't see me, however strange and strong she may be.

"Come back here, Strig," says Professor Baranyi. "Keep us company."

The owl tilts his head and looks at me, as if asking permission. I glare at him, and he flutters over to his master and sits on his shoulder. Theo is more interested in the owl than in me now, thankfully.

"I wanted to speak to you because I know Mrs. Och is holding back," says Bianka. "I hope you will be more candid."

The professor looks startled, takes his glasses off nervously and cleans them.

"I'm sorry," she says. "She has been very kind—you all have—and I understand that you are protecting me. But she tells me nothing beyond that she is working to find a safe place for me and Theo. I want to know what is *happening*. I want to know *why* it is happening. I want to know about Gennady."

Professor Baranyi puts his glasses back on and smiles

183

wanly. "Surely I cannot tell you anything that Mrs. Och cannot. As for Gennady, I have never met him."

Theo fights his way off Bianka's lap and hides under the desk.

"Well, I mean, what *is* he? He's not some kind of manwitch, is he?" asks Bianka, slipping her foot out of her shoe and wiggling it at Theo. He grabs her toes.

"No, he isn't that," says Professor Baranyi cautiously. "But he is a very unusual man."

Bianka sighs and slumps back in her chair. "You're all so blasted secretive," she says. "He was too. I wish I knew what happened to him."

"We all do," says the professor.

"I knew he wasn't going to stay," says Bianka. "Of course I knew *that*. But I didn't think he'd disappear so completely. We went to Sirillia for a holiday right after Theo was born. He changed our plans midway, put me on a train and went to get something from the dining car, and he never came back. I've had no word of him since. You don't think . . . well, with all the death following me around, I can't help but fear he's dead too."

"I am as certain as I can be that he is not," says the professor.

"How can you be certain?" says Bianka. Then she throws up her hands. "Mrs. Och said the same thing. But then what has happened to him? Why would he disappear without a word?"

"Gennady has enemies," says Professor Baranyi. "He may have gone away to protect you."

"It didn't work," she says sharply. "Now I have enemies too, it would appear."

"Yes. We are working on that. Tell me again about the man you mentioned to Mrs. Och, the one who was looking for Gennady."

"I'd lost my job at the dance hall. They replaced me while I was pregnant, and then after Gennady disappeared, I had to tell Magdar that Theo was *his* son. I didn't know what else to do. Magdar took good care of us. He got me a nice house by the sea to share with his lover, Kata."

"Magdar was the banker, the second victim, yes?" asks the professor. "And Kata—this is the dancer who was killed? The first victim?"

"Yes. Magdar had a taste for dancing girls. Kata and I were friends, even though she was Magdar's new lover and I was his old one. She didn't seem to mind any of it—my being there, Theo. I suppose it might have been a relief to her to see Magdar took care of his castoffs. It's something girls like us need to worry about."

The professor looks a bit uncomfortable at this. "And the man who came to see you?" he prompts her.

"Yes, so then this man turned up at the house, well-spoken, handsome, except he had an eye patch, and his other eye was yellow. Quite ruined his looks. He sat in my parlor and asked me all these questions. I didn't tell him much, but he knew a fair bit about the two of us already. He knew about Theo too, and seemed very interested in him. He snipped a bit of his hair without asking me, pricked his finger so it bled, and

I kicked him out then. The whole thing scared me witless, of course. I wanted to get out of town, and I'd heard about a troupe doing sort of avant-garde circus performances in Falleri, up the coast. I went to look for Gennady, or to see if any of them had heard of him. It was a long shot, of course: he wasn't there, they didn't know him, and when I came home, Kata was dead. You know what happened. I saw it, and I *knew* somehow it was my fault—that it was meant to be me. I packed my things and had Magdar take me to the train right away. I met the governess at the station, just by chance. I didn't know, how *could* I have known just how unlucky it was for her, meeting me that way? Her name was Jani. Magdar put me on the train—we waved to him from the windows— and not long after I got to Spira City, I saw in the papers that he was dead as well. Then the governess, Jani, and the cabriolet driver who took us from the station, and the innkeeper, and the messenger boy. Everyone I meet seems to turn up dead in the same horrible way." Her voice is rising now. "Mrs. Och didn't seem terribly surprised by that. Are you?"

Professor Baranyi's face is stony now. "Someone is hunting you," he says. "That is all."

"But why also hunting my friend, my old lover, the woman I share a blasted cabriolet with?"

"I believe that before he disappeared, Gennady must have done something to protect you, to hide you from the killer. But still he searches, hoping those who have met you can lead him to you."

"Is it the man with the yellow eye?"

"No. But I'd wager that they have the same employer."

"But who? Why? What do they want with me?"

Tiring of his mother's toes, Theo is making toward me now, crawling across the room. Very slowly I lower myself to the ground and settle myself in a plausible position for having fainted, in case he draws attention to me. Luckily Professor Baranyi is far too engrossed in his conversation with Bianka to notice the movement, and Bianka has her back to me still.

"That is what we must find out," says the professor. "My own best guess is that they want Gennady, and they hope you will either know where he is or, together with your son, serve as bait to lure him."

"I don't know where he is, and I doubt he would come to our rescue," she says bitterly. "So the killer is wrong on both counts. If you know who it is, can't you stop him?"

"We are doing what we can," says the professor again.

"Mrs. Och said the man with the yellow eye probably wanted to test Theo's hair and blood to see if he was really Gennady's son. Is it possible?"

"Such tests do exist, yes. Is he . . . you're sure, then, that he *is* Gennady's son?"

I can't see her face, but her shoulders slump a bit. "Yes, quite sure."

An uncomfortable silence follows, interrupted by a knock at the door.

"Ah," says the professor, leaping to his feet, clearly relieved. "There is Mrs. Och."

My blood turns to ice. She'll come right in and see me, as

she did before. As quickly as I dare, I crawl behind the divan piled with books. I can't see them now, but I hear Mrs. Och's voice greeting Bianka. Theo joins me behind the divan, batting at my apron string like a kitten.

"We'd like you to give us a little demonstration," says Mrs. Och. "Just to see if there might be something unusual about you besides your association with Gennady—something that might be drawing all this unwelcome attention."

"There is plenty unusual about me," says Bianka. "As you know. I haven't hidden anything."

"Mrs. Och may be able to recognize something you cannot," says the professor. "Have you heard of transmogrification?"

Silence from Bianka, and the professor supplies the answer: "Turning a living creature into another kind of creature. I thought we might try it on Strig here. Owl into cat. Do you think you can do it?"

"I've never tried any such a thing," says Bianka. "It seems rather cruel. But if it will tell you something you need to know, give me pen and paper and we'll see."

My heart starts to pound. No wonder she is so strong. I peer over the top of the books. Mrs. Och is facing Bianka, not me. Professor Baranyi is fetching pen, paper, and ink for Bianka. I watch her dip the pen and sigh. Everything seems to slow down.

"I do not often write anything down," she says, almost dreamily. "Not unless I need to. When I hold a pen in my hand, I feel the whole world tremble before me. I want to follow the trail of ink to a thousand places. The temptation of it frightens me. The power of it. And so I do not write letters, or lists, or anything else. Because I might find I am writing something different altogether. I hold the pen and do not know which of us is master."

The professor and Mrs. Och are watching her closely, tensely. It would serve them right if she turned them both into toads, if you ask me. But I find I am a little afraid myself, riveted by the sight of her with the pen in her hand. She twists the pen in her fingers and begins to write. Then she stops, and blood gushes from her nose. I force myself to keep still, not to clap a horrified hand over my mouth. The professor rushes over, proffering a handkerchief, which she presses to her face. The room pulses, once, filling with the smell of rotten flowers, and I feel as if I am seeing everything anew, eyes washed clear.

"There!" cries the professor. "It's working."

Strig has fluffed up his feathers and is leaping about on the floor, blinking furiously. *"Hoo!"* he cries. *"Hooo hoo!"* Then all at once he lengthens out, forepaws extending from his chest, talons growing into hind legs. He looks up at them, and they look at him.

His size has not changed, only his shape, and so he is really the size of a kitten. His beak has become a little brown cat nose, but he still has great big yellow owl eyes, and an odd blend of feathers and fur. His face is a strange, squashed, wide-eyed sort of face for a cat.

"Meow?" he tries out hesitantly. A second time, with more confidence: *"Meow."*

All right, he seems to be saying. So I am a cat. Meow, then.

"Are you all right?" Mrs. Och asks Bianka.

"Rather dizzy," she says. "Was it helpful?"

Mrs. Och shakes her head. "I did not see anything unusual in it," she says.

For heaven's sake. Only in this house might turning an owl into a cat be considered the usual sort of thing.

"Impressive, though," says Professor Baranyi. "Most witches could not change a living creature so completely."

"No?" asks Bianka, her voice muffled by the handkerchief. "I've never known any other witches. I don't even know what I can do. I'm afraid to find out."

"You are strong for a witch," says Mrs. Och. "But you are no more than that. It does not explain your situation."

Professor Baranyi strokes Strig's head. Strig purrs.

"Shall we undo it?"

Bianka hands him the pen somewhat reluctantly. I notice that although she is holding it out to him, he has to tug a bit before she loosens her grip and lets him take it. He snaps it in two, and the cat yowls, fur and feathers standing straight up.

"You're hurting him!" cries Bianka.

Professor Baranyi looks at the two pieces of the pen, and at the cat.

"Breaking the pen used to write the spell ought to be sufficient to break it," he says.

"I don't know," says Bianka, still holding the handkerchief to her nose. "I'm not in the habit of writing spells at all, let alone breaking them."

"Such a powerful spell may require a more complete destruction of the writing implement," says Mrs. Och. "Immolation, perhaps."

"I could write another spell to change him back," says Bianka. "Later, perhaps. I don't think I could manage it right now."

"He seems all right for the moment," says the professor, looking anxiously at the little owl-cat, who sets about washing his paws.

"I asked you this before, but I must ask again," says Mrs. Och. "Please, try to remember. Did Gennady give you anything—anything at all—that you still have with you?"

"I've told you, nothing," says Bianka, exasperated. "He wasn't the sort to go in for jewels and love poems and that kind of thing. He was just . . . well, he was himself, and that is what he gave me."

"I know the sort of man he is," says Mrs. Och, rising abruptly. "If you will excuse me, I must go and lie down."

"She lies down a good deal, doesn't she?" says Bianka after Mrs. Och leaves.

"She is not well," says Professor Baranyi in an odd voice.

"I could use a rest myself," says Bianka. "I don't know about your poor owl, but that took a bit out of me. My head is pounding."

Theo creeps closer and touches my cheek. "Lala," he says very seriously. "Abla ba ba ba. Lala."

I pull a lock of hair free of my cap and dust his nose with it, feeling an odd kind of elation. Bianka is a witch, just like my mother, and whatever else, she loves her son, just as our mother loved us. Theo giggles, then hoists himself up using the edge of the divan and goes wobble, wobble, wobble over to the fireplace. I look anxiously at Bianka and the professor, but neither of them is paying any attention to Theo.

Bianka is staring up at the ceiling now, still holding the handkerchief to her face. She talks as if to the air, in her slow Nim accent. "Gennady told wonderful stories. He built a little cabin right by the water, and he always smelled of the sea. His performances were odd, a bit slow-paced for Nim's audience, his sense of humor unusual. He never seemed to make much money. He wasn't my type, really, but he made me laugh. We were careful. I wasn't expecting Theo. And then all of this, and yet I can't bring myself to regret it. Being with him, I mean."

Theo is crawling alarmingly close to the fire, blinking at the flames. I want to shout: *The baby is about to crawl into the fire!* I should, of course. I should stage a dramatic awakening. Say I fainted while dusting (except I am not supposed to be dusting in here), opened my eyes, and there he was. My heart thuds in my throat, but I say nothing. I watch, paralyzed with horror, as he reaches out to touch the flames.

An awful howl as he falls backward, and Bianka is on her feet, rushing over to him.

"We have some salve," says the professor, leaping up also.

"It's all right," says Bianka, examining his hand. "He pulled it out quick." She laughs wryly. "That answers one question. I hadn't been able to bring myself to check, you know."

"If he would burn?" asks the professor.

"It's not bad, but he'll have a blister," says Bianka. "So that settles *that*." And almost absentmindedly, she passes her own hand through the flames, slowly. Then she hoists the crying baby onto her hip and takes him over to the desk.

"Lala!" he half sobs, pointing at me over her shoulder. I can't help myself—I pull a silly face at him. Even through his tears, he gives me a wobbly smile.

∾

"Well?" Florence backs me against the wall as soon as she sees me on the landing.

"Well," I say. "Well what?"

"Are you going to pretend you've just been doing your job? I've been searching high and low for you."

I sigh. "It doesn't sound like you've been doing *your* job, if that's the case," I say.

"That *is* my job, in part," says Florence. Her little eyes are flashing with anger and triumph. "I am in charge here."

"You know, Mrs. Och never mentioned that to me when I started," I say. "She told me to do as Mrs. Freeley said. She never told me, 'You will report to Florence and follow her instructions.' Why do you suppose that is?"

Her jaw hardens. "I'll speak to her," she says. "I'm going to tell her how you disappear all the time, how you do not do your share of the work here. I could have you fired if I wish."

"Mrs. Freeley has no complaints about me," I say, sounding more confident than I feel.

Florence narrows her eyes and steps in front of me as I try

193

to go past her. With a not insignificant effort, I master the urge to shove her down the stairs. It's not her fault that she's stuck being pious, ratty Florence, after all.

"What's the matter with you?" she demands.

"Nothing," I say. "Look, I'm not feeling well and I took a short nap. I'll make it up."

"You didn't," she says. "I checked our room."

"Of course you did." I try not to roll my eyes.

Her expression changes slightly. "It's Mr. Frederick and Bianka, isn't it?" she says.

"What is?" I am so preoccupied that for a moment I truly have no idea what she's talking about. But she is starting to look a bit pitying, and it hits me. "Oh. Oh. No."

"You should have known better," she says. "Mr. Frederick is above you in every way. It would never have worked. And it's been hard on Chloe and me, you know. Having to pick up your slack."

"I'm sorry," I say. I almost mean it; she looks so put upon. I know what hard and miserable work it is here, and she doesn't have the luxury I have of knowing she's getting out soon and will have a nice pile of silver in exchange for her treachery. "Are they actually involved? Frederick and Bianka, I mean?"

"I wouldn't know," she says loftily. "But you've seen the attention he pays to her at dinner. He's obviously in love with her."

I shrug, although there's a surprising little sting to that. I hadn't noticed at all, but then my attention has been elsewhere. Not that I mind, really—I don't have feelings for Frederick—but I suppose it's always nice when someone takes a fancy to you.

"I won't go to Mrs. Och this time," she says magnanimously. "But you're going to have to pull yourself together and start doing your job properly. Especially as I may not be here much longer."

"Oh?" I follow her down the stairs to the scullery. "Have you found another position?"

She looks around to make sure the scullery is empty and then turns to me again, eyes dancing suddenly as if I am her best friend. "I'm engaged to be married," she says.

I am so startled, and can't imagine what kind of man would want hard-edged little Florence, that for a moment I say nothing. Then I manage, rather insincerely, "Congratulations! That's wonderful."

"I'm sorry. I know it's hard for you to hear right now," she says, which is laughable, but I don't contradict her. "We probably won't get married until the summer."

"Who is the lucky man?" I ask with just the slightest hint of sarcasm, which of course she doesn't pick up at all. She is eager to confide, as if she hadn't been threatening to have me fired less than a minute ago.

"He has a grocery," she says. "Well, it's his father's grocery, but he basically runs it, and he's going to inherit it. It brings in a decent wage, and I'll work there once we are married, as his mother died this autumn."

"Oh, what a shame," I say perfunctorily.

"Well, that's why he needs a wife," she says. "To help in the shop."

I try not to laugh. "Is that the reason?"

"Well, and for having children." She smiles a very superior sort of smile. "I'm not a romantic like you. I don't go chasing after impossible prospects. We'll both have better lives once we're married."

"Then I'm very happy for you," I say. I am starting to feel rather sorry for Florence and her practical grocer, but she brings me up short.

"The problem with your way is that it gets you nothing but pain, in the end. The wrong man, and he won't commit to you, and then when somebody prettier comes along, he'll forget you. With Nil . . . well, he's solid. I know he's honest, and he'll take care of me. I can trust him. I don't mean to say that Mr. Frederick is not honest. But men can be fickle, and finding a good man who will stand by you is no small accomplishment in a place like Spira City, where there's always a fresh face. Oh, look, these are things you have to think about. . . ."

I turn away from her. I'm thinking about what Dek said. *You can't trust him. He's out a lot.* I'm thinking back to the Cleansing, that flash I saw of Wyn with his arm around the waist of a laughing Arly Winters. I'd convinced myself it didn't mean anything, but that poisonous doubt is worming its way back into my heart.

"You'll find a good man someday," says Florence comfortingly. I resist the urge to strike her hard across her smug, pointed little face.

196

THIRTEEN

It is the coldest night of the winter so far. The snow has frozen underfoot, and the crunching beneath my boots as I walk is the only sound in all the city, it seems. The river is frozen solid, the moon a yellow sliver in the sky. Even if it weren't for the murderous thing terrorizing Spira City, nobody would be out tonight besides soldiers; it is too cold. I see the soldiers all over the Scola, huddling in their blue and white, stamping their booted feet, their breath rising up into the frigid air in great white plumes. I take the side roads, the unlit roads, where the frozen snow piles up high, blocking the doorways.

I have been shivering since I stepped out of the house, but now I feel as if the cold has seeped deep into my bones, like I have ice on the inside, radiating out from my core. I can barely use my fingers when I arrive at the flat. I can see I am holding the key, but I don't feel it. I fit it into the lock and fumble it open with nearly as much difficulty as if I were picking it. One foot heavy in front of the other; though I try to walk softly, I cannot tell if I am quiet or not. Lifting my legs is painful in a distant sort of way, all the way up the narrow stairs to Wyn's attic flat, and here I do have to pick a lock with frozen fingers.

The room is dark and cold, but I do not light the fire. I walk from hearth to table to bed, touch the icy sheets. It is midnight. I want to lie down in the bed but instead I find my way to the far corner and sink to the floor. It is no warmer in here than outside, but I am one with the cold now. I disappear. My eyelids fall closed, heavy as anvils.

∽

I have loved Wyn half my life now. I loved him immediately, like everyone does. But I was like a little sister to him, of course.

"You'll marry me when you grow up, won't you, Brown Eyes?" he'd tease. "I can tell you're going to be a beauty."

While I may not have become a beauty, I am not bad to look at, and though I got older, he didn't seem to see it. I was still a little girl to him, and I didn't know how to make him see me any other way. Then I saved his life, which is not bad, as aphrodisiacs go.

I wasn't supposed to be on the job at all. It was, according to Esme, a very standard burglary. There were no guards, only dogs, and that was no trouble—animals adore Wyn. Some Prashan jewel thief had turned up in West Spira and bought a house, looking to sell his stolen treasure. Wyn was the best crook in the Twist when it came to scaling a wall, picking a lock, cat burglar stuff. I loved to see him, so fluid and fearless on a job. As a pathetic ploy to spend time with him, I had made myself his apprentice. I swore I wouldn't slow him down. I said I would stay vanished the whole way. He said no. "Not this time, Brown Eyes. I need to focus." I went anyway. He couldn't see me, after all.

The wall wasn't a problem. Nor were the dogs. He had drugged some meat; they went for it right away and then went to sleep. He slipped in through a window, and so did I. He found the safe in the basement and broke the lock apart with some of Dek's quiet explosive powder. I had assigned myself the task of keeping watch, but really I was watching Wyn, watching his profile in the shadows as he pulled a heavy bag out of the safe and opened it to have a look at what he was stealing. Then we both heard the thick voice from the corner of the room: "Before I shoot, you haf anything to offer me for your life?"

A shadow with a pistol stepped forward. We formed a triangle in the room, the Prashan, Wyn, and me. I was the invisible corner. They saw only the line between them, the line the bullet would travel.

"Give me a moment," said Wyn. "I'm sure I can think of something."

I remember how steady his voice was, and my own terror that I would see him die.

"Not good enough," said the voice.

I didn't think. I pulled the knife from my boot and threw it. I was aiming for the Prashan's chest, but it caught him in the shoulder. He swung toward me, but I was on him already, grappling for the gun. His grip was poor, perhaps because of the knife in his shoulder. I got the pistol easily enough but lost my balance wrenching it away and fell to the floor. He lunged after me. I had never fired a gun before, but I shot him. The recoil and the smell of gunpowder and the horrible scream from the Prashan all jolted me so badly, I must have dropped the gun. At least, I was not holding it anymore, and Wyn had me by the arm, hauling me up. We were running, a mad scrambling, sliding sort of run, up the stairs, out the door, past the sleeping dogs. I hadn't killed the Prashan, for we could still hear him roaring, and then a gunshot overhead, and another. But we were out in the street, tearing out of there. Wyn never let go of my arm, turning down one street, then another, then another. I had no idea where we were until we emerged on the road by the river.

Wyn leaned against a wall and stared at me for a long moment. Then he began to laugh. He laughed and laughed. I laughed too, with what breath I had left, shaking and laughing from sheer relief.

"Bleeding Kahge, Brown Eyes! Where did you come from?"

"I told you, I wanted to go," I said.

"You could have been killed."

"You *would* have been killed."

He got a funny look on his face then. "So I owe you my life, is that right?"

I was giddy and bold. "You owe me something."

"What's that, then?" he asked. He was so close, half bending toward me. He used the sleeve of his jacket to wipe the Prashan's blood from my face. I went on my tiptoes and kissed him.

He laughed, and I kissed him again, a chaste sort of peck on the mouth.

"You need kissing lessons," he said.

"So give them to me."

I was a quick study.

$\sim$

I wake with a start. A crashing sound has me half scrambling to my feet before I remember where I am, and it is only the door anyway. I slide back down against the wall, vanishing again.

His voice. That gorgeous voice, gentle and smooth, only sharpened a little by Spira's hard vowels.

"Kahge's hounds, it's cold!" he says.

"Light the fire."

And even though I knew, of course I knew, my heart sinks like a witch through dark water. I bite my frozen lip to keep from crying out.

He fumbles with matches, and soon the fire blazes up. He lights the lamp by the table. Arly Winters—of course it's Arly Winters—stands shivering by the door in a heavy fur that can't possibly be hers, a fur hat squashing her dark curls. Wyn is wearing a fur coat as well. They look half animal in the firelight.

"Come on close to the fire," he says, pulling her to him. "It'll warm up soon."

"We shouldn't've been out at all," she says. "It's dangerous, with a madman on the loose!"

"You're safe with me," says Wyn, taking his pistol out of his pocket and giving it a spin before putting it down on the table. "And how else were we going to get these fantastic furs?"

She giggles.

"And this too!" He takes a dark bottle from his pocket, pulling out the cork and swigging from it.

"Think I would have died on the way here without it," she says, and he hands it to her. She takes a swig and giggles again. "It's strong."

I'm going to go out on a limb and say that he isn't with her for her wit and scintillating conversation. I have to stop biting my lip before I bite it off. I release it slowly, and it throbs. Instead I clench my teeth together, all my rage in my jaw.

"Have a bit more," he says. "Warm up. That fur is very becoming, but you'd be even more so without it."

"You're such a scoundrel," she says, and has another swig.

"I am no such thing," he says. "Come here, my beautiful, dark-eyed girl."

As the fire blazes, the room slowly warms and my bones begin to thaw and ache. I have seen what I came to see. I have seen enough. But I do not leave. I stay and watch the whole thing. The furs falling to the floor at last. His familiar, tender look, the way he touches her face and then slides his hand down her neck and farther down, the way he unbuttons her dress with one hand while he holds her chin in the other hand and kisses her softly. She is beautiful, milky white with heavy curves, laughing and tossing that dark mane back. I watch them the way I watch every Cleansing. I do not leave until the fire is down to embers and they are sleeping underneath their furs. It is not in my nature to turn away. Not I—I look my nightmares in the eye. And if my nightmares should look back, they see nothing but shadow. I am not there.

∽

The moon and stars have gone into hiding when I stumble out into the street, which is, unbelievably, even colder than when I left it. But the cold is nothing. I am in a blazing cocoon of pain, and the cold can take me or not for all I care. I don't feel a thing—I don't even know where my feet are taking me. It's as if something is calling me, and I follow the call, blinded by tears that freeze on my cheeks. Down one street and then another, half running. I stumble and fall, landing hard on the frozen snow. Through the haze of my tears I can see a shape at the end of the street. Something tall. Something beginning to move toward me. Some inner voice tells me: *Run.* But I find I can't obey, my horror freezing me where I lie.

A glint of metal in the dark, though I can't think what light it might be reflecting, for there is none. I know what this thing is. I pull back, vanish, but the creature keeps coming.

It does not need eyes to find me. The pain and the cold make way for the rush of adrenaline. The voice within telling me *run* gets louder and stronger, and I force my limbs into compliance, scrambling to my feet, slipping. I run.

A soft snarl behind me. I know without looking that I cannot outrun this creature, whatever it is. But we are in the Twist and I know every corner, every alley, every abandoned stairway. I turn up a dark staircase and race up to the empty apartment where some Ishtan traders keep their wares. The smell of spice is overpowering. There is an open window and a pulley here. You cannot see it in the dark, but I do not need to see. This spot has not changed since I was a child, when Dek would send me sailing over the street to the apartment across the way in the crate attached to a wire.

I stub my toe on something and go sprawling. A soft hand touches my neck, then pulls me up by the collar of my coat. White eyes with black pupils, long-slit pupils like a cat's. A panther face, almost—black and feline, yet expressive as a human's. Almost kind. A crest of white in its hair, or fur. I can feel the blast of winter from the window gap behind me. The creature raises his blade.

"I know who you are," I gasp, making a fist over the weapon Dek made me. "I have a message for you."

The blade hovers.

"You can go straight back to Kahge," I say, pulling the mechanism at my palm so that capsicum gas shoots out from the nozzle at my wrist. A great cloud swallows up the creature, and it lets out a strangled howl. The gas burns at my eyes, my throat, and nose as I kick free and send myself sailing straight out the window, grabbing for the wire with frozen fingers. By sheer luck I find it, kicking wildly at the crate. I let myself fall into it and I push myself off, gliding across the street. The capsicum gas does not slow the creature for long—I can see it climbing down the wall, loping across the street with a terrible, swift grace. There is more space between us now, at least. I sail straight through the window across the way, and as soon as the creature enters the building, I send myself whizzing right back. I dive through the window, run across the room and down the stairs, out into the snow again. The Twist is like a maze engraved into my very being. I let it swallow me up, one corner and then another, through the buildings I know to be empty or open. I'd scream for help, but who would help me? I feel the pull, the call, once more. I have to fight myself, force myself each time in the opposite direction of where my feet are trying to take me. Too many times I realize I am letting myself be drawn, and I turn and run, turn and run, turn and run. I hear it before I see it again, the crunch of snow behind me. But I am almost at my destination, tearing down the hill, the Edge dark before me.

"Liddy!" I scream, even before I reach the door. "Liddy!"

I hammer at the door, and the shadow keeps coming, blade aloft. The door opens and I fall inside. The creature is in the doorway, staring at Liddy with those inhuman eyes. The doorway I've just passed through lights up with golden webbing, and three poison-green spiders, like the ones I got for Professor Baranyi from Torne in the Edge, drop down on golden threads. But these are larger—the size of my fist—and they raise their front legs and *hiss*. The blade lowers. Liddy shuts the door then, and helps me to my feet.

∾

It is half an hour or more before I feel able to talk. Liddy wraps me in blankets and furs, lights the stove, makes coffee. I sit and sip the coffee mechanically while my heart tries to batter its way through my rib cage and the cold eases out of me, biting at my fingers and toes as it departs.

"It can't come in?" I say at last.

"My home is protected."

"By giant, hissing spiders."

"Not spiders. They are rhug. Very fast, very poisonous, nearly unkillable. They breed quickly, bond to a place, guard entry points. A handy sort of pet. Given time, the Gethin could break the rhug's bond to the house, but it would take longer than the few hours left before dawn. And the Gethin is a creature of night." Liddy gives me a searching look. "Why is the Gethin coming for you, Julia?"

"The Gethin," I repeat the name she is using. "What the blazes is that thing, Liddy?"

"The last of its tribe, as far as anyone knows," says Liddy. "The Gethin were soldiers and bounty hunters thousands of years ago, often employed by the Eshriki Phars. The story goes that Marike, the Eshriki witch who founded that ancient empire, called the Gethin from Kahge, but nobody knows the truth of it anymore."

"Is there really such a place as Kahge? All fire and demons under the earth?" I told the Gethin to go back to Kahge, but I didn't think I was being literal.

Liddy snorts. "That is Kahge reimagined to fit a particular worldview," she says. "Lorian cosmology made a nightmare of it, and the Rainists treat it as a metaphor, but it is neither. It is . . . how shall I put it? Like the shadow, the echo, the reflection cast by magic in the world. There are beings there, to be sure, but we know almost nothing about them. It is not distant like the stars, nor does it lie beneath the earth. It is all around us and yet separated by . . . well, what you might like to call our reality." She waves a bony hand in the air, like she might be able to catch some of it to show me. "Magic flows out of the world through Kahge. In that sense, it also functions as a release valve, maintaining balance. Witches have always had an interest in the boundaries between the known world and Kahge, as a place where magic accumulates. But the nature of Kahge is a question for philosophers, not the likes of me, and you have dodged my question. Someone has called the Gethin. Why is it hunting you?"

"It's looking for a guest at Mrs. Och's house," I say. "And the holies only know why, but it's killing people who've met her."

"I've heard it said that the Gethin can drink the memories of its victims," says Liddy. "Perhaps each victim is a clue in its hunt, leading it ever closer. Oh, Julia. You should leave Mrs. Och's house."

That startles me. "What do you know about her?"

There is a long silence, so long that I think Liddy will not answer me. I feel so far away from my own body, weak with exhaustion and cold and fear. My eyes fall shut and I think that none of this is possible, this cannot be my life. Then Liddy begins to speak, and it takes me a moment to remember what she is talking about.

"You have heard of the Xianren, yes? *Xianren* means, literally, 'the before people' in the language of Yongguo. There were three Xianren in the beginning—immortals who spoke their magic and ruled the world. The magic they spoke could alter even death and time, back when the world was new and great lizards were crawling from the seas while dragons battled in the skies. They are called immortals, but all life has an end point, even theirs. They have been fading for centuries now, and their power is much diminished. Och Farya is the eldest of the three."

"Mrs. Och," I say. "Is her brother Gennady one of the Xianren too?"

Liddy inclines her head. "Zor Gen, the youngest, and the wildest, according to the stories. Prone to stealing lovely princesses, and father to some of the greatest kings and warriors throughout history."

"And the third?" I ask. "What's his name?" I think I can guess.

"Lan Camshe," she says. "A scholar and art lover. A recluse. He built himself a castle with a great library on the Isle of Nago, off the coast of Sirillia."

"Casimir," I say, remembering the unfinished letter in Mrs. Och's desk. "Hounds, Liddy, how *do* you know all this?"

"I have been around a long time," she says, which is as unsatisfying as every answer she's ever given me to similar questions. She looks at the clock, then rises and climbs some wooden steps that lead through a hatch in the ceiling.

"Wait," I say, and follow her, afraid to be alone.

The room at the top of the steps is full of wire hutches. Inside them, silvery pigeons nestle, sleeping. Liddy scrawls a quick message and ties it to the ankle of one pigeon, then opens a window onto the gray predawn night and sends the pigeon out into the cold. Unprotesting, the pigeon flies straight into the Twist and is gone.

"What are you doing?" I ask.

"Esme should know where you are and that you are in danger," says Liddy. "I can protect you tonight, but if the Gethin wants you, you'll need more help than I can give in the nights to come."

"Can Mrs. Och help me?" I ask, a coldness twining about my heart.

"Mrs. Och is known for helping people," says Liddy. "Indeed, I have sent a few desperate souls her way myself, over the years. But she is *not* known for having a forgiving nature. If you are working against her for her brother Casimir, would she be inclined to help *you*?"

Probably not. I imagine going to her and telling her everything, and shudder. We go back down the stairs to huddle by the fire.

"Ah, Julia," sighs Liddy. "How did you come to be in the employ of such people?"

"Gregor told me it was a lot of money," I say, and then, like a fool, I begin to cry. Liddy doesn't say anything. We sit by the fire and sobs shake me, wring me out, leave me empty and shuddering in the chair, too warm now under the furs but too exhausted to cast them off. I cry for Bianka and whatever will become of her and her little boy; I cry because of Wyn and Arly Winters laughing as if I didn't exist; I cry because I feel sometimes that I barely exist, barely touch the world I walk in; I cry because Dek is unhappy and Gregor is a drunk and Esme is lonely; I cry because Florence thinks she is lucky to be marrying a grocer to take care of his shop; I cry for my mother and the brown-haired witch I saw last month, falling to her death in the unforgiving river Syne. I cry because I am exhausted, because I fear for my life, and I want to live, more than anything I want to live. I fall asleep in the chair and am woken not long after by, of all people, Gregor.

"Better get you back before you're found missing," he says.

It shocks me how glad I am to see him. I want to throw my arms around his neck, but don't, of course.

FOURTEEN

I don't know what to say to Gregor as we trudge through the gray half-light, the snow crunching underfoot. *Well, Gregor, it seems that a monster just tried to kill me and will likely try again tonight, probably because I'm working for an immortal wizard who is interested in this witch I'm spying on, but lucky for me, my mysterious, secretive friend has some giant, ugly pet spiders guarding her shop. . . .* It just doesn't make for easy conversation, but it's almost impossible to ignore one's near-death experience of a few hours past and talk about something else.

Since I don't know what to say about my brush with death, I raise the subject of my heartbreak instead, the easier of the two to face now. Nothing like nearly dying to put losing your lover into perspective.

"Wyn is shagging Arly Winters," I tell him.

And suddenly, unexpectedly, I find myself remembering Wyn in the dark, a year ago or more, stroking my cheekbone with his rough thumb and telling me, *You're lucky, you remember your mother.*

"Ah," says Gregor, hands deep in his coat pockets. He doesn't sound surprised.

"I suppose everybody else knew about it already."

And now I'm remembering Wyn and me sitting together at his open window in the summer, feeding the pigeons on the roof, and how I thought, This is what it means to be happy, *this.*

"I didn't know, Julia, but I can't pretend to be surprised," he says. "I'm fond of Wyn, but he's a rake and always will be."

"We were just having a good time," I say lamely.

Wyn and me, laughing our way home after burgling a West Spira house, me draped in the stolen jewels.

"I'll tell you, when I fell in love with Csilla, I knew every other woman would be a shadow to her after that, and I was right. She stole my heart and it's been hers ever since. She's stuck by me through everything."

"How lovely for you," I say sarcastically.

"What I mean, Julia, is that if you're going to fall in love, you make sure it's with somebody who knows how to love you back the same way."

"It's not like that," I say, because my pride hurts as much as every other part of me. "I don't care what he does when I'm not around."

Gregor says nothing to this. I suppose he knows I'm lying. We cross the bridge, Cyrambel Temple looming over us. I can see snowy lumps on the low path, indigents and Scourge survivors frozen to death and covered over by snow. Soldiers will take them away soon, but sometimes in the spring, after a sudden melt, you'll find a few thawing corpses before they are tidied away.

"I've sent word to Pia," he says. "As soon as we hear back, I'll have Solly fetch you with a good story—he could say the police need to question witnesses of a theft or some such thing. We need to make sure this business is all taken care of by tonight. Liddy thinks you'll be safe until nightfall."

"Liddy seems to know everything there is to know about it but only tells what she wants. As usual."

"She's never steered anyone wrong that I know of," he replies curtly. "Now, do you want to tell me what in Kahge you were doing out in the middle of the night in the first place?"

"How is that any of your business?" I ask.

"It's my business because you work for me," he says. "You shouldn't be taking stupid risks. You were almost killed, and now we have to beg for help. It's unprofessional."

"I work for Esme, not you, and I'm so sorry that my nearly dying strikes you as unprofessional," I shoot back. "What an embarrassment and inconvenience it must be for you."

"By the holies, Julia, stop being sarcastic for a minute, would you?"

"Fine. Here it is. I'm not asking for your bleeding sympathy, but I don't need to be scolded for nearly being killed either. You got me this job, and it's the most horrible, *dangerous* job I've ever worked. *You're* the one who as good as threw me in the way of this beast. 'Just go and work as a maid, have a look around, heaps of silver,' you said. You didn't say the client's a lunatic and there's magic involved and you may find yourself next on a beheading monster's hit list, did you? You failed to mention that in the job description, and you'd met Pia, so you *knew* this was no ordinary job! Stop blaming *me* for what's happened. *I'll* talk to Pia. This has nothing to do with you, besides being your fault."

We walk on in angry silence for a time—or, at least, I am angry. When Gregor speaks again, his voice is surprisingly soft.

"I'm sorry," he says.

"I should hope so," I answer tartly, though in fact I'm rather startled to get an apology at all.

"I never meant to put you in harm's way, and I shan't forgive myself for it." He clears his throat. "You know that Esme watched her husband and her son die within five days of each other, don't you?"

"Yes." If he's trying to change the subject, this is a dark direction to choose.

"It broke her heart in such a way that now it swings open and shut at random, letting in unexpected strays. I didn't understand until she just scooped Wyn off the streets one day. He'd run away from that terrible orphanage, was living by his wits, if that's what you want to call it. Esme brought him home, started calling him her son. Then, a few years on, I come by after a job and find she's acquired two more children—young ones too—a crippled boy and a girl with a scowl that would turn any heart to stone. I figured she'd lost her mind, and said so. She told me what you could do, your vanishing act, and she told me she had a feeling about Dek, that he was cleverer than any child she'd ever known. 'They'll be useful,' she said. She was right, but even so, I knew it wasn't for your skills that she took you in, exceptional though they are. It was the Scourge marks on his face, his blasted limbs, and those motherless eyes of yours. One look at your eyes, Julia, my dear, and anyone with a heart and soul in them can see you are motherless."

"Shut up," I tell him. I don't want to hear this. He keeps on talking.

"Esme always said you were the one who'd take over from her someday. No doubt in any of our minds about that. You were made for this work. You were tough as nails, even back then. Quick wit, quick feet, quick to laugh, but sharp, *sharp*. I mean to say—look, you work for Esme, but you're family too. Hers, and mine, and Csilla's. You know that, don't you? That you have a family?"

"Of course I do," I say a bit numbly. It would have meant the world to me just weeks ago, days ago—knowing I was being groomed to take over for Esme. I don't know what it means now. Is this the work that I am made for? And if not this, what else is there for a girl like me?

"It's all right, Gregor. I know it's not really your fault. I'm just . . . I don't want to die. I *really* don't want to die."

"Nor shall you," he says, and when he takes my hand I let him, because it's blasted cold. "Look, what I'm trying to tell you—I'll stand between you and that thing myself, if it comes to that."

"Well, let's hope it doesn't, for it would make very short

work of you and do me no good at all," I say, which isn't very kind, but true. "But thank you—for the sentiment."

I am about to make a joke about how drunk he must be when I realize that he *isn't*. There is no trace of liquor on his breath or in his face or gait. He is stone-cold miserably sober.

"It's not like you to be up so early without a hangover," I say, suspicious.

"I've given it up," he says. "For good. Not another drop to pass these lips."

Something in me hardens at this. I pull my hand away and say, "I've heard that before."

He gives me a sad look, but I don't care, not a whit, not for everything he's said or for his struggle with the bottle or any of it. The first lesson I ever learned, and I learned it well, was never to trust a man who is a slave to the bottle or the poppy or anything like that, because he will choose it over those he professes to love, over and over and over again.

"People don't change," I say.

"You're sixteen, and you're so sure of that, are you?" he says.

I say nothing to that. He knows I'm right.

"You don't need to believe it. You will eventually. Csilla believes it."

"If she does, I'm sorry for her," I say feelingly.

Gregor looks at me sideways. "You're too young to be so cynical," he says. "We have to live in hope, you know. What else do we have?"

"We have exactly what we *have*," I say. "I'm not interested in playing pretend."

"What do you have, then, if you're so keen on stark realities?"

Love, I might have said, just yesterday. A love unlike any other, so rare and strange and wonderful. Now I know better, for whatever that's worth.

"I have Dek," I say. "Soon I'll have lots of money too."

My life, for the moment.

"We're all about to have lots of money," says Gregor. "That's a fantasy too, you know."

"No it isn't," I say. "I'm working a job and I'll be paid for it, and I don't gamble my money away. Then Dek and I can go on holiday."

"Dek can't go anywhere, and you know it," says Gregor.

He's right. Scourge survivors are not welcome anywhere. We are lucky to have a home; we would never find another decent place that would take us in.

"I'll buy myself a fur coat and eat hot cakes every day till spring," I say.

"Sounds like bliss," says Gregor dryly.

∽

Florence and Chloe are already up and heating water in the scullery when I get back. I come in with an armful of firewood from the shed in the yard, hoping they haven't fetched it already.

"You were up early," says Chloe, startled to see me.

"Just a little before you," I say.

Florence looks suspicious, but not even she would imagine

I'd be mad enough to spend a night like the last out in the cold.

"You don't look well at all," adds Chloe. She glances at Florence. "Perhaps she ought to lie down?"

Florence puts her hands on her hips and glares at me.

"I'll be fine," I say, avoiding her gaze, though in fact I am feeling a bit feverish. I begin to assemble the coffee things.

"I've got everyone upstairs," says Chloe. "Take that one to Bianka?"

I do not want to see Bianka, and I hope she will still be asleep. I let myself into the back parlor gently, balancing the tray of coffee and sweet buns and fruit on one hand.

Baby Theo is nestled among the blankets, one arm flung back, dark curls in disarray, breathing deeply. Bianka is awake, sitting by the window and looking out thoughtfully at the snow. When I come in, she looks up but does not smile.

"Breakfast, ma'am," I say softly.

"You've had a bad night," she says.

"I'm feeling a little under the weather, ma'am," I say.

"I should say so." She rises and takes the tray from me, putting it down on the table by the window. "Sit a moment," she says. "Have a bun."

I don't want to talk to her, but I do want the bun, and so I sit and take it before she can change her mind or indicate she didn't mean it.

"You've been up all night," she says. "And crying."

"I have a cold," I say. "It makes my eyes red."

"I know the difference," she says. "I've had my heart broken before, you know."

The bun sticks in my throat. "I'm fine," I say, forcing myself to swallow.

"Well," she says with a shrug. "If you say so."

I eat the rest of the bun while she pours a cup of coffee and sips at it. Baby Theo sighs in his sleep, and we both look at him. I wish I could ask her about being a witch—all the questions I never asked my mother about discovering such a power, what it means, how it feels, using it or choosing not to, being hated and hunted. I want to shake her and cry: *Do you really believe that you're safe here? Don't you know your enemies are closing in on you? That I am here to do you harm?* But, of course, I can say none of that. I stare at the rest of her breakfast longingly.

"The first time I fell in love, I was about your age," she says, giving me a shrewd look. "But then I found out he had another girl. That old story."

"What did you do?" I ask.

"I cut him loose," she says. "I thought I was done with love after that. But two years ago, I fell in love again. It was beautiful for a while, but he disappeared after Theo was born. Now I think I really am done with love." She laughs, as if this is funny. "I said that to Mrs. Och, you know. I told her this man had broken my heart and I was done with love. She told me, 'You are never done with love.' How old do you suppose she is?"

"I've no idea," I say, thinking about what Liddy told me. Older than she looks. Old as the hills, quite literally.

"Do you think it's true? That you and I will love again? It's hard to imagine anyone as perfect and beautiful as the one I lost."

I don't even want to imagine somebody other than Wyn.

"I suppose it must be true," I say, my voice brittle. "We'll go on to be married, perhaps, and forget them."

Bianka shakes her head, smiling. "We won't forget them," she says, and hands me another bun. "I like a girl who keeps her appetite no matter what. Food is a great comfort. Honey cakes won't break your heart, will they?"

She winks, and I manage half a smile. We might have been friends, I think. Then I stop myself thinking it.

∽

Solly comes at noon in his uniform, with his story about needing me as a witness, and takes me to the hotel. Pia is dressed entirely in brown tweeds, including a fitted cap, today. Even without those disturbing goggles, she would be the strangest-looking person I have ever met.

"The Gethin came after me," I tell her.

If she is surprised, she doesn't show it. She seems almost cheerful. "But you got away," she says. "That is lucky. And unusual."

"He's looking for Bianka, isn't he?" I say. "And I'm, what . . . a way of finding her? He chews on my brain a bit and knows what I know, is that the idea?"

Pia settles back in a chair, crossing one long, trousered leg over the other and grinning up at me like I am terribly amusing. "Something like that. Who told you all this?"

I don't want to give Liddy away, but I say, "I have a friend. She knows a lot about . . . well, folklore and whatnot. Everything."

"Everything!" says Pia. "What a useful friend to have. Does she happen to know who sent the Gethin, this friend of yours?"

"No," I say. "I thought you could tell me that."

"No. I wish I could."

I lower myself shakily onto the sofa and struggle to keep my voice even. "Well, I nearly got my head sliced open last night, and I'm in a very poor mood as a result," I say. "I'm doing my job as best I can. You might have warned me."

"I did not think of it—that he might seek you out. Did he catch your essence from the messenger boy's memory?"

"I don't know. I don't know how it bleeding works."

"It is interesting. Something keeps him from Bianka," says Pia conversationally. "Some spell, I suppose. The Gethin can sense a person's essence, but he cannot seem to sense hers. And so he finds only those who have seen her, been close to her. He follows one to the next; he hunts them down and takes their memories in the hope that they will know where she is hiding, but she keeps moving, and so his search continues. But now he has found you." Her goggles whir, in and out. "Do you have a report for me?" she asks.

Partly this makes me want to spit with fury, but I pull myself together. After all, I need to be worth saving, if I am going to ask it of her. I recite my list of Bianka's belongings (not much); I tell her that Mr. Darius is actually Sir Victor Penn Ostoway III and give her the letters from Agoston

Horthy; I tell her about the rhug spiders and the silver bullets I collected from Torne for Professor Baranyi; I tell her all I saw and heard in Professor Baranyi's study, the owl turned cat, and so on. She listens impassively, interested in Agoston Horthy's letters but otherwise showing no reaction, even when I tell her about Torne sending his regards.

"Do you know him?" I ask.

"From another lifetime," she says.

"Why are all these people after Bianka, anyway?" I venture. "I mean, us, and the Gethin."

"She has something," says Pia.

"You're sure about that? Because I told you, besides her clothes, a few trinkets, and romance novels, she doesn't have anything."

Pia tilts her head to one side and looks at me for a bit before saying, "She has a small boy. He wasn't on your list."

And just like that, I feel my whole body turn to lead. "Theo? What *about* Theo?"

Pia shrugs. "I don't know. Nor does the Gethin, I'll wager, for that creature too is a slave, like me, like you. We do as our masters bid us. You are to bring me the child."

I can barely get the word out. "*Why?*"

"Ah, curiosity," says Pia. "You are young. I have reached a point where I know more than I wish to and am incurious. In fact, I long for ignorance. Perhaps you will feel the same one day. The grander purpose is this: My employer now believes that there is something inside the boy that he wants. We must bring him the child so he can get it out."

"Inside him? What does that mean?"

"I do not know. Nor do I want to."

"Why didn't you tell me . . . before?" It sounds so pathetic. "I mean, I was going through her underthings."

"I received a telegram about it only this morning," says Pia crisply. "We did not know what we were looking for, not exactly, not until now. A shadow, my master said, but it might look like anything. Now our source says it is the boy, and because we do not leave a trail of bodies like the Gethin, we can achieve our own ends quickly, without drawing any attention."

"How does your source know it's Theo?"

Pia spreads her hands, palms up, in the Lorian gesture of accepting the mysteries of the Nameless One. Very funny. Unless she's actually Lorian, but that seems unlikely.

"What about the Gethin?" I ask desperately. "He'll be sniffing me out again tonight, won't he?"

Pia nods slowly. "I wish we knew who sent him. But I do not want him stalking us once we have the boy. We had better take care of the Gethin first."

Well, I won't deny I am very glad to hear it. For the moment I put aside that chilling *once we have the boy*. "How?"

"I will have to kill him," says Pia.

"Can you do that?" I ask, startled and relieved.

"I do not see another way around it. If I let him kill you, your memories will lead him straight to the house and Bianka."

"No need to be so sentimental about it," I say sarcastically, and am surprised when Pia cracks a tiny smile.

"You are still important," she says. "Don't be afraid."

"So you'll just go out and kill him?" I ask. "How will you find him?"

"You will find him," she says. "Or, more accurately, he will find you."

FIFTEEN

And so, for a second night I find myself out in the freezing cold after midnight, this time with Pia at my side. She is wearing a long coat made of coarse grayish fur. It is not like the fashionable fur coats ladies in West Spira wear. Not like the coats Wyn and Arly stole.

"What is your coat made of?" I ask. My voice sounds too loud in the silent street.

"Wolf skin," says Pia.

Not, as I said, a fashionable choice. I shiver and stomp my feet.

"You feel nothing?" she asks.

I shake my head. "Should we walk? Just to keep warm? It might help if I'm moving. Last time I was moving."

"As you wish," she says. "It will make no difference. As soon as you feel the pull, follow it."

We are waiting for the Gethin to find me, but we have been waiting for almost an hour already at Molinda Bridge, looking over the frozen Syne.

"My mother is down there," I hear myself say, nodding toward the river. Pia frightens and repulses me, but to whom else could I so freely admit what my mother was? Easy to say to somebody who deals with much worse, probably *is* much worse.

"A witch?" she says, and I nod. "How old were you?"

"Seven," I say.

"Very young," she says, and I say, "In a way."

"What of your own power? Where does it come from?"

"I don't know," I say. "I'm no witch, if that's what you mean."

"I understand," says Pia. "Like you, I have certain abilities. Our power sets us apart. You'll feel that more, as you get older." She adds, almost reluctantly: "I too have lost people I cared for to the river Syne."

The moon is out tonight, brighter than the night before. Pia looks ghostly white, her tweed cap pulled down over her ears and leaving her face a pale oval between fur and cap, goggles adjusting and readjusting. Looking at her, I feel a mix of revulsion and something else, perhaps recognition of whatever we share. I sense that her hardness, like mine, is hard-earned.

"How will you kill it?" I ask. "Just with that knife?"

She nods. "Silver," she says. "To kill the Gethin, you must pierce the heart with silver and then cut off the head. Safest then to keep the head and body separate and burn them both."

"What happens if you don't do all that?"

She grins at me in the moonlight. "You may find the Gethin coming for you again," she says.

"Aren't you worried about Bianka coming after you?" I ask her.

"Why would I be?"

"I don't know. Mrs. Och says she's strong for a witch. Suppose she spells you dead, like Sybil the Bloody killed all those people?"

"Bianka does not know me," says Pia. "And Sybil the Bloody was an invention of Agoston Horthy's. No witch alive has such power. Or perhaps only one."

"What do you mean, an invention?" I say, stunned. "He made her up?"

"Yes," says Pia. "And a very successful story it was too."

I mull that over a bit, and then, since we are chatting so amiably, I am bold and ask her, "Is it true that the man you work for, Casimir, is one of the Xianren?"

She turns her head toward me sharply. So I guess Liddy knew what she was talking about. We are almost into the Plateau now.

"Who told you that?" she asks. "Your friend who knows everything?"

"Yes," I say. "There are three of them, aren't there? Casimir, Gennady, and Mrs. Och."

"Giants," says Pia. "And we, their pawns."

"I'm not a pawn," I say. "I work for pay."

"We are all paid for what we do, in some way or another," says Pia. "And in our own ways, we all pay for it too. That changes nothing."

"Well, who's trying to change anything?" I say.

"Not I," says Pia. "Still nothing?"

I shake my head. And so the night passes slowly. I grow so cold that it hurts to move. Pia removes her long wolf-skin coat and wraps it around me casually. It radiates warmth. She is taller than I am, and the coat drags in the snow after me. I want to protest that she will surely freeze, but I am too grateful for the fur to offer it back. We wander the Plateau, Mount Heriot rising up above us, avoiding the miserable, freezing clusters of soldiers. Pia moves easily, apparently impervious to the bitter winter night. Then she stops and sniffs.

"Blood," she says. "Fresh."

Nameless One help me, I am wandering the city at night with some bizarre woman-thing that can smell fresh blood. *And* counting her my friend and protector. Gregor's fault, indeed. What has become of my life? I follow Pia at a trot, for she has quickened her pace and I want to stay close. Down an alley, next to a closed warehouse, we find the body. The snow around him is dark with blood. Before I turn away I see that the top of his head is missing.

"Look at him," says Pia harshly. "Do you know him?"

When I do not look, she catches me by the shoulder. She pulls my chin around and forces me to face the man, who stares up at me, eyes wide and still, big buck teeth in his long jaw. My stomach churns, and I taste iron.

"Do you know him?" she repeats, giving me a shake.

"Yes," I gasp, and she releases me. I stagger against the warehouse wall, turning away again and trying to blot out the image of his face. "The hackney driver," I say. "His name is Jensen. He brought Bianka to the house."

"Then the Gethin knows where Bianka is," says Pia.

I nod, swallowing hard and trying to still my heart and my stomach. Pia glances at the moon descending behind Mount Heriot.

"We have an hour till daybreak," she says. "Run."

~

We run through the dark, icy streets, back toward the river. I have always been a good runner, but I am slowed by the cold, and nauseous with horror at what I have seen. Pia, long-legged, is much faster than I. Trying to keep her in sight, terrified of being left behind, I stumble twice and then fall flat. I cry out, not a word exactly, though if I could make words I would say something undignified and pathetic like *Don't leave me out here alone.* Pia turns back for me and hauls me to my feet. I wheeze, "I can't." She does not pause but tosses me over her shoulder like a sack of grain. I gasp with pain as I jounce against her, the ground flashing by below. Despite the ice and the snow and the dark, her booted feet never slip but keep pounding the ground, propelling us through the city, across the bridge and into the Scola.

She slows at Lirabon Avenue, letting me slide to the ground. My ribs and belly are bruised and sore. I stagger but manage not to fall.

"Someone is working magic," she says.

I smell sulfur. We round the corner to Mikall Street cautiously. Across from Mrs. Och's house, a figure in a heavy fur is huddled on the ground, perhaps writing, but it is difficult to say. A hat obscures his or her face.

"Not this way," says Pia, pulling me back around the corner.

"Who was that?" I ask, but she doesn't answer. We take an alleyway that leads along the back wall of the garden. Pia climbs up the wall and disappears over it like a spider. It is incredible to see. I try to climb the wall, but it is high and sheer and I cannot. I sense something and turn. There, down the alleyway, is the Gethin, watching me.

I scream. In an instant Pia is back over the wall, clamping a hand over my mouth.

"Hush," she says. "He does not care about you anymore."

She drags me up the wall with her, heaves me over, and I fall into the snow in Mrs. Och's back garden. Pia climbs partway down and stops, just hanging from the wall like gravity means nothing to her.

"I cannot touch the ground here," she says, and then I see them, the rhug shining in the snow, scampering toward the wall, toward us—many, many more of them than I brought back from the Edge the other day. They move around me like I am not there.

"They won't harm you—you belong here," she says. "But someone is trying to break their connection to this place. Go and warn Mrs. Och. Quick. If the Gethin gets past me, they will need to be ready. They must not let him take the boy."

She draws her long knife, placing it neatly between her teeth, and disappears back over the wall before I can thank her or wish her luck. I make my way as fast as I can across the snowy garden, my boots sinking deep into the unpacked snow. I let myself into the scullery through the side door, run straight to the back parlor, and throw open the door. Bianka is curled against Theo, both of them buried in blankets. She sits bolt upright when the door opens.

"There's something," I say, lost for words. "Something outside. A monster."

Bianka gives me a look of blank horror, then scoops Theo up in her arms and tears past me out of the room, straight up the stairs to the bedrooms. She bangs on Professor Baranyi's door, and then on Mrs. Och's.

"It's here!" she cries. "It's come for me!"

Everybody comes stumbling out into the hallway in their nightclothes.

"What do you mean?" says Mrs. Och.

"Ella says there is a monster outside," says Bianka, her face rigid.

Mrs. Och looks at me. "Why are you dressed?" she asks, very reasonably.

"I heard something," I say. "I went to see, and—" I don't need to finish my lie. There is a sound like ice splintering. The smell of sulfur fills the house. Professor Baranyi looks wildly at Mrs. Och.

"The house is unprotected now," she says coolly. "You have the bullets?"

"Yes, yes," he says, and I remember the box I got from Torne. "Frederick, quickly, the gun, the bullets."

Frederick runs down the stairs toward the study as the

front door crashes open. We all stand in the hallway, just waiting.

"Shouldn't she hide?" I say of Bianka, but nobody seems to hear me.

"Get me a pen," says Bianka.

"A pen, Frederick!" Professor Baranyi shouts down the stairs. Then he says, "Nameless One save us," and backs away from the stairs. I hear the attic door open and Florence's footsteps descending, her voice: "What is happening?" Followed by a blood-curdling scream.

The Gethin appears at the end of the hall, blade shimmering in his hand. Those eyes. That strange, kind face. The face of death, in my mind now, perhaps for always. I wonder what has become of Pia then.

"This is my house, and you are not welcome here," says Mrs. Och in a deeper and more resonant voice than her usual voice. I have curled myself against the wall, disappeared without really thinking, and she steps past me so she is between the Gethin and the rest of us. She is transformed. Great gray wings are folded on her back, fur marked black and gold along her arms. There is a crest of feathers on her head too, but I cannot see her face. She holds a golden hand up, and the Gethin raises his blade and swings it toward her. She leaps back, then says again, "You are not welcome here," and steps toward him.

"Bleeding hurry, Freddie," mutters the professor. Bianka is backed up against Mrs. Och's bedroom door, clutching Theo tightly. He has woken up and is staring at the scene before him with bewildered brown eyes. The Gethin gives a snarl. Mrs. Och sways slightly; a wind rises in the hall. Quick as lightning, the Gethin raises his blade and slashes at her. She staggers, buckles, the wind dying. I see blood and close my eyes. Bianka screams. I feel the Gethin brush past me, and I don't know what compels me but I stick a leg out to trip him.

Well, it would have worked on a soldier or a bully in the Twist. Instead, I have the Gethin's soft hand on my throat again. His eyes search my face almost tenderly for a moment; then he drops me, gasping for breath, on the floor.

A gunshot, deafening. The Gethin spinning around. Mrs. Och rising from the ground, her face terrible, half human and half cat, her wings filling the hall. Frederick beside her, holding a gun in shaking hands, his face white. The Gethin moving toward them. Bianka calling again for a pen, Baby Theo crying now, Florence still screaming on the stairs. A second shot, and the ring of metal as the Gethin deflects the bullet with his blade. He sends Frederick crashing to the ground with a blow from his black-furred hand. He drives his blade into Mrs. Och, who crumples. The Gethin whirls around and springs down the hall toward Bianka. Professor Baranyi steps before him and is swatted easily aside. A dark shape whisks past me—the Gethin tumbles. I see Pia, teeth bared, blade aloft, standing over him. One arm hangs oddly and she has blood on her face, but she seems not much the worse for it. The Gethin swings his own blade from the ground, and Pia runs halfway up the wall before leaping onto him again. He throws her off, and she rolls elegantly, back on her feet in an instant. They face each other, blades ready. Pia lets out an animal hiss and pounces once more.

I crawl past the fallen, bleeding Mrs. Och, over her wings. Frederick is only half-conscious from the Gethin's blow, but I can see he is alive. I pick up the gun. I do not trust my legs enough to walk, so I crawl back toward the battle in the hall. Professor Baranyi and Bianka and Theo have barricaded themselves inside Mrs. Och's bedroom while Pia and the Gethin swing at each other with shining blades. From floor to walls to ceiling and back again, they are light as air, quick as light. Pia fends off a blow from the Gethin's blade, but in the same instant he catches her with that lethal hand, a blow to the throat. She makes a choking sound and falls, gravity claiming her suddenly. He does not stay to finish her off but goes crashing straight through Mrs. Och's bedroom door. I raise the gun, aim for the left side of his back, and shoot.

The Gethin falls straight forward. I crawl as quickly as I can past Pia, who is struggling to rise, one hand to her throat. The Gethin is still moving, but I pry his shimmering blade from his hand, the one that nearly took off the top of my own head just yesterday night. It weighs hardly anything. I close my eyes and hear myself scream as I lift the blade and bring it down on his neck.

The Gethin's head rolls to the side and his body falls still.

"Burn the body." Pia's voice is hoarse. She staggers past me, catching the Gethin's head under her arm. I see his face for the last time, white eyes sad and staring. Pia is making straight for Bianka and Theo. I try to shout out, to warn them, but no sound comes from me, and Pia stops a few feet away from them, straining against the air. She is thwarted by something, though I do not see what at first. Then she lets out a snarl, and with one booted foot she kicks out the window. It shatters, and she leaps out of it. Bianka must have found a pen in the room, for on the wall above them, she has scrawled: *STAY BACK.* The smell of rotten flowers—the smell of her magic—still lingers in the air, mingling with the acrid smell of gunpowder.

And there we all are. The headless body of the Gethin, bleeding blackly onto the carpet in Mrs. Och's room. The professor huddled in the corner with Bianka and a wailing Theo. Mrs. Och, wingless and quite human now but with blood all over her torn nightdress, standing behind me in the doorway. Frederick groaning and getting to his feet down the hall.

And still the sounds of Florence screaming and the wolf man raging impotently in his locked room.

∿

"Did you see who that was?" says Mrs. Och to the professor, indicating the broken window. She sways and half falls against the wall. The professor lifts her in his arms like she's a child and carries her to her bed, lays her down. Her eyelids flutter.

"Rest," he says. "The Gethin is dead."

"She . . . she belongs to Casimir, that one who was fighting the Gethin!" she whispers. "Who but Casimir could command the Gethin? If *he* did not call it, who did?"

"Hush, now. Rest," says the professor.

"I will not stay!" Florence is shrieking in the hallway. "Fetch me a hackney immediately! We will not stay a moment longer in this place!"

The professor sighs and says to Bianka, "Are you all right?"

She half nods, Baby Theo whimpering in her arms now and sucking his thumb. "And you, Bessie?" he asks me. "Are you hurt?"

"No," I say. I start to say "It's Ella" for the hundredth time but can't be bothered. I am shaking all over. I want to disappear until morning, but it's too late for that.

"We owe you a debt of gratitude," he says. "What you did was very brave." He pauses. "How did you know to cut its head off?"

"That . . . woman told me to do it," I say. Still playacting, still lying. It feels so pointless now. I want to tell him everything and then sleep for a week.

"It was brave and may have saved our lives," he says. "I know you must be very frightened of what you saw here tonight." He looks as if he is considering saying more, then shakes his head slightly. "Frederick will get you a drink downstairs to help settle your nerves."

"I think he's hurt," I say, but then I see he is beside me looking terribly concerned.

"You aren't injured?" he says.

"I thought you were," I say.

"A bit dizzy," he says. "But I'll live."

"Me too," I say, and I smile up at him, which is silly, but the fact that I am alive delights me suddenly. The Gethin is dead. I am safe. Even Theo is safe, for tonight at least.

"Come on." He helps me to the door.

"That woman . . . she said to burn the body," I say to Professor Baranyi over my shoulder.

He nods. "I'll see to it."

∿

Frederick gives me a brandy in the parlor and pours one for himself. Florence has tossed her belongings into a bag and dragged Chloe out into the night to fetch a hackney. I feel numb.

We sit in silence for a bit, Frederick next to me on the sofa, holding his brandy glass between both hands, head bowed.

"I wish I could think what to say to you about what you saw tonight," he says at last. "You must be horrified."

Well, he's not wrong about that. I sip at the brandy and it burns its way down my throat, warming my belly.

"There is more to the world than you realize," he begins slowly. Heaven save us, he's about to launch into some dry lecture about supernatural forces. I don't have the patience for it.

"I'm not some naïve little girl," I say sharply. "My mother was a witch, drowned in the Syne when I was seven."

He looks up at me, white-faced. "I'm sorry," he says, his voice as thin as paper.

I can't seem to stop myself. "I've seen things. . . . *You* can't imagine the things *I've* seen. I'm not a child!" I slug back the rest of the brandy and nearly choke.

"It's all right," he says gently, taking my empty glass and putting it with his own on the side table. "It will be all right."

I realize I have tears on my face, which makes me feel foolish and angry.

"It won't be," I say harshly. "Give me another drink."

"One is enough," he says.

"Don't tell me what is enough!" I cry. I want to strike him, as if all of this is his fault somehow. I raise my hand, and he catches it in his, lowers it to his chest. His hand is big and warm. He is very close to me, his ever-startled face inches from mine, the round spectacles over clear, sad eyes, the untrimmed beard.

"Do you remember asking me about my work?" he says. "I did not explain it clearly, but I am assembling a comprehensive record of the role of witchcraft in the Porian kingdoms. History as it is written now emphasizes the Magic Wars, the competing covens and the terrible abuses of witchcraft in that period, and the Purges, when witches were drowned in vast numbers and witchcraft of any kind became punishable by death. Historians ignore the long period before the Magic Wars, when magic was an integral and controlled part of society. Indeed, even today, in Yongguo, witches are seen as gifted, special. I hope that if we can bring out this history, study it and share it, we can work toward a new Frayne that understands and accepts witchcraft as part of the natural world."

I just stare at him. No wonder he didn't want to tell me before. He could be executed for saying such things.

"I mean to say . . . whatever you may have been told about witches is false, Ella. It is a terrible thing that happened to your mother. I am sure she was a good woman, an honest woman. Most witches are." He is still holding my hand. "No child should lose a parent the way that you did. I am so sorry for your loss."

Nobody has ever said that to me. Even those that *were* sorry were too afraid to say so. I don't think about what I am doing; I lean forward and kiss him. After a moment's hesitation, he kisses me back. It is soft and warm and rather a relief, like the brandy. I shut my eyes and forget everything but the feel of his lips on mine. But the moment doesn't last. His mustache prickles me; he does not kiss like Wyn. I pull away and burst into ridiculous tears.

"I'm sorry," Frederick is saying, distraught. "I'm so sorry. Unforgivable. I'm a lout. I just . . . you looked so . . . I'm sorry. Please, Ella, you're quite safe with me; it won't happen again. A sweet, innocent girl like you . . ."

I can't take it anymore.

"I'm *not*!" I cry. "I'm not sweet or innocent. You have no idea!"

For a terrifying, vertiginous moment, I think I am really about to confess everything. It is all there, on the tip of my tongue, when I see a shadow at the window.

"Frederick, look!" Half-mad and fearless with brandy and the kiss and brushes with death and my near confession, I find myself pouncing after it. The shadow disappears, but I throw open the window, scrambling out after it, and Frederick is right behind me. The fur-clad figure is running for the gate. I tackle it in the snow. It is a woman, I see when we turn her over, probably in her fifties, with gray hair escaping from underneath her fur hat.

"I am unarmed," she gibbers, but when we search her we find a modern cartridge pen and several sheets of paper covered with symbols. Unarmed indeed.

"I think you had better come inside and speak to the professor," says Frederick.

∽

They question the witch for an hour in the parlor. She broke the rhug's bond with the house, and the eerie creatures have wandered off. She confesses everything, sobbing loudly, and I can easily make out her answers from my place at the keyhole. She'd been three weeks in Hostorak, she says, and was released unexpectedly this very night on the condition that she perform this task. The man who spoke to her had an eye patch and one yellow eye, she says, and I remember the man Bianka described, the one who came and asked her about Theo, took hair and blood samples from him. She says she was outside the window hoping to catch one of the lingering, confused rhug and sell it.

After some hushed consultation, they take her up to Mrs. Och, and I follow, staying vanished in the hall when the two men go back down to the parlor. I can hear Mrs. Och—"You knew this was my house and yet you used your magic against me"—and the witch sobbing and begging forgiveness.

She does not get it. "No!" I hear her gasping, then shouting: "No! No! No!" There follows a horrible scream that ends suddenly, smoke pouring out from under the door with an awful stench. I clamp a hand over my mouth and stumble back downstairs, where the professor is saying to Frederick, "She cannot afford to be merciful; you *know* this," while Frederick weeps into his hands. Neither Mrs. Och nor the witch emerges from the reading room. Frederick and the professor remain in the parlor, talking in low voices. I am too nauseous and exhausted to stay huddled outside the door trying to catch snatches of their conversation. I go upstairs to the empty attic room and lie down, fully clothed, on the screeching cot. When I wake it is midmorning and the little owl-cat, Strig, is curled up against me, purring.

*T*he room is full of yellow smoke. Or perhaps it is his mind that is full of the smoke. His thoughts move slowly through it. He cannot see; he cannot move. He can think, very slowly: Move. Fight. But they are just words he is thinking, as removed from reality as dreams are. You may dream that you are walking down the street at sundown watching the bats swoop overhead, but you are only lying on your bed, still as the dead.

She is writing on his skin with fire. The silver she sometimes uses is nothing. He could fight the silver if not for the things she writes on his skin. Things that still him, freeze him, rob him of himself. She does it swiftly, her manner detached and professional, as if she were a doctor performing some minor surgery.

"Almost done," she may say, comfortingly.

Then the yellow smoke clears, and she is finished. He can see the ceiling, and a chair lying on the ground. He thinks he knocked it over; he thinks he tried to fight, before the smoke.

"He wants to see you," she says. "Shall I call him? Tell him you're ready?"

The sheets are pulled halfway off the bed. There has been a struggle in this room. He is lying on the floor and his tongue is too big for his mouth. The smoke is gone, but the place she has written on him, on his shoulder, is burning.

"Can you get up?" she asks.

Then she sighs and leaves the room.

Minutes, hours, days, there is hardly a difference anymore. And then a pair of boots by his head, the swirling edge of a cape. He forces his eyes up to where Casimir's head looms near the ceiling, frowning down at him.

"It looks as if you tried to give Shey some trouble this morning," Casimir says.

He tests his tongue, to see if he can speak. "Ffff . . ." is all he manages.

"You never told me that you'd had a son recently," says Casimir. "You have been far too clever. The witch is very pretty too. But you ought to steer clear of falling in love with witches. It never ends well."

To tear this room apart, to tear down these walls, to unleash this rage upon Casimir—but he is defeated, utterly, utterly. He had not known he could be so undone. That there existed this place between life and death. That such despair was even possible.

Casimir bends down to examine Shey's writing on his shoulder.

"My, my," he murmurs. "I sometimes wonder if I oughtn't to be a little afraid of her myself! Well, it will wear off, and you'll feel more yourself soon enough."

It does wear off. And when he can move again, he lifts himself painfully from the floor. He rights the chair. He makes the bed. He weeps.

SIXTEEN

Nobody tries to pretend for my sake that we are living in an ordinary house anymore. Small scrolls of paper with unfamiliar script on them are pasted by all the doors and windows, and smoking pockets of herbs and who knows what dangle from the ceilings in unexpected places. The house stinks of magic.

Mrs. Freeley treats me to a rare, wry smile when I appear in the scullery late morning. "Had a nice lie-in?"

But she says it without malice. She herself seems unperturbed. I don't ask her what she knows, what she has come to accept, living here. I don't know what to do besides continue to work. I help with the lunch preparations, then serve the baked fowl with scalloped potatoes and asparagus spears, pouring apple wine for everybody. Mrs. Och remains in her room, her blood all over the upstairs hallway, the singed smell of whatever she did to the witch still lingering in the air. Frederick's face is bruised, and his head is bandaged. Theo is sleepy in Bianka's lap, and nobody speaks much. Both the professor and Frederick have pistols strapped to their chests. Sir Victor eats with them and does not ask questions, so either he knows better than to ask or they have already told him what happened. A letter comes for Sir Victor—everybody jumping at the sound of the mail carriage in the street—and he goes out soon after in his hat and coat, mumbling some excuse. It is the first time I have seen him leave the house since I came here, which would have interested me greatly just yesterday, but I have too much else on my mind to wonder much at the wolf man's movements.

The parlor is still closed up, and so I go in to light the fire. When I open the curtains I see an electric hackney pulling up at the gate. Two figures in long, fur-collared coats are climbing out.

"Frederick!" I call, running back to the dining room. "A hackney."

"I will meet them at the door," says Mrs. Och, descending the stairs. She is upright and dressed, her hair pinned back, as if she hadn't been run through with a sword the night before. I gape at her.

"Go on to the scullery, Ella," she says to me sharply. I bob my head and duck past them, but I hear her say to Frederick, "I want Bianka and Theo in the cellar tunnel. Give her a pen and paper. Then come to my reading room with the professor."

Cellar tunnel? This house still has more secrets than those I have uncovered. I slip out of the scullery and dart up the stairs, making straight for Mrs. Och's reading room. It's no good vanishing here—Mrs. Och would see me—but I can hide like an ordinary snoop. I look around the room wildly, for it doesn't offer much in the way of hiding places. I hear voices below. I remove some large reference books from a cabinet under the bookcase and put them behind the curtains. Then I race back to the cabinet. For a horrible moment I think I will not be able to fit. I can hear them in the hall and I am terrified they will come in to find me stuck halfway out of the cabinet, but I manage to cram myself inside it and slide the door shut as they enter, leaving myself a crack to peer through.

I hear the creak of Mrs. Och's chair as she sits down in it. I can see the professor's and Frederick's trousers and shoes by the door and two other sets of legs in front of them—a tall man's and a short man's. I ease the cabinet door open a crack farther.

"I intended to ask the Gethin's master why he sent his creature to my home," says Mrs. Och. "But now you are standing before me, I wonder how you commanded the Gethin at all."

"I inherited him, shall we say," says a deep male voice—a voice I know. "He is dead?"

"Dead," replies Mrs. Och. "Perhaps I should have guessed it was you when I heard you took care of the victims' families. Still, I wonder at your selective guilt. There are others in Spira City who are destitute because of you, who have died because of you, if less directly."

"I do what I can to protect the innocent. Sometimes evil can only be fought with evil."

I am trying to place the voice—its resonance, its country vowels. It is so familiar. Squashed as I am inside the cabinet, I vanish and slide the door farther open, slowly, carefully. I see Mrs. Och's ankles, the edge of her desk. I pull it wider, craning my neck, and almost let out a cry of surprise. There in the middle of Mrs. Och's reading room, wearing the same shabby coat he wore at the Cleansing, stands Agoston Horthy. A man with a sweep of gray hair and one yellow eye towers behind the prime minister. He wears a patch over the other eye. Frederick and the professor are at the door, both of them armed, but the conversation takes place entirely between Agoston Horthy and Mrs. Och.

"I have puzzled over you for a long time, Mrs. Och. You have done a great deal to help the innocent, the destitute, and the powerless, and I have admired you for it. And you have done a great deal to help the evil and the vengeful, the criminals and the unbelievers, and I have loathed you for it."

"We have different methods of categorization."

"I imagine we do. But I have a country to take care of, and you have only your own interests. I have left you alone for twenty years. Suppose that now I surrounded your house with soldiers, filled it with investigators. What would I find?"

"Very little, because you wouldn't know how to look."

"Your brother Casimir warned me long ago that making you my enemy would be a waste of resources."

"What do you want from me?"

"You are harboring a witch and her son. I want you to hand them over."

"Why send the Gethin instead of merely asking me?"

"I am asking you now."

"Well, since we are playing 'suppose'—suppose that a woman with a baby came to me asking for help because someone was hunting her. Suppose we established it was the Gethin hunting her. Still, we did not know who sent the Gethin, and we did not know why. Suppose we put the woman and her boy on a train to Sinter, or perhaps on a boat to Ingle. Suppose I can give you an address, if you can persuade me that your cause is just."

"The witch concerns me less than the child. You know who the boy's father is?"

"Yes."

"My man here sees very well with only one eye, and he keeps that eye trained on certain things within my borders. Unpredictable things. Things like you. Your brother Gennady was in Frayne not long ago."

"I had heard."

"He was posing as a clown, doing subversive performances in the south. Then he disappeared, but our eyes and ears are everywhere, and though we could not find him, we found the witch and her little boy. What do you know about the child?"

"I know nothing, except that he is my nephew."

"My man here obtained some samples. We had them tested. Every cell in that child's body is coded with *something*. Something powerful. Something magical. He is a vessel for something, and this is no mere witchcraft. I thought perhaps *you* could tell me what it is."

"I know nothing of this. I have not seen my brother in years and learned of his son only very recently."

"It is essential that he be examined and the witch questioned."

"If they have left Frayne, why does it concern you?"

"Because we do not know what he is. That makes me uncomfortable."

"Give me a few days to think it over. Then I can give you an address in Sinter. Or Ingle."

"Suppose my man has a look around your house right now?"

"I do not recommend it. The house has teeth today. You understand, surely—after an intruder, one must take precautions."

"Suppose we do not find the witch in Sinter, or Ingle?"

"It's true, she might move on quickly. How am I to know?"

"Suppose I give you until tomorrow, and if I do not have the witch and her son by sundown, I march the Fraynish army to your doorstep?"

"Are you so sure that you will still have an army at your command tomorrow?"

"Are you threatening me?"

"I am interested in you. Does Casimir know that you command the Gethin and that you are looking for this witch?"

"I do not report to Casimir."

"Oh no? I rather thought you did."

"You are mistaken. We have an understanding. Our understanding extends to you, as a matter of fact. It is out of respect for him, as well as for your good works, that I have tolerated you within my borders. And out of respect for him, I am doing you the courtesy of this visit, an attempt to resolve this matter peacefully."

"I'm sure he would be delighted to hear how much you respect him, and while I am touched by your visit, I feel that your borders have nothing to do with me."

"You believe you are above our laws, but you are like the great sea lizards. Your time is done."

"I wonder if you have expressed this view to my brother."

"He knows who I am, just as I know who he is. For now, we have our understanding."

"Your alliances are not what one might expect from a man who abhors magic."

"Desperate times lead to strange bedfellows, Mrs. Och."

The man with the yellow eye laughs at that—a rather nice laugh, as if he is genuinely amused.

"You have until tomorrow," says Agoston Horthy. "I will be back at sundown, and it will go better for you if you have found your witch and her son by then."

Mrs. Och rises, and her voice is terrible, like when she spoke to the Gethin in the hall. "It will go better for *me*? You command the Fraynish army, you rule while the king prays, but you are still a little man with a little life and you know nothing, nothing at all, and you can do nothing to me. Frederick, show our guests out. If they do not go gently, you are very welcome to shoot them."

"Sundown tomorrow," repeats Agoston Horthy, unperturbed.

I watch three pairs of feet filing out into the hallway. Professor Baranyi shuts the door, and he and Mrs. Och are silent for a moment.

"Well," says Mrs. Och at last. "Horthy has gone rogue. How interesting."

"What will we do?"

"If we can get them north, Livia will keep them safe at the farm for a time. I will need you to send a telegram. You heard what he said about the boy? A vessel."

"Yes. What could he mean? I'm sure Bianka doesn't know—she's quite desperate to solve the matter herself."

She cries out, making me jump: "He wouldn't! He couldn't, surely."

"Wouldn't couldn't what, my dear Mrs. Och?" asks the professor. "And to *whom* are you referring?"

"Gennady," she says.

"Ah," he says.

"It's impossible," she says. "And yet, there is only one thing that Casimir wants."

He waits.

"We must find Gennady," she says. "How can he have disappeared so completely from the face of the earth?"

A soft knock, and Frederick comes back in.

"We're going to be hung, aren't we?" he says.

"Oh dear, I hope not," says the professor, as if he'd never thought of that.

"Agoston *Horthy*!" says Frederick. "I've just been pointing a *gun* at Agoston Horthy!"

"It is a twist I was not expecting. Casimir will *not* be pleased when he finds out," says Mrs. Och. Then she asks, "What do you make of the maid, by the way?"

"What—Ettie?" asks Professor Baranyi.

"Ella," Frederick corrects him.

"Yes."

"Remarkable, isn't she?" the professor says. "Showed nerves of steel last night. She must have very good aim or very good luck—she hit the Gethin straight through the heart with that bullet. Bright too—or so Frederick says."

"You know her best, Frederick," says Mrs. Och. "If we explain a few things, will it frighten her off? It will be difficult, in the days to come, to maintain any façade of normality, and she might be useful."

I don't like the sound of that. I am up to my neck in usefulness already.

"I think she would take it very well," says Frederick simply. He makes no mention of my mother, and I'm rather touched at his treating it as a confidence.

"Still, there is something about her that strikes me as odd," says Mrs. Och.

"In what sense?" asks the professor.

"She has secrets," says Mrs. Och, and my blood runs cold. "That is nothing terrible in itself. Many people have secrets. It may be time to find out more about her, however."

I think of the witch screaming for mercy last night—no trace of her left in the morning but a terrible smell. Mrs. Och is not known for her forgiving nature, said Liddy. I need to get well away before she finds out that I am not who I claim to be.

"I'll vouchsafe that she's trustworthy," says Frederick stoutly, which gives me a little pang.

"That may be," says Mrs. Och. "Her references were thorough, but, Frederick, perhaps you can visit the family tomorrow morning, just to be sure. For now, we have work to do."

"What about Pia, Casimir's creature?" asks Professor Baranyi. "What will we do if *she* returns?"

"Alazne's Blind," says Mrs. Och.

"Really?" The professor sounds as if she's just proposed dining on the moon. "Is it . . . *can* you?"

"Not alone—but with Bianka, yes. If she can transmogrify, she ought to be strong enough to manage it. I doubt it will last us more than twenty-four hours, but that will be enough. The house will be quite impossible to find."

"My! Well!"

They leave the room, still talking. Professor Baranyi goes out straightaway, presumably to send a telegram to this Livia Mrs. Och mentioned. I make a halfhearted start on the dishes in the scullery, while Bianka and Mrs. Och shut themselves up in her reading room, Frederick entertains Baby Theo in the library, and Mrs. Freeley snores loudly in her room off the kitchen.

My mind is racing, and the house is quiet, so I abandon the dishes and go upstairs to let myself into Professor Baranyi's study. Strig comes bounding in after me with a cheerful *"yowww!"* and I scratch his feathery little ears. I have no lockpick with me, but a hairpin does fine for the locked cabinet of books. I sit myself down on the floor behind a divan, disappearing, and begin to flip through *Legends of the Xianren I.*

◠

I pass the rest of the afternoon skimming through the long, dry, semi-comprehensible tomes. The first book, as best as I can tell, is all overwrought tales of the exploits of these winged wizards in the old days: taming dragons, battling sea monsters, corralling wrongdoing witches, and such. The Xianren have been in the thick of things throughout history, if these books are to be believed. Mrs. Och was advisor to the first emperor of Yongguo, Hna, and that empire, the book claims, has thrived for millennia on cooperation between humans and witches. It wins for longevity, in any case. Not to be outdone in the founding of empires, Zor Gen, or Gennady, married the Witch of Parna and together they started the Parnese Empire, which lasted three hundred years, but by then Gennady had gone off walking and swimming around the world, fathering kings and warriors here and there, battling enchanted bears and rebellious witches, as one does, I suppose, if one is an immortal thrill seeker, and the empire fell. The third book tells me that the Xianren joined forces and spent centuries looking for something called Ragg Rock, but, I quote, "they could never find it; they were not welcomed by Ragg Rock, and this showed them the limitations of their power." The fourth book is largely preoccupied with the Eshriki Empire, second only to the Yongguo in lasting power. The Eshriki Phars were witches and wanted something called *The Book of Disruption,* a magical text the Xianren had divided among them. The Xianren were all imprisoned at various points and forced to give up their part of the text, but it turned out that the witches could not read it—only the Xianren could—so that settled that, and the Xianren won out in the end simply by outliving the empire. Points for immortality. The book deems this conflict a turning point for the Xianren in that it became obvious their power was waning dramatically. They remained influential, however, and Lan Camshe helped found the Sirillian Empire, the first great empire to outlaw witchcraft. Och Farya goes quiet. Zor Gen leads various rampaging insurrections around the world. The Sirillian Empire falls and Lan Camshe retreats to the Isle of Nago, off the coast of Sirillia. They all seem to stand back from the Magic Wars, the Purges, and the rise of New Poria. The letters are starting to blur, and I can find nothing to suggest why Casimir might want to kidnap a little boy or why he would ally himself with the likes of Agoston Horthy while Mrs. Och quietly rescues the odd witch from their clutches.

The house is cold, none of the fires set, none of the lamps filled for evening. I put the books away, fetch water from the pump, and light the stove to heat it, then lug firewood up the stairs to lay the fires. The smell of rotten flowers—Bianka's magic, as I've come to recognize it—is everywhere. I can hear Bianka, Frederick, and Theo playing hide-and-seek in the music room now, sounding quite merry, all things considered. They've lit the fire themselves, so I do not disturb them. I carry the warm water and a rag to the hallway upstairs, where I kneel down and begin to scrub Mrs. Och's blood from the walls and rug.

～

I slip out after midnight, cross the river, and walk through the Plateau to West Spira. The windows of the hotel blaze with light. The doorman stands outside in a long fur, his breath puffing out of him white. He recognizes me, lets me by. There is hardly anyone in the lobby, though someone is tinkling away at the piano for the entertainment of the guests who aren't there. The uniformed staff behind the desk huddle together and stare, but nobody stops me. It is a different man at the elevator than usual.

"Top floor," I say. "Room ten. She's expecting me."

"She isn't really a foreign royal, is she?" he asks me as the elevator goes *clank-clank*ing upward.

"Is that what they say?" I ask.

"They say all type of thing," he says. "But she's paid for the whole top floor. Distant relation to the Magyar king, I heard."

I laugh, and he looks offended, lets me out without saying good night. I'd forgotten coins to tip him with.

Pia opens the door as soon as I knock. She is fully dressed in her long boots, trousers, and fitted leather coat. I wonder when she sleeps, *if* she sleeps, what she would wear to bed. Impossible to imagine Pia in a nightgown.

"I didn't know how to send you a message," I say.

She gestures for me to sit, so I do.

"Are you all right?" I ask her.

The goggles whir. She pauses a moment before giving a short, bemused laugh. "I am," she says. Another pause. "And you?"

I shrug. Pia sits across from me, slings one leg over the other, waits.

I tell her, "Frederick is supposed to visit my family in the morning to find out more about me. But they aren't real, which he'll find out, of course, when he goes to see them."

Pia smiles as if this is amusing.

"And I know who sent the Gethin," I add, feeling somehow that I owe her information. Not owe it in the sense that she is paying me for it, but owe it to *her*. She did save my life, and I suppose I am asking her to save me again. I am terrified of what Mrs. Och will do when she finds out the truth about me. "It was Agoston Horthy. He came to the house today."

Pia's goggles whir in and out rapidly.

"What did he say?"

"He gave them until sundown tomorrow to hand over Theo and Bianka, but Mrs. Och kicked him out. I suppose he doesn't know about you yet. There was a creepy-looking fellow with him, one yellow eye and an eye patch."

"Ah," says Pia.

"That's all? Ah?" I say. And then, rather pathetically: "Anyway, I'm out. I can't go back there. She'll murder me."

"Bring me the boy, and you never need to go back again."

I have never been to sea, but I imagine this is what it feels like to be on a ship that is going down, and no land in sight to swim to.

"What's going to happen to him?" I try to keep my voice calm and steady.

"That is not my business," she says. "Nor yours." And then she is next to me, cupping my face in her cold hand as if she is going to kiss me. "Put it out of your mind, Julia. You are bound to your part."

"I'm not," I say, pulling my chin out of her hand. "I didn't know it would be kidnapping. I never agreed to that."

Pia taps her fingernails against her knife, surveying me blankly. "You took the job and some money in advance and now you must complete it," she says. "The boy will go to Casimir or to Agoston Horthy, in the end, and my own guess is that he will fare better with Casimir. Your Mrs. Och cannot protect him, and you might ask yourself if that is truly what she intends. It is far too late for second thoughts, Julia. There will be a hackney waiting for you at the corner all morning tomorrow."

"There are probably soldiers watching the place now," I say desperately.

"I'll make sure there aren't any tomorrow morning."

We just stare at each other for a moment, and then with a rapid hiss of metal against leather, Pia draws her knife and holds it to my throat. I try to pull away from the sharp edge of the blade, but her other hand has closed around the back of my neck.

"You have two choices left: silver or death," she says into my ear. "Do not attach yourself overmuch to one little boy, Julia. Do you weep for every child who meets a hard fate in this city? You have until noon tomorrow to bring him to me. If you do not, I can assure you that he will die by Agoston Horthy's order, and for a hundred nights to follow, you will find the fingers, toes, ears, and noses of a hundred little boys turning up on your pillow. They will die, those little boys, the ones you do not know or care for, because of your failure to obey me. And when I am done, I will find *you*, Julia, and I will show you how good I am with this knife, how long I can make dying last."

She rises and puts away the knife, striding over to the window, hands clasped behind her. She speaks with her back to me.

"What do you think? Is he worth a hundred children? Is he worth your own life? Is it enough, or shall I add to the cost of mutiny?"

I am shaking so hard, I cannot speak. I manage to nod my head a little.

"Answer me out loud, Julia. If you don't care about little boys, I can find other means of persuasion. Shall I choose girls your own age to cripple and mutilate? Shall I burn down the Twist, one house at a time? Shall I butcher your employer, Esme, and make you watch? There is no limit, and the only alternative is obedience, for which you will be paid. Tell me when you agree."

"Yes," I whisper.

"I cannot hear you."

My voice is a strangled thing, barely a voice. I push the words out: "I'll bring him."

"Good. I will expect you in the morning."

I get up and leave. Pia must have sent down a message, for the doorman has fetched me a motor cabriolet.

"I've no money," I say.

"I'll be paid," he answers, so I get in. He drives me back to the Scola, but when we turn down Mikall Street, the house is not there.

"Which one is it?" he asks, puzzled.

I'd laugh if I weren't so exhausted and terrified. The houses are all familiar, with their forbidding gates. There is no gap where Mrs. Och's house was before; it is simply gone, as if it had never been there at all. Alazne's Blind.

"I'll get out and walk," I say.

I half hope that I will not be able to return, that Mrs. Och's strange spell will lock me out forever and this impossible choice, not really a choice at all, will be taken away from me. But once I am on foot, I come to the house immediately. The spell does not apply to me, I suppose, any more than the rhug considered me an intruder. I stare at the house, all its windows dark, and I cannot go in. I turn around and head for the Twist.

I let myself into our flat. The room smells like stale liquor. Dek is snoring in his little bunk, under a mound of blankets. I climb the ladder to my own bunk, where I haven't slept in weeks. I pull the blanket over me, and for a brief moment I feel like a small child again, home and safe. It only lasts a moment, though, and for all that I'm bone-weary, sleep takes hours to come.

SEVENTEEN

I wake with a jolt, cold to my bones and fleetingly confused before I remember where I am. Fear comes back instantly, twisting me into knots: Pia's threats, Agoston Horthy, my cover about to be blown. The pale winter sunlight is coming in between our ragged curtains, and Dek is still asleep. I imagine never going back to Mrs. Och's house. Telling Esme what happened. Going into hiding, perhaps. But then would Gregor, Esme, and all the others need to go into hiding too? I touch my throat, where she pressed her knife last night. *I will show you . . . how long I can make dying last.* Suppose I went to Mrs. Och, told her everything, begged for her help? But I remember the witch who disappeared, her terrible scream. No, I cannot tell Mrs. Och that I have been a spy in her house. I fleetingly imagine murdering Pia—I know where to buy poison—but that is a ridiculous idea. I am out of options, and I am out of time. Every way out of this nightmare, every way back to my old life, is closing against me. Every way but one.

I can't stomach breakfast, so I just pull my coat and boots on over my wrinkled clothes of the previous day.

"I'll come back rich by noon," I tell Dek, who carries on sleeping, and my voice sounds odd to me, not like my own.

I am crossing Fitch Square when I see Wyn coming toward me. He looks as if he's slept as poorly as I have, and I reckon I know why.

"Hullo, Brown Eyes!" he cries out when he sees me, a little too effusive.

"Out all night?" I say.

"Figured it was safer than walking home at night, what with a serial killer on the loose," he says. "Now I've got an awful crick in my neck from sleeping on Ren Winters's floor."

Smooth as smooth, that's my Wyn. If there's anyone who can lie as quick and easy as I can, it's my boy here.

"Come on, let's go out for breakfast," he carries on, slinging an arm over my shoulders. "You've got some making up to do, haven't you? You left me waiting in your room the other night. Dek had to kick me out when he came to bed!"

"Right. Sorry about that." I shrug his arm off.

"What's wrong, Brown Eyes?" he asks, peering at me. I look at him straight on then: his beautiful face, the way his eyebrows come together comically when he frowns, the way his mouth quirks, like it's waiting to smile even when he's se-rious. The truth is that I've hardly thought about him since the Gethin came for me. Almost dying has a way of taking a girl's mind off her other troubles. But when I look at him now, it hurts again, the way it hurt when I watched them together, the way he touched her, the way he spoke to her. I swallow hard, trying to force down the lump in my throat.

"Julia! Say something, will you?"

So I push the words out past the lump: "Look—this thing between us—it's over, all right?"

He looks as if I've slapped him, and I know if I keep looking at him I'll start crying, so I push past him, make it most of the way across the square before he catches up to me. He spins me around to face him.

"By all the stars," he says. "You're not ending it like that. Tell me what's wrong. You owe me that, at least."

"Fine. Arly Winters."

Just a flicker of . . . *something*, but he recovers fast. Smooth as smooth, like I said.

"It's Arly, then, is it?" he says. "Why didn't you say something?"

"I'm saying something right now. I'm saying it's over."

"I should have told you," he says. "Look, it's just . . . you know how that girl is. She said she'd pose, just like for the art class, and I could draw her, and it . . . well, I missed you, and you've been so busy. You forgot all about me the other night."

"It's my fault, then, is it?"

"That's not what I'm saying. Honestly, I'm glad you know. I didn't know how to tell you, but I've been feeling rotten about it."

The ridiculous thing is, he looks so sad that I almost want to comfort him. But I've got other things to do.

"Well then, that's both of us feeling rotten about it," I say, and walk around him. He grabs my arm, and I shake him loose.

"Julia, wait, just come upstairs so we can talk." He reaches for me again, and I step away, sliding a bit in the snow. "We'll light the fire. Please."

He keeps stepping in front of me, trying to keep me from walking away.

"Hounds, Wyn, let me go!" I cry, shoving him hard in the chest, my anger swooping in late to rescue me. "If you're the kind of man who'll shag some tart behind my back, then I want none of you, and there's nothing more to talk about. You can go scurrying back to that idiot if you like, but by all the holies, don't you dare touch me or get in my way again. I've got somewhere to be."

I leave him staring after me, let the alleys of the Twist swallow me up and lead me back to the river. I stop there under the shadow of Cyrambel and try to weep, but I've used up all my tears of late, and so I just stare down at the ice for a while. When I look up, the sky looks gray, flat, hanging low over the city, but I know better. I remember the pictures Frederick showed me; I know about the wheeling planets and dying stars out there, the empty space that goes on and on. I feel a small, mean, pathetic sort of thing, here on the bridge, pinched between the earth and the heavens. I imagine I can feel my heart, all my warm feelings, calcify and freeze. Better not to feel, not to weep. Better to be dead inside until all of this has passed. I walk the rest of the way to the Scola and Mrs. Och's house, to do the thing I have to do.

"Where have you been?" demands Mrs. Freeley when I let myself in through the scullery side door.

"I was feeling dizzy," I say. "Needed some air."

She puts her hands on her hips and stares me down. For a strange moment, I envy her. Because she seems unafraid, and because she seems to have found satisfactory answers to whatever questions may have once plagued her. Because she seems to know herself. Because she sleeps all day long.

"Look, nobody minded you taking a day off yesterday, after everything that happened," she says more gently. "But now you've got to decide if you're still working here or not. You can't have room and board and a copper a week for nothing."

"I know," I say. "I'm sorry."

"If you want to leave, nobody's going to stop you," she says. "Least of all me. I've had better help than yours. But I'll tell you what—there's nothing to be scared of here. The world is a terrible place, and we all know that. Mrs. Och, she's made it her business to help folks who need help, and that's all there is to it. These are good people, and a girl like you could do a lot worse than keeping house for good people."

"Yes, ma'am," I say.

"All right, then," she says, nodding at a pile of laundry. "I'll do lunch by myself. You help Chloe."

For there is Chloe, smiling wanly at me. Mrs. Freeley disappears into the kitchen.

"You're back," I say, stating the obvious.

"Florence is furious with me," says Chloe. "But there are so few positions now, and I need the money. I'm not getting married soon like she is. I need to build up a little something for myself. They were shocked as anything to see me this morning."

I'll bet they were. She must have walked; a cabbie wouldn't have found the place. I guess that, like me, Chloe is still considered a friend by whatever magic hides the house.

"Well, it's good to see you," I say, meaning it. Chloe is not bad.

"I know they must be very wicked here," she whispers to me. "Florence says the house is haunted, or they keep a monster, or some such thing. She says she saw it on the stairs, the thing that Clarisa saw. We heard fighting and gunshots."

"I don't know what she saw," I say. "I know there was a wolf in the house, and Frederick shot it. Do you know there have been more and more wolf sightings in the city? They're starving in the woods, it's such a brutal winter, and so they're coming into the city for food. That door in the cellar is broken. . . ."

I trail off and wonder why I'm bothering to lie to Chloe about all this anyway. It's such a habit now, the endless lying. I'm covering tracks that aren't even mine.

"Well, whatever is the case," says Chloe doubtfully, "we are paid well, and on time, and treated fairly. That's enough for me."

"Me too," I say. Because that is what it means to do a job.

You may not like it, but you are paid money to do it, and so you do it. We fold the laundry together, and she talks with great excitement about the shop Florence will work in, as if it were every girl's dream come true. My stomach rumbles, but still I can't bear the thought of food.

Bianka comes in to warm some milk for Theo.

"He has a cold," she says crossly. "He never got sick in Nim. It's the blasted northern winter, the rotten, filthy air here."

Theo trails after her, his nose streaming snot.

"Poor thing," I hear myself say. "I'll give him the milk, shall I? You could have a rest."

She gives me such a look of gratitude, I almost crack right there.

"I could use a lie-down," she says. "I didn't sleep a wink last night, and it's been such an impossible couple of days. I've had him with me nonstop. But I know he's safe with you."

I can't speak, so I just nod. She gives my arm a friendly squeeze, then says to Theo, "You be good for Ella, won't you? You know she'll smack you if you're naughty." She gives me a wink and sails out.

"Lala," says Theo, looking up at me.

"There, you be a good little fellow," I tell him, wiping his nose with my handkerchief. "I'll have your milk ready in a jiff."

I warm the milk and sit Theo on my lap by the stove to give it to him. He nestles into me sweetly and guzzles it back, gasping for breaths in between gulps. Afterward he is drowsy and sits calmly on my lap, playing with my apron string.

When Chloe takes the laundry up, I grab my coat, wrap it round us, and slip out the side door.

My heart is in my throat, and I don't know if I'm terrified they'll catch me or terrified they won't. I hold tight to Theo and run. As Pia promised, there are no soldiers on Mikall Street, and a sleek electric hackney is waiting at the corner. I climb inside, and the hackney slips away. Theo chirps excitedly and looks out the window.

"There's the river," I tell him inanely as we cross the bridge, my heart going so fast it is making me dizzy. "That's where they drown witches like your mama and like mine. And here we are in the Plateau. You can see Capriss Temple up there, at the top of Mount Heriot. Look, aren't the streets grand in West Spira?"

"Pira," he repeats cheerfully.

The doorman lets me by without a word. I go straight up to Pia's room with Theo in my arms. She opens the door but does not invite me in this time.

"Well done," she says, without emotion. She hands me a heavy leather purse. The silver clinks inside it. I sling it over one shoulder and stand there, silver on one arm, Theo in the other. Then she takes Theo from me, and it's as if she's pulled my heart right out.

"Don't let them hurt him," I choke.

"Lala," says Theo, twisting in her arms to reach for me. "Lala!"

"Does he sing?" asks Pia dryly.

"He's saying Ella."

"You are finished here, Julia," she says.

"Don't forget to bleeding feed him!" I cry. "It's nearly lunch-time! And he takes a nap in the afternoons."

I see his snotty little nose and wide eyes staring out at me for a half second more before she closes the door on me and I am alone in the hall with my silver.

EIGHTEEN

There aren't many people out in the streets, and those I see look unreal, moving too slowly, frozen faces clouded by the white of their breath. I feel out of sync with the world, my heart rabbiting and my hands trembling while the fine folk of West Spira drift by me in a dream. The driver of an electric hackney stuck in the snow examines the ice-clad wheels helplessly, while a man in thick furs leaning out the window says, "This is just the trouble with these fancy ee-lek-tric hackneys. A good strong horse is what we need now!"

They wouldn't let me in the first shop I tried, nor the second, and I knew if I showed them my silver they'd probably call for a cop. But there are furs to be bought elsewhere. I walk to Mount Heriot, my toes and fingers numb with cold so I can't feel them at all by the time I get there. I buy myself a pair of fur-lined boots that go up to my knees, a gown of heavy blue velvet with matching gloves, and a long brown fur coat and hat, beautifully soft. Mink, the shopkeeper tells me, glancing uneasily at my trembling hands.

I am leaving the shop in my finery when a ghoulish figure comes staggering toward me across the snow, bound in rags. He moves with a jagged gait, his legs rigid, his arms hanging limp at his sides. His face is horribly disfigured, mottled with Scourge spots and scar tissue. He has no eyes, only a mess of scars, but still it seems he is looking right at me, his aim unerring, as he croaks, "Forgive me! Forgive me, love!" I back away fast, toward the shop, but he keeps coming, and then a man in a fur coat comes running and clubs him with a walking stick, *crack*, right over the head. He crumples into the snow like a boneless pile of rags and skin, and my knees buckle under me. The man helps me to my feet. The shop-keeper is at my side as well.

"Are you all right, miss?"

"Can I fetch someone to take you home?"

"I'm fine," I say, steadying myself between them. My voice sounds far away from me. "I just need to eat something."

In an elegant café with a view of the city, I force down as many garlic snails and fluffy pastries as I can, though I barely taste them. Then I seek out an expensive electric hackney and flag it down, even if a horse-drawn is safer in the snow. I'll live like a rich lady as long as this silver lasts—fine clothes, fine food, a plush seat in a hackney whenever I want to go somewhere. This is what I've been dreaming of for weeks now.

The thought comes to me unbidden—*He must be so frightened*—and the inside of the hackney spins, my stomach lurching. I clamp my heart shut around the thought, like a trap with a screaming animal caught inside. Pia is right—what business is it of mine? Worse things happen to small children every day in Spira City and I don't go around crying my eyes out for every tot that gets beaten or starves or freezes or falls ill and dies. Terrible things are happening all the time. I know. I have not escaped the world's frivolous cruelty either. I have a job that affords me a better life than most girls born into my circumstances in the Twist. So I do my job, like a professional. It is ugly, but it's no good dwelling on it. She left me no choice—none at all. I was nearly killed, and I've bleeding earned this silver.

I return to the flat with a great, juicy ham, a honey cake, a few bottles of expensive rum, and a silk scarf for Esme. It is a hero's welcome I get. Dek hugs me hard and says he is to vet every job I take from now on. Esme thanks me for the scarf, but she is more interested in counting out her share of my silver. For the first time in my life I resent seeing her take it. Wyn comes down and tries to take me aside, but I shrug him off, sharing out the ham and cake. Gregor and Csilla arrive, kissing my cheeks and laughing and congratulating me, and the fire is too bright, the room too hot; I can hear my voice pitched too high, my laughter false and ugly.

The first time somebody asks me how I wrapped the job up, I ignore it. The second time, I call it a state secret. I pour a glass of rum out for Gregor, and he says, "Well, just one, to celebrate Julia's return to the fold!" I see Csilla's fine, clear brow crease, her eyes on him as he downs the drink, as his large hand reaches for the bottle to pour himself another. Her fingers tremble a little as she lights a cigarette and moves over to the window.

I am not usually keen on liquor, having watched since I

was a tiny thing the way it makes men into fools and slaves, but I drink it tonight, glass after glass, until the room sways around me and I can hear my awful laughter ringing in my ears. I see my reflection in the window, my hair wild and ragged, my face red, the silk gown falling off my shoulder. I laugh at Wyn scowling in his chair; I dance with Gregor; I let Csilla powder my face and paint some lurid color on my lips. The third time somebody asks me how I finished the job, I tell the truth: "A boy—they wanted a little boy in the house. So I kidnapped him and handed him over."

The room goes very quiet then, and I throw up all over Esme's fine rug.

～

I wake up in my own bed at dawn, wrung out and miserable. My stomach has turned itself virtually inside out several times, ridding itself of all the rum and rich food. My hands won't stop shaking, whatever I do. I put on my new clothes, tuck my knife into the lining of my gorgeous new boot, and find a hackney to take me to the Scola.

It is dangerous to come back here, of course. Who knows what they would do to me if they found me. But I have to know what is happening. I find the house easily, so either Alazne's Blind has been lifted or I am still exempt from it. I slip through the gate as the sun rises, vanish next to the pump, and wait.

Chloe comes out for water, fills the bucket right next to me. I grab her arm and clamp a hand over her mouth, drag her into the outdoor privy while she struggles and tries to scream. But I am stronger than she is.

"Hush now," I hiss, holding up my knife so she can see it. There is something incongruous about the ugly knife in my velvet-gloved hand. She looks at me like I am some kind of monster, her eyes glassy with horror. Well, I know how she feels.

"Why?" she sobs. "Why did you do it?"

"Never you mind," I say. "Tell me what's happening. What are they saying?"

"They say . . . you and Mr. Darius ran off with Baby Theo."

"Mr. Darius?" I gape at her in bewilderment. "What do you mean, Mr. Darius? Isn't he at the house?"

She shakes her head. "He's gone. Disappeared yesterday morning." She seems to take me in properly then, and blurts out: "What are you wearing?"

I shove the knife closer to her face. "Tell me what's going on in there."

She shrinks away from me, still staring at my fur coat. "Bianka . . . they had to give her some medicine or something to make her go to sleep. She was nearly mad, and she had a pen. . . . Oh, I'm afraid to say it!"

"She's a witch," I say impatiently, and Chloe's eyes widen.

"They had to take the pen by force—she was screaming; it was so terrible!" says Chloe, her shining eyes locked on me, speaking half in terror, half as if she is confiding in me. "Then they gave her a drink of something, and she's been sleeping on and off ever since. Mr. Darius's things are all gone. Mrs.

Och is bedridden. She said they should have guessed about you, and Frederick wept. But that was all at first, right after. I didn't hear much after that, because they were always in private." She starts to cry again. "That sweet boy! Will he be hurt?"

"That's not my business, nor yours."

Pia's words in my mouth taste like iron.

"How could you do it?" she blubbers. "He's just a baby, Ella."

"My name isn't Ella, you stupid fool," I say, and I shove her out of the privy. I run all the way to Lirabon Avenue, certain that someone will be in pursuit. But if they come after me, they are not quick enough. I flag down a cabriolet. It's over, I tell myself. You did your job and it's over. It's too late to take it back now. But my hands are trembling still, and I don't know how to make them stop.

❦

Liddy pours me some coffee, gives me a fresh bun. I try to eat, but I can't get it down, and the coffee roils in my empty stomach.

"I heard the Gethin is dead," she says, watching me with those hooded eyes.

"How do you know?" I ask.

"This city crawls with watchers and knowers and rumor speakers. My friends."

Of course.

"I gather from your fur coat that you have been paid too,"

she continues. "And yet you do not have the look of someone who has reached the happy conclusion of a difficult job."

I could tell her everything, but what would be the point? Or maybe I am too ashamed to confess what I have done for all this money. Not that I had a choice. Surely Liddy would understand that I had no choice.

"It wasn't a good job," I say.

"Of course it wasn't."

"What are you, Liddy?" I've danced around this question with her for years, never daring to ask quite so bluntly, but I have no such qualms anymore. "Are you a witch?"

Liddy laughs.

"No. I am something else."

"Something else?"

"There are a great many something elses in the world; you will learn if you look carefully," says Liddy. "Looking carefully is something that comes with practice. Seeing things that others often don't—like you, when you step behind whatever curtain hides you from ordinary eyes."

"Mrs. Och could see me too. And the baby, Theo— Gennady's son."

"Odd that the baby would see you. It may be *because* he is Gennady's son, and sees as the Xianren do. Or perhaps all babies see the way that animals do, their minds not yet filling in the blanks for the eye."

"I wonder why I can do it," I say in a small voice. I'm not entirely sure I want the answer, even if she has it. But she offers no hypothesis.

"Your trouble, my dear, is that you've been born into a time of very few choices for a girl of your talents and character and social class. Perhaps it is my fault for taking you to Esme in the first place. I thought . . . well, I supposed she would educate you. I supposed it would be better than the alternatives. And it seemed that it was, for a while at least. But I wonder sometimes what kind of life your mother hoped for you. Unlike the rest of us, she never learned to live without hope."

Liddy has never once mentioned my mother in all the time I've known her, not since she plucked me out of the market, a ragged little apple thief, and handed me over to Esme.

"Did you know her?" I ask, stunned by this possibility.

"Everybody knew her," says Liddy. "Those who didn't know her knew *of* her, at least. I met her once or twice."

"You never told me that."

"There is little to tell," Liddy replies. "I thought of it now only because when I knew her, she was in trouble. I never saw so much of her in you as I do now."

"Trouble? What kind of trouble?" I have to grip the edges of the chair so I don't leap up and try to wring the answers out of Liddy. Her eyes are disappearing into the wrinkles of her face, her lips tightening; she is shutting up like a clam again, and I can't bear it.

"Ammi thought she could change the world. She was an idealist. She tangled with forces too strong for her, but she did so with open eyes, and those who cared for her could find some peace in knowing that. She knew what it might cost her. It was a risk she was willing to take."

I feel suddenly dizzy and have to put my head down to my

knees. When I close my eyes, I see Theo's face staring out at me before Pia shut the door. Yesterday I wanted only to survive this, but I didn't know then all the ways there are to die inside.

I feel Liddy's hand, cool on the back of my neck. Shuddering there in her back room, trying not to throw up again, I have two thoughts. The first is that if what Liddy says is true, it was not fair for my mother to risk her life and leave us orphaned in a place like Spira City. What chance did we have, Dek marked by Scourge and both of us marked as the children of a convicted witch? What choices did she leave us with? The other thought is that I am not hopeful or brave like my mother. I've caught a glimpse of the powers that trample the rest of us, and I am no idealist, just a thief and a spy.

Still, like her, I've tangled with forces stronger than I am, and they haven't killed me yet. I may not be able to change the world, but I am the best thief and spy this wretched city has ever known, and I reckon I can bleeding well steal Theo back.

The dizzy spell clears. My heart slows. My shaking hands go still.

∾

I call a meeting, and by noon we are all assembled in Esme's parlor. Gregor is sipping from a flask again, Csilla fidgeting with her gloves. Esme sits like a statue, arms folded across her chest, her face a thundercloud. Wyn is still giving me this hangdog look, while Dek is all furrow-browed concern.

"What I did—it wasn't about the silver," I say, almost pleading right off the bat. "Pia threatened to do such terrible things, and she would have too . . ." I stammer, then come to the point: "What's done is done. Now I've got a job prospect that'll see us not just through this winter but well beyond."

"You're finding the jobs now?" asks Gregor. "Nameless One help us."

"What do you know about our former client?" I ask him.

"More than you, I'll wager," he hedges, looking uneasy.

"I doubt that," I say. "Do you know who she works for?"

He just stares at me, slack-jawed. "Look, I know she's not to be meddled with, that's all."

"Pia is just a slave," I say. "She works for a man named Casimir. Not quite a man, in fact. He's one of the Xianren."

Silence, and then Wyn gives a short laugh. "You've gone bonkers," he says.

"Ask Liddy, if you don't believe it," I say. "There are three of them, and Mrs. Och is one too. They can do magic without touching a pen. I don't know much about all that, but I do know they are very, very rich, and I know it wasn't just Casimir after that kid. Agoston Horthy wanted him too. There's something about him that's got them all chasing him down. Casimir paid me a lot of silver to snatch that boy away, and I'll bet you Mrs. Och will pay us even more to get him back."

There. That's it. I clench my fists and sit rigid to keep myself from trembling, for I can't do this without them, and they won't do it if they're not to be paid for it.

"Well," says Gregor heavily. "None of us liked how it ended

up, but you did what you were paid to do. Turning around and undoing it sounds bleeding unprofessional to me."

"You've stolen paintings and sold them back to the owners," I say, cool as I can. "This is no different."

"Hold up, hold up," says Dek. "Are we really talking about the Xianren? This is sounding a bit . . . well, isn't that just an old story?"

"Some old stories are still around," mumbles Gregor. "More of them than you might think. Liddy is sure of it?"

"She's sure," I say. "And with the things I've seen the past few weeks, so am I."

"Has this Mrs. Och asked to hire us?" says Esme.

I shake my head. "She's never heard of us. All she knows is that I took him. If you'll all agree, I think we should set up a meeting. I have a plan, but I need Gregor and Csilla to be part of it."

"And what of the rest of us?" asks Wyn. "Are we needed?"

"I don't know yet," I say, avoiding his eyes. "Probably. It will depend on Mrs. Och."

"I don't like it," says Gregor. "We do not want to cross Pia, let alone one of the Xianren, if that's who she's working for. Our lives will be worth nothing."

"They won't know it was us, and frankly I don't think it was a good idea to cross Mrs. Och and Bianka either," I say. "What do you think, Csilla?"

"It sounds rather dangerous, getting mixed up with these sorts of people," she says, winding a flaxen curl around her finger. "How much silver are we talking about?"

"Maybe gold," I say. "But we have to meet with Mrs. Och to get an offer."

"Csilla, I don't like this," says Gregor.

"Go on, bossy boots, there's nothing wrong with a meeting," says Csilla, smiling up at him. "And look at Julia's lovely fur coat!"

"Let it go, Julia!" Gregor looks at me imploringly. "You've got your silver."

I shake my head. He stares at me wordlessly for a minute or two, then throws up his hands and leans back in his chair. "Does everybody want to do this?" he asks. He looks at Esme. "Do *you* want to do this?"

"There's no harm in a meeting," she says, suddenly brisk.

"There might be," grumbles Gregor, but he won't fight Esme.

"We'll have it somewhere safe, neutral," she says. "I'll talk to Liddy. We could use her shop."

Once Esme has spoken, it is settled. She leaves the room without even looking in my direction.

*T*hey stand side by side on the dock, watching a small ship approach. He is nearly twice her height, wrapped in a long fur cloak. His storm-cloud eyes never break their hold on the boat, as if he can draw it to him by watching it. And perhaps he can—who knows what he can do? She wears a coat of gray muslin and a scarf wrapped around her head. Small and hunchbacked, she appears in every way the weaker of the two, though it would be a mistake to think so.

"You are all that I was told you were, and more," says Casimir. "You have done all that I asked. If you can do this final thing, I will keep my promise to you."

Does she tremble a little at that? It is a moment before she answers, and her voice is steady: "Thank you, my lord."

"I wonder how he did it," he goes on. "I would not have thought it possible."

"He had help, my lord," she says.

"But whose?" says Casimir. "Who in this world, besides you, could do such a thing?"

"There are others besides me who could do it," she says. "But perhaps none other who could undo it."

"You are confident, then?"

"I am, my lord. The vessel makes no difference—be it lake or tree or child, the unbinding is the same."

"How long?"

"The unbinding itself, an hour perhaps, but I will need some days to prepare."

"Not more than a week?"

"Not more than that, my lord."

"Good. That is good."

"My lord—you understand, I take it, that the vessel will not survive the unbinding? To separate them, either the text or the vessel must be destroyed."

"I am sorry to hear it," he says.

"If you wish me to look for another way . . ."

"Is there another way?"

"No, my lord. There is no other way."

"Then do what you must, and I will honor our agreement."

"Yes, my lord."

They both look to the boat bobbing closer, everything they have been waiting for and working toward drawing at last into view.

NINETEEN

It is late afternoon and the sun is getting low in the sky. There aren't enough chairs for us all to sit down, so we stand around awkwardly in Liddy's shop, drinking coffee and not speaking much. Dek suggests a game of King's Heir, and Wyn joins us in the back room. I play without looking at him; I play carelessly and fast and I lose every hand until there is a knock at the door and we fumble the cards away and go back out into the shop.

Liddy opens the door and says to the group assembled on her doorstep, "This place is mine, and you are welcome here."

At first this seems to me a very odd greeting, but then I wonder if it has something to do with the rhug. Esme told me nobody would be able to do magic in Liddy's shop, and I hope she's right. In they come, into my world, where I am not Ella the illiterate housemaid, but Vanishing Julia, thief and spy, kidnapper of Baby Theo. Mrs. Och is followed by Professor Baranyi, Frederick, and, Nameless One help me, Bianka.

Bianka's eyes fall on me and my knees go loose. I think I'm going to be sick. I have never seen such raw hatred in a person's eyes before. They are all looking at me, of course. Mrs. Och, though as always it is impossible to know what she is thinking; Frederick, with a sort of stunned sadness; and Professor Baranyi, with almost friendly curiosity. I try to meet Bianka's gaze, thinking to show her I am not afraid, but have to look away immediately. What does it matter if she thinks I am afraid or not? She can crush me with a stroke of the pen.

Esme steps forward, towering over all of them, even Frederick. "I am Esme," she says. "Julia works for me."

"Julia," says Mrs. Och, looking at me again. "That is your name?"

I nod.

"Julia *what?*" hisses Bianka.

Nobody answers her. I have a sudden wild hope that she needs my full name to curse me. I will ask Liddy as soon as I have a chance.

Mrs. Och turns back toward Esme. "Who asked you to place a spy in my house? Was it my brother Casimir or the prime minister?"

"Pia got in touch with me," Gregor answers, sitting back in the only comfortable chair, his long legs stretched out in front of him. "She'd heard a rumor about Julia, wanted to know if I really had a vanishing girl in my employ. But Julia tells me that Pia works for Casimir."

This surprises me. I hadn't realized that Pia knew of me

before approaching Gregor. I didn't think anybody knew about me. I'm not sure whether to be pleased or alarmed that I've acquired, apparently, a reputation.

"Who are you?" asks Mrs. Och.

"Nobody much," says Gregor. "But crooks know other crooks. Julia was the obvious choice for the job."

Mrs. Och looks at me curiously. "Yes. This ability to go unseen. It is interesting."

"It didn't work on you," I say.

"No," says Mrs. Och. "I should have realized something was wrong when I found you in my study. But then, I have never heard of a skill such as yours, and I have been around for a long time, as you may know."

She gives me a questioning look, as if asking how much I do know. I don't answer that. I want to apologize to them all, but it would sound so stupidly feeble, and I can't, anyway, not in front of Bianka. Because, of course, I can't apologize to her. I glance at her and look away again. It is like touching flame.

"Where is my son?" she says in a voice not at all like her own. It is a hoarse, trembling, dreadful voice. Not a young woman's voice.

She takes a step toward me, and it is everything I can do not to turn tail and run. Professor Baranyi catches her arm, and Wyn moves quickly in front of me.

"I handed him over to Pia," I say, more to Mrs. Och than to Bianka. "She'll be taking him to Casimir, I reckon. He lives on a Sirillian island called Nago, doesn't he?"

Bianka looks at Mrs. Och, who nods briefly, raising an eyebrow at me.

"I came to your house on a job," I continue. "There was no malice in it. I did what I was paid to do, that's all. Now the job is done, and we're available for more work. We can get into any place and steal anything. Including Casimir's place, and including Theo."

"That is confidence indeed," says Mrs. Och.

"With a little more information, we can do it," I say.

Bianka's eyes widen. I think her pupils actually tremble. She looks at me and then at Mrs. Och. There is in that look both the desperation of the prey and the ruthless hunger of the predator. A long moment passes, and then Mrs. Och says, "What of Mr. Darius? What was his part in this?"

"I don't know anything about that," I say. "You know who he is?"

She nods.

"Perhaps he was still working for Agoston Horthy," I suggest.

"Impossible," says Professor Baranyi. "He *did* work for the prime minister, it's true, but after his accident—"

"The wolf bite," I say, and now his eyebrows go up.

"It seems you know as much as we do. He came to us for help, but I failed him."

Something about this doesn't sound right to me.

"Why would you help somebody who was working for Agoston Horthy? Best I could tell, he was some kind of high-level anti-magic officer. Not really your kind of fellow."

"Yes, true." He glances at Mrs. Och and she nods, as if giving him permission to continue. He clears his throat and explains: "His daughter is a witch. He worked for her sake, to keep her safe. The real payment for his work was her life. If he becomes a wolf, he will no longer be any use to Agoston Horthy and her life will be forfeit. So he came to us in secret, and he promised secrets in exchange. We thought it might be useful to have a man on the inside. We said we'd help him in exchange for information on Agoston Horthy's activities and targets and started working toward getting his daughter out of the country. But he disappeared the same day you did."

This is a loose end I don't like, but I don't know what to make of it.

"What does he matter? What about *Theo?*" Bianka's ragged voice puts an end to this line of questioning.

"I will need to hear your plan," says Mrs. Och. "How would you approach the island undetected? How would you enter Casimir's castle? How would you find the boy and release him? How would you make your escape?"

"Julia," says Esme, giving me the floor.

I clear my throat. I can hardly bear Bianka's hungry gaze. It is worse than her fury. I am finding it difficult to look at Frederick too, so I address myself mainly to Mrs. Och.

"I had in mind a pleasure boat with rich, lost honeymooners aboard, docking by accident, maybe shipwrecked. Would they not be given shelter, at least?"

"Perhaps," says Mrs. Och.

"The castle doesn't worry me," I say. "If we can get onto the island, we can get inside the castle. I'll scout ahead, unseen, and figure out what we need to do to get Theo." I don't say *if he's still alive*. "We can get past any locks or guards, whether it's stealth or force that's required. We will be out and away before they know what has hit them."

"It won't work," says the professor. "Casimir's castle is like a fortress! This isn't some pretty West Spira house."

"The Duke of Cranfell's castle was highly fortified, but we went in and took the duchess's morasanti diamonds from her locked dresser while she slept," says Gregor breezily. He shaved this morning and is only very slightly drunk. "The collector Lord Elrich keeps his most prized art objects in a safe under guard, but those too ended up in our hands. We stole Izza's *Misty Dawn* from the very wall of the Anderov Scole Museum."

"*You* took *Misty Dawn?*" cries the professor.

"It was the Crown's gold that bought it back," says Gregor.

"Hounds," says Frederick, staring at us. "You don't look like much."

"That helps, actually," says Gregor.

"You are bragging of exploits more than a decade past, and none of it means anything, dukes and museums and so on," says Professor Baranyi. "Casimir's fortress is different. It won't work."

"We shall see if it works or not," says Mrs. Och. "Casimir's forces are mostly abroad; he cast a wide net in his search for Theo. He knows my usual contacts, would see them coming. This, at least, is something he will not expect, and we are short on time. Can you be ready tomorrow?"

I look at Dek, and he gives a brief nod.

"We'll take the train to Nim," says Esme. "We can find a boat there."

Mrs. Och looks us over. "Is there a witch among you? Do you have any other unnatural powers?"

"Only Julia's ability," says Esme. "And it goes no farther than you know."

"There will likely be enchantments protecting whatever Casimir wishes to keep hidden," says Mrs. Och. "You will need Bianka if you are to break them."

My skin prickles with alarm as Bianka turns her eyes on me, slowly. I do not want to do this job with her at my side.

"We will come with you," says Mrs. Och. "I can help the boat to approach the island, but I cannot get too close, or he will know. There are some smaller, uninhabited islands nearby, and I will wait for you on one of these. Bianka can cope with enchantments within the castle itself."

I look desperately at Esme. She says, "Fine. But I'm in charge of this job, and you'll all need to do as I say."

"Name your price," says Mrs. Och.

"Fifteen gold freyns," she replies.

Wyn covers his exclamation with a cough, and I wonder if she's joking or trying to sabotage the job, but Mrs. Och only nods.

"We would need four gold freyns up front," Esme continues. We all goggle at her in amazement. Mrs. Och reaches into her purse and counts out four large gold coins. We all stare at them on the table, and then Esme scoops them up.

"We will leave for Nim tonight," says Mrs. Och. "Agoston

Horthy is coming to my house this evening, and I would prefer not to be there. I will give you an address and you will join us tomorrow. Julia!"

I jump.

"What were your instructions in my house? Why did you wait before taking the boy?"

"I didn't know it was him they wanted, at first," I say. "I mean to say, they didn't know either. Pia told me I was to find a shadow but that it could look like anything."

"A shadow," she repeats. For a moment she looks quite lost, like an old lady who has wandered into the wrong place and can't remember what she's doing there. Then her eyes clear, and she says, "Casimir has been assembling a bit of a collection. Theo will be the priority, of course"—she glances at Bianka—"but Casimir stole something from me too, some time ago. If you can retrieve it, I will double your payment."

A long, stunned silence follows this. Then Esme says, "What is it?"

"A tree," says Mrs. Och, and then she smiles wryly. "But it could look like anything."

∿

The conversation turns to boats, weapons, lockpicks, and so on. My nerves are shot and I need a breath of air, even if it is a freezing cold breath, so I slip outside. Frederick follows me, hands tucked away inside his wool coat.

"Julia," he says, trying it out.

I say nothing. What can I say?

"It's a pretty name," he says. His voice has a cool edge that is new to me. "Hard to get used to. It suits you, I suppose. It's odd, though—I find myself missing Ella. I liked her a great deal. Now it turns out she doesn't exist."

"I don't miss Ella much," I say.

"She and I were friends," he says. "You look just like her, in spite of that ridiculous dress, but I don't know you at all. You're a stranger, and what I do know of you ranges from the unsavory to the horrifying."

I shrug. Absurdly, I am a little stung by his dig at my dress. I pull the fur coat tighter around me. He keeps talking, this new Frederick, with his remote, hostile expression.

"Since coming to work for the professor, I've seen things I never would have believed in once. I've met people who are often called evil—people like Bianka or Mr. Darius. They are gifted or cursed in ways that set them apart, but they are not evil. They are simply people, with good and bad, like all of us, struggling like all of us. Evil, to me, has always been rather an abstract thing. I never felt myself touched by it before now. But I look at you, wearing the face of my friend Ella, and I think of what you have done, and I wonder, is this girl evil? You do not look it, and yet I think the answer can only be yes."

I stare at my new boots, the soft toes already scuffed from tramping around in the snow. I can think of no reply, and when I look up, he has gone back inside. I stay outside until I am too cold. His words have opened up something dark and horrible inside me. My limbs are heavy as I go back in too. Frederick has not joined the others—he is standing by himself, moodily examining a woman's lambskin boot on display.

"That would suit you well," I say.

He looks up warily.

"So what about this tree of Mrs. Och's?" I ask.

"I know no more than you," he says. "There was a beautiful old cherry tree in the garden, and then one day it was gone, torn up by the roots."

"And she says Casimir stole it. Why would he want a tree?"

"Why would he want a baby boy?"

Silence falls between us. He makes to walk away and I stop him, catching him by his sleeve.

"I'm not evil," I say. I don't know why it matters. Why I should care what he thinks. What else *could* he think, after all?

"I was thinking aloud," he replies coolly. "I know you are capable of doing evil. I do not know what that says about the state of your soul, whether or not you have a conscience and feel things as other people do."

"I don't know how other people feel."

He gives me a look of vague interest, like I am a specimen in a jar. The conversation is making me feel queasy.

"Do you feel remorse?" he asks. "Do you see Bianka's suffering, and feel pity?"

"Of course I feel . . . pity," I say. "Look, I didn't know what this job was going to be like. I do what I'm paid to do."

"There are other kinds of work. As you know."

"Bleeding housemaid." I shake my head. "Not a chance in Kahge. I figured I was just snooping, or maybe stealing something. I didn't know what they wanted until after the Gethin, and Pia would have killed me if I hadn't done as she said."

"So you are not evil but a coward, perhaps?" he suggests, unsmilingly, and I have no reply. I don't know how to begin to explain to him every moment that led me to this one, how I needed Dek to be safe too and the home we found with Esme, how the job spiraled out of control and I was so confused and so afraid all the time, squashed in a cabinet staring at the man who ordered my mother's death, Pia's knife against my throat, her grotesque threats, all of it. I don't know what to say to him, but somehow I can't bear for him to think me evil. Or perhaps I can't bear the possibility that he's right. What kind of person hands Theo over to Pia?

"I'm going to get Theo back," I say.

"For fifteen gold freyns," says Frederick, and he walks away from me again.

∽

"You want some?"

I shake my head, and Wyn puts the expensive brandy back on the table, staring into his own half-full glass.

"Julia," he says sadly. "Always such a paragon of strength and self-control. You make fellows like Gregor and me look like such dismal weaklings."

"Speak for yourself," says Gregor, who is stoking the already blazing fire—probably not a safe thing to do if you're as drunk as he is, but we don't stop him. The flames rise up and he lies down right there and starts snoring.

We are back home now, thank the Nameless One, after that awful meeting. I say awful, but I suppose technically it was a success, as we are to go ahead with the job and meet Mrs. Och and the others in Nim tomorrow. Esme has gone straight to bed, and Dek has spent the evening at a workshop in the Edge belonging to an associate of Esme's, an illicit gunsmith with an innovative flair.

"I miss you," says Wyn. "Are you ever going to stop hating me? Even if I can't have you back, won't you at least smile at me now and then?"

I miss him too, but I don't say so. Frederick's words are still buzzing in my head, and so instead I say, "That boy could be dead already, for all I know. Do you think . . . am I evil, Wyn?"

"Evil?" He gives a bark of laughter. "Hounds, Julia, you did a job. It wasn't a nice one, and I feel bad for you; I'll bet it was awful. But we're crooks for hire—that's our business—and what else were you to do? Back out and get your throat cut? You're not evil, Brown Eyes."

"Esme won't look at me," I say.

"Esme just asked a bleeding fortune for this job. I'd say you've brought her the best business she's ever had."

Csilla comes in then, bundled in a fur coat and hat.

"You two had better get some sleep," she chides us. She

kneels next to Gregor, strokes his face, and whispers, "Come home with me, love."

By the firelight I can see the faint lines around her eyes, strands of silver among the gold of her hair.

"We can help carry him down," I offer, but Gregor rouses, mumbling something about a horse.

"Lean on me, darling," she says, helping him to his feet, and he lurches out on her arm, stinking and stumbling.

Wyn shakes his head. "He made a real go of it this time. Poor old Csilla."

I don't say anything to that. This is the story I grew up on, and I know it by heart.

"Look, it was a rotten job," he says to me. "We've both done plenty of rotten things, but that doesn't make us rotten people. Or maybe it does, I don't know. I'm no philosopher. Are you going to walk out on me if I tell you I'm sorry?"

I shake my head, try to force a smile.

"I know I'm no good at saying it. . . . I don't know why not—the holies know I feel it—but the words stick in my throat when I think them. But I do love you, Julia. You're everything to me. We're so alike, the two of us. We love the world, but the world doesn't love us back. The truth is just that I was bored and I was lonely and Arly Winters is pretty and I didn't think you'd find out."

"You need to work on that little speech," I say dryly. "The first bit is better than the last bit."

Laughter plays across his beautiful mouth before he turns

serious again. I've always loved that, how close he seems to laughter, even at the worst of times.

"If I thought it would make a difference, I'd spew remorse and beg and make promises," he says. "But I want to be straight with you. I'm sorry because it hurt you, but I don't think what I did was anything so terrible. We aren't betrothed. It was just a good time, and it's over. She means nothing to me."

I know he wants to make me feel better by saying this. It doesn't matter now, and so I don't tell him that there was no joy as great as his nearness, never has been, for me, and to have him treat it so lightly, give the very same of himself to stupid Arly Winters like it was nothing at all, that is what hurt. I look out the dark window, snow drifting past it. I am not even sure myself what thing has been broken between us by his dalliance. It's just that the beauty of what we had, the rarity and wonder I believed in, seems a lie now, and though I want to go back to him, I know it won't be the same.

"Well, you've said your piece," I say, rising, and I kiss him on the cheek to show him I'm not angry anymore.

"Don't go," he says, but I shake my head, pulling away.

"Csilla's right, we need to get some sleep. Big day tomorrow."

Still, it hurts to walk away from him. It would be a comfort, tonight, to hold him close, to lose myself in him, to hear him tell me that he loves me, that we are alike. Instead I go downstairs holding Frederick's words close to my heart: *I think of what you have done, and I wonder, is this girl evil?*

Dek is back from the gunsmith's workshop. He is sitting at his desk and scribbling figures on a sheet of paper, his hair pulled back so the dark Scourge blots stand out starkly, a crescent around his missing eye. Before him there is a metal cannon no bigger than my forearm, and seven small canisters lined up next to it.

TWENTY

I have always wanted to see the sea. Now I cannot see anything else. Mrs. Och says our boat is a sturdy vessel, but it seems to me a poor sort of thing, pitching this way and that on the great gray swells, lost between the sky above and the water below. The horizon is a dark line where the sea meets the sky, encircling us. It is foolhardy, I think now, to leave behind the solid earth. This is a place for fish and for birds, not for us.

When Frederick shows me on a map the small distance we have traveled, I can hardly believe the world is so large. The first night, I lie on the rocking deck looking up at the stars, and I fear my own smallness will simply be snuffed out, extinguished by the vastness surrounding me. I feel it then, unexpectedly: that thin membrane through which I can disappear. I feel it all around me, tugging strangely at me, and a part of me wants to push through it and disappear farther than I have ever disappeared before. I can feel another infinity there, another eternity, but anything seems safer than these stars that don't care and the cold depths we ride our boat across. The following night is clouded, and though the sky seems less vast, it is darker.

It is a strange journey, very busy at times but with great long stretches with nothing to do at all but watch the sea pass by and listen to the surprising conversations that spring up between Mrs. Och's crew and my own. Here on the boat, the quarters are too close and the work required of us too immediate to keep a chilly distance. Frederick teaches me how to use the compass and sextant; we learn to read the sails and adjust them as needed; Dek and I compete over the telescope, marveling at how it brings things at a great distance up so close it seems you could reach out and touch them. My own gang steers clear of Bianka, clearly wary of her, but she keeps to herself and does not join in any of the conversations. Mrs. Och herself stays in a cabin below, resting, and we do not see her.

The coast of Sirillia comes into view, a reddish hump in the distance, and we sail alongside it. Even at sea, the air is warmer here than in Spira City, and we all shed our coats. Frederick talks about the fall of the Sirillian Empire. Gregor rhapsodizes about Sirillian wine. Csilla tells a story about visiting the ancient monasteries carved into the cliffs above Fiatza, the capital. Gulls wheel overhead, and it feels as if we are returned to the world, almost.

I slip belowdecks and find Mrs. Och lying very still in her cabin, eyes wide. For a horrible moment, I think she is dead, and I gasp. Her eyes flit toward me.

"Julia," she says.

"What are you doing?" I ask. "Are you all right?"

"I'm preparing," she says, almost in a whisper.

"Oh." I linger in the doorway a moment; then the boat hits a wave and lurches and I stumble into the room, coming to an awkward stop right by her little bunk. "Do you think Theo is still alive?" I ask her, because I can't ask anyone else, and because I can't keep the question locked inside me anymore, burning its way through everything that used to matter to me.

"I don't know," she says. "If he is still alive, I do not think he will be for much longer."

The room sways, and I don't know if it's the boat or my own horror robbing me of solid footing. I clutch the side of the bunk.

"Then Casimir means to hurt him."

"Casimir means to take him apart and rip out the thing that is woven into his being," says Mrs. Och. "I can only guess the result will not leave much of Theo behind."

"What is it?" I whisper. "Why Theo?"

She props herself up on her pillows, and I think, I have never seen a person look so tired.

"Memory can only hold so much, and mine is not what it used to be," she says. "When I recall the beginning, I have only flashes now. The smell of the soil, how the waves of the ocean were as tall as mountains, how the mountains were full of fire. I remember riding the wing of a great dragon, and always, I remember my brothers with me. Everything had a will back then—even the elements. The story goes that Feo, spirit of fire, wrote the first magic, becoming lord of the other spirits, but I do not know the truth of it. What I do know is that the Book shaped everything that followed, and shapes it still."

"*The Book of Disruption*," I say, remembering what I read in Professor Baranyi's study.

Her eyebrows go up. "You know about it."

"Not really. I read that the Eshriki Phars tried to take this book from you, but they couldn't read it."

"The Book can only be read by the Xianren, and we knew better than to read it. At least, back then we did. My brothers and I were each charged with a fragment of the Book to keep safe and separate."

"Charged by who?" I ask.

"Some have called them the gods of the elements. I do not know what to call them, but they have long since faded, passed into the earth, as the Xianren are doing now, and as the Book has tried to do. According to legend, the other spirits rebelled against Feo and broke the Book in three, releasing magic into the world. They birthed the Xianren to protect the fragments and keep them separate. After the Eshriki Phars tried and failed to read it, the fragments seemed more alive than ever and began to change, becoming unreadable even by us. Casimir's part, I remember, became a glorious green lake in the foothills of the Parnese mountains. Mine, a great tree. Kingdoms rose up and fell around it, and I stayed in what much later became Spira City, next to my tree. Gennady's was the strangest: a shadow that attached itself to him, a small winged thing, dark, and moving wherever the light struck it, like a mischievous child."

"He put it in Theo?" I whisper.

"I do not know how, or if it is even possible, but Casimir seems to believe so," she says. "If he can truly reassemble the Book, make it text again and read it, he will be master of the very magic that binds and balances the world as we know it. I know Casimir. I love Casimir. But now I fear Casimir."

"Does Bianka know?" I ask.

"I told her," says Mrs. Och. "For her, this is only about her son, but I am telling you so that you understand there is more at stake than a boy's life. There is a hunchback in the castle, a witch named Shey. You must be careful of her. She is more dangerous than Casimir. The lake is no longer a lake, my tree is no longer a tree, and I do not know if Theo will still be Theo, but you must make sure to obtain at least one fragment, if not all of them. I do not know what you should look for. Perhaps text. Something written. The castle will have many books, for Casimir is a great collector."

"Pia told me I was looking for a shadow that might look like anything, and it turned out to be Theo," I say. "Hard job for a thief, when the thing you're meant to steal doesn't keep on being the same thing."

"I suppose that is the spy's job, then, to find what the thief must steal," says Mrs. Och.

"I'm going to look for Theo," I tell her. "If I see a book that looks as though it might have been a tree or something, I'll grab it, but I'm not going looking. I won't risk it. I'm looking for Theo and getting him out of there."

She looks at me for a long time then.

"You aren't doing this for gold," she says.

I try to answer but can't. I sink to my knees before her. A bubble rises up through my chest and bursts. My body shakes with awful, gulping sobs; tears wet my face and hands, but I feel oddly as if I've stepped out of myself and this is not really me—and thank the Nameless for that. I can't bear to be Julia anymore—Julia, who is a fool and a coward, Julia, who understands nothing, Julia, who sold a boy for silver and who will get him back for gold if he's not dead yet, if he's not dead yet, if he's not dead yet.

I feel her hands in my hair, and I go still. She strokes through the sea-tossed tangles with gentle fingers. Nobody has combed my hair for me since I was seven years old. I feel like I'm falling, my heart plunging toward the water. I can hear the crowd roaring as the water closes over her; I can see Theo reaching for me as Pia shuts the door, and the weight of silver and gold pulling me down, down. I think I sleep a little, there in the dark cabin, half on the floor, with my head on Mrs. Och's pillow as she strokes my hair.

I wake when she whispers in my ear: "It's time."

∿

The coast of Sirillia is gone, but through the telescope I see a gray hump in the gray water, which the professor tells us is the Isle of Nago, and several smaller islands surrounding it. Dek, Bianka, Frederick, and the professor go belowdecks. Beneath the rug in the main cabin, there is a trapdoor to a storage room, and the four of them squeeze into it together with a small gas lamp, the spare sails, and the weapons. The others have their parts to play. Esme is cook and crew, Wyn the boat's captain. Gregor and Csilla, of course, are the rich newlyweds. As for me, I will not be there at all. The sea gets rougher; soon we find ourselves staggering, sometimes unexpectedly sprawling, as we are tucking away all evidence of those hiding below.

When I go back up on deck the sky is almost black, even though it is early morning, and the waves are rising higher and higher around us. Gregor, relatively sober for the first time on the journey, is bundled up against the wind, trying to control the wheel.

"Great hounds!" I hear Esme cry out somewhere to the side of me. Gregor lets the wheel go and the boat tilts madly. Mrs. Och stands middeck, arms wide, great gray-white wings spread out behind her. Her face is more animal than human, catlike, her own features surprisingly distinctive in spite of it. She is looking up at the sky as if she were looking into somebody's face, and she is speaking. I don't understand the words, but her voice is like some unearthly music, entreating and commanding all at once. The air seems to ripple and crackle and move in great circles around her. She is speaking magic.

The clouds come rushing to her, and the waves rise up to meet them. Rain pours down upon her. Lightning forks white and terrible onto the black sea around us. I cling to the doorframe while our poor vessel is lifted up high on a wave like a cliff, and then we go crashing down to the water below.

Another wave rises up over us, a mountain ready to tumble. I hear myself scream, and the wave falls. Water pours down the stairs, cold and dark, sending me sprawling and soaked into the narrow black hall below. I struggle up the steps, still sloshing seawater as the boat tilts so far to the side I think we are capsizing. I will drown like her, I think, and I will know if Liddy was telling the truth that it is a peaceful death. I will never see Spira City again. I will never atone for my crime. I will never set it right.

I reach the deck on all fours. Another wave is rising over us. Mrs. Och is gone. A tearing sound, and the mainsail is suddenly flapping across the deck. I cannot see the others anymore. I hang on to the ropes binding the lifeboat in place, cleave there as our poor vessel rides the storm, helpless. The world is all black water and sudden flashes of white light that illuminate the waves towering around us. I hear somebody shouting my name, but I don't know who it is. I think of Dek shut away in the belly of the boat with strangers, and I weep because I am too afraid to leave my spot and find him, to help him or to die with him. I can only hang here, waiting to know what it is to be taken by the water, to swallow the sea and be swallowed by it, to die. I think to myself, the fear is the worst part. Let go; let it be over. But my arms cling fast—they cannot be reasoned with. Something strikes me on the shoulder and I cry out but do not loosen my grip. I vanish without thinking, pull away from it all, as if I can hide from the storm, but the storm did not see me to begin with and does not care. I taste salt, the sky heaves and roars, and the terrible sea mocks our folly in venturing out upon it.

And then it is over. I think it must have been more gradual than that, but it feels sudden. Eyes pressed closed, arms worked through the ropes, I realize: It is quiet. And then: It is still. I open my eyes. The sky is no longer so close, but high and gray. The waves are long swells that do not threaten to topple us. And there before us sits an island, gray stone and shrub rising up out of the water, a walled castle perched upon its jagged shelf.

∾

The waves carry us to shore, kind and helpful now. By the time the prow of the boat touches the rocky beach, there are three men in gray furs and tall boots waiting for us. They wear swords at their hips, rifles slung over their shoulders.

There is no time to check if the others belowdecks are all right. Gregor is bleeding from a cut on his forehead, Wyn pale and cradling his arm as if it might be broken. Blast him, I think unreasonably, what good is he with a broken arm? Mrs. Och is still nowhere to be seen, and I wonder if she's flown off to one of the nearby islands on those big wings of hers—I wonder if she *can* fly. We climb out of the boat, clamoring and terrified—I must credit Mrs. Och for the realism, I suppose. In spite of the panic of the storm, everyone is now in character.

"Good sirs, thank you!" Csilla is crying, practically falling into the arms of one of the guards. Unsurprisingly, he doesn't seem to mind one bit.

"Boat is done for," laments Wyn.

"We'll have it repaired here," says Gregor. "We can pay. Sirs, can you tell me where we are?"

"You are nowhere. An unlucky place to come ashore," says the shortest and, I'd guess, the eldest among the three. "Where are your papers?"

His Fraynish is heavily accented. They are all three very dark-skinned, perhaps from Eshrik or North Arrekem.

"I'll fetch them, sir," says Esme, still on the deck of the boat. Gregor looks proud and affronted. Esme returns with the forged papers. Her expert hand and false seal are unrecognizable as fakes. The guard goes through each one, reading the document and then looking up at the owner.

"Congratulations," he says to Gregor and Csilla. There is a kind of menace in his voice that I do not like at all. "You are recently married."

"This is our *honeymoon*," says Csilla indignantly. "Please, I don't care where we are—may we come inside? We are soaked; it is cold; our boat is a wreck."

"It will sail again, I think," says the guard, looking it over with vague disinterest.

"Sir," says Csilla, growing shriller. "We have been shipwrecked! How long must we stand here? We will freeze to death!" And then she faints, most convincingly. Gregor catches her and cries, "Please! My wife is not well!"

"It is odd that you came ashore here," the guard says to him. "Nobody comes ashore here."

"I can see why not," says Gregor, every inch the insulted aristocrat. "Is there a doctor here?"

"We'll light a fire in the Terra Room," says the guard. He turns abruptly and walks back toward the castle, saying something to the other two in another language. They lead our frightened, sopping little group up the hill. I go right behind Esme, whose movement seems to open up the widest swath of margin-of-the-world space. Walking, she parts the air like the Lorian prophets parted water, so they say. I can follow her and remain hidden, a blurred membrane on either side of me, like I am walking through an invisible tunnel. Still, I am not used to moving this fast while vanished, and it requires fairly intense concentration.

The stone wall around the castle is high, and spiked with vicious-looking iron blades along the top. Heavy chains draw up a thick wooden door, which then lowers behind us. I can't immediately see who has opened it or how. This is unsettling, as it will be my job to get back out and then back in again if we need weapons or Bianka's witchcraft. Then I spot a guard by the door we are heading toward, an unassuming side door, with his hand on a lever between two stones in the wall. We pass through the door into the castle itself.

The guards take us through chilly, lamplit corridors to a room with tall beveled-glass windows all along one wall, which let in the light but allow no view. There are divans to sit on over by the windows. A middle-aged woman in white muslin comes in to light the fire. She looks unwell, skeletal. As she turns away I think I see a flash of something on her wrist, almost like a hinge, but then she is gone. The fire blazes up. We cluster near it and look around us. I do not know what kind of room this is supposed to be, what use it could possibly have. Paintings depicting hunting parties and sailboats and giant birds hang on the walls, along with scenes from folklore stories. A huge jade urn sits in one corner, a marble statue of a wicked-looking imp in another. Perched on pedestals around the room, a stuffed wolf with horns, a giant lizard twice the size of a man, and a small tiger-like creature with long fangs watch us with their shining dead eyes.

"How long must we wait here?" demands Gregor angrily. "We need dry things, something to eat. What kind of hospitality is this? Do you not know who I am?"

The guards say nothing.

"How about a privy?" says Wyn. "I've got to go."

The guards glance at each other. One of them shakes his head.

"I've been drinking the wine stores all morning—I'm desperate for a piss, come on," he begs. The guards are unbudging, so he shrugs and heads over to the large urn, opening his trousers.

One of the guards actually laughs, but another grabs Wyn roughly by the arm, saying something in their language, which I do not recognize. I move with them quickly, staying close to Wyn, like his shadow. His other arm dangles at a bad angle, and I can see it hurts him with every step. We hurry down the hall, where I come an inch from crashing straight into a shoulder-high urn painted with war scenes in reds and blacks, down some carpeted stairs, and then along another narrower hall to an indoor privy. I go in with him, and he shuts the door. The guard gives a warning rap, as if to say, be quick.

Wyn looks for me, and I come back with a sigh of relief, so he can see me again. I mouth *Well done*, and he puts his unhurt arm around me, buries his face in my hair.

"Be careful," he whispers in my ear.

"Is your arm broken?"

"Yes. It's all right."

"Stick together, and I'll be back for you."

I don't want to let go of him, but the guard bangs on the door again. I step back against the privy wall. Wyn runs his thumb along my jaw, mouths *I love you*, and swings open the door. The guard drags him back down the hallway. I wait until I cannot hear their footsteps anymore. Then I slip out.

∽

I keep to the walls, move slowly and listen well, but I meet nobody. The walls and rooms are rich with tapestries, marble and bronze statuary, strange animal heads, old maps, bright pre-Lorian paintings, star charts, and Yongguo-style ink paintings. I suppose if you live for thousands of years, you accumulate a few things. Most of the doors are locked, and so I pick them one after another, finding more corridors, more wide rooms packed full of art and books and antiques, more winding stairways. I have a good sense of direction, but the twists and turns are so numerous that I begin to shift things to act as reminders, my own trail of breadcrumbs to follow back: an ivory table's corner pointing toward the door I came through, the dry dead nose of a stuffed jackal directing me back down the corridor, a gold statuette of a dancer with her leg kicking out in the direction I must return by.

I am in a hallway lined with suits of armor, great iron things with dramatic feathers on the tops of their helmets—how anyone could ever move in them is quite beyond me—when I hear footsteps. I slip behind a suit of armor just as she rounds the corner. She is past me before I have a chance to disappear, her eyes fixed on the floor: a diminutive woman with fair, graying hair. A hunchback. My breath catches, remembering what Mrs. Och told me. She shuffles by, carrying a black leather bag. I wait until there is a good distance between us and then I follow as softly as I can. The floors are thickly carpeted here, and it is easy to move without much sound, which is how she caught me nearly unawares.

She does not look up or to the side. She goes up, up, up one stairway after another. We are climbing to the top of the castle, it seems. Her breathing is labored, and I feel confident following a little more closely, for she surely can't hear me over her own gasping breaths. We come out into a bright corridor full of windows, high above the sea. I catch a glimpse of the turrets below, the beach, and our own little boat tilting on the shore, but I don't venture after her into the hall. There are four guards at the end of it, heavily armed before a bolted steel door. They step aside for the woman, heads bowed. Something in the way they move, the swiftness of it, the tension, makes me think they are afraid of her.

She removes a chain of keys from her waist belt and opens three different locks on the door. Then she stands still, head bowed, muttering. She raises one hand to cover her face, and with the other she traces something on the door with her finger. The pungent smell of damp, freshly turned earth wafts down the hallway, and the door swings open. I can't see beyond it. She enters and it clangs shut behind her. The guards exchange uneasy looks but say nothing.

A guarded room with so many locks on the door—and enchantment too, by the looks of it—any thief knows that's the door you want to get through. I will need Bianka after all. I can do nothing by myself, and I do not know how long the woman may be inside. I have to find my way back—easier said than done. I run down the stairs, back to the suits of armor where I first spotted the woman. I follow my landmarks and pointers back the way I came: great head of elk, twisting staircase, jade urn, large clock, alarmingly lifelike lion, small jeweled crown in case, star map hallway, and so on and so on.

I pause in a hallway lined with calligraphy in various languages. I don't know if it is a shadow of movement or some other sense that alerts me. I look up. And there she is, all in black, hanging from the ceiling like some kind of giant, awful spider.

"You see, I can be invisible too," Pia says.

And before I can run, she drops straight down onto me.

TWENTY-ONE

She drags me by the hair down the hall. I am wearing Dek's wristlet of capsicum gas but I don't know that it would truly incapacitate Pia, with her mechanical goggles, and I daren't risk revealing it. I unhitch it from my hand and slide it farther up my arm, under my wet sleeve.

She bangs on a door with her fist. A sonorous voice calls out some reply that I don't catch, blood rushing in my ears. Then we are through the door, and she sends me sprawling to the floor before a pair of tall, shining black boots.

I look up. A great fur cape, gold buttons on his jacket, a black beard and black brows framing a pale face with full red lips, eyes of the deadest, flattest gray imaginable.

"Is this the girl you were telling me about?" he asks.

"This is Julia."

Pia walks around me to his side, and they watch me stagger to my feet, dizzy from the hair-pulling run, my clothes still soaked through. Casimir, for I assume that is who I am facing, is very tall, and slender as a dancer. He might even be handsome, in a severe sort of way, if his coloring were not quite so stark and bloodless.

"The girl who can vanish," he says. "The one who brought us the little boy."

I don't bother to answer. He knows who I am. I scan the room. There are windows, and the door behind me is unlocked, but Pia is watching me with a tiny smile, and I don't think much of my chances if I try to make a break for it.

"And now you are here to steal him back again," says Casimir. "Pangs of remorse?"

"Pangs of liking money," I say, for it seems a safer answer, and he laughs.

"My sister is paying you," he says, not a question. "How much?"

"Fifteen gold freyns," I answer. There is no reason to lie.

He raises his eyebrows. "That is a fine price indeed," he says.

"More than you paid me," I say.

"The risk is greater," he says. "Our job was easy by comparison, was it not?"

I shrug. That remains to be seen.

"I hate to see wasted talent," says Casimir. "Now that you are here, I can't decide if I should cut your throat or hire you."

My heart skips a beat. I don't trust myself to say anything to that.

"She would be useful," says Pia.

"Trustworthy?" says Casimir.

"The contract would hold her," says Pia.

"I do what I'm paid to do," I say. "You paid me, and I got you Theo. Now Mrs. Och is paying me, so I work for her."

"And if I doubled her price, would you work for me again? What would you say to thirty gold freyns?"

I lick my lips and keep my voice steady. "It would depend on what you were hiring me to do," I say.

"There are limits to what you'll do for thirty gold freyns?" he asks, raising one black eyebrow.

"I don't like to accept a job without knowing what it is," I say, although of course I did just that for him before, and for far less.

"I am not talking about a job," he says. "I am talking about a retainer fee. After accepting my contract, you would then be paid by the job. Do you speak any languages besides Fraynish?"

I shake my head.

"You would have to learn a few; no great matter, you are young and intelligent, I can see that. I have a pet in a position of power, but he is unpredictable and strong-willed. He needs to be kept on a tighter leash, and a vanishing girl would be an asset indeed."

"This pet of yours . . . you're talking about Agoston Horthy, aren't you?" I say, mainly to keep him talking while I try to think of a way out of this.

He smiles at me. It is not a nice smile, and I get the uncomfortable feeling he knows exactly what I'm thinking.

"Doesn't it bother you that he spends all his spare time drowning witches?" I ask.

"A harmless hobby," says Casimir. "Witches and I have not been on good terms since the rise of the Eshriki Empire. My sister thinks she can work with them, steer history alongside them, but she has never been very pragmatic. If Agoston Horthy wants to drown them like vermin, let him." Then he raises an eyebrow and says, "But perhaps you don't feel the same way? You may have personal reasons for thinking the drowning of witches an unsavory practice."

I feel a little chill around my heart and wonder how much Pia has told him about me.

"So, for thirty gold freyns, you want me to go spy on Agoston Horthy for you?"

"Thirty gold freyns would be, as I said, the sum paid for you to abandon your current job and agree to a contract with me. There would be more gold for every job. You would also be under my protection"—he pauses very slightly here—"should you have enemies."

He promises wealth, relative safety, and adventure. I know a girl who would have said yes to that in a heartbeat and considered it a dream come true, but I've buried that girl in her ill-gotten finery and barely remember what it felt like to be her.

"The world hates magic," continues Casimir. "Frayne is leading the march to stamp it out. People like you need to find a safe harbor. At my side will be the safest, luckiest place to be."

I don't like the way Pia is looking at me. That gleam in her electrical goggles. Did young Pia stand here once, reeling at the thought of so much gold? Pia, who calls herself a slave. Pia, who prefers ignorance beyond her particular instructions.

"What if I refuse?"

"I'll let you go," he says, looking affronted by the question. Then he adds, "Not your friends, though. I'll feed them to the birds."

"I'll need to see this contract," I say, keeping my cool.

"Of course," says Casimir. "Pia remembers what it entails, don't you, my dear?"

Pia says nothing.

"I'm famished too," I add. I can't do much on an empty stomach, after all.

Casimir laughs. "I like her," he says to Pia. "Fearless little pup, isn't she?"

Pia's goggles whir. Pia knows I am not fearless.

"I will ask my man to prepare a contract for you." Then to Pia, he says, "Take her upstairs. Put a guard on the door and have the girl send some lunch up."

She grabs me by the hair again, unnecessarily rough, and drags me out of the room.

"Let go of me; I'll walk!" I cry, twisting in her grasp. She hurls me to the floor and stands waiting, hands on her hips. I stagger to my feet and face her.

"You stupid girl," she spits.

Whatever glimmers of kinship I felt for her at one point, it is all terror and loathing now.

"Is this how you started out?" I ask her. "Casimir telling

you how special you are, offering more gold than you'd ever dreamed of?"

"You shouldn't have come here," she says.

"I suppose not. Is he going to dress me up in leather and put goggles on my eyes?"

Her mouth twists. "Your choices are limited now, but there are worse fates than what he offers, for a girl like you."

"What kind of girl am I?"

"You are like me," she says. "Or perhaps I should say that I was once like you."

And maybe that explains it, her almost kindness, and her cruelty.

"I'm not like you," I say. "And you were never like me."

My fingers are itching for my knife. I'm not sure I've ever wished someone harm in this way. I want to erase her.

She grins now, like she knows what I'm thinking and finds it reassuring.

"I was *just* like you," she says.

❦

There is a bed with an iron frame in a corner of the room. A tall chair and a table by a window. The window overlooks the sea, facing the opposite direction from our boat, if our boat is still there at all. An unlit chandelier, spiked with long white candles, hangs from the domed ceiling, beams climbing up to the center of the ceiling like a spider's web. A chest, locked. A tapestry depicting a rearing unicorn in a wood. I walk despondently about the room, pushing at the walls as if I might discover a secret panel. I consider breaking into the chest, but that's absurd, of course. Why would they put me in here if the room had anything useful or interesting in it?

The servant we saw earlier brings me a white muslin dress like hers, a pair of coarse stockings, and ill-fitting black shoes. She does not stay to watch me change out of my wet things, thank the Nameless One, and they did not bother to search me, so I still have my knife in the lining of my boot, Dek's lockpick in the heel. I take the pick out and slip it into the stocking, up by my thigh, and then I fasten the capsicum gas wristlet back around my hand. I don't think I can run in the shoes, so I opt to keep my wet boots, uncomfortable as they are. I've nowhere else to conceal my knife anyway.

The sky clears, the sea flattens, and the pale winter sun rises up toward midday. The maid returns with a tray of cheese and fruit and bread and a small flagon of what smells like beer. I watch her as she puts it on the table, looking for that flash of silver at her wrist. It looks as if the skin is pulled back around a shining little disk, but she moves quickly, and I can't get a good look before she goes out again.

Halfway through my meal, there is a heavy thud outside the door, like a body falling. The door opens, and the guard posted outside slides onto the floor, unconscious. I leap up, backing toward the window as if I might escape out of it, and then freeze. Sir Victor Penn Ostoway III steps over the body and into the room.

"Ella," he says. "I'm not here to hurt you."

"Good," I say, my voice shaking in spite of myself. I keep my back to the wall and my finger on the nozzle of the capsicum wristlet. "What *are* you here for?"

"I've been talking with Casimir," he says.

"Have you?" I hear myself laugh shrilly. *Steady, Julia,* I scold myself. "You were working for him all along?"

"No. I met him only yesterday. He had a proposal for me. It's complicated, and I don't know that we have much time. . . ."

The pieces click into place all at once.

"Let me save you the trouble. He wants you to keep tabs on Agoston Horthy. But aren't you about to turn into a wolf any day now?"

His jaw drops.

"My name isn't Ella," I add.

"No, that's right, he told me. What is it? Julia?"

I nod.

"He told me you are his employee, that you would pose as my niece at court and take your orders from me. That you can disappear. But then why have they locked you up? He is not telling me everything—and I prefer to know everything."

"He's kidnapped Theo," I say, a bit of a dodge, but there we are. "I don't work for him anymore. I came for Theo. To get him back."

Sir Victor yanks the sheets off the bed and uses them to bind the unconscious guard very efficiently to the chair. He gags him with the pillowcase.

"What are you doing?" I say, though I'm nearly ready to weep with gratitude. "You're going to get killed."

"He didn't see me," says Sir Victor. "Don't worry—I'm quite good at this. Why Theo?"

"I don't know. Some part of a magic book inside him. Blasted if I understand it; all I know is, they're going to hurt him to get whatever it is Casimir wants out of him."

"I have a daughter your age," he says, straightening up and looking into my face, his expression rather sad. "You remind me of her, a bit. She's a good girl—clever, gifted, kind, but the world is not on her side."

"I know," I say. "I know about her."

"Then you are a gifted spy, but you can still choose to be free. You don't want to belong to these people. Not if you can help it."

"But you belong to them?"

"I ran out of time. Casimir, or rather his witch, Shey, was able to do for me what Mrs. Och and the professor could not do."

"She cured you," I say, and in spite of everything, I am rather glad for him. I suppose Pia got to him after I showed her the letters.

"I have been bound to Agoston Horthy for a long time, and now I am bound to Casimir too. But you don't need to be bound to anyone. Not if you can get away. I'm afraid I can't do more than this for you." He hands me the guard's gun and gestures at the open door.

"It's more than enough," I say. "And I'm grateful. I . . . I did spy on you and don't deserve your help."

"I don't have many chances to help people," he says. "So I am grateful too."

"Why don't you come with me? I know where Theo is. We

can get out of here; I know it. If you're cured, then maybe Mrs. Och can still help you with your daughter."

"It's too late. I've struck my bargain, and I need to get back to my room. They have to think you got out on your own."

"Why too late?"

He shows me the inside of his wrist. Purpled, scarred flesh surrounds a disk of shining metal. I touch it with my finger and withdraw sharply. To my horror, it is as hot as a pan on the stove.

"What in bleeding Kahge is that thing?" I ask.

"My contract," he says. "You should hurry."

༠৬

It takes me longer than I'd hoped to find my way back to the door we entered the castle by. I find the metal prong between the two stones in the wall and give it a tug. The wooden door in the outer walls begins to lift, hauled up by great rolling chains. Tucking the gun into the sash of my dress, I run for the wall and then along it so as to be unseen from the shore, and search among the rocks for a good-sized boulder. Once I find one, I roll it toward the door, straining and sweating. The door is beginning to lower again already. I huddle by the wall, waiting as the door comes down, then wedge the rock under it, stalling its descent. I vanish and crawl under the gap. The two guards by the boat have their pistols out of their holsters, while a third is coming toward the door to investigate.

I move down the hill toward him, slowly, carefully, staying

behind the curtain of the visible, until we are barely a foot from each other, and then I spray him with the capsicum gas. He drops screaming, and the other two panic, running in my direction, though they cannot see me. I stay still, since that is easier, and get both of them as soon as they are close enough, holding my dress up over my face, but even so, the proximity of the gas makes me gag, my eyes tearing. I wait for the gas to clear a bit before disarming them. Then I run for the boat and clamber aboard, leaving the three men blind and howling near the wall. Down the cabin steps, I pull up the rug and open the trapdoor.

The first thing I see is the barrel of a rifle. Then, four faces staring up at me. The gun in Dek's hand lowers. They are huddled around a book with pictures of sails in it, a single lamp lighting the grim little cellar. They look damp and battered. I can hear water still sloshing on the floor below them. Frederick has a strip of wet cloth around his head, and Dek's jaw is swollen, disfiguring his face even more. The storm was not any easier to weather down here, I gather.

"Theo," says Bianka in a strangled voice.

"He's alive," I say. I don't know if it's the truth, but I know she needs to hear it.

"Did you see him?"

"No, but I saw where they're keeping him," I say. "You fellows get the boat ready to sail again, and quick. I need Bianka with me now. We'll have this thing done in a jiff."

Bianka has a piece of chalk. I did not know, would have been terrified had I known, but I am glad to see it now. She holds it like a weapon as Frederick and I tie up the guards and drag them down the slope and around the side of the boat, so they are hidden from view.

"We should toss them in the sea," says Bianka harshly.

"They're just doing their job," I say. "They aren't your enemies."

"Those of you *just doing jobs* that involve taking and keeping my son from me are very much my enemies," she says acidly.

I don't answer that. I lead her up the slope toward the castle.

"How do we get in?" she asks. My boulder has shifted under the weight of the door, which has fallen several inches farther. There are but a few inches left open, not enough space for us to crawl under.

"Hounds of Kahge," I curse, scanning the wall. It is too high and too smooth for me to scale.

"You go first," says Bianka. She squats by the great door, gripping the bottom edge. My mouth falls open as it begins to budge and rise.

"Hurry," she grunts.

"Wait there," I say. "I can get it open for you once I'm through."

I get down on my belly and squeeze under the door as she struggles to lift it, hoping desperately that her strength doesn't give way when I am halfway through. The bottom of the door scrapes against my back. I wriggle beneath it into the castle grounds, run up the hill to the side door, and pull the lever. The chains start to roll and the door lifts with a groan. Bianka comes through it like vengeance personified.

"Take me to him," she says.

I'm afraid of what she'll do if we get lost. The castle is a bewildering maze, but my mind is sharper for having eaten a bit, and I find my way back to the suits of armor where I first saw the hunchbacked witch. From there it is easy to find my way to the top of the castle.

"Wait," I murmur as we near the top of the last staircase. I vanish and peer into the hall. Four guards still. The lack of commotion in the castle and their easy posture reassures me that no one has discovered my escape or noticed the activity out by our boat yet.

"Four guards," I tell Bianka softly, returning to the stairs where she is waiting for me. "I can pick the locks, but there's magic on the door too. No matter what, we need to take care of the guards first."

She bends and writes something on the step with her chalk. I wonder if the guards will notice the smell of rotten flowers. Even in the dim light, I can see the sweat standing out on her brow. The walls seem to shimmer a little.

"Are you all right?" I ask. "Do you need to sit for a moment?"

She looks at me as if she's going to tear my head from my shoulders, and I quake.

She steps out into the hall, and I follow.

The guards are, all four of them, sound asleep, slumped around the door.

"Very nice," I say. "Bloodless. Will it last long?"

"I've no idea," says Bianka.

I set straight to work on the locks. They are sophisticated, but Dek's pick is a match for them. Bianka is writing on the floor with her chalk again, breathing heavily. When I have all three locks open, I look and see that she is just writing *open open open open open open*, over and over again, all over the floor, along the walls.

"Is that going to work?" I ask, doubtful.

"I ... don't ... know," she grinds out. "I don't know how it works ... any better than you do. I've not had much ... practice." Sweat drips from her brow onto the ground and the chalk words.

I can do no more to help, so I sit there on the floor by the enchanted door and watch her sweating, trembling, writing. The words are all over the walls, stretching farther back down the hall, her breath coming ragged now, blood trickling from her nose. *Open open open open open.* I think of my mother, the wild, falling sheaves of paper as she hunched over Dek's sickbed, staving off death. Bianka will write this word until she breaks, and I do not know when that might be. But the door's magic breaks first. There is a sound like ice cracking. The door swings open, and before I can move, Bianka hurtles through it. She freezes, then gives a sick little laugh. I scramble to my feet and follow her.

It is a round room with windows and a bed and a chair and table. Slumped against the wall is a large shirtless man with fair hair. He opens his eyes—they are blue as the sky—and stares at us. He has silver bands on his wrists and on his ankles and black writing all over his body, though it's no kind of writing that I recognize. There are scars on his torso, some old, some fresh and red.

"Where is Theo?" I cry. All my hopes that he is still alive dashed now, I run to the center of the room and look around wildly, then sink to my knees, weak with a despair whose power amazes me, undoes me.

The man says, "Bianka. Are you real? Not a dream?"

His voice rolls across the room. The kind of voice you want to hear singing, it carries such a sweet resonance. He rises slowly, a huge man, and passes me to walk to Bianka, his arms outstretched. His bare back is deeply gouged with crisscrossed crimson scars, as if something has been cut out between his shoulder blades.

"Gennady," says Bianka, stepping out of reach of his arms. Her voice is terrible. Like his name is a curse.

TWENTY-TWO

Even if she had not spoken his name, I would have been able to guess that this is Gennady: Zor Gen, Bianka's lover, Mrs. Och's brother, Theo's father. I can see now that the writing on his body is not ink but made of thin black scars, as if the strange script has been burned into him. On his side, a darkly fresh piece of writing still smokes slightly. He moves, not easily, and yet with a kind of lithe power. With his startling bulk and his great golden mane, he looks like a wounded lion.

"It's you," says Gennady. He reaches for her again, and again she steps away. His hands fall to his sides. "You are not a dream."

"No," says Bianka. Her voice shivers with some emotion I can't name. "Not a dream."

"My son is here," says Gennady. "They have him."

"You didn't think I'd come for you, did you?" says Bianka. "Where is he?"

"I don't know." His voice goes a pitch lower than I've ever heard a voice go—like the growl of a great cat. Bianka stands before him, shaking. I don't want to see what it looks like when a witch and some kind of wounded immortal fall apart completely. I get up off the floor.

"Let's not all start blubbing," I say, hoping I sound less like blubbing than I feel. "We'll find him." I hold out to Gennady the gun Sir Victor gave me. "Can you shoot straight?"

He takes it. It looks like a toy in his huge hand. "Who are you?" he asks me.

"A wicked, treacherous wretch, and also, for the moment, a friend," Bianka answers for me.

"That, and I've got an idea of where to start looking," I say, drawing my knife out of my boot. I am more comfortable with the knife than a pistol.

We step over the sleeping guards, Bianka's chalk *openopen openopenopen* all over the floor, and her *go to sleep* scrawled on the steps. Bianka's eyes are fixed on Gennady's mutilated back, but she does not ask him about that. I lead them in the direction of the room I was held in. If the bread in my lunch was still steaming when it got to me, it had not traveled far through these chilly corridors. I figure whoever makes the food here must have some idea of where it goes.

We walk several minutes in silence, and then I hear him murmur, like a distant thunder roll: "Bianka. Look at me."

Bianka spins around and strikes him so hard that he falls to the ground and lies sprawled there, staring up at her with those dazzling too-blue eyes.

"You didn't tell me. You didn't warn me." She bites out the words, her voice ragged with rage. "You put my son in danger and then you disappeared. Can it be undone, what you did to him?"

He rises slowly, towering over her, but she is straight as a pike and does not tremble before his terrible gaze. Still, the chalk is crumbling to dust between her fingers and her thumb. I know I should stop them but I can't move, can't look away.

"I never asked if it could be undone. You don't know Casimir. If he wanted my shadow, he would stop at nothing to get it from me, and the witch in his employ has power beyond what any witch should have. Ko Dan—the man who did it, a monk from Yongguo—told me that my shadow could not be fully separated from me, that it *refused* to leave me. The only way to create distance between the shadow and myself would be if some part of me, linked to my own life and essence, carried it apart from my body. A child, in other words. I rented the house in Sirillia and pretended it was ours so that they would not know who you were, where you lived. Ko Dan bound the text to Theo while you slept, bound it to his life, to live and die with him. He wanted to kill the baby immediately, thus destroying the fragment, but I wanted Theo to have a life first. He was still my son, after all. I hid your essence with magic and left you behind so they would never trace you to me. Even once they had me, I thought I could hold out against Shey, but I couldn't. She reached so far into me, took me apart, took what she wanted. I gave you up. I told her everything."

"You told this someone everything, but you told me *nothing*. You made use of me. You made use of Theo, like he was a thing and not your son."

She raises her fist again, but this time he catches it in his gigantic hand and pulls her close to him.

"I chose you because I knew you could protect him. I knew you would be strong enough. I knew you would love him."

She makes a funny sound in the back of her throat. "Not because you loved *me*?" she says.

"My dear." The ferocity goes out of him, and he looks only sad. "That was . . . a secondary consideration."

I hear the sharp intake of her breath—and something else. I find my voice and step between them: "Stop. *Listen*."

Through the awful silence of the castle, something like music. I beckon them on, following the sound, and after a momentary hesitation, they obey. No more words pass between them. As we draw close, it becomes more obviously a woman's voice singing. I gesture at them to stay in the hall as I make my way toward the sound.

Down a few steps, there is a large empty kitchen. A fire burns in the hearth. The singing comes from the room behind: the scullery. There I find a girl with dirty blond hair, hanging laundry and singing a foreign song in a pretty but strained voice. I edge around behind her, then grab her by the hair and put my knife to her throat. Her singing gasps to a halt, her body tensing. Good. She is of the freeze rather than the fight variety.

"Not a sound or I'll cut your neck right open," I hiss. She

trembles against me, rigid with fear. I think again of Pia—*I was just like you*—but I don't falter. "Where is the little boy? If you do not tell me, even if you *cannot* tell me because you do not know, I will cut your throat. For your sake, I hope you do know."

She whispers it: "I can show you."

She takes a lantern from the wall and lights it with shaking hands. I keep my knife to her back, forcing her back up the steps.

"No wild-goose chase, no taking us to Casimir or the guards," I warn her. "I can kill you faster than anyone can help you, remember that."

"They can kill me too," she whispers.

"They won't know a thing," I say. "Once we've found the boy, you can run and hide. Or come back here and finish hanging the laundry. Whatever you like."

Her wide eyes take in Gennady and Bianka in the hall. She takes us down, deep into the castle. I think we must be below the ground, for there are no more windows. We come to a large room with a cold hearth and nothing but a couple of rotting tapestries on the walls and a great oak table off to one side. The girl points at the rug on the floor.

"Down there," she whispers.

"Pull back the rug," I say, and Bianka does so. There. A bolted trapdoor. She tears it open and makes a noise like a sob. I take the lantern from the girl, all of us crowding around the empty square in the stone floor.

There are no stairs, just a long drop down to a sparse room, though "room" might be too generous a word for it. A curly-haired little boy lies sleeping in a bed down there. Whether it is the sudden light, the sound Bianka makes, or a draft from the open trapdoor, he wakes, staring up at us with his dark eyes.

"Is that him?" whispers Gennady.

"Mama!" cries Theo, scrambling out from under his covers and reaching pitifully. "Mama!"

"How do we get down?" Bianka asks. It is too far to jump.

"There must be a rope," I say. "Or some mechanism, some hidden stairs."

"Or another way in," says Gennady, looking around the room we are in.

"Stay where you are, my sweet boy," Bianka calls down to Theo. "Mama is coming for you."

I shove the girl toward the far corner. "You stay there. Don't try to run or I'll cut you to ribbons. Not a sound, not a sigh, do you understand?"

She nods wordlessly at me, stumbles to the corner. I put the lantern down by the trapdoor, tuck my knife back into my boot, and begin tearing the tapestries from the wall, knotting them together to make a rope. Bianka calls reassurances down to Theo.

"Bring me that table," I say to Gennady, pointing at the oak table in the corner. "Pull it over by the trapdoor."

He starts to drag it. He is a powerful man, but it screeches slowly on the stone floor. Bianka rises to help him. Theo begins to scream the moment she is out of sight.

"I'm here!" she calls to him. "I'm coming!"

Gennady lets go the table when they are halfway across the room, straightening. Bianka drags it to the trapdoor on her own, shouting at him, "What's the matter with you?"

"Someone is here," he says.

My heart plunges into my gut. There in the doorway is Pia.

"I am surprised at you, Julia," she says. "I did not believe you were so sentimental. Casimir's offer was a generous one."

I feel Bianka's eyes on me.

"You made the choice easy," I say. "I won't be like you."

There is real anger in her expression for the first time.

"Are you so noble that you prefer death?"

"Death isn't my plan either," I say. A gunshot, and at the same moment Pia darts up the wall in that mind-boggling way she has of defying gravity. Another shot as she flies to the floor, rolls, and kicks the pistol from Gennady's hand.

Gennady takes a swing at her with one of his gigantic fists, but he is much too slow for her. She runs up the wall to the ceiling and leaps down at him, her boots striking his knees so they buckle beneath him. Bianka and I both scramble for the pistol, but Pia gets there first, kicks it aside, and hurls Bianka into me so we both go sprawling to the floor. Gennady is struggling to his feet, but she kicks him in the face, knocking him back, then takes hold of one of his legs and twists it so it cracks. He lets out a bellow. Bianka is on her feet faster than I am, still gasping for breath. Pia aims a kick at her head but Bianka dodges it, catching her by the foot and throwing her halfway across the room. Pia rolls elegantly to her feet, her knife flashing in her hand now. Bianka places herself between Pia and the trapdoor. Between Pia and me.

"Hurry," she says to me.

I tie the tapestry rope to the table leg with shaking hands. Once it is as secure as I can make it, I throw the rope down into the little room. Bianka and Pia are on the floor now. For a moment Bianka has Pia pinned. She is the stronger of the two, but Pia's agility and speed outdo her easily. With a twist she is out from under Bianka, dealing her a lethal-looking kick to the head. Gennady is dragging himself toward them. I can't watch. I pray the rotten tapestries will hold, and I swing down into the room, where Theo stands screaming blue murder on his little bed.

"Hold on to me," I tell him. "We'll go get your mama."

Poor Theo doesn't seem to remember it was me who took him away, or at least he doesn't understand that this is all my fault. He stops screaming.

"Lala!" he says, his little voice hoarse and trembling.

"That's right, it's Ella," I say, and pick him up. He is wearing the same clothes I last saw him in, fouled, reeking of shit and piss. He is filthy and rumpled and thinner than a few days ago, his eyes red-rimmed and his nose crusted with snot. I think it will crush my heart, the way he looks at me, the way he wraps his arms around my neck.

"Hold on tight," I say, and he does. I begin to haul us up the rope, arm over arm. I am barely a quarter of the way before I feel as if my arms will give out. I am sweating, and I can feel his little arms sliding against my damp neck.

"Don't let go," I grind out, to him or to myself, I'm not sure. I keep going. My hands burn. My arms burn. But there is the trapdoor, and with reserves of strength I'd been sure halfway up I didn't have, I pull us through it.

Gennady lies in a great golden heap, both his legs broken. Bianka has fared somewhat better and is still standing, but bleeding heavily from her side. As we emerge she lands a blow to the side of Pia's head that sends Pia staggering. I think it must be the first blow she has struck, for Pia begins to weave, retreat, dodge, trying to gather herself again. Bianka is too slowed to hit her again but does not stop trying to corner her, swinging her fists, unafraid of the knife.

"Mama!" Theo cries, trying to run to her. I grab him and put him under the table.

"Hush, hush," I whisper. "Your mama is very busy. You're all right now. Just sit tight and don't move, do you hear me?"

He stares at me, wide-eyed. I pull out my knife and vanish, counting on the blur of movement in the room to help hide me. I make straight for the grappling form that is Pia and Bianka. Bianka shoves Pia against the wall, and Pia kicks out, sending her reeling backward, stumbling to the ground. I come at Pia from the side and shove my knife deep into her belly.

It goes in so easily, through the leather, through her body. Right up to the hilt. She doubles over it. Dizzy with the horror and strangeness of putting a knife into someone's flesh, I pull the blade out and bring the hilt smashing down on her goggles as hard as I can. The lenses shatter, and she screams. I turn tail and run. Pia makes chase, her own knife still in her hand. She is following the sound of me, or for all I know the smell of me, blind or nearly blind with the goggles smashed. I leap right over the opening of the trapdoor, holding my breath and praying I've jumped far enough to make it over. I hit the ground on the other side and relief floods me. Pia staggers straight into it and falls with a terrible cry. Quick as I can, I pull up the tapestries, and as I do so I hear a sickening thud as she hits the ground. I don't want to look, but I can't help it. She lies there, a tangle of black, my nightmare reflection at the bottom of a pit. I think she must be dead until I hear her voice.

"Don't leave me here, Julia."

I slam the trapdoor closed and shut the bolt.

Baby Theo is in Bianka's arms, weeping and babbling into her neck. She clutches him close, rocking back and forth, bleeding all over him. I go to Gennady, broken and grimacing on the floor.

"How will we lift him?" I say.

"We won't," says Bianka. "There's no time. That girl is gone. She'll sound the alarm. We have to go *now*."

Gennady grabs my wrist.

"Shey is the one who can take the text out of Theo," he says. "Casimir can't do it without her. Kill her."

"I'll do my best," I say, though I have no intention of looking for the hunchback. "We'll be back for you."

"No we bleeding won't," says Bianka.

She runs faster than I can, even hurt, and I find myself fixating on Baby Theo's terrified face staring at me over her shoulder as I try to keep up.

"Go left; go left!" I call out, pointing her to the stairs. When we get closer to the room that the guard called the Terra Room, I catch up to her. Blood is seeping down her dress all the way to the hem.

"Stop," I whisper. "The others are near here. There will be guards."

"The others?" She turns on me, murderous. "I thought you were getting us out of here."

"We won't get far without anyone to sail the boat," I implore her.

"Take Theo," she says between clenched teeth. "Stay behind me. Stay unseen. Keep him away from any fighting."

"Can't you use magic?" I ask.

She shakes her head. "Lost my chalk. Too dizzy now, anyway."

Theo clings to my neck, presses his face to my cheek. I point the way and disappear, folding myself into that invisible place, tucked behind Bianka's limping, pained walk.

When we round the corner, a single guard draws his gun and shoots. I flatten myself against the wall, but Bianka runs straight for him. He shoots again. She staggers but keeps moving. I crouch behind the large urn I nearly knocked over earlier, as if it might offer protection, and press my face to the wall. Two more shots followed by an awful sound like bone cracking. Wood splintering. I open my eyes, peer around the urn. The guard is on the floor and Bianka is charging through the broken door.

Then silence. Awful silence. I stand in the hallway, holding on to Theo, staring at the guard's body. Bianka does not come back.

TWENTY-THREE

I have never felt so alone in my life, clutching Theo in the hall of Casimir's fortress, just a few feet from the dead guard. His eyes are open, his neck twisted back so it seems he is staring right at me, his legs a jumble on the floor. Whoever he was, gone with a snap of the neck. I wonder what brought him to this place, who will grieve for him. I think to myself: He is like me. The great players here are the Xianren, Bianka, even little Theo. This is their story. This guard and I, we are just caught up in it. We are the ones who get left behind by the story, left on the floor with our necks broken while the story rolls on without us, uncaring. I think it will be my neck next, or perhaps a bullet in my head, or perhaps something else.

I feel Theo's little hand on my face.

"Stay here," I say, putting him down. I creep down the hall and grab the dead guard under his shoulders. He is very heavy. I drag him over to Theo and pull off his jacket. Theo reaches out and touches the guard's hair.

"Don't touch him," I say, slapping his hand away. He stares at me, drawing his hand up toward his mouth. "You shouldn't touch him," I say more gently.

I don't know why not, though.

I lie him down next to the guard's body and whisper, "Hide-and-seek, all right, Theo? We're playing hide-and-seek!" Then I drape the guard's jacket over him and tip over the urn so that it lies across the guard's back and obscures the lump under the jacket. As long as he stays still, anyone passing in a hurry is unlikely to spot him. They will just see a dead guard under a knocked-over urn.

"Mama." He peers out at me with pleading eyes.

"Mama's coming," I say. "You keep hiding, and Mama will find you. Do you understand?"

Bleeding Kahge, Julia, of course he doesn't understand. But when I pull the jacket over his head, he snuggles down like he's taking a nap.

"Good boy," I say. I have to pry the guard's fingers from his gun to take it. His fingers are warm, and the bile rises in my throat but I force it back down. There is still no sound at all from the Terra Room. I vanish again, quiet my breathing, and edge into the room.

They are all there. The last of the sunlight is filtering through the windows, illuminating the swirling dust motes, whose slow dance is the only motion in the room. It is like looking at a painting, or a room full of statues. They are frozen in place: Wyn facing the other door, the one the maid came through this morning, Gregor lunging toward Csilla, who has thrown her arms up before her face, Esme turned toward me, mouth wide as if she is shouting something. She is looking right at me, but I cannot tell if she sees anything at all. They look like people fending off or fleeing an attack that came from every direction at once.

Bianka made it halfway across the room. Her hands are in fists. The blood soaking her dress drips onto the carpet. I cannot see her face.

"Who is there?"

It is a woman's voice, low for a woman but certainly not a man's. She speaks Fraynish with a country accent. I did not see her at first, but now she steps out in front of Wyn's frozen form, looking around the room for me as if she can smell me. It is the hunchback, Shey.

Bianka takes a sudden staggering step forward. Shey traces something quickly in the air with her index finger and Bianka halts midstep.

I raise the gun, take aim.

I am too slow. I hear him, or sense him, a moment before he gets to me. But in that second or two, I do not pull the trigger. I am dealt a swift blow to the shoulder and the gun clatters to the ground, my hands buzzing and stunned. Casimir has me by the throat, yanking me back into the world.

"This is the vanishing girl, Shey," he says to the hunchback. His voice is jagged, a little breathless. Not the sonorous, calm voice from earlier in the day. "Ammi's daughter."

The woman he called Shey says nothing in response to this, but I think my heart actually stops for a moment.

He gives me a little shake. "I rather liked the idea of Ammi's daughter contracted to me, to do my bidding. It seemed a fitting conclusion to our story. But maybe she is too much like her mother after all."

I think I must be dreaming this, the way he talks so casually of my mother, like he knew her. The remaining light is fading fast.

"Where is the boy?" he asks, his grip tightening on my throat so I cannot breathe. It occurs to me, as my vision narrows, that this is a very poor technique for getting someone to talk.

"Ghhhh," I rasp, working my tongue. The whole world is just those terrible eyes and the need to breathe. His other hand grabs my hair, and he loosens the hand on my throat. I gasp in a few quick lungfuls of air.

"The boy," he says again.

"Gone," I say. "Where you'll never find him."

A blow to the side of my head, and for a moment everything is entirely black. My hands are scrabbling against something hard, and then I realize it is the floor. I look up and see a boot, which smashes me in the face and sends me rolling back, pain splintering through my nose and eyes. My mouth is full of blood. The boot comes down on my arm and I hear a scream that must be mine. Through a fog of tears I can see only his face right over mine, his flaring nostrils, his full lips and white teeth.

"Do you remember what it was like, Shey—being young?" he calls to the hunchback.

"I do, my lord," says Shey gravely.

"So sure of everything, so brave. We are all that way when we are young."

I do not feel sure of anything, let alone brave, but I am in no condition to argue the point. He pins me to the ground, one knee across my right arm, and then takes my left hand in his as tenderly as if he were about to propose marriage.

"Do you know why I chose you, Julia? Shall I tell you the story?" He bends my little finger back so I scream again. "I had a uniquely memorable encounter with your mother, once upon a time, before you came into the world and had fingers."

He snaps my finger like a twig. It is an awful, animal sound that comes out of my mouth. Somewhere, hazily, under the agony of it, I am surprised that a little finger could hurt so much.

"Ammi was ambitious. I recognize and respect ambition," he continues languidly, as if breaking my finger has relaxed him. "Most truly ambitious people are driven by their desire for one of two things: vengeance or power. For some of us, it is both."

He breaks the next finger suddenly, and I howl, the pain exploding in my hand and behind my eyes.

"A long time ago, my brother, sister, and I were stronger than we are now," he continues. "The world was ours and none could stand against us. But times have changed. You have never heard of the Sidhar Coven—such things are not spoken of—but your mother knew them. They sought to bring the most powerful witches in New Poria together, to overthrow the various kingdoms and establish another empire led by witches. They were behind the so-called Lorian Uprising. Did your mother tell you that?"

He waits politely. I make an attempt to shake my head, and he snaps another finger. I would like to deny him the satisfaction of my screams, but it turns out that screaming is entirely involuntary when your fingers are being broken. Nausea sweeps over me. I rather hope I am going to faint, but I don't.

"Agoston Horthy was an experiment, but he proved to have a real talent for uncovering secrets. His spies learned of the uprising before it was even under way. He decimated the coven and all their witless allies. The survivors were scattered, in hiding, gone underground, but they identified me as their primary enemy. They were underestimating Horthy, I think, but never mind that—I've made the same mistake myself. Ammi was the second assassin they sent after me. The first was little trouble, but Ammi nearly succeeded. To this day, I do not know how she came in secret to my island, how she entered my fortress, past all my guards and enchantments, how she came undetected to my very bedside, armed with all the magic the coven could give her. She didn't manage to kill me, but she put me inside a great rock and buried me in the sea. That was the first time . . . that was the only time that I have felt myself defeated."

He is caressing my index finger now. He twists it in his hand, and I hear the bone crack, the pain zagging up my arm. This time I throw up all over myself, my body rejecting everything, trying to escape itself. He cradles my broken hand in his like something precious.

"Eventually my sister heard of it and got me out, but still she would not see the threat that witches posed to us, to the world. For years, then, I had fixed in my mind the image of this young, dark, nameless witch. It took me seven years to find her, keeping her head down in the Twist, whispering revolution and trying to reassemble the coven. The truth is that I was afraid of her, this witch who nearly ended me. I could not face her. I left her to Agoston Horthy. I went to the Cleansing that day—I watched the whole thing—but there was no way to make her suffer like I did, alive for months at the bottom of the sea."

All at once he bares his teeth and with his two hands, breaks my wrist. I roar like a beast.

"But all that was years ago, and you are just the coda. Where is the boy?"

I don't know how, but somehow I come back to myself just enough to gather a gob of spit in my mouth and send it spraying right into his face. He snarls and twists my snapped wrist so that the whole world is just broken stars of pain and my own ragged weeping.

"Look at me," he says, and I do, or I try. Through a haze of tears, I see a blade in his hand. "You look like her, but not so pretty," he says. "I am going to cut your throat, and you will bleed to death here on the floor. Or you can take me to the boy. These are the choices."

The truth is that even now I am afraid to die. Still, I've

had a practice run with this particular gruesome choice, and I know better, this time, than to prize my life above all else.

His voice hardens. "Keep in mind there are five throats here for me to cut before I get to yours."

I close my eyes. I think I am moaning, but I'm not sure. We are all as good as dead, and he'll find Theo too, but he'll do it without my help, by the holies.

"Ah, well," he says. "Pain always works in the end, you know."

He grabs my other hand and no, no, *no*, with all of my being I pull back from his awful face, from the pain in my hand and face and arm, from the pain to come, from this relentless fear. It is not the floor beneath me anymore. I smell the river Syne, and blood, then smoke.

At first I think it is something he has done to me. The pain is gone. The thought comes to me slowly: He has killed me. I find myself on a rocky ledge, but I am not myself. My hands are dark, clawed things, and far below, a river of fire pours through a ruined, flaming city. I scramble back from the cliff's edge and everything shifts. I am back in the Terra Room, but like that time in Mrs. Och's reading room, I have no body at all. I can see everything, from every direction, including Casimir straightening, calling out: "Shey! Where is she?"

"I do not see her, my lord."

And I realize he did not do this, whatever it is. I did it.

The last of the light is gone. The frozen figures of my friends, my family, are shadows now in the dark room. But

I can see Wyn's face, and Esme's, as close as if I were next to them. I can hear Bianka breathing, struggling against the spell that holds her. If I listen carefully, I can hear her bleeding. I do not know where I am. I do not know what has happened to me. It's as if I don't exist beyond my exaggerated senses. Panic takes me. I seek the door, I try to run, and in so doing I find my legs, my body. All the pain comes back at once.

"There!" cries Casimir, pointing. "Stop her, Shey!"

I am near the door, which is a good place to be, but I get no farther. Shey writes something in the air and I am stopped, still as the others. Casimir looms over me, nostrils flaring.

Again, no, no, I recoil, pull away from this man or whatever he is who arranged my mother's death, or so he claims, who has had his awful eyes on me for longer than I knew, who will break me piece by piece if I let him. It is like the vanishing I have always done, but complete. Not a careful step back to some in-between space but a crossing over to someplace else altogether. I pant for air on the expanse of black rock above the burning city. I recognize Mount Heriot, Capriss Temple a blackened husk. A hot wind blows over me. Fire fountains up from distant mountains, and beyond those, filling the horizon, a roaring grayish swirl, like a spinning, sucking mouth that seems to pull the wind toward it, over me. Steam pours up from between the cracks in the rock, and I see my feet, not my feet; those aren't my feet. . . .

"Where is she? Where has she gone?"

Casimir. I lean toward his voice. I hear Shey, impassive: "How remarkable."

It is too frightening, this non-being, this other-being. I lunge back to my body in the Terra Room, all the parts of me that are and that hurt, my shattered hand. I land on the floor. My hand and my face and my guts blaze with pain but I move faster than I have ever moved in my life. I run for the gun I dropped. As soon as I feel it in my unbroken hand, I vanish.

Ashen sheets flap like ghosts around me. This is the courtyard behind the flat where we used to live with our mother. That distant roar fills my ears. I have the pistol in my hand—my clawed, monstrous hand.

I hear Shey whispering, "Where are you; where have you gone?"

If I think about the Terra Room, I can see it, like looking at a room reflected in a dark window, superimposed over this place, this ruined memory of a place. I try to aim myself, focusing on the door, and indeed, there I am when I step back into myself. That is good.

Not good: Theo is standing there screaming, "Mama! Mama!" and Casimir is taking great strides toward him. There is no time to think. I grab Theo and pull him with me to that other Spira City, broken and burning. Flames gutter in dark windows; lava bubbles up between cracks in the street. We are in the Edge now, where shadows dart along the alleyways, ash rolling and blowing on the hot gusts of wind.

"Lala," his voice is a whimper. I feel his heart against mine, *thud-thud-thud-thud-thud*. When I struggle to see the room again, I can see only Casimir, wheeling and screaming words I do not understand. I lunge back to the world, to the hall where I hid Theo before, clutching him and his *thud-thud-thud-thud-thud* against me. We hit the ground and I pull away again immediately, trying to take myself to the very edge, to that place where I am nowhere and see everything, beyond my usual vanishing but before I disappear completely into that burnt Spira City. I move down the hall in wild, vanishing leaps, back down to the bottom of the castle, all the way to where Gennady lies, eyes wide, arms spread, on his back on the ground. I have Theo in my arms, the gun in my good hand, and it is my own hand now.

"We need you," I plead.

His eyes find me, slowly.

"I cannot walk," he murmurs thickly through bloodied lips.

I kneel at his side. His broken legs twist out from his body at horrible, impossible angles.

"My boy?" He lifts a great hand to touch Theo, who pulls away, buries his face in my neck. Gennady lets his hand drop to the ground again with a thud.

"Bianka?" he asks.

"Casimir has her," I say. "Or, that woman, Shey."

"Drag me there if you have to," he says. "I will break him, and then Shey also." Desperation brings some strength back into his voice, but the idea of dragging him is ludicrous. He is too large.

"I can't," I begin.

He rolls over with a groan, starts to pull himself along the floor with his mighty arms.

I don't know why I think it possible.

"Hold on to me," I say. I help him to put his great arms around me, Theo between us. He smells of blood and burnt skin. I wrap an arm around his thick neck. He is massive and heavy and it is hard to think of anything but the pain in my hand and wrist and face, but longing to be free of that pain is what saves me. I pull our three bodies embracing on the floor right out of the world. We are at the edge of the river Syne, but the river is boiling, and nightgowned figures fall into it from a burning boat, again and again, silent. They stare at us with black eyes that mirror the flames. I draw away from it again and we land heavy down the hall. Theo cries out.

"What are you?" Gennady asks me, his blue eyes amazed.

"I don't know," I say truthfully.

"You can go farther," Gennady says, and I think he must be right. I pull them with me. The pain disappears with me. The hot wind screams, the streets steam, and winged monsters wail above us. A transparent whore with maggots in her eyes beckons from a burning doorway, her dress singed. Something with antlers moves toward me down the street, calling out to me.

"This is Kahge," whispers Gennady, and without knowing why, I know that he is right. I carry them both, half in the world, half out, back to the Terra Room. There I hang, bodiless.

Casimir, part man, part winged beast now, is pivoting slowly. I return us to the world just above him, effectively dropping Gennady on top of him. Gennady's giant arms wrap themselves around Casimir's neck, pull back, one hand over his mouth. The two of them fall in a struggling mass to the ground, and I land next to them, with Theo, with the gun.

Shey is holding one finger in the air and looking at me curiously. The kind of look someone might give you at a party if they wanted to strike up a conversation. This time I do not hesitate. I cock the hammer and shoot her in the neck. She falls to her knees, one hand clamped to the wound, blood pouring between her fingers, over her hand, over her shoulder. I was aiming for the head, but never mind—there are more bullets. I shoot again and she falls backward with a creaking sort of gasp. There is such sorrow in the look she gives me as she falls. I shoot her again, and then again.

With the fourth bullet, everyone in the room collapses, whatever had held them in place suddenly gone, like puppets whose strings have been cut.

"Mama!"

Theo struggles free and I let him go. He runs for Bianka and she scoops him up.

"Go!" she cries, shoving me toward the door.

Casimir, his head locked between Gennady's arms, Gennady's big hand clutching his mouth, stares at me with his deadly gray eyes. I run.

We make our way in a scrambling mob out of the castle. I've dropped the gun, I don't even remember when or where, but I yank the lever on the wall with my good hand and we all pour out through the rising door in the outer wall. Nobody in pursuit. Not yet, anyway.

"What about Gennady?" I shout at Bianka.

"No," she says, not looking back. I hope Sir Victor will be all right, but there is nothing I can do for either of them.

Frederick, Dek, and the professor have got the new mainsail rigged, and Frederick is waving his arms at us as if we might not be able to spot the boat otherwise. Nobody pauses; nobody speaks to consult. Gregor and Esme push the boat deeper into the water, Frederick unfurls the sails, and the professor takes the helm while the rest of us splash through the dark water and scramble over the side. Bianka is weeping freely, covered in blood, collapsed against the lifeboat with Theo in her arms. The wind fills the sails and the boat begins to move swiftly through the water. I feel it fully then— the pain in my wrist, my hand, pain in my face, my arm, my side. Every part of me hurts, and unconsciousness beckons, a respite from pain and terror.

"You all in one piece, Brown Eyes?" Wyn's hand is on my shoulder. I nod, though I don't know if I am or not. And there is Dek, smiling in spite of his swollen jaw and a long day of being soaked and trapped in the belly of the boat.

"I can't believe you pulled it off," he says. "You look like you've been to Kahge and back, though."

I hug him, squeezing my eyes shut. For a moment, holding my brother tight, I let myself imagine that yes, we've pulled it off, it's over, we're safe—Kahge and back is only an expression. But when I open my eyes, I see under the rising moon five sleek boats setting out in pursuit.

TWENTY-FOUR

We do not speak. What is there to say? The boats are fast, and none of us are experienced sailors.

"Chalk," rasps Bianka. The professor scurries belowdecks to get her some more. Esme is bent over her and is trying to do something about the knife and bullet wounds. Bianka ignores her, watches the boats, Theo clutched to her breast.

Gregor hands out pistols. Dek readies his little cannon. Frederick has the telescope, but he hands it to me when I go to his side. His eyes are all questioning concern. It is not easy to see anything in the dark, even with the moon nearly full, but through the telescope I can more or less make out the figures on the boats. These are not the guards we encountered on the island. I do not know what these things are. White-skinned, white-haired, naked, covered with tattoos. I can see Casimir on the deck of the nearest boat, arms behind his back, fur coat flapping in the wind. I wonder what has become of Gennady. I give the telescope back to Frederick and wipe blood from my chin with the sleeve of my dress. I know my nose is bleeding too, but it is throbbing too much for me to touch it.

"You ought to have Esme look you over," he says. "Great Nameless, what happened to your hand?"

"He broke my wrist and every finger," I say. I mean to sound cavalier, but it comes out a sad little bleat. My hand doesn't look like a hand at all anymore, rather a swollen, bloody mitt. Every time I move, the pain rips up the length of my arm. Frederick touches my other arm, about to say something, but then Gregor shouts out: "Everybody stand back; here it goes!"

Dek is peering through the eyehole at the top of his little homemade cannon. He swivels it slightly, then pulls a switch. A hiss, and one of his canisters goes shooting out in a great arc, a trail of yellow gas billowing out behind it. This is not capsicum, but sleeping gas. The aim is true, and it lands with a thunk on the deck of Casimir's boat. Casimir surges up on great wings and spirals above the boat. The ghostly, tattooed savages fall to the deck, unconscious and soon hidden by the cloud of yellow smoke turning brown.

"Remarkable!" cries Professor Baranyi. "Surely the Crown would pay you a fortune for this?"

"I've never approached the Crown," says Dek. "Not sure I'd trust them to pay me, though." He calls out to the rest of us: "Masks in the bag here by the lifeboat! If we end up too near the smoke, put one on!"

"How many do you have left?" asks the professor.

"Six," says Dek.

He hits a second boat, and it too falls out of the line, drifting away in a brown-black cloud. I am watching Casimir above, circling higher and higher, a dark shape against the dark sky.

"Are you a good shot?" I ask Frederick.

"I'm fair," he says. "Not as good as you."

"That . . . thing," I say, pointing. I don't trust my own aim right now. "Keep your gun trained on it and shoot it if it gets close enough."

Frederick nods and looks up. The stars are coming out now.

A third canister just misses the next boat, lands hissing in the water next to it, smoke pouring off the waves and then extinguishing.

Bianka is trying to write something on the deck, but her chalk breaks and she falls against the lifeboat, her breath fast and ragged.

"Let Esme take care of you, by the holies," I tell her. "You're going to die if you keep trying to fight with those injuries."

Bianka gives me a lopsided little smile. "Not unless you throw me overboard," she says.

"Well, you're too weak to do magic," I tell her.

"And I don't know what happens to witches who've lost as much blood as you're losing, but I don't think even a witch can walk around with no blood in her," says Esme sternly. Bianka is too weak to resist. Baby Theo clings to her, hiding his face against her.

Bianka stares at me over Esme's broad shoulders and says, "Whatever happens, don't let them take Theo."

I hold up my gun solemnly, like a promise. Bianka nods her head, eyes drooping.

A fourth canister, a third boat out of the pursuit. I see another winged shape in the sky. It tangles briefly with Casimir, way up above us. Then he breaks free and dives.

"Shoot!" I shout at Frederick. "Shoot!"

Casimir is a great shadow overhead, his wingspan nearly equal to our boat's width, when we both fire on him. He veers off to the side, circling up again.

A fifth canister is shot out of the air and falls, billowing smoke. I can see wide white eyes now in the blank faces of the creatures on the nearest boat. There are six of them, rifles in hand, taking aim.

"Everybody down!" I cry. I throw myself down on the deck, and for a moment it hurts so much I think I've been shot. Wood flies here and there as bullets pepper our boat.

"Get belowdecks, all of you!" Gregor roars as soon as they stop to reload. "I'll hold them off!"

Wyn is at my side, and with the arm I can use I shove him toward Theo. "Take the baby down!" I shout at him. He gives me an entreating look, and I scream with what little voice I have left, "The bleeding *baby*, Wyn! I'm right behind you!" He takes Theo from a half-conscious Bianka. The professor and Esme lift Bianka between them. Dek is putting another canister into the cannon when a rifle shot rings out and he falls to the deck screaming. It is raining bullets again.

I don't know where he's been hit, but Frederick has him already, good fellow, and is taking him below.

Casimir is circling closer and closer again, and I've lost the other winged creature, which I can only hope to be Mrs. Och, come from whichever island she'd waited on. I scramble for Dek's cannon and take shelter by the wheel. I find Casimir through the spy hole. Circling, circling, then diving, and he is out of my sight. I find him again, horribly close, fix him in the crosshairs, and pull the lever.

The canister shoots straight up and lodges itself in his chest. He falls straight onto our deck, so fast I barely get out of his way before he lands, feathers flying. I scramble for the bag of masks by the lifeboat as the yellow smoke pours right over our boat. I taste it, acrid and hot, and for a moment there is no up or down—I feel myself floating quite painlessly. Then the mask is over my head. I take a sharp, metallic breath, my senses returning to me. Casimir thrashes weakly and then falls still, his wings collapsed on the deck. I push my way through the smoke, breathing hard through the mask. The air feels thin and strange. I drag him with one arm toward what I hope is the side of the deck. He is not as heavy as I would have expected, but still it is slow going. Through the goggles of the mask I can see the smoke turning brown. My back hits the edge of the gunwale and I nearly tumble into the water myself. I don't know how I will lift him. Perhaps with both my arms I could do it, but not with one arm. I heave and heave, uselessly. Then suddenly his body lifts, tilts, falls into the water with a splash. I see another wicked-looking mask next to me as the smoke begins to clear, the boat moving out of the cloud of gas. She pulls the mask off as soon as we are in open air: Mrs. Och. Gregor is out cold on the deck, his pistol beside him.

She points at the two boats still in pursuit, closing on us. "I want to call the wind," she says. "Give me your strength."

She takes my good hand in one of her furred, leopard-spotted hands. She begins to speak words I don't recognize. My vision narrows suddenly and then widens, spreads out an alarming 360 degrees. I try to pull my hand away, but she doesn't let go. I cry out and struggle uselessly. Not because I do not want to help her, but because I feel as if my life is being pulled out of me. It is painful, but not only painful. It is not just energy or strength being sapped, but something more elemental than that. Thought. Self. Breath. My very pulse pulling away from me. I am begging, though I am not sure for what. For it to stop. For my life. For forgiveness.

And so I remember later, but barely register at the time, the wind that rises behind the boat, the wind in our wake, a great roaring gale. I see the remaining two boats pursuing us tossed aside, capsized. I see Casimir emerging from the waves, wings outstretched, but he is blown back, out of sight.

It seems to last forever. When Mrs. Och lets go of my hand I fall limp to the deck, my vision closing to nothing, the world spinning into darkness. It occurs to me from a very great distance that I am dying. I am terribly sad but can do nothing, and I am sorry but cannot say so.

∿

When I wake up, Wyn is there. His face looks unnaturally large, and he says, "A man can change, Brown Eyes, if he finds something worth changing for," and I say "ghhhhrg" and he says, "Have I really lost you, Julia?"

The answer to that is more complicated than I have the strength for. It occurs to me that I might be dreaming or hallucinating, but I reckon I'd better say something anyway, in case I'm not, so I just say, "Yes." Overlarge Wyn-face starts to cry, and it is all too much, so I pass out again.

∾

The next time I wake, Dek is beside me, his own regular size, and I am in a bed. My broken hand is bandaged, each finger like a great gauze sausage. The first thing I do is lean over the side of the bed to retch. Nothing comes up. The world is swaying. Gradually I realize the movement beneath me is the movement of the boat. I recognize the room, the narrow bunks.

"Thank the Nameless One," says Dek. "Have some water. Or some broth."

I make a rasping sound, which alarms him slightly, then manage to say, "Water. Please."

I force myself up, and he holds the cup to my lips. My throat is very dry and the water feels good, at least until it hits my stomach and then comes straight back up. A splitting headache takes hold, wrapping around my skull like a vise. I weep with the pain, but when it passes I am able to drink some water and some broth and feel somewhat restored.

"What's happening?" I ask Dek.

"We'll be landing in Naripi soon," he says. "A Sirillian port town. You haven't missed much. Repairing the boat, tending to the ill and wounded, keeping a lookout for that mad fellow with wings."

"Casimir," I say.

"Mrs. Och figured we'd make it to Naripi before he'd be able to find us again. We're splitting up after that. They're taking Bianka and the baby somewhere. Gregor's up in arms because he thinks we aren't getting our money. I have a feeling your Mrs. Och is good for it, though."

"I expect so," I say.

"Esme did a nice job patching up the witch. Set the bones of your fingers right too."

"Is Bianka all right?"

"Moving slowly, but she seems it."

"And Theo?"

"Right as rain, by the looks of it."

I swallow my tears and ask, "What about everybody else?"

"Everyone's a bit beat up, I guess, but no worse than that," says Dek. "Wyn's got a broken arm from the first storm. I took a bullet to the leg, the good one too. Still, I'd say we got off lightly, for the most part."

He stays and chats with me awhile, and once or twice he tries to ask me about what happened in the Terra Room, but I find I cannot answer.

∿

The professor helps Mrs. Och into the cabin, lies her down on the bunk opposite mine, so I have the odd sense we are bunkmates taking a rest. She looks ancient and very frail.

"I have come to apologize," she says. "I do not like to borrow the life force of another, especially when you have been through so much already. I could see no other way."

"What does that mean, borrowing my life force?" I ask.

"It is exactly as it sounds. Every person has a life force, an energy. It is strongest in the young, of course. Borrowing it is something I learned to do long ago and have needed more as I got older. But the demands of the storm I summoned and your own weakened state resulted in a rather close call for you. I am sorry."

"I'm all right. Or, I reckon I will be. What now?"

"We will take Theo somewhere safe. But he will not be safe for long. Casimir will be looking for him again."

"But that witch or whatever she is, the hunchback, Shey, is dead," I say. "Doesn't he need her?"

"I highly doubt that Shey is dead," says Mrs. Och.

"I shot her four times," I say. "She was bleeding everywhere."

Mrs. Och says nothing to that, and I am thinking, these terrible people, nothing seems to kill them.

"I suppose Pia isn't dead either," I say gloomily.

"Pia, I think, has nine lives," says Mrs. Och. "I do not know how many she has used."

I can't tell if she's joking, but I get the gist. I am not safe from her, not yet.

"Will you go back for Gennady?"

Mrs. Och shakes her head. "I cannot save Gennady," she says.

"But he's your brother."

I would never leave Dek behind in a place like that. Never.

"Casimir is my brother too," she replies.

I take a deep breath. "Casimir said he *chose* me for the job in your house, because he knew my mother. He said she tried to kill him. Is it true?"

Her brow furrows. "Who is your mother?"

"She's dead," I say. "She was drowned years ago. Her name was Ammi Farian."

Mrs. Och makes a sound like a long sigh. "You are Ammi's daughter. I did not know. Oh, Julia. I do not think Casimir will want to let you go."

"You knew my mother?"

She shakes her head. "I knew of her," she says. "I never met her. But I think she knew how it might end, Julia, in choosing to be his enemy."

"That doesn't make me feel any better," I say.

"No, of course not."

"How do you choose witches to save?" I ask her. "Why Jahara Sandor, but not the other witches who were drowned that day?"

I'm thinking of the young witch with brown hair. I'm thinking of my mother. I'm thinking of the witch she killed, but I don't dare ask about that.

"I can't save everyone," she says, and some childish part of me wants to demand *Why not?* "If there is to be change in Frayne . . . I try to help those who might best effect it, when the time comes."

"The time for what?"

"The time for change."

"My mother wanted to change the world. Nobody saved her."

If Casimir was telling the truth, then Mrs. Och's rescue of him is what cost my mother her life. She saved him, and he hunted my mother down. I am torn between hurling accusations at her and feeling gratitude to her for saving us today.

"No," she says calmly. "I didn't save Ammi. I didn't want to involve myself too closely in Casimir's business, at the time, but Casimir's business is becoming unavoidable. I am responsible, in a way, for his desperation. I'm dying, you see."

"Oh," I whisper. I still don't know how to feel about Mrs. Och. I don't know how to respond to her almost casual dismissal of my mother's death, the idea that she *might* have helped her and chose not to, and I don't know if I am sorry she is dying.

"It is taking rather a long time. Still, it has put in Casimir a fear of his own death. He thinks he can restore us to our earlier power with *The Book of Disruption*, that death will not be able to claim me, or him, or any of us, if he can reassemble it. Perhaps he is right, but I do not want to see the world that Casimir would make."

Neither do I.

"Tell me what happened at the fortress," she says. "Shey was able to immobilize all the others, except you. How did you escape them?"

I don't want to talk about it—I don't want to say aloud what happened—but then who else might know what any of it means? So I tell her everything. I describe what I saw, how it felt. When I am done, she says nothing, which is annoying, given what it cost me to get it out.

"Gennady told me . . . he said that other place was Kahge," I say.

"Impossible," she says, though her expression tells me she believes him. "Not even the Xianren can cross into Kahge."

But I can. I come to the point. It is not easy to say, and so I whisper it: "What *am* I? What am I, that I can do such things?"

For the first time, I see a hint of something that might be fear in her eyes. She says, "I don't know what you are, Julia."

∾

Frederick comes to help Mrs. Och go up on deck.

"The Naripi harbor is in sight," he says. And then to me, "You look better."

"Yes," I say. A strangled little yes, in lieu of crying out *I'm so sorry* or *Please forgive me.* I find I can hardly look at him, and yet I must.

"Shall I come back down to help you?" he asks me, a little taken aback by the intensity of my gaze, I think.

"No," I say. "I can manage on my own."

"Well, I am glad to hear it." He bends over Mrs. Och, helping her out of the bed. They are halfway into the little hall when I manage to get the words out: "Please don't think me . . . what you said."

They both turn to look at me, Frederick looking puzzled, Mrs. Och faintly amused.

I make myself say it: "Evil."

There is something terribly like pity in his expression, and I shrivel.

"Taking Theo was evil," he says softly. "What you did to get him out—that was very brave."

I follow them out into the brilliant sunshine. Everybody comes crowding around to greet me, and there is a great deal of frantic talk, exchanging of stories, and so on. When I meet Wyn's eyes, I cannot be sure if he wept at my bedside or if I dreamed it. He squeezes my good hand once and says, "Stars, Brown Eyes, it's good to see you up and about." I bob my head stupidly, and we are awkward and silent until the others break in talking again. Gregor hugs me so it hurts, weeping drunkenly, but I manage to hug him back.

Naripi is all low buildings around a sparkling harbor. The coast is dotted with islands. Fishing boats and trade boats traffic the water here.

"Our first foreign country," says Dek, grinning at me. But I can't find joy in it, not yet. I search the sky for a winged man, scan the boats for Pia's ghoulish smile. I think I will never be free of fear again, as long as I live.

Everybody takes a turn looking at Naripi through the telescope. I join Csilla and Esme, leaning on the gunwale.

"Shame about your pretty nose," says Csilla to me. "But I can't tell you how relieved I am to see you walking about. You looked like death for a while there."

"What does my nose look like?" I ask, touching it tentatively. It still throbs.

"At the moment? Hideous." She smiles warmly.

"It will be a bit crooked, I expect," says Esme. "But it could be worse."

"War wounds," says Csilla. "Everything heals a little crookedly, and then you forget how it was before. Your friend Frederick was terribly concerned about you, by the way."

I look over at Frederick in some surprise. "We're not exactly friends," I say.

"I'd say he feels otherwise," says Csilla, raising an eyebrow at me. Then she looks toward the harbor again. "We've got to go to the market for Sirillian silk! We might as well get some lovely dresses, after all this unpleasantness."

"I'm sorry," I tell her awkwardly. "I didn't know . . . how awful it would turn out."

"Oh, Julia." She gives my arm a friendly squeeze. "I've had worse days, believe me. I'm going to have a go with the telescope!"

She flounces over to where the others are taking turns looking at the harbor through the telescope. I watch her go, thinking that I know nothing at all about her life before she took up with Gregor.

"I couldn't ask them to do it for less," Esme says then, in a low voice. "There was no question about the danger. The reward had to be equal to it."

Is she explaining why she asked for so much gold?

"I don't think they'd have gone along with it if you hadn't."

"If Mrs. Och comes through, I'm retiring," she tells me. "I'd like to set Wyn up with an apprenticeship, or even his own studio. Give him a shot at something else. I'd send Dek to the university if I could, but they'd never take him. Still, he might do well with his own workshop, a laboratory, if he can make a few connections. It's you I worry about, Julia. You could take over for me, if you wanted to. You'd be good at it. But you're still young, and you don't have to go down this road."

"I'll give it some thought," I say. I can't go back to my old life, my old self, but nor can I think of any other kind of life. I don't know what else I'm good for. *Your mother never learned to live without hope,* Liddy told me. But I don't know what to hope for.

"You've done well." Esme nods to where Bianka sits playing with Theo, covering a marble with a cup and lifting it again, the marble rolling with the deck as soon as it is free. "A mother should be with her children."

When I look at Theo, not quite the chubby imp from Mrs. Och's house, but clean, laughing, reaching for the marble, my heart clenches in my chest like a fist. I make my way over on wobbly knees and lower myself to the deck next to them. Bianka slams the cup over the marble and gives me a scorching look.

I will not ask for her forgiveness—I don't deserve that. But I cannot stop myself from kneeling before her and whispering fiercely: "I'd die before letting anything happen to him again. I swear to you, I'd die first."

To my surprise, she reaches out and takes my good hand in hers, twining her fingers between mine. She says, "I know."

I clutch her hand, but I can't meet her eyes. I can't undo any of it, but to see him well and happy and playing at his mother's side again—for that, I feel a gratitude I think will overwhelm me. Though I am not generally prone to prayer, I squeeze my eyes shut and offer my silent thanks and my wordless remorse to the Nameless One, the wheeling stars, the universe and whatever there may be in it that listens or cares. And I ask the universe, though I have no right to ask for anything: *Protect him. Protect him. Protect him.*

TWENTY-FIVE

The snow is coming down swift and thick, and the sky is black. I walk through the Edge and all the way down to Forrestal before turning north again. Moving keeps me calm, or something like it. Cyrambel Temple's great bulk rises up before me now, looming in front of the moon, and I quicken my pace. I stop on the bridge where I saw the murdered governess just a few weeks ago, though it feels like lifetimes. I am not that girl anymore.

From the bridge I stare down at the frozen river, the snow lying heavy and untouched over the ice. They will come to clear the snow and break the ice at dawn, for there's to be a Cleansing here tomorrow morning. This one will draw a crowd in spite of the cold, as Marianne Deneuve is to be drowned along with the other witches. It will be the first Cleansing in years that I will not attend; we are leaving early on a train to the south.

Liddy found us a place to stay, a place to hide, when we

returned; we did not dare go back to Esme's, where Casimir would surely know how to find us. And Liddy directed Professor Baranyi to the unprepossessing house on the outskirts of the Plateau a few days after our return to the city. He brought with him eleven gold freyns and a new offer, which we unanimously accepted. We are to travel with Mrs. Och and the others to Yongguo. They intend to seek out Ko Dan, the monk Gennady spoke of, in the hope that he can undo what was done to Theo, somehow remove the text fragment from him without harming him. We are to act as bodyguards, spies, or whatever the situation requires. We will be well paid, Professor Baranyi assures Esme, and we all feel safer leaving Spira City for a time.

Every night since his visit, the others feast and drink while I go out and walk the empty, snowy streets. I don't begrudge them their delight in their new wealth, but I can't share it. I asked Liddy to give my share of Casimir's silver—what's left of it—and Mrs. Och's gold to an orphanage or some worthy cause so that I won't have to touch it or look at it. She raised one white eyebrow archly at the idea of me as a philanthropist but said she would do as I asked. I can't even wear the awful gown or the fur I bought, given what I did to earn them. I looked ridiculous in them, anyway. I am wearing my old gabardine coat over the mended dress Torne's fellows ripped open. Not as warm as a fur coat, but I feel more myself.

Casimir told me that all great ambition finds its root in the desire for vengeance or power, but I suspect it is the nature of a certain kind of man to think his own truths universal.

He would not understand how powerful remorse can be, the desire for atonement. He didn't mention love, or grief. Still, we are not altogether unalike. Power doesn't interest me, but vengeance, yes. I understand what he said about vengeance. Mrs. Och said Casimir would not want to let me go, and nor will I let go of him, of what he did to me, to my mother.

I flex my hand, which feels stiff and strange—Esme took the bandages off this morning—and remember that other hand, in that other place. I told Dek a little of what Casimir said to me about our mother. I could not tell him, or any of them, about my vanishing to Kahge, if that's truly where it was. I can't bear for him to doubt who and what I am. Not before I know, myself.

I look up into the falling snow, and it feels like I'm flying, sailing up into the sky, leaving Spira City far below me. Goodbye, then, to the streets of my childhood, the streets where my childhood ended. Goodbye to the Twist, goodbye to the Edge, goodbye to the rats and the thin stray cats. Goodbye to the sparkling Spira City nighttime, and to the frozen water underneath the snow. Goodbye to the bones of witches at the bottom of the river. Goodbye to the bones of my mother. Goodbye to the witches who will drown here tomorrow.

Goodbye to the Julia who would sell a boy for silver. Light on my feet, I run the rest of the way home in the snow.

ACKNOWLEDGMENTS

First thanks go to my agent, Steve Malk, who took a chance on the scrambled manuscript I was calling a book, and from whom I learned so much while revising it. I've heard authors say things like "I could not have written this book without old So-and-So," but before working with Steve, I never really understood what they meant. Now I do. Thank you.

To my wonderful editor, Nancy Siscoe, to everyone at Knopf who has worked on *Julia*—I could write sonnets of appreciation for copy editors!—and to Amy Black and the team at Doubleday Books: I am so lucky to be working with you, and so grateful.

Thank you to Dan Gilman, Samantha Cohoe, Kip Wilson Rechea, Dana Alison Levy, and Katie Mei McCarthy, who read and critiqued various parts of the book at various stages. Tremendous gratitude also to Jim and Janet Hunter, whose generosity gave me an extra two mornings a week to write and saved me from losing what I like to call my mind.

My thanks and my infinite love to the following people, who read and shaped my writing and so much more: my parents, who are not just in my corner but pretty much built my corner; my brothers, without whom Julia's love for Dek would be a shadow of the truth; my grandmother Kato Havas, who has taught me so much about the joys and perils of the creative life; Jonathan Service, who is both the most serious and the least serious person I know— thank you for taking me more seriously and less seriously than anybody else at exactly the right moments all my life; Gillian Bright, thank you for incisive critiques and tireless cheerleading; Mick Hunter, my partner in all the very best and worst—thank you for brainstorming sessions, for keeping your cool through every storm, for doing all the hard stuff as if it isn't hard, for making me laugh every day, and for everything else, too. You leave this would-be wordsmith speechless.

Finally, all the love in the world, but no thanks at all, to James and Kieran, who have, from the very first draft, stood—loudly! exuberantly! irrepressibly!—between me and the completion of this book. Finished anyway. Smooch.